T0365116

Lemon Creek Chronicle

Lemon Creek
Chronicle

L. L. CLAASSEN

WESTBOW
PRESS®
A DIVISION OF THOMAS NELSON
& ZONDERVAN

Copyright © 2013 L. L. Claassen.

All rights reserved. No part of this book may be used or reproduced by any means, graphic, electronic, or mechanical, including photocopying, recording, taping or by any information storage retrieval system without the written permission of the author except in the case of brief quotations embodied in critical articles and reviews.

WestBow Press books may be ordered through booksellers or by contacting:

WestBow Press
A Division of Thomas Nelson & Zondervan
1663 Liberty Drive
Bloomington, IN 47403
www.westbowpress.com
844-714-3454

Because of the dynamic nature of the Internet, any web addresses or links contained in this book may have changed since publication and may no longer be valid. The views expressed in this work are solely those of the author and do not necessarily reflect the views of the publisher, and the publisher hereby disclaims any responsibility for them.

Any people depicted in stock imagery provided by Thinkstock are models, and such images are being used for illustrative purposes only.

Certain stock imagery © Thinkstock.

ISBN: 978-1-4908-0642-6 (sc)
ISBN: 978-1-4908-0644-0 (hc)
ISBN: 978-1-4908-0643-3 (e)

Library of Congress Control Number: 2013915345

Print information available on the last page.

WestBow Press rev. date: 08/13/2021

Table of Contents

Acknowledgements. . . . . *vii*

Dedication . . . . *ix*

Prologue . . . . *xi*

Chapter 1   Journey down the Lemon 1

Chapter 2   Facing the Blade 14

Chapter 3   Past, Present and Future. 27

Chapter 4   Gearing Up. 35

Chapter 5   Reunion. 43

Chapter 6   A way of escape 55

Chapter 7   Last flight of the Lemon Lady 64

Chapter 8   Havens reunion. 74

Chapter 9   A new leader 88

Chapter 10   The escarpment trail. 99

Chapter 11   Laying the Lady to rest 108

Chapter 12   A new back door. .118

Chapter 13   Wedding bells and the bear 128

Chapter 14   Avalanche. 136

Chapter 15   A prophetic word 142

Chapter 16   Black tail hunt 150

Chapter 17   Meat and greet 158

Chapter 18   Mid-tribulation Eschatology 101 167

Chapter 19   A conclusion and a new beginning 175

Chapter 20   Big cats and ravens. 185

Chapter 21   Scavengers 194

Chapter 22   Family time and reconciliation 202

Chapter 23   Staying ahead of the storm 210

Chapter 24   Down to the Gastineau banks. 218

Chapter 25   A perilous journey home 228

Chapter 26   Home and counting coup 238

Chapter 27   A day of Thanksgiving 247

Chapter 28   Jenson plans for revenge. 253

Chapter 29   Battle for the Mark-less 261

Chapter 30   The Lemon Creek Massacre 269

Chapter 31   Peace in the eye of the storm 276

Chapter 32   Jenson's grand reception 283

Chapter 33   In Clouds of Glory 296

Epilogue: Scarlet Thread 299

About The Author *301*

Acknowledgements

In any worthwhile endeavor, one is blessed to find himself or herself under the knowledgeable and watchful eye of a mentor. As a writer and nascent novelist, I am blessed with two. It is with deepest respect and appreciation that I wish to acknowledge the men who have guided me to the fulfillment of this endeavor, **David T. Peckham,** and **Rolfe Korsborn,** both now reside in the presence of their Lord and Savior. Without their expertise, dedication, and encouragement this work would have remained a dream, written only on the tablet of my heart.

Dedication

This book is dedicated to my Heavenly Father who wrote it on the tablets of my heart, before the first stroke of my pen ever touched paper. To the memory of my Father, who taught me the meaning of commitment, and unconditional love. To my mother, whose prayers, support, and encouragement, fill my life with a sense of purpose, which only a mother's love can give. And, to my precious wife Talafaipea, my never-ending story, and the fortress in which I dwell.

Prologue

The Eschatology contained in this fictional work is intrinsically woven throughout every chapter. It is not offered as an absolute, but as a very plausible possibility. As we enter what many believe to be the end of the church age, the only true and undeniable interpretation of God's word and end time events must come from Him who set all things in motion, and this through the leading of the Holy Spirit.

Lemon Creek Chronicle looks at end time events through the eyes of common people and simple faith, taking God's word at face value. It is a story about fictional characters in a real place, living in a not-too-distant future. Seeking truth, and clinging to their hope in Christ, they battle against a one world socialist government, which has risen out of worldwide economic collapse and chaos. Like the Jews of the 20th Century, 21st Century Christians have become the targets of intolerance and hatred, the scapegoats of a Godless and dying world. The rest of humanity will either submit, or face extermination.

Too often, we study the word of God through the lens of theological theories, based on man's own understanding. What part of "Lean not to your own understanding" needs interpreted? God never intended for his word to bow to interpretation but be raised up in obedience.

Rightly dividing the word of truth does not find accomplishment in simply seeking deeper understanding, but through the daily and practical application of Christ's precepts to our lives. Truth becomes manifested, by living out, the living word. God's word can and will substantiate itself.

Lemon Creek Chronicle: is written to vicariously connect the reader through the lives of its characters, with a viable reality few Christians today are prepared to embrace. My prayer for those who read this work, is to encourage them who have called upon the name of Christ, "to make their calling and election sure", in the dark and perilous times ahead. For those who live in fear outside of God's matchless grace, I pray this story might be a harbinger of hope and inner peace, which can only be found in a personal relationship with Christ.

Like Rahab the harlot, who by faith hung a scarlet cord from her window, believing for deliverance from destruction, we by faith in Christ do the same. Clinging tenaciously to our hope and trusting that He will bring us through whatever lies ahead, our great commission is and will remain to seek and lead the lost to Christ, right up to the last moment before the sky rolls up like a scroll and the trumpet sounds! Louis L, Claassen

CHAPTER 1

Journey down the Lemon

Pastor Bowens, his wife Sarah, Alice Foster, and Ben Huskins, gathered around Ellen and Jessica. Laying their hands on the two young women, Pastor Bowens prayed for God's blessing and hand of protection over them, as they prepared to send them back down the Lemon.

"It's taken the better part of two years, to come to this moment," Pastor said, after concluding his prayer.

"We've made more forays into the Lemon Creek community for provisions, than I care to remember. With this last trip down the mountain, we'll be prepared to stand in the gap for one more year, or until the rapture, whichever comes first."

Ben took Ellen by the arm and ushered her aside.

"Ellen, do you remember everything I've told you about the truck?"

She nodded.

"The truck is located at the Southeast corner of the big bend in the creek, just before the old quarry. The keys are in a small box attached to the inside of the rear bumper of the truck on the driver's side. The map is in the pouch on the driver's seat, and the fuel additive is behind the seat."

"Praise the Lord, the rest I know you can handle. Your one tough cookie, he said with a twinkle in his eye."

With last minute instructions and hurried hugs, the women made their way across the rocky plateau. Entering the forest, they began the first leg of their descent down the mountainside, with Ellen leading the way.

Although it was, only five miles as the crow flies from their retreat to the small town of Lemon Creek, it was still going to take almost six and a half hours to make the torturous 3500-foot descent to where the old truck was hidden, just a mile and a half outside of town. Ellen and Jessica slowly worked their way along the steep and rugged mountainside.

Ellen followed a trail indelibly etched in her mind but invisible to the naked eye. Her only landmarks were those that indicated where the turns were made as their path zigzagged across the forested, and nearly vertical landscape. It was almost two and a half hours into their descent, and the women had crisscrossed the mountainside four times. They had covered about five miles, and only descended a little over a thousand feet. Neither woman spoke during the descent, except to encourage each other to be careful. Now, Jessica spoke up as they stepped out onto a large flat rock where turn number five would begin.

"Ellen, it's time for a break, and I could use some water."

"So could I," Ellen responded, removing her pack, and tossing down her walking stick.

She sank to her knees, and in one simple motion rolled over on her back, with Jessica mimicking her sister. They lay there almost fifteen minutes before Ellen rolled up on her side and looked down at her watch.

"We had better have some water and a little snack she said, pushing herself into a sitting position. It's almost eleven, and we've got to be at the truck before nightfall."

With that, the women savored a couple of biscuits Alice had baked for their breakfast that mornings, washing them down with bottles of ice-cold glacier melt.

Continuing their way down the mountain, Ellen and Jessica arrived at the first of three crossings; two across a tumbling mountain stream, they had aptly named Slip Creek. The third was down on Lemon Creek, across a log, three-feet wide, and thirty-five feet long.

At the creek where they now stood, the stream was only twelve feet wide. The water wasn't deep, but it was swift. One slip on the stepping-stones could send a person over a thirty-foot waterfall to the rocks below. As Jessica followed Ellen over the creek, she labored to keep her eyes on the stones in front of her, and not on the roaring torrent disappearing to her left.

"One down and two to go," Ellen shouted, over the roar of the water.

They had now descended almost 1300 feet, and the distance between the last three turns would be less than three quarters of a mile each. The kicker was, the two most dangerous crossings of slip, and Lemon creek still lay ahead of them.

Stepping onto the bank, Jessica reached out to Ellen for a hand up. Suddenly, a great Alaskan brown stood up behind them and announce his presence with a roar that made the sound of the waterfall disappear.

Ellen and Jessica froze as the words "sweet Jesus," formed in their minds but never escaped their lips. The bear, bouncing on its forepaws lunged forward into the water, but never made it to the middle of the creek. Slipping on one of the large rocks Jessica had just crossed over, it plunged into the water nose first, and with a gurgling roar, disappeared over the waterfall. Clinging to one another and sinking slowly to their knees, the women whispered a prayer and thanked the Lord for His ever-saving presence in their lives.

Taking a deep breath Ellen sighed and hugged her sister.

"I think we had better pay closer attention for sign she said," as she stood.

"That's a big for-sure," Jessica responded, but it's awful hard to keep your eyes on where you're stepping and placing your hands and still watch for other dangers with teeth," she said laughingly.

"Then watch with your ears," Ellen said, adjusting her backpack and helping her sister to her feet.

The remainder of the two and a quarter mile descent brought the women back to slip creek on the edge of a sloping hundred-foot precipice of cascading water. At this point, the water spewed out of a twenty-foot-wide overhang of rock, shaped like the spout of a pitcher. It was on a narrow ledge, which ran under the spout that Ellen and Jessica had to pass. Pushing aside the low hanging boughs of a small evergreen, the women stepped into a clearing about four feet square. Jessica was the first to step onto the ledge with her face to the wet rock.

"Watch your step," Ellen said, trying to raise her voice above the sound of the cascading water.

Moving sideways and clinging to the natural handholds, Jessica inched slowly across, carefully feeling for each step she kept her eyes fixed on the safety of the other side.

Seeing that her sister had safely maneuvered herself to the trail that would carry them down to the bank of Lemon creek, Ellen carefully began moving across the wet slippery surface.

If it weren't for the fact, the ledge sloped back and down into the mountainside, fording the raging stream at this point would have been impossible for them, and an arduous task, even for a seasoned mountain climber, she thought.

As Ellen reached the other side, Jessica grabbed her hand and pulled her to the safety of the descending trail. From their vantage point, the women could see the sun quickly sinking in the west toward the tops of the lower island mountains. It was now only a quick hundred-foot descent to lemon creek, and a thirty-five-foot balancing act across the last major obstacle, the old log.

Stepping into the clearing at the edge of the creek, Ellen again looked at her watch. It was now three thirty in the afternoon. By six, the valley would be plunged into deep shadows, too dark to find their way safely.

They had to hurry. This time Ellen led the way as she climbed up on the huge log. Inching forward, she carefully stepped over the patches of lose moss that would surely spell disaster. Every few feet the snag of an old branch would lend itself as a point of balance, but Ellen didn't dare put any real weight on them, for fear, they would break and send her plummeting fifteen feet, into the icy water below. Turning when she reached the other side, she motioned to Jessica.

"Be careful when you come across, keep your eyes on the log," she called out.

Only then did Jessica climb up, to begin her exodus across the swiftly moving creek. As she neared the other side, Jessica's heels found a piece of lose moss. Helplessly straddling the log and clinging to the broken end of one of the old branches, she caught her breath.

"Jessica, Jessica… Ellen shouted, are you alright?"

"Yes … yea I'm ok," she called back!

Realizing she wasn't going to get back to her feet, Jessica carefully began to shinny across the remainder of the log, until she was able to reach out and slip into Ellen's waiting arms.

"I was terrified, are you alright," Ellen questioned?

Jessica nodded her head and winced a smile.

After careful examination, Ellen was satisfied that aside from a few scrapes and some possible bruising, Jessica was going to be ok. Light was fading fast, as the women repositioned their packs, and started out on the last three-mile hike to the old truck, and a well-earned nights rest.

It was dark, by the time, they made the last quarter mile stretch to the truck, and Ellen had to use her flashlight to find their way through the thick underbrush. As the chrome on the bumper glistened in the darkness, the women sighed with relief.

The old ford 4x4 belonged to Ben Huskins. It was right where Ben had told Ellen they would find it. Taking off her backpack, and lying down, with the flashlight in her mouth, Ellen pulled herself under the rear of the truck. Looking where Ben had directed, she found the box, popped the latch, and removed the keys.

"I found them," she said, sliding out from under the truck.

To her delight, she found Jessica diligently working at starting a fire. Few people ever ventured very far past the end of the old quarry road. There was a trail about two miles long, but no one ever ventured off of it because of the dense brush and rugged terrain, not to mention a local population of Alaskan brown bears who guarded the upper reaches of Lemon creek with a vengeance. The browns were content to stay in their realm, and the local Juneau population was for the most part, happy to stay in theirs.

Unlocking the driver's door and looking in the pouch on the front of the driver's seat, she found the small notebook. Opening it, she saw the crude but simple map on the inside of the cover. There was no road or trail from where they were, back to the quarry bridge, and the road into town. Early in the morning, they would have to drive out over dense brush, small boulders and between an array of trees and snags, for over half a mile.

As Ellen unlocked the tonneau cover that secured the box of the pickup, she quickly found to her delight the sleeping bags, pillows and camping gear Ben had left, when he made his last trip up the valley over a year earlier, everything was still wrapped and sealed in the plastic trash bags, where Ben had left them. Bowing her head and thanked the Lord.

Opening a small carton, she pulled out two MRE's. *Meals ready to eat she mused.* They really were not her idea of meals, ready to eat or not, but they were better than nothing, and she was starving!

Jessica already had a fire going at the mouth of a small shallow cave, where Ben had previously made camp. The fire not only drove away the darkness and provided some security for the women, but its warmth was appreciated the most. As Ellen and Jessica huddled behind it, they ate their meals in silence. It wasn't until they had finished, the fire was stoked, and they had settled down at the back of the small cave, that the women began to converse and make tentative plans for the next leg of their odyssey.

"It seems so strange to be down on the banks again," Jessica said, pulling the collar of her jacket up around her neck and ears. I miss Max; he was all I had after Andy left. Andy and that dog were inseparable, and now Max has been gone since the day we left for the Havens. That's been over fourteen months ago," she said with a sigh.

"Probably went looking for Andy, Ellen said, stirring the coals of the fire with a small stick. I really loved Andy, Ellen went on, and I know that he loved you with all his heart, I just can't understand why he left the way he did, and then never called or wrote. It just doesn't seem right she said," tossing the stick into the fire and leaning back against the now warmed stone of the cave.

Jessica stood up from the fire and backing up sat down next Ellen.

"I don't understand either she said, leaning her head on Ellen's shoulder. He's still my husband and I've never stopped loving him, he was just so troubled and disappointed about work and everything ... I pray every day that he's ok, and the Lord will keep him safe, but I've given up hope of ever seeing him again, in this world."

"Well, we've already decided how we're going to deal with tomorrow," Ellen said, as she stood and rolled her sleeping bag out with the foot towards the fire. "All we can do now is deal with each day as it comes and believe that the Lord is in control. Everything will unfold according to His plan for our lives; we just have to continue to trust in Him."

Reaching out for another piece of firewood, Ellen tossed it on the fire.

The women's goal for the next morning was to get in, get the supplies on their list and get out, as soon as possible. The alternative plan was simple, run and make their way back to the retreat either alone or together, but none the less run.

Stoking up the fire, the women slipped down into their sleeping bags. Ellen with her hand lying across the breach of the .22 caliber survival rifle she had found in the back of the truck, slipped into a light and restless sleep. Jessica, sore and exhausted drifted to sleep, feed by the warmth of the fire. Jessica didn't awaken until first light when Ellen gently shaking her shoulder, called her back into the chilly reality of a new day.

"It says scrambled eggs, hash browns and ham," Ellen said, as she slid the aluminum trays off the wire rack hovering over the hot coals. "I just hope that's what it looks like … if not, we'll have to eat with our eyes closed."

Responding to Ellen's remark, Jessica sat up and rubbed her eyes.

"I really don't care what it looks like, as long as it's hot," she said drowsily.

Ellen had the fire crackling again, and the camp pot on the fire was spewing steam, signaling that the water was ready for the tea bags whose tags dangled over the edge of the tin cups next to the fire.

"Breakfast is ready," Ellen touted, trying to coax Jessica out of her sleeping bag.

Huddling next to the fire, the women began their day with a devotional from the small Bible Ellen carried in her vest pocked, and prayed for the Lord's guidance, protection and grace through the day that lay before them. After praying, Jessica pulled a small book out of her backpack, along with a pen, tucked into an inner pocket, and began writing in her diary.

After a few minutes, she lay it down on a large flat rock next to her and joined Ellen for breakfast.

With newfound strength from God's Word and a good night's rest, the women savored their tea and MRE's, as they discussed their plans. When they were finished, Jessica doused the fire with the remaining water from the camp pot and stirred the smoldering embers with a stick to make sure the fire was completely out. Loading everything up in the truck, the women climbed in, and buckled up. Starting the truck, Ellen put it in gear and cautiously pulled forward, glancing up at the crude map that now hung on the visor.

Pastor Bowens and Ben left the Havens a few hours after the women, following the same trail they had taken down the mountainside. They arrived at the old log crossing on Lemon Creek shortly before Jessica and Ellen arrived at the base camp, and the old truck. It didn't take long for

Ben to get a small fire going under an overhang of rock near the creek, as Pastor Bowens gathered larger pieces of wood to stoke the fire.

"Pastor," Ben said loudly. "Don't go out too far, the browns fish in this creek, and they don't do much sleeping."

A few moments later Pastor Bowens appeared with an armload of large dry limbs and tossed them down by the fire.

"Ben Huskins," Pastor said, hiking up his trousers. "I'm five years your senior and I do know a few things about bears. I know for instance, that they don't eat Pastors, says so in the Bible. It's there in Second Kings, chapter two. It says they only eat mouthy younger men that tease older men of God," he chuckled.

All Ben could do was shake his head and try to subdue the telltale grin that was forming across his face. Pulling the small coffee pot out of his pack, he walked down to the creek and scooped up a pot of water.

Back at the fire, he sat the pot down on a flat stone and shoved it up against the red-hot coals. When the water was ready, he pulled out a jar of instant coffee, and added what he thought was enough to make four cups, stirring it with a small stick.

"Suppers ready," he said.

As Pastor Bowens held out his cup, Ben served him with a smile.

"Traveling light is a bummer," he said, filling his own cup.

"Not as light as you think young whipper snapper, Pastor said", pulling a bag of jerky from his knap-sac.

"It's from my private stock," he said with a smile.

Ben almost spilt his coffee, as he gazed hungrily at the large bag of jerked meat Pastor was holding out to him. As he reached for the bag, he didn't care if the meat was beef, venison, bear or kangaroo, he just wanted to sink his teeth into some.

The men sat for a good while, savoring the coffee and jerked meat as they talked about their plans for the next day.

"Crossing here in the morning isn't a problem, but when we get down to the quarry, we're going to get wet, making two crossings with the girls and the stores they'll have with them," Pastor Bowens said.

"I talked it over with Ellen, and there's been a little change in plans," Ben interrupted. "The winter weather is on us, and it's not a good time to be getting wet, we would stay wet all the way back to the Havens. Ellen and Jessica will meet us at the South end of the bridge, he said, holding his hands out to the warmth of the fire."

"Ben," Pastor said, with a surprised look on his face. "That will put us less than a mile out of town, if there's any trouble, we'll be hard pressed for any kind of safe retreat."

"You're absolutely right." Ben said, swilling down the last of his coffee. "You and I will wait up on the hillside, where we can see down the road. When the women come, we'll be able to see if there's anyone following, then we'll go down to meet them, load up and head for back to the crossing here."

"Sounds good to me," I wasn't looking forward to dipping my backside in that freezing water anyway. I'm assuming that Sara and Alice will still be waiting here for us with some supper when we get back, right?"

"Yea, nothing else has changed, we'll have a good breakfast the next morning, divide up the supplies between the six of us, and make the climb back up to the Havens." Ben said, poking the fire with a stick.

With that, Pastor Bowens un-laced his boots, pulled them off, and set them by the fire.

"I don't know about you Ben, but my old bones need some rest."

Rolling out his sleeping bag and unzipping it, he slid inside and pulled the top over his head. Within minutes, Ben could hear Pastors muffled snoring. Standing, and throwing some wood on the fire, he followed Pastors example and slid into his own sleeping bag.

By five thirty, both men were up, booted and chewing on some more of Pastors jerky. Ben poured the remainder of the morning's coffee and a little more water from the creek on the dying embers of the night's fire, and both men climbed up on the old log. Ben led off, and Pastor Bowens followed about six feet behind. As Pastor Bowens teetered across the last four feet of the log, he grabbed onto Ben's waiting arm, panting.

"I'm getting to old for this sort of thing, he said. When we get back to the Havens, I won't be going down again, cause my only desire is and will be to go "UP," he said with a grin.

As Ben and Pastor hiked the last three miles to the base camp where Ellen and Jessica had spent the night, only a trained eye like Ben's could see where the women had passed.

"You sure can tell these girls were raised in the bush," Ben said, as they made their way down the same path the women had taken the day before.

"Just like their parents," Pastor said, between breaths. Don and Joanne spent more of their lives in the bush, than they did at home, but they never missed a Sunday. I really miss them … they were such a blessing."

"Yea, I miss them too. As quickly as things are happening now, we'll be together again though, before we know it!"

It was a little before eleven when Ben and Pastor Bowens walked into the small opening where the shallow cave was, and the truck used to be.

"Looks like they made it out ok," Ben said, as they continued following the path the truck had made. "We don't have time to stop now if we're going to be at our rendezvous by noon." Turning to see if Pastor Bowens was keeping up, he paused. "I'd rather be a little early than late, for their sakes more than ours."

"Ben," Pastor said, stopping and leaning up against a large rock. If you don't give me a five-minute breather, you're going to have to carry me the last quarter mile, and I won't let you have any more of my jerky either."

"Ok Pastor," Ben said, turning and walking back to where Pastor Bowens was sitting on a fallen log. You know I'm in no shape to carry you, but if you want, I think I could help you out and carry the jerky for you.

Pastor Bowens looked at Ben over the top of his glasses and took a deep breath before clearing his throat.

"Brother Ben, he said in his Pastors voice, when we get back the Havens, please remind me go get out my anointing oil. I think I'm going to have to pray you through all over again, but until then, I think we had better get moving."

Standing up Pastor Bowens took the lead, but only for a short distance.

"You had better move up here Ben," Pastor said, turning around and standing in the middle of a small clearing. "I do pretty well, leading from the pulpit, but out here in the woods, I'm kind of out of my comfort zone. I just wanted to help get you on your way again he chided, leaning heavily on his walking stick.

Ben stepped forward, giving Pastor Bowens a pat on the shoulder, and a little nudge.

"You're doing just fine for an old duffer," Ben said, as he led the way down the trail left by the truck.

"I love you too," Pastor said, tossing a small cone that nearly knocked Ben's hat off.

Forty minutes later, Ben and Pastor Bowens stood in the shelter of some fir trees overlooking both the road and the bridge, about twenty yards up the hill.

"Praise the Lord, Ben said; looking at his watch, we made it here with ten minutes to spare."

The men made themselves comfortable and began their vigil, glancing down the road every few minutes and listening for the sound of Ben's old truck. Minutes turned into hours, and by two PM, Pastor and Ben were convinced that something had gone terribly wrong.

"I'm sure something went wrong when they tried to use Ellen's smart card so close to the deadline, Ben said, they probably had plain clothed militia lurking around the checkouts. We should never have tried this last attempt for stores, and just trusted in the Lord's provision!"

Pastor Bowens put his arm around Ben's shoulders.

"We've done everything we could do Ben; we still have two other women waiting for us in a very dangerous area, we have to think about them too," he added. "Let's turn to the one who knows everything and can accomplish anything. Let's do what we do best, "pray!"

Knowing that they would have to leave before two thirty if they were going to make it back to the crossing before dark, the men bowed their heads and began to pray.

"Lord," Pastor spoke tearfully. "We've waited as long as we can for Ellen and Jessica. Father, we pray that your hand of mercy will remain upon them, whatever their circumstances might be, and that in your timing and power, you will restore them to us according to your will and purpose. Lord, please extend your grace to us, and in this time of despair, fill us with your peace and give us the strength we will need on our return to the Haven you prepared for us. We ask this in your precious name, Amen."

Without further conversation, the men pulled their packs up on their shoulders, and began the arduous trek back up the Lemon.

CHAPTER 2

Facing the Blade

ELLEN AND JESSICA WALKED BRISKLY as they made their way into the Lemon Creek Costco, flashing Ellen 's membership card, as they went in. The mile and a half drive into town along Lemon creek had been uneventful. The drive back down to the quarry bridge following Ben's map, was a different story, and had left the women visibly shaken. They were thankful that on the return trip, the quarry bridge would be as far as they would have to go. Ellen and Jessica knew they would be abandoning the vehicle, with no intention of anyone ever coming down again, at least on this side of the rapture! It still didn't lessen the anxiety they both felt, after all, they were evangelical Christians, and the deadline for exchanging their smart cards for the embedded mark of the New Collective, had come, and gone. Now the amnesty period was almost over and purchasing much needed supplies would be impossible without the mark.

"In and out", Ellen quipped.

She longed for the safety of the forest, the security it provided, and the other four members of their group who had fled into the Mendenhall wilderness with her and Jessica. Fleeing was the only way to escape the growing persecution and constant harassment of the Collective Militia. Ellen knew their names were already on the list for arrest when the amnesty period ended.

Already many of the marginal Christians and those who were only Christian by association had crossed over. Rather than face being ostracized by their neighbors and community, or harassed by the Collective Militia, they received the mark. Some of those people were once friends, who Ellen had worshiped and fellowshipped with, since she was a child.

After today she thought, *the choices would only be the mark or death.*

As Jessica placed the second twenty-five-pound bag of sugar on the cart and headed for the large bags of flour on the other side of the isle, Ellen's attention returned to the task at hand.

Cooking oil Ellen thought, where is the cooking oil?

Going down the list and gathering the items with a growing sense of urgency, Jessica and Ellen pulled two large bags of salt off a pallet and headed for the checkout. Ellen could feel the muscles tighten in the back of her neck, and her lips pursed as the checker scanned their items.

Pulling out her smart card, Ellen presented it for payment. The middle-aged woman who had checked her purchases gazed at her in amazement.

"Honey, you're cutting it close, she said, deeply concerned. Noon is the end of the twenty-four-hour amnesty, and things are not looking too good for those who have waited until the last minute. You had better hurry down to the Collective Center when you leave and get this taken care of."

With those words, she took Ellen's card and completed the transaction. Ellen and Jessica wasted no time getting their purchases to the old truck. They quickly popped the tonneau cover, and hastily stowed everything away. When the tailgate was up and the cover securely locked, the desperation in their faces slowly gave way to sighs and then uncontrollable laughter.

As their elation began to subside, Jessica sat down on the rear bumper of the truck. Dropping her chin, she patted her tummy.

"I'm so hungry I could eat roadkill," she breathed.

Looking into her forlorn face, Ellen placed her arm around her sister's shoulders, and again broke into laughter.

"You know Jessica, if we would have hit all the tasting stations a couple of times while we were shopping, we could have eaten for free Ellen grinned," too bad.

Looking at her watch, Ellen pulled Jessica to her feet and walked her around to the front of the truck.

"It's only 10:30; I know we're supposed to meet Pastor and Ben at the bridge at Noon, but let's go over to Abby's Kitchen, for a quick bite. It's just a block, Ellen added. We can walk there and back, and then we'll head out of town well before noon… I'm hungry too."

Leaving the truck parked in the Costco lot, they walked arm in arm down Bent Street, past play it again sports, and turned into the diner.

As Jessica and Ellen walked into the restaurant, Molly Dixon dropped the menu's she was holding and stared at Ellen and Jessica as if she had seen ghosts.

The last time she had seen the women, was at least a year and a half ago, she mused.

Quickly picking up the menu's, Molly stammered a quick greeting and motioned Ellen and Jessica to follow her to a booth. Seating them, Molly handed the women each a menu and quickly scurried away, returning moments later with water and a barrage of questions.

Coyly, Ellen managed to evade most all of Molly's enquiries with vague, but what she thought were reasonable answers.

"What's the special today," she quipped, trying to change the subject.

Molly rattled off a couple of choices, neither of which sounded good to Ellen or Jessica, so they settled for cheeseburgers, fries, and water. Molly again scurried away, with their order. Ellen sensed that there was more on Molly's mind than just getting their order to the kitchen. Jessica leaned over the table and whispered.

"Does Molly seem to be acting a little strange, or is it just me?"

Taking a sip of her water, she watched as Molly disappeared around the corner.

"It's not just you," Ellen whispered back. She was always so two-faced when we were in school, no one ever really trusted her. She would act like your best friend one minute and then spread malicious rumors about you the next. Your right, she's not acting like herself."

After turning in her order, Molly quickly stepped around the corner and began to re-read the flyer posted on the bulletin board in the kitchen.

"NOTICE" 250 credit reward for information leading to the arrest and conviction of anyone not bearing the mark of the Collective. Contact a Collective agent at 209-MARK [209- 6275]

With a deep breath, Molly exhaled and adjusted her apron. She knew that Ellen was a Christian and knew enough about Bible prophecy to know that Ellen would never take any kind of mark, let alone a chip under her skin. The same went for Jessica, and Molly could see the credits multiplying as she dialed the number on the flyer.

As Ellen and Jessica sat and quickly consumed their meal, a sense of foreboding suddenly caused Ellen to shiver.

"Jessica," she whispered, I think it is time we get out of town."

Jessica nodded, and with that, both drank down the last of their water and slid out of the booth. As they walked to the counter, Molly handed Ellen the check, which she presented to Abby at the register, along with her smart card.

"Another thirty minutes and this card will be worthless," Abby said, with a twinkle in her eye. It's better that I get your money than the Collective."

Taking back her card with a sigh, Ellen said "thanks", and turning with Jessica, headed for the door. The door had barely closed behind them when Molly quickly whispered into her cell phone.

"Agent Thomas, they just walked out the door."

Walking down the street past a large white van, Jessica was just starting to speak when two men stepped out of a car in front of them.

"Ellen Michaels," said one of the men? Sensing danger Ellen spun Jessica around, and cried, "Run!"

Before she had moved three feet, Ellen fell writhing to the ground, every muscle in her body screaming in pain. Stunned, she lost consciousness.

When she and Jessica came to, they found themselves lying in the back of a moving van, their hands bound behind them with what felt like zip ties. Transported to the Lemon Creek Correctional Center a few miles away from the restaurant, they were weak and unable to raise themselves, as the van rolled to a stop. Guards dragged them from the van, muscling them through a large red door, and into a small white room containing two metal chairs and a table. Thrown into the chairs, their captors turned out the lights and left them sitting in the dark as the door slammed shut. Jessica was the first to speak.

"This doesn't look good sister," she said, struggling to push herself erect in her chair. It's so dark in here; I couldn't see my hands in front of my face, even if they weren't tied behind my back!"

Even though her body ached, Ellen could not hold back the chuckle that emerged.

As Ellen pushed herself up in her chair, the light in the room suddenly came on. After being in the dark, the light was blinding. The women squinted, as the door opened to reveal two uniformed men and a woman, wearing latex gloves. Carrying what looked like a plastic toolbox, the uniformed woman tossed it on the table.

With their hands still bound, the guards forced the women to stand, as they began to cut off their clothing with shears and examine each piece before stuffing them into a large black trash bag. Naked and shivering, the women watched, as a guard pulled their smart cards out, laying them on the table beside a hole punch and two large zip ties. Punching holes in their cards, they inserted the ties. These they placed around their necks and after cinching them loosely, cut off the ends. Ellen and Jessica then endured the shame and humiliation that followed.

Weeping bitterly, they were drug to the table one at a time, where the woman roughly performed cavity searches, as the guards held them securely. Only when their bonds were cut and they were allowed to put on the blue scrubs tossed to them, did the weeping subside to muffled sobs.

The women, then given ankle sox to put on their feet, followed their captors out of the room and down a dim lit hallway. Their cells contained only a wide metal bench and one wool blanket.

Evidently, they were not going to be here long, Ellen thought.

Neither Ellen nor Jessica dared utter a word, as they were place in adjoining cells.

With the guard's departure the lights went out, and again the women were plunged into darkness. Both Jessica and Ellen curled up in the rough wool blankets and attempted to find a position of comfort on their hard metal beds. Ellen could hear Jessica sobbing in the cell next to hers. She wanted to express some words of comfort, but simply could not find any, even to soothe her own pain. She lay in the darkness, thinking about Pastor Bowens and Ben. By now, she was sure they had waited if they could and had returned to the log crossing where they were to meet up with Sarah and Alice.

As her eyes began to adjust to the darkness, she could see a faint glow reaching down the hallway. Peering around the edge of her cell, she could just make out the window of the guard station. Standing in front was a uniformed guard, talking to the jailer inside.

"Convicted felons are being pardoned and given positions in the Collective Militia if they willingly take the mark," he said. All but a few inmates, who have become Christians, have taken the offer. Most of the correctional center, is now filled with believers, or those who hadn't made a choice before the end of the amnesty period today. They'll be given one last chance to cross over or be put to death by decapitation. The last two women came in today, numbers 97 and 98. Sounds gruesome to me, he concluded!"

"It may be Gruesome the jailer replied, but quick and not as messy as other options. They bleed out fast, and the fire hose makes clean-up a snap." With that, the guard turned and walked out of sight, his footsteps fading into silence.

Trembling Ellen jerked her head back from the bars and leaned against the wall.

Making the choice to lay down her life for Christ had come sooner than she had anticipated, she thought.

Ellen lay back down on the bench and threw the other half of the blanket over shivering body. She longed to be somewhere else and fell into a fitful sleep.

ELLEN LAY ON HER STOMACH for the longest time, her cheek pressed against the soft warm grass. Again, and again, she inhaled deeply, savoring the scent of rich moist earth that wafted up through the field of green, cradling her body. Raising her head and supporting her chin in the palm of her hand¾wisps of hair brushed against her face. The warm evening breeze seemed to caress the landscape unfolding before her half-closed eyes.

Like a Thomas Kinkade painting, the soft glow of a waning afternoon sun filled the canvas stretching out before her, with dancing rays of light. Gleefully, they teased the amber shadows of evening, and a hush soft as babies' breath seemed to fill the air. Ellen rolled on her back and gazed into an azure sky, her heart soaring, as the words and music of a favorite chorus flooded her mind.

He is my, everything, He is my all. He is my, everything, both great and small. He gave His life for me, made everything new ...

Suddenly, with the ringing of steel sliding against steel and the jolting sound of impact, tranquility exploded into a scene, of grey scale reality!

Sitting on the edge of a cold metal bench Ellen struggled to regain her composure. In the hazy twilight of morning, the muffled voices of those conducting hastily preformed tribunals, already echoed down the dimly lit hallway. With a trembling hand, Ellen reached for and clutched her only remaining possession, a smart card that now dangled from the plastic collar around her neck. Embedded in that thin rectangular piece of technology was her entire life's history, evidence that she really did exist, at least for the moment.

"Ellen, Ellen! Are you awake?" Jessica whispered.

A soft muffled voice suddenly pulled her thoughts out of the shadows and into the stark reality of the moment.

"Yes, she whispered, I am, but I wish I were dreaming!"

Recalling the reverie from which she had been so abruptly awakened, she slumped back against the wall, and prayed.

Jessica, with her face pressed against the cold bars of her cell, courageously fought back the tears that coursed her cheeks. Trying not to reveal the building anxiety, which flooded her heart, Jessica whispered slowly and deliberately.

"Ellen, do you think they'll come for us today?"

"I don't think so; I just heard them call for number 27. You and I are 97 and 98, Ellen sighed. Unless all those ahead of us choose the mark, it will take some time for those felonious members of the new collective, to accomplish their gruesome tasks."

"Let's have a Paul and Silas moment Ellen touted, and with that, she began to sing the song that had filled her dream with joy." He is my everything, He is my all.

As Ellen and Jessica sang, their subdued chorus found new strength. Even the harsh voices from the distant end of the hallway, seemed to pause and listen to the loving refrain that poured from their hearts.

"Like honey in the rock, O` He tastes like honey in the rock ..." Jessica paused, as Ellen finished the chorus.

"I love you Ellen," Jessica whispered. I'm so proud of you; I could never ask for a more wonderful sister, you've always been there when I've needed you!"

Twilight had given way to morning, and now a faint ray of sunlight began to flicker through a dirty windowpane on the far side of the hallway.

Ellen dropped her gaze to the floor. There surrounded by the morning light, was the shadowed silhouette of a cross. With a sudden burst of emotion, Ellen squealed.

"Jessica, look at the floor!"

By mid-morning breakfast arrived in the form of a small bottle of water and two slices of crudely buttered bread. As they prayed and slowly savored each bite, Ellen and Jessica recounted the flurry of events that had led to their captivity and prayed together for the safety of Pastor and Ben as they made their way back up to the crossing, and retreat at the Havens.

Throughout the day, Ellen and Jessica sat back-to-back against the wall that separated their cells, reminiscing about growing up with the rugged Mendenhall wilderness in their back yard. They talked about school days, church camps, and all the wonderful friends and people who had made their lives in the great Pacific Northwest, a treasure-chest of memories. It was in the middle of this vast, wild and overwhelming beauty that Ellen and Jessica had learned about the unfathomable love of Christ; through the example their parents had set for them. The women had both received Christ as their Savior, side by side at Bible camp when they were young girls, Jessica was five, and Ellen seven.

Even without her watch, Ellen could tell by the fading light that it was getting late in the afternoon. The torturous sounds that had echoed down the hallway throughout the day were beginning to show on the women's faces. Pleading, weeping and the periodic sound of a gavel as it bounced off its wooden anvil, were continually separated by either a brief silence, or the sound of the ringing steel of the guillotine. It was in the middle of this heart wrenching experience, that the women made their pact with each other and before God. They would stand together and face their persecutors with confidence in Christ, and His redeeming power, in life or in death.

As Jessica and Ellen sat and prayed together, the floor beneath them began to move to the sound of a deep rumble. Dust filled the air and slowly settled upon them and the floor. As quickly as it had left, silence returned preceded by the sound of ringing steel and a deadening thud.

The women sat listening to the commotion, which ensued after the tremor, but it wasn't until they heard the shuffling steps coming down the hallway toward them, that Ellen and Jessica suddenly sprang to their feet. Within seconds, four guards appeared, two in front of each cell. The doors were rolled open, and the women ushered down the hallway and into a fluorescent-lit room which resembled the one they had found themselves in the day before. This time however, it contained a long rectangular table, behind which, sat three solemn faced men, and a computer workstation attached to a card reader and another machine, with Micro Technology Laboratories Inc. emblazoned across its face. The women watched as another prisoner, was ushered over to the table. His smart card was removed and swiped through the card reader, as the technician keyboarded information into the computer and waited as it was transmitted to the third machine. When the transfer was complete, the technologist placed the man's right hand over a stainless-steel ball mounted on a short pedestal and pressed a red button on the machine.

"Done," he said, and turned to face the women as guards led the man out of the room, and back into the hallway.

On the table were two piles of papers, one noticeably higher, and in the hand of the man in the middle were two remaining documents with large numerals visibly printed at the top of each, 97 and 98.

Ellen and Jessica reached out to grasp each other's hand for support but were quickly jerked farther apart by the guards standing behind them. The man holding their documents, fixed his gaze on Ellen, and spoke in a cold and uncaring tone.

"Ellen Michaels, you have been arrested and brought before this tribunal for failure to comply with the edicts of the World Collective, and our sovereign leader, Lord Chris. It is the desire of his Lordship, that you be given one last opportunity to receive his mark of allegiance or be put to death as a part of the religious cancer that has prompted his divine intervention … make your choice," he said.

Ellen, with her eyes looking directly into those of her accuser, pursed her lips and spoke unwaveringly. "I choose death she said, only my Savior Jesus Christ is Lord!"

"So be it", "Go to your savior and lord," her accuser said, and hit the wooden anvil with his gavel.

One of the guards behind her stepped around with a knife in his hand.

Pulling her smart card away from her neck, he cut the collar and removed her identity, tossing it into a large plastic box in front of the table. Then, as quickly as she had been brought in Ellen was ushered through another door, and into the chilling air of the prison yard.

Moments later Jessica stood beside her, guards gripping their arms on each side. The women stood, forced to face the guillotine. Before them, two militiamen callously removed a limp headless body from the narrow bench where it lay strapped. Following them, a man with a fire hose, slowly erased the evidence of the violent act, washing it down through a grated hole beneath the stainless-steel structure.

One elderly man remained in front of the women, flanked as they were by two guards. He stood as erect as he could, and with his chin raised in a defiant gesture, glanced toward Ellen and Jessica. With trembling lips, he spoke four words that sent Ellen's mind racing back to that morning in her cell, "He is my, Everything!"

Half walking half dragged, the man was led up the steps and thrust face down on the narrow bench, his head placed in a stock, his hands shackled to the platform and his body synched to the bench. In unison, the guards took two steps back, one pushed a large black button, and it was over. With what appeared like military precision, the guards stepped forward, undid the restraints, and removed the lifeless body as the fire hose and its operator fulfilled their duty.

As the two guards returned, walking toward Ellen, they stopped suddenly. In an instant, a low rumble exploded into a violent shaking that sent everyone staggering and sprawling to the ground. During the confusion, and clinging to Ellen, Jessica staggered away from the collapsing building, as the women fell face down on the cold shattering concrete. All around them the earth heaved, buckled, and tore. Jessica clung to Ellen as they both huddled together in a fetal position. Burying her face in Ellen's hair, Jessica covered Ellen's with her hands.

Minutes later, the violent shaking melted into a deafening silence. The choking air brought the women to their knees, coughing, and spitting the muddied dust that clung to their lips and eyes as they wiped away the debris from their faces. Ellen was the first to stagger to her feet, and reaching down, pulled Jessica up, wrapping her arms around her. Slowly the women turned, gazing in unbelief at the devastation unfolding around them.

Turning to face their captors, "there were none!" The prison had been destroyed, and only a smoldering heap of ruble and twisted metal remained. Everything else lay swallowed up into the chasm at their feet, including the guillotine and those who had served its insatiable appetite.

The small platform of concrete, which Jessica and Ellen stood on rose several feet above everything else around them, giving them a commanding view in every direction. Behind them and to their left, lay Lemon Creek. Beyond, they could just make out the silhouette of the Costco store as flames lit up the evening sky behind it.

"Costco", Ellen's mind raced as she thought of the truck! Hope welled up in her heart

. "Jessica," Ellen blurted out, our truck, it's in the Costco parking lot, we have clothing and food in the back. We've got to get to the truck," she said, looking around her for a way of escape.

The twelve-foot fence, surrounding the prison, although leaning and twisted, remained intact as far as the women could see in the growing darkness. Ellen continued looking for a way out, as Jessica tugged on her arm, pointing to a section of fence near the main gate.

"Thank you, Father,", Ellen sighed.

Sitting down on the cold slab, and pulling Jessica down beside her, she began to pray.

Just to the right of the main gate, the bottom of the fence hung in the air over the end of the chasm the earthquake had created.

It took some time in their stocking feet and flimsy clothing, to climb down from their island of concrete, and make it across the fifty yards of broken and twisted earth, to the main gate. Maneuvering into the chasm and up through the crack torn under the hanging fence, left Jessica clinging to Ellen for support. With a great deal of painful effort, the women were able to slip under the fence. Crawling up the crumbling bank and over the jagged edge of the ripped asphalt, Ellen turned, and pulled Jessica to freedom.

The women shivered in the chilly evening, as they moved through the debris and up-heaved pavement, which separated them from the brush and tree lined bank of Lemon creek.

"Ellen, look at the fire, I don't think it's Costco that's on fire, it's got to be the Home Depot, the flames are too far away," Jessica said.

"I think your right," Ellen replied, pausing to momentarily look up in the direction they were going.

Moving toward the glow from the fire behind the Costco store, Ellen's mind raced ahead to the freezing water that she and Jessica would have to ford in order to get to the truck and warm dry clothing. When the women reached the edge of the creek, the water was raging, and appeared to be about thirty feet wide. Without hesitation, she waded into the icy water with Jessica following close behind, the fear of being caught again, driving them relentlessly forward. Suddenly they found themselves shoulder deep in the creeks channel and having to swim against the current as it carried them down stream, away from their intended destination.

The women, were swept over two hundred yards before they were able to pull themselves up onto a small sand bar, jutting into the creek. Freezing cold, they struggled over boulders and snags, desperately seeking in the darkness for a way through the brush and trees to the buildings and road above. After fifteen shivering minutes, they emerged from the brush to find themselves standing behind Ben Huskins Outfitters Store and staring into the blinding lights of a running vehicle. Time seemed to stand still, until a familiar voice rang out.

Jessica, Ellen … is that really you, "Praise God!"

CHAPTER 3

Past, Present and Future

CLUTCHING THE PAPERS TIGHTLY IN his hand, Joshua walked out of the Juneau courthouse, breathing a sigh of relief as he slid into the driver's seat of the van, and made his way across the city. Josh knew Juneau like the back of his hand. Turning north on Glacier Avenue he hung a left on Highland Drive at the north end of Douglas High School and made a quick right into the parking lot of the Breakwater Inn. Looking at his watch, he quickly grabbed the court documents lying in the passenger seat and slid out. Locking the door with the push button on his key chain, he walked into the restaurant.

Scanning the booths and tables on both sides, Josh looked for what he hoped would be the familiar face of an old friend.

The night before, Josh had received a phone call from an old school mate, Andy Bridgeport. He hadn't seen Andy for almost three years. Andy had no hooks, as the old timers used to say. He was always disappearing for a year or two at a time, seeking his elusive fortune. That was Andy's way, until he fell head over heels in love with Jessica Michaels. Josh paused in his reminiscing as a smile began to curl up at the corners of his mouth. Six months later, Andy was a born-again Christian and standing at the altar with Jessica at his side.

"Just yourself this morning," the server asked.

Josh paused for a moment in his musing, and replied with a smile to the waitress standing in front of him,

"No, I'm expecting a friend," he said, and followed the waitress to a booth by the window. Seating himself, he faced the doorway so he could see when Andy came in. Quickly looking through the menu, he made his selection and laid it down. Picking up the documents he received that morning; he began to re-read them for the third time.

"Josh, Joshua Huskins?"

Josh looked up into Andy's smiling face and quickly rose to his feet, giving him a hug and a hearty slap on the back. As Andy removed, his knap-sac, the two men slid into the booth. Josh couldn't hold back his excitement.

"Andy, where in the …, (Josh paused, reconsidering his choice of words,) where have you been?"

The smile on Andy's face quickly faded and his eyes dropped to the menu in front of him.

"It's a long story Josh," Andy said, taking a deep breath. "I'll try to explain it as best as I can, but the most important thing in my life right now, is I'm here to find Jessica, and I really need your help!"

Josh responded as reassuringly as he could.

"You know I'll do everything I can, but first let's order something to eat. You look like you could use something, and I'm starved."

After the waitress poured their coffee, and returned to the kitchen with their order, Josh again pressed Andy about his disappearance, waiting in silence as Andy searched for a place to begin.

Josh stirred his coffee, his mind drifting back to where Andy and Jessica's lives together, first started.

Andy spent the first two years of their marriage working in the fishing fleet, struggling through two seasons trying to make ends meet, and never felt he was able to provide for Jessica the way he wanted to. Finally, frustrated, and desperate Andy began to fall back into his old ways, spending more and more time away from home. Then one day Andy disappeared, leaving Jessica a letter that he had gone to the oil fields in Barrow and would return when he had made enough money to take care of her properly.

A year after he left, Jessica's parents were beaten to death by a gang of young men from the newly formed militia of the New World Collective, and their home burned to the ground. Shortly after that, Jessica's sister Ellen arrived, and the women lived together until their disappearance four months later. For over a year Jessica waited for Andy, without a phone call or a letter, and now he's appeared out of nowhere.

"Come on Andy, open up", Josh urged!

Andy picked up his cup. Taking a sip, he began with a sigh.

"Josh, I've been back for a little over a week now, about ten days to be exact, and I've done a lot of digging around. I know that after Mom and Dad Michaels were burned out and killed, that Jessica and Ellen hooked up, and eventually fled into the interior. Those I've talked to seem to think they're up the Mendenhall or maybe even up the Lemon, but nobody knows for sure. In the last year and a half, they've been seen here on the banks a few times, but nobody seems to remember when, you know, out of sight out of mind. Josh, I want to go up the Lemon and search for them, I just have to find Jessica and I am flat. I need your help man; can you grub me? There's no way I can make it without some tack," Andy said pleadingly, dropping his gaze back down on the table.

As Josh reached over and grasped Andy's wrist, he looked up with tears forming in his eyes.

"Andy, you're more like a brother than a friend, and I have no problem outfitting you, but I need to know why you left and where you've been for the last two and a half years. You've got to fill me in brother, you owe me that much."

Pulling back his hand, and taking another sip of coffee, Josh waited for Andy to pull himself together. As Josh sat down his coffee cup, the waitress slid their breakfast in front of them and walked away to bring back a pot of coffee for their table. It was then that Andy folded his hands, bowed his head, and began to pray. With an Amen, Andy raised his head to see Josh looking at him in wide-eyed amazement.

"What's with the praying, Josh queried? The last time I saw you, you were half stoked on Jose Cuervo, and when you used the name Jesus Christ, you weren't praying."

Andy's eyes suddenly dimmed a little.

"That's a fact," he said, with what appeared to Josh, to be legitimate remorse. "But I'm not the same man I was thirty months ago, and that's a fact too," he said, punctuating his statement with a deliberate nod of his head.

Andy now had Josh's undivided attention and continued as he reached out for his coffee cup, wrapping both hands around its warmth.

"Two weeks after hitting Anchorage, I was broke, homeless and hungry. To make matters worse, I was angry with God, hating myself, and too proud to call or write Jessica and let her know where I was, or my condition. All I could think about was getting to Barrow and filling my pockets with my share of the dollars flowing out of those new oil fields they discovered. Eventually, I got hooked up with a couple of drillers, who were in Anchorage on furlough, and was able to get on through them."

"That's awesome," Josh retorted. "But what's that got to do with you not being the same man you were when you left here?"

"Don't get your shorts in a bunch," Andy said, grinning, as he took a sip of his coffee. "I'm getting to that in a few minutes."

Andy shifted himself in the booth. Sliding his hips forward, he leaned back, toying with the handle of his coffee cup.

"I made good money," he said. "I worked nearly a year and a half without a furlough and put all my money into the bank in Anchorage." Taking another sip of coffee, he licked his lips.

"I had accrued almost three months of furlough and decided it was time to come home to Jessica with my savings, almost a hundred and forty thousand dollars, less taxes and living expenses. I flew out of Barrow in the middle of a snowstorm, and never made it to Anchorage. The plane went down in a remote area of the state, and I was the only one to survive."

Josh looked at Andy in disbelief, swallowing the last bite of his omelet, and quickly washing it down with a mouth full of coffee.

"I REALLY DON'T KNOW WHAT happened after the crash," Andy continued. "When I finally came to, I was in the lodge of a tribal elder and leader of a small native village in the middle of nowhere. I found out later that I was about three hundred and fifty miles north of Anchorage, and about eighty miles from the nearest forest service airstrip. It was only manned from mid spring into the fall."

"The old man who took me into his lodge, said that I was so near death, that they didn't believe I'd survive. They figured that when I died, they would just bury me in an ice vault and haul me out with the spring thaw. Between fevers, multiple fractures and lacerations sewed together with waxed thread, it was almost five months before I was recovered enough to be brought out of the interior."

"It was during that time, as the old man and the villagers nursed me back to health, that my life began to change. Preacher Tom, as the villagers called him, would sit and read the bible to me. I explained to him that I had accepted Christ as my savior at one time, but left him behind along with my wife, when I made my way to the oil fields. The more he read from his Bible the more I came to realize how much I needed Christ back in my life. One day as he was reading, I bowed my head and prayed that God would forgive me, and really make my life worth living."

"When it was time for me to leave, old Tom told me that I should consider staying with them, because the outside world was getting very bad, and not a good place to live in. It was then that he began to read to me about end time prophecy and speak about the radical changes that were sweeping around the world."

"From that time on, all I could think about was getting to Anchorage, back here, and to Jessica, if she would still have me."

By this time, Josh had eaten all of his breakfast and half of the toast on Andy's plate. Waving his hand in an upward motion, he urged Andy to continue his story, and took another sip of coffee. Andy poured another cup, fortifying it with some cream and sugar. Leaning forward he continued, focusing more intently on the signs of the times, what a difference Christ had made in his life, and what a difference Christ could make in Josh's.

"So, what did you do with your money?" Josh queried.

"It's in the Bank," Andy said with a grin, and as worthless as a man without Christ! In less than two hours, it will belong to the Collective!"

Holding up his hands, and pointing to his forehead with a finger, Andy leaned forward and whispered ...

"No marks of the Collective Beast never had any and never will. My treasure is in Heaven, and the Collective will never take that from me!"

As Josh and Andy sat engrossed in deep conversation, two grey pickups sporting the emblem of the new collective pulled into the parking lot. A reflection from the windshield of one of the vehicles caught Andy's eye, and motioning to Josh, both turned and looked out the window.

Four men climbed out of the trucks wearing fatigue style camouflage uniforms matching the color of their trucks. As Josh looked at the emblems on the side of the vehicles, and the shoulders of the uniformed men walking into the restaurant, he spoke with a tone of disgust in his voice.

"I Hate those people, and everything they stand for!"

This time Andy looked at Josh with wide-eyed amazement!

"Look at that emblem," Josh blurted out. "They corrupt everything they touch."

The Alaska State Troopers emblem shrouded with the banner, Loyalty, Integrity and Equality hovered over the State Seal, with the new blue, and grey mark of the World Collective now emblazoned in its center. The picture, which reflected all that the great state of Alaska represented, was gone.

"Let's get out of here," Josh suggested. With that, the two men slid out of the booth and headed for the register.

Josh waited patiently as the cashier attended to the customer in front of him. As the cashier rang up the total, the customer reached out, and passing his hand over a scanner on the countertop, turned and walked out the door. Josh stepped forward and presented his smart card and guest check to the casher. Glancing up he noticed that the militia who had just been seated, seemed a little too preoccupied with how he was paying for his and Andy's meals. The casher scanned and returned Joshes card, then quickly hurried away to retrieve an order waiting in the kitchen window.

As Josh and Andy turned to leave, one of the new militiamen stood up and met them at the door.

Coughing into the back of his hand, he spoke.

"Gentlemen, could I see some ID please?"

Andy and Josh both reached into their hip pockets and produced their smart cards, handing them to the officer. The officer then removed a small electronic device from his belt, and one at a time slid their cards through the reader, studying the screen. Returning their cards, he fixed his gaze on Josh and then on Andy.

"Gentlemen," he continued. Yesterday was the deadline for turning in these cards and receiving the International Mark of the World Collective. Noon today will end a twenty-four-hour grace period for you and others who have not received the mark and pledged their allegiance to Lord Chris. I would strongly suggest, you take care of this matter this morning, if not, our next meeting I'm afraid, will not be as cordial."

With that, he walked back to the table, seated himself with his comrades, and then passed around the reader as they all examined the two new reports it contained.

As Josh and Andy made their way out the door, and climbed into Joshes van, they could sense the eyes of the collective following their every move and writing down the license number of the van. Josh quickly backed up and drove out on to Highland, hung a right onto Egan Drive and headed out of town.

It was only five miles to the outfitters store in Lemon Creek. Joshes father had built it back in 2013, on Anka Street. Joshua had struggled to keep the business going ever since his father's disappearance, while he fought in court to get his father declared legally dead so he could make the necessary changes to keep the store open. If it had not been for his own delivery and freight business, and half ownership in the bush plane belonging to him and his father, he would have had no source of livelihood at all. After a year of jumping through all the legal hoops, Josh now had the papers in his hand, but he knew in his heart, he would never have that opportunity.

Andy and Josh didn't say much as they drove up the highway, but as they pulled up behind the store and parked, Josh's hands slipped into his lap, and he leaned his head against the top of the steering wheel. Putting his arm across his back, Andy leaned his head on Josh's shoulder and began to pray. It was then all the pain, the heartache over losing his father, and the overwhelming fear, guilt, and emptiness in his heart, that Josh burst into a cascade of sobs that left his chest heaving. When he was able to regain some of his composure, he wiped the remaining tears from his eyes and leaned back against the seat. Turning and facing Josh, Andy made his appeal.

"Josh, you and I sat all morning in that restaurant, talking about how things are, and how God has changed my life, and given me a peace and joy that will last forever. It's the same peace and joy your daddy spoke so often to you and me about, when we were kids. The same grace and strength that made Ben Huskins the man he was and can make you the man God wants' you to be, especially now, and in this time."

Andy pleaded.

"Don't hold back anymore, ask Him into your heart!"

It was Andy this time who burst into tears. Josh turned and reached out, grasping Andy's hand, with tears welling up in his eyes as well.

"Yes, yes Andy I will," he said.

Almost forty minutes went by, before the two men opened their doors and stepped out of the van. Josh danced up to the rear door of the store and let out a howl that echoed across Lemon creek.

"I am not the man I used to be," he shouted!

"Amen Brother," Andy echoed. "You're a New Creation!"

CHAPTER 4

Gearing Up

J OSH UNLOCKED THE BACK DOOR of the store. Swinging it open, he turned on the light and motioned Andy inside. Locking the door behind them, Josh turned on the monitor for the security system and quickly scanned the images for any sign of movement around the premises. Satisfied everything was quiet, Josh put on a pot of coffee and the men sat down at a small kitchenette against the back wall of the storeroom.

As Andy looked around, surveying the stores that filled the shelves, Josh cleared his throat and spoke with a sense of foreboding.

"Andy, I know your plan is to head up the Lemon, but things are happening to fast, I'm not sure that's the thing to do right now."

Hesitating for a moment, Josh continued.

"Look at me! Look at my life, everything I've worked for is gone and what's more, I don't even care, cause I'm not the same guy I was this morning, and the Collective 's deadline has changed everything anyway!" Again, Josh paused.

"Andy I ... I guess I'm just afraid, I've been alone for such a long time and you're the only friend, Brother, I've got... We need a plan Bro; we need a plan big time!" Josh jumped to his feet and began to pace the floor.

"Whoa, Andy stammered." "Calm down a minute, let's have some of that coffee you put on, chomp some of these chips here on the table, and we'll put something together, after all, "Gods on our side," remember?" Stopping in mid-stride, Josh looked down at Andy's grinning face and began to laugh.

"I'm right, you know I'm right", Andy chided.

Josh sat back down and poured them each a cup of coffee, pushing the cream and sugar to the edge of the table. Pulling down a map from the wall, Josh placed it between them, and cleared his throat.

"This map covers approximately two hundred square miles, with the airport as center zero Josh said," pointing at the satellite view of the airport and surrounding terrain.

"Let me have a closer look" Andy said, lifting up the map' and holding it close to his face.

"Either the light is really bad in here, or I need glasses," he moaned.

As Andy held up the map to get a closer look, Josh suddenly noticed another map, which was hand drawn on the back. Josh knew immediately that the wavy blue line was a good rendering of lemon creek, and the four blue splotches on the Northeast side represented the small melt lakes at the end of the Lemon Creek glacier. What Josh was not sure about was the small x at the top and bottom of the map.

"I can't begin to imagine where Jessica and her sister could have gone, where they would feel safe Andy muttered," his eyes scanning back and forth across the map.

"I think I can, flip the map over and take a look at the other side," Josh said.

Andy flipped over the map and rotated it so he could see what it was that Josh was pointing out. He inhaled sharply and placed the map down on the table. Picking up his coffee cup and taking a sip, he and Josh leaned intently over the new revelation. Tracing the blue line with his finger, and then jumping over to the small x at the bottom, Andy began muttering to himself.

"This x looks like it's only a half mile or so Southeast of the old quarry," he said.

"Nothing up there but thick brush and boulders, Josh added. One trail, no road, just a lot of rough going, not to mention the lemon creek bear clan, he chuckled."

Andy straightened up in his chair and looked at Josh questioningly.

"Yea, there's about a six Alaskan browns up the Lemon now, moved in about two years ago, and they stay awake year-round just looking for somebody ... err, I mean something to eat," Josh said with a grin.

"The elevation of that other x at the top of the map has got to be at least 3500 feet if not more, there's nothing up there but snow, ice and bitter cold. On top of all that, the climb to that area is almost straight up," Andy said ... taking another sip of his coffee.

"I've flown over that area hundreds of times, there's hardly any trees, and then only a few patches here and there. From there on up to the ridge, there's nothing but bare cliffs, rockslides, and avalanches in the winter," Josh added.

"There might be an old gold mine up there," Andy proposed.

"Or a cave, Josh said, look up here in the corner."

Andy turned the map to get a better look; there in the upper left-hand corner were printed two words, "Haven Caves."

Josh leaned back in his chair, and lifting his cup paused, taking a long look at the map before sipping his coffee.

"Andy, let me show you something, I never thought much about it until now, but I thought it was a little odd when I found it."

Pulling out a drawer under the small folding dinette table they were sitting at, Josh pulled out a five by seven post card, dated April 22, 2017. The front of the card had a picture of the little UP church established in Lemon Creek in 2013. It was addressed to Ben Huskins, from Pastor Bowens.

Andy read the four handwritten lines on the back.

Ben, the women are packed and ready to make the ascent. E and J will be joining us at the rendezvous point as planned on the 26th. See you there. In His Service, Don

"Andy, tomorrow we need to drive up the old quarry road and take a little hike up the creek. I think we should try to find out what that x represents before we make any decision about tackling the lemon, no one I know has ever gone very far up, it's just too rugged, and the old trail to the glacier doesn't exist anymore," Josh said, pushing his empty cup to the side of the table.

"I'm with you," Andy agreed. "But there's one thing we need to remember."

"What's that," Josh responded questioningly.

"The amnesty period ended two hours ago, we're wanted men," Andy said flatly.

"I guess we had better start packing up our gear then," Josh said, pushing back his chair and getting to his feet. "Choose whatever you think you'll need, just remember, it's all going to be on … your back." With that, Josh walked over to the end of one of the shelves and pulled down two mountaineering packs and sleeping bags, placing them in the middle of the floor.

"The rest is up to you," he said. Knives, rifles, handguns, ammo and other survival equipment are in the cases up front, grub on the shelves to the left."

Andy rose from the table and walked over to where Josh was standing. Reaching out and taking Joshes hand, he pulled him into his chest, hugging him as he patted his back.

"I am so thankful that God has blessed me with such an awesome friend as you, he said, and "blood brothers in Christ to boot … we are a team!"

It took almost five hours for the men to gather, re-check and load their packs with the supplies they thought they would need. Josh suggested and Andy agreed that they each pack for themselves in case they were to be separated for any reason. By the time they were finished, both had packs more than forty pounds.

"Josh," Andy called out. "I've been going through all of these handguns, and I can't make up my mind about which one to pack, could you give me a little help here?"

Josh stepped around the corner, and without a word, slid open the gun case and pulled out a .45 caliber pistol, laying it on top of the counter.

"The Judge," he said with a grin. "Shoots .45 cal. Colt ammo, and 410 shot he continued. It's good for all kinds of varmints, two legs, four legs or no legs at all."

"Have a lot of kick?" Andy asked holding and pointing the pistol with both hands.

"I don't think so," Josh said. "It's what I've carried for over four years now, I think you should try it, he said reassuringly."

"Gotcha", "where's a holster and the ammo?"

"Right here Josh said, handing Andy a Grizzly Tough holster and two boxes of 410 shells. One loaded with #4 shot, and the other with slugs.

"Josh, why the slugs instead of the .45 Cal. Colts," he said questioningly.

"Personal choice for one," Josh replied. "There also cheaper than the .45's, but in this case, it doesn't really matter does it, whatever you prefer."

Leaning his head back around the corner, he added … "I also use smooth cartridges instead of ribbed, they chamber easier, and the slugs work just as well as the colts."

"What about a rifle," Andy said, turning around and facing the rack behind him.

Josh stepped back around the corner, and nudging Andy aside, pulled open a large drawer under the rifle rack. He quickly pulled out two new AR7 survival rifles and four boxes of 22 caliber long rifle hollow points.

"We already have fire power," he said. "We need these for groceries."

Now that Andy and Josh had their gear ready to go, the only thing left was to get their clothing ready for the next day.

"Warm, but light," Josh, said, pulling some long handles and sox down off the shelf. Remember layers, and don't over dress. Looks like you could use some new boots too, there up front, next to the snow suits."

It was 7:30 in the evening, when Josh pulled the MRE's out of the oven, and he and Andy sat back down at the kitchenette. It had been a long day and neither of them said much, both lost in their thoughts as they listened to the traffic on Joshes scanner and ate their meal.

Andy sat pensively, stirring the cream and sugar into his coffee as he reminisced about days when things were different, when he, Jessica and Max would walk together along the Banks.

Max, Andy mused, would be in his prime if he were still alive. About four and a half years old he thought. Max was his dog and they had been inseparable since he was a pup. The only time him and Max were apart was when he had to be at work, and Max would always be waiting patiently at the gate when he came home.

"What are you thinking so hard about Andy," Josh said, grinning over the top of his coffee cup. Andy pulled the spoon out of his cup and laid it down on the table, sliding it aside with his finger.

"Nothing really, I was just thinking about Jessica, and Max," Andy replied, scratching his head and repositioning himself in his chair.

"Max ... are you still pinning over that overgrown Terrier? If I didn't know better, I'd think you loved him more than Jessica," Josh said teasingly.

Andy grinned. "He was our baby boy, and a smart one to, jutting out his chin in a defiant gesture.

"I don't know about you, but I am one tired hunk of flesh Josh breathed, pushing back his chair and rising to his feet. There's folded cots back in the corner, I think now would be a good time to try out those new sleeping bags."

As a precaution, Josh set the store alarm, while Andy set up his cot and climbed into his sleeping bag. Sliding into his own, Josh reached up and turned out the light. As they lay there in the dark, Andy began to pray.

"Father," thank you for your mercy, your wonderful love, and your awesome grace. Thank you for bringing Josh into your kingdom and preserving our lives throughout this day. Father, we don't know where Jessica and Ellen are tonight, but we pray for their safety, and that you would watch over them. We commit everything into your hands and pray for your help, as we search for them, and in our service to you … Amen."

A LOUD CRASH BROUGHT ANDY and Josh scrambling out of their sleeping bags, and leaning against the door, listening intently to the noises emanating from outside. Josh quickly stepped across the room and turned on the monitor for the security system, checking the camera for the back of the building.

"It's only a dog," Josh said with a sigh of relief. "You must have taken our leftovers out with the other trash last night, lots of strays now days with so many people dying or disappearing."

"No food went out that I know of all I took out to the trash was my old clothes and some papers, I'll go run it off," Andy said, opening the door. As he prepared to step outside, he hesitated for a moment watching the dog rolling around on his old clothing and tossing his old boots.

"Haaa, git outa here," Andy shouted waving his arms in the air. The dog suddenly rolled over, and crouched, looking at him intently. Without a sound, he suddenly lunged, and ran toward Andy. Leaping into the air the dog hit him square in the chest, knocking Andy through the door, and sending him sprawling to the floor. As he struggled to get to his feet, the dog lunged again, only to begin licking his hands and face in an excited frenzy.

Josh quickly closed the door, and sitting back in one of the chairs, let out a belly laugh that brought tears to his eyes. Andy on the other hand, finally getting a hold on the dog, pushed it back and gazed for a long moment into the face of a long-lost friend.

"Max!" "Max," he shouted, pulling the dog to his chest, as tears welled up in his eyes. Andy sat on the floor, rocking Max back and forth in his arms. After regaining his own composure, Josh stood up and walked over to a row of shelves. Pulling down a case of canned dog food destined for delivery to a client who later canceled his order, he carried it to the counter.

"I guess this is a good time to break out this old case of dog food," Josh said, grinning as he twisted the handle on the can opener.

Things had calmed down a little by the time Josh placed a bowl on the floor filled with dog food. Max was quiet now, but held his muzzle firmly under Andy's chin, licking occasionally, with a whimpering tone of affection. Andy just sat there in a daze.

"Andy, maybe Max could use a little grub. Why don't you see if he'll eat something," Josh said?

Maneuvering to his knees, Andy pulled the bowl of food over, and offered it to Max. Without hesitation, Max voraciously emptied the bowl, prompting Josh to open another can.

Andy stood to his feet, shaking his head. "I ... I just can't believe this is happening he said." Walking over to the table he sat down.

"I'm not as surprised about Max showing up, as I am about a twenty-pound dog knocking you on your butt," Josh said with a twinkle in his eye.

"Wasn't the weight that knocked me down," Andy responded. "It was his excitement that took me to the floor; I can't believe this is happening!"

"It's 2:30 in the morning," Josh said yawning. "Why don't we try to get a little more sleep before we start our day? I have a feeling there's going to be more surprises than this ahead of us, and we need to be ready!"

CHAPTER 5

Reunion

WITH ALL THE EXCITEMENT, NEITHER Josh nor Andy woke until late in the morning. Max was pawing at the back door of the shop. Andy figured even though he had been on his own for so long, Max still had enough manners not to relieve himself inside. Slipping out of his bag, he staggered to the door and opened it. With a bark, Max darted out and disappeared over the bank toward the creek. Andy had barely gotten his pants and boots on before Max was scratching and announcing his presence at the door.

"Hold on Max, I'm coming, I'm coming," Andy groaned, as he pulled on his new flannel shirt and stepped to the door.

Opening it, Andy stood back in amazement.

"Josh, you've got to see this," he exclaimed!

Max was sitting at the door, sopping wet from head to tail. In his mouth was a trout, almost as big as he was.

Josh stood and looked at Max, shaking his head and grinning from ear to ear.

"Looks like Max has taken care of breakfast for all three of us, he said, I'll get the skillet."

As soon as Andy took hold of the fish, Max let it go, and he handed it to Josh.

"Now let's take care of you mighty Max," Andy said, wrapping the dog in an old towel Josh had tossed him. Carrying him into the bathroom, Andy stood Max in the shower.

"You had better strip down, if you don't, your new duds will smell like old Max," Josh said with a chuckle. "I know your bosom buddies and all, but smelling like each other, is going too far."

It was almost eleven thirty by the time, Max was a new dog, and the three had finished breakfast.

After placing their gear in the middle of the floor, and suiting up, Josh and Andy sat down at the table to begin making plans for their hike up the Lemon. Josh pulled out the map they had look at the night before and flipped it over. Laying it down on the table they studied it again before Josh spoke.

"There's a trail that winds up the Lemon for about two miles," Josh said, the forest above the creek is dense, and most everyone who hikes up there never leaves the trail. This x look's to be about two or three hundred yards up over the rise, above the creek. If we hike up the trail, it'll be a lot easier going, except for the last few hundred yards once we turn off."

"If we park the van on this side of the bridge, can we put it where it can't be easily seen," Andy asked.

"Yea, I know a spot that can't be seen coming or going, and it's easy to get to, but we won't be taking the van. Josh said. "I've got a four-wheeler in the next room!"

"We had better get going then if we want to have any daylight left to look around up there," Andy said, getting to his feet.

Josh stood, and the men began carrying their gear through a side door and loading the back of the large ATV. Rolling up the metal door, Josh pulled out and Andy closed it behind him. After he and Max climbed in, Josh quickly drove around the building, and hung a left, heading up Anka Street and on to the old quarry road.

The trip to the bridge took less than four minutes, five minutes later the ATV was hidden in some dense trees, and Max and the men were making their way up the trail along the Southern bank of the Lemon. It was two in the afternoon, after forty minutes of searching, that Josh and Andy walked into the campsite, where Max was already sniffing and rolling around in the dirt at the back of a small shallow cave.

"This was one hard place to find," Josh said, taking off his pack and laying it down at the back of the cave where Max lay whimpering. Andy knelt on one knee examining the fire pit and the stones that surrounded it.

"These stones have been around this pit for several years, it was built to be used more than once," Andy said, stirring the ashes with a stick, as he looked for sign.

Even with Max's rolling around, in the cave Josh could see where two campers had laid out their bedrolls, maybe two or three days earlier. To his right, was an area of freshly moved soil. Picking up a stick, he removed some dirt, and discovered the ruminants of some of MRE's and a couple of plastic water bottles. It was when Josh's gaze circled back around to his left, that he saw the book and pen laying on a rock on the other side of the cave entrance.

Quickly walking over, he picked up the items, and opened the cover of the book.

"Andy," Josh shouted. "This looks like something for your eyes only! ... "Get your buns over here, 'Now' brother," Josh added.

Four strides and Andy was at Joshes side, peering over his shoulder. As both men looked down at the first page, Andy read aloud.

"This *is the Diary of Jessica M. Michaels/Bridgeport ... For Her eyes only!*

Josh closing the book turned and handed it to Andy.

"I'm going to do a little more looking around, and I think I'll start a fire so we can warm up a little, have some coffee and maybe a snack."

"Take your time my friend," Josh said, and walked toward where the truck had been parked.

Andy worked his pack off one shoulder, letting the other strap slide into the crook of his arm, and laid it against the back of the cave. Sinking to his knees, he opened the diary and slowly skimmed through the pages, until he arrived at the last entry, dated October 15, 2019.

"Yesterday," Andy thought his mind racing. *Jessica was here in this camp, yesterday!*

As the tears welled up in his eyes, Andy wiped them and tried to focus on the words Jessica had written below the date.

Everything went well yesterday, we arrived at the camp a little after dark, started a fire, ate and bedded down for the night. I don't know what I would do without Ellen, she was up early and had breakfast ready before I woke up. It will be a long day today, and rough going once we get started. Ellen is calling me to breakfast, more later...

Andy stood and looked around hoping to find something more that he and Josh might have missed. It was then that Andy noticed Max's strange behavior, running back and forth across the area of the camp, and then disappearing out of his sight to the Northeast.

"Max, Max," Andy called. Moments later Max was back at his side, whimpering, and looking around with his ears raised, as though he was listening for something.

"Looks like there was a rig parked over there," Josh said, walking to where Andy was standing. "It had to be four-wheel drive to get in here. It's strange though, there is only one set of tracks going out, and none coming in. That means that it had to be sitting here for a long time, at least a season or two he concluded."

"According to the last entry in Jessica's diary, her and Ellen were here yesterday morning, and then headed out, but to where," Andy said questioningly.

"Beats me," Josh mumbled, but I also found two more sets of tracks around where the rig had been parked. They were deeper and larger, not more than a day old I think… "Men I'm sure, they were too small for the women."

"Have you noticed how Max has been acting," Andy asked." "I think he knows something we don't."

Josh took a long hard look at Max, scratching his chin.

"Remember how Max was acting last night when we found him rolling in the trash. He was rolling on your clothes. I'll bet he's on Jessica's scent as well, and he probably knows which direction her and Ellen went."

"Max was going up trail to the Northeast, when I called him back, Andy said, and Jessica wrote in her diary that it was going to be a long day and rough going. I'm thinking that maybe they were on their way back up the Lemon to where that other x was, on the map."

"Still doesn't explain the rig, and the direction it was going, looks like back towards town," Josh said. That scent could have been coming down the Lemon instead of going up!"

"Let's get that fire going that you were talking about, and make some coffee," Andy said, we have to do some serious thinking, before we make a move in any direction right now, and I could use something to eat.

"Me too," Josh echoed. Hey Andy, was I prophetic this morning or what? Didn't I say I had a feeling there was going to be more surprises ahead of us than Max showing up, and that we needed to be ready?"

"Yes, you did," Andy said, pausing and taking a deep breath. I'm not sure I am, and I just pray that the Lord will give me the strength and wisdom I need to carry on! … Jessica is so close, and yet so far away. Let's get that fire going."

It wasn't long before another fire was going in the fire pit Jessica and Ellen had huddled around two days earlier. When the coffee was ready, Josh poured Andy and himself a cup. Squatting next to the fire, Andy tossed another piece of wood into the flames.

"Josh," Andy said pensively. I'm really torn between which way to go. If we head back to the banks, I have absolutely no idea of where to begin looking for Jessica and Ellen, and all we know is that there used to be a

4x4 parked here at one time, but no make, model, color, or anything else to look for, and two men, who could be friends or foe. On top of all that, it's a death sentence if we're caught by the Collective."

"That should answer your question, Josh said, tossing another piece of wood on the fire. Personally, I think we should head up the Lemon and let Max show us the way. Everything seems to point there, even Jessica's Diary, not to mention Max's nose."

"Your right," Andy said, poking the fire with a stick. I just needed you to confirm what was already in my heart to do, I guess. Hey josh, I was just thinking, did you pack any rope, carabiners, or camming wedges? I know I didn't."

"No, he said. Standing to his feet and stroking his chin. But those should have been the first things I tossed into the middle of the floor last night! Where we're going, I'm sure we'll need them. I'm going to have to go back, I've got to go back and get them,"

"It's three o'clock now," Andy said, looking at his watch. "I guess if you leave right now, you could get there before dark, but you'll have to wait until first light before heading back, it just won't be safe trying to get back here in the dark. You could leave you pack here with me and travel lighter going back down."

"Not a good idea brother," Josh said, putting on his pack and hiking it higher up on his shoulders. "If something was to happen, and I couldn't make it back to you, I'd be in deep trouble. Just in case something does happen, and I am not back here within an hour and a half after first light, you and Max head up the Lemon. If I'm late, I'll catch up with you! You'll be tracking, so you won't be moving too fast."

Andy stood and handing Josh his walking stick, gave him a hug.

"Take care of yourself Josh," I'll keep the home fire burning, Andy said with a smile."

As Josh headed through the brush following the trail left by the 4x4, and disappeared out of sight, Andy began collecting broken branches and dry wood to keep the fire going through the night.

An hour later, after he and Max had shared a MRE together, Andy rolled out his sleeping bag next to the fire. Lying down on his stomach, he pulled out Jessica's Diary from inside his vest, and began reading by the light the fire provided, with Max curled up at his side. Not long after he began reading, Max suddenly sprang to his feet, alert and waiting. It was then that Andy heard the rumble and felt the earth beneath him begin to move. Jumping to his feet, he grabbed his sleeping bag, and lunged into the shallow cave with Max on his heels, as the earth began to shake violently.

He huddled in the back of the cave with Max securely cradled in his arms, until the ground stopped moving. The view from the cave entrance looked surreal through the dust and settling leaves, which were backlit by the still burning fire. The ground in front of the cave lay littered with rocks and a few small boulders, but everything else seemed to be all right as far as he could see in the darkness. Max still wasn't as sure, and walked cautiously out of the cave, with his ears raised and his nose in the air.

Throwing some rocks out of the way, Andy stoked up the fire, and retreated to the back of the cave where he laid out his bag and secured his backpack. Andy was sure there would be aftershocks, and the back of the shallow cave was the safest place to be. Two aftershocks did follow … one a little after 11:30, and the other just before first light.

As the shadows began to disappear, Andy had the fire blazing again, and a pot of coffee brewing.

After all, didn't he tell Josh that he would keep the home fire burning?

Andy poured himself a cup of coffee and settling down by the fire, shared a few pieces of jerked beef with Max, and waited.

As the darkness continued to retreat from the morning light, Andy looked at his watch. He knew that time was running out for Josh's return. Knowing what he was going to have to do, he bowed his head and began to pray.

"Father," I know what I have to do, and I know that it won't be easy. I need your help Father, I'm alone and I'm desperate. Things have been happening so fast, with changes in plans and circumstances beyond my control. Father, I'm in your hands, and I surrender myself to your direction

and guidance. I have to believe that Josh is ok, and that Jessica and Ellen are safe as well. I pray that you will bring us all together soon, and I ask this in your name, Amen."

Andy poured the remaining coffee on the fire and pushed the smoldering coals into the middle of the pit. Pulling on and adjusting his pack, he picked up his walking stick, and with Max leading the way, began his journey up the Lemon.

IT TOOK JOSH ABOUT AN hour and twenty minutes to hike back to where the ATV was parked. Maneuvering it down to the South end of the bridge, he headed into town. Minutes later, as Josh passed the old Anka street scales, the earth suddenly began to shake violently buckling the street in front of him and tearing it apart. The violent shaking hurtled Josh and the ATV into a newly formed crevasse in the road, throwing Josh into the air, as the ATV burst into flames.

Dazed, and disoriented, he found himself lying next to a ruptured fire hydrant, his backpack beside him, with one strap twisted around his right arm. Rolling out from under the spewing water, he slowly rose to his feet, making sure everything worked.

Nothing broken and no bleeding he thought to himself, thank you Jesus!

Traversing his way down the torn and up-heaved street, for the last hundred and fifty yards, he made his way to the store, climbing over mounds of earth, and broken pavement. Making his way to the back door, Josh found the van was still upright. With the exception of broken glass, and obvious structural damage, the building was still standing.

Unlocking the door Josh stepped inside, and without thinking reached over and flipped on the switch. Amazingly, the lights came on, much to his joy and surprise.

God, Josh thought, I'm sure glad you and I are on the same team! Thank you for protecting me ... and Lord ... thank you for the power, it's good to have some light.

Looking up he saw the keys to the van hanging on the wall by the door.

I had better try to start the van he thought just in case I need it to get away from here in a hurry.

Grabbing the keys off the hook, he stepped back outside and slid into the driver's seat, putting the key into the ignition. The van started without a problem, and he let out a deep sigh of relief. Out of habit, he turned on the headlights, unprepared for what they revealed as he sat momentarily in utter amazement! Pushing open the van door, he jumped out, shouting with wonderment, and disbelief.

"Jessica, Ellen… is that really you, Praise God!"

Without hesitation he rushed forward and embraced the women, one in each arm. Cold, wet and shivering, they slumped into his arms clinging to him, as they both broke into tears.

"I've got to get you two inside," he said, spinning Jessica and Ellen around.

Half carrying them, he ushered Ellen and Jessica through the back door, and sat them down on one of the cots. Returning to the van, he shut it down, turned off the lights and entered the back door, quickly closing and locking it behind him.

"I have so many questions," he said, pulling blankets down from the shelf and wrapping them around the women.

I've got to get them warmed up, and fast he thought to himself. Water, a hot shower will warm them up faster than anything!"

Muttering to himself, he darted into the bathroom and reaching into the shower turned the faucet on, holding his hand under the water until he could feel its warmth. Returning to the other room, he pulled the women to their feet and led them into the bathroom, pushing them both into the shower, wet dirty scrubs and all, and closed the shower door. Pulling out a stack of large towels he placed them on the counter.

"Don't come out until the hot waters gone, "he said, and closed the door.

Thirty minutes later, Jessica and Ellen emerged from the bathroom, wearing the robes, they found hanging on the back of the door and their heads wrapped in towels. Josh was happy to see smiles instead of tears.

"It's a little drafty in the front of the store," he said. I hung some blankets over the broken windows, and they'll have to do. Everything you'll need as far as clothing, you'll find in the ladies section, just help yourself to whatever suits your fancies!" I'll have some grub on the table by the time you get back in here," he said, turning back to the sink.

Ellen and Jessica quickly disappeared through the door, closing it behind them

Josh could hardly contain himself as he slid three MRE's into the oven, and opened a couple of cans of sliced peaches, pouring them into a large bowl. By the time the food was hot, and the Coffee was ready, Jessica and Ellen opened the door and stepped into the room. As Jessica started to speak, Josh couldn't hold it in any longer and erupted with an avalanche of words that all seemed to run together.

"Slow down Josh, it's ok, we're listening," Jessica said, stepping forward and embracing him with a kiss on the cheek, "It's ok," she said.

"There's so much I want to know, but before that, there's something I've just got to tell you he said.

Taking a deep breath, he looked at Jessica.

"Andy's back, and up the Lemon waiting for me to return."

Tears suddenly filled Jessica's eyes, as she grasped Josh's hands.

"Thank you, Father," she said, looking upward, and then burying her face on Josh's shoulder, she began to cry softly. Josh looked up at Ellen pleadingly as he continued to speak.

"We were on our way up the Lemon to look for you and Jessica, when I had to return to pick up some things we forgot. Then the earthquake hit, and here we are. Andy will wait until first light for me, and if I don't return, he and Max will ..."

"Max! Jessica blurted out, Max?"

"Yea," Max showed up here last night, rolling around in Andy's old clothes out back. When Andy opened the door to chase him off, Max took him down and licked him silly," Josh said, harboring a grin he could no longer hold back.

Jessica stepped back and wiped the tears from her eyes with the back of her hand, as a smile began to light up her face. Turning quickly, Josh raced to the stove, dropped the oven door, and pulled out their dinner while it was still eatable.

"We had better eat," Josh said. The Collective Militia will be out in force soon and we need to have a plan."

With that, the three sat down to the table and quickly devoured their meals. As they shared with one another the events, which had occurred over the last three days, they rejoiced in how God's hand had been in every facet of their lives, and how He truly does work everything for the good of those who love and serve Him. Leaning back in his chair, Josh looked up and studied a picture of the company plane hanging on the wall.

"I think we should try to get to Andy before he heads up the Lemon. I'm sure we could make it to him before first light," Ellen said, looking at Josh.

"I don't know," Josh said reluctantly. "Things are torn up pretty bad between here and the bridge, God only knows what things are like farther up, and I don't think you ladies are really up to that kind of climb after what you've been through. Besides, what about the supplies you left in the back of Dad's old truck, I still can't believe he's alive, he said. I think I have an idea that will make life a whole lot easier for all of us, if we can just pull it off!"

Josh went on to explain, chances were good that the businesses bush plane, "Lemmon Lady," would still be good for one more flight. She was sitting over at the airport, fueled and ready for making a delivery the Collective's deadline never allowed. Josh went on to explain his plan.

"Over in the other room, I've got three small pallets that we use for aerial drops at remote locations. They're three feet square and two feet deep," he said. I will take one in the van and see if I can make it to the truck to fetch the grub and things in the back. Quickly jotting down a number of items on a piece of paper, he continued. You and Jessica fill the other two with the things on this list, and anything else you want, and think will fit, to fill them up. When I get back, we'll seal them and load them in the van."

"There's no place to land a plane up there," Ellen chided.

"Not one with wheels, but mine has pontoons, he said teasingly. Here's my plan he said, putting his arms around the women's shoulders.

"There are drop chutes on the plane for the cargo, and one parachute for me. We'll load up and drive over to the airport, cut the locks at the Southeast gate and pull down to the plane on the float pond by the runway. We'll load up, cast off, and wait out on the water until first light. My idea is to fly up over the Mendenhall, swing around over the Lemon glacier and drop the supplies over the havens. Then I'll bank left, come around and land on the upper melt lake. I'll drop you and Jessica on the beach and take off again." Jessica interrupted …

"Those melt lakes are too small, you'll never get back up in the air," she said.

"The larger of the two lakes is just over a thousand feet long," Josh replied, and the mountain begins to rise, not too far from the end of the lake, it'll be close, but I'll be fine he said. "Once I'm back up in the air, I'll swing around over the Lemon glacier, gain some altitude, and bail out after setting the auto pilot.

I think the plane should come down somewhere over the pacific, maybe ten miles out or so. Well, what do you think?"

"You're so crazy Josh, it will probably work," Ellen said with a smile.

CHAPTER 6

A way of escape

As Josh headed out the door, Ellen and Jessica laid the list Josh had given them on the counter, and began gathering items, as they loaded up the pallets.

Josh started up the van and pulled around the West end of the building. Driving across Ana Street he cut across the equipment lot, through the parking area for Pet Nanny's and down Bent Street, to the intersection at Ralphs Way. Despite heaved earth, cracks and fallen debris, Josh was able to navigate his way into the Costco parking lot and to his dad's old truck, which now lay on it' side.

Pulling up beside the truck, Josh turned off the engine and lights. Grabbing the crowbar, he had tossed into the passenger seat, he climbed out of the van. Looking toward the Home Depot, which was fully engulfed in flames, he could see the entire front of the Costco Store had collapsed along with the roof. Between him and the mouth of the Lemon creek valley, the earthquake had ripped open an enormous chasm.

Prying open the tonneau cover, Josh allowed the contents of the truck to spill out onto the pavement. Opening the side door of the van, he began loading the pallet with the groceries Ellen and Jessica had risked their lives to acquire.

With the contents of the truck safely stowed in the van, Josh looked at his watch. It was almost eleven thirty, and there was still no sign of militia or any emergency vehicles in sight.

This was a good sign," he thought to himself.

Without warning, an aftershock hit, sending Josh tumbling to the ground. Moments later, as quickly as it came, it subsided. As Josh got to his feet, to his dismay he could see that his retreat back down Bent Street was blocked by a gaping tear from one side of the street to the other. Climbing into the van, Josh started the engine, and with his headlights on high beam, hung a left down Ralphs Way and turned right onto Commercial.

So far so good, Josh thought to himself.

The streets thank God, were undamaged, and he was able to drive all the way down to the West end of Ana Street without confronting any obstacles. As Josh approached Ana Street, his mind raced to the bridges across Lemon creek on the Glacier and Egan highways. If they were out, there was no way they were going to get to the airport and the plane. A last hope would have been the little bridge down off the old business center access road, but that washed our years ago.

I'd better check them out before heading back to the store, he thought, it'll only take a few minutes.

Turning left, he drove the two blocks to Glacier and hung a quick right.

Two minutes later, Josh was staring down into the Lemon as the now raging water was pouring over what remained of the bridge. Turning around, he made his way back down the highway and on to Ana Street. Finding the lower portion of the street blocked, Josh began snaking his way through the parking areas of adjoining businesses until he was able to reach the store.

In less than half an hour, and despite the tremor, Josh was back at the rollup door behind the shop and rushing inside to see if Jessica and

Ellen were ok. Although shaken and apprehensive, the women were fine, seeing now that Josh was back. The pallets were filled, and Jessica was placing the cover on the second pallet when Josh walked in.

"The Glacier Highway Bridge is out," Josh said. Pray the Bridges on Egan Drive are still standing." As he helped Jessica clasp down the lid on the pallet he continued, "if they're not, we'll have to climb the mountain he said ruefully, and all this will have been for nothing."

While Jessica gathered their coats and some bottled water, Josh and Ellen loaded the two pallets into the van and closed the doors.

"Before we head out, let's pray, and wait on the Lord together," Jessica said, motioning Ellen and Josh back into the storeroom.

"Josh," Ellen said. "Would you lead us in prayer?"

"I'm not sure I know how," Josh said. I've only been a Christian for a day, but I'll give it a shot."

"Just Pray like He is right here with us," said Ellen. "Just talk normal."

"God," Josh began. I'm not sure I know what I'm doing, but I just want to thank you for watching over Jessica, Ellen, and me. We're about to step out, not knowing what we're up against., but we're going to go, trusting that you will continue to be with us, and watch over us. I pray that you'll keep watching over my brother Andy and keep him safe as he makes his way up the Lemon, and Lord …I thank you for knowing my father is still alive. I ask these things, believing that you'll watch over us… Amen.

"Amen," Jessica and Ellen said in unison.

Putting on their coats, and grabbing the rest of their gear, Josh followed the women out, locking the door and closing it behind him. Jessica climbed into the back of the van and sat down on a pallet behind Ellen, as Josh slid the door shut behind her. Jumping into the driver's seat, he and the women could hear sirens in the distance. Looking at the dash, the clock read 1:05.

"We've got to get across the Lemon and off the highway before those emergency vehicles get here, hold on tight," he said … "This part of the trip might get a little rough!"

Josh stepped on the gas, and sped around the building, following the same route he had taken when returning from checking out the bridge on Glacier. Turning left, he raced down the Glacier Highway and onto Vanderbilt Hill Road, dodging debris and flying over the cracked and rippled pavement. When they arrived at the Egan Drive intersection, Josh made a bouncing right turn onto Egan, and hit the gas, as they sped toward the Lemon creek bridges.

ELLEN AND JESSICA GASPED IN unison as Josh suddenly hit the brakes and came to a sliding stop at the edge of a chasm, where the North bound lanes of Egan Drive used to cross the Lemon.

"Dear God, the bridge is gone," Ellen moaned.

"Now what," Jessica said, wrapping her arms around Ellen, and leaning forward, peering out the windshield.

Josh put the van in reverse, and backed up, turning the wheel so that the headlights were shining toward the south bound lane.

"Look," he said, the other bridge is still standing! Dropping the van into low, he crept forward, pulling down into the median and up into the south bound lane.

Slowly he pulled onto the bridge, looking for any sign of cracks in the concrete. When they were about two thirds of the way across, Josh floored the gas pedal, and sped over the remainder of the bridge. From that point on, Egan Drive was clear, and the trip to the Yadkin exit, took only a few minutes. Once off the highway, Josh stopped and turned off the headlights.

"I've got to let my eyes adjust to the dark," he said. "I don't want anyone to see our head or taillights going in. We're going to be in stealth mode, until we get into the air at first light."

Putting the van into gear, he hung a left onto Maple's den Way, and moments later, came to a sudden halt at a chain-link gate, blocking the way to the runway, and the floatplane access road.

"I'll be right back," Josh said reassuringly, jumping out of the van with a pair of bolt cutters he had thrown between the seats earlier with the grow bar. Quickly cutting the lock, he pushed the gate open and climbed back into the van. Pulling out Josh turned right onto the taxiway, and then making a quick left across the runway, headed down the float pond access road parallel to the runway.

Almost there, he said, patting Ellen on the knee … Almost there."

Before Ellen could respond, the van rolled up next to a silver twin-engine bush plane, with its pontoons lashed to a floating dock.

Ellen sighed, as Jessica leaned forward. Wrapping her arms around her sister's shoulders, she gave her a gentle squeeze.

"What a ride, Jessica said, straightening up and patting Josh on the back. I was just thinking about asking you a question Josh, when we pulled up to the plane."

"What was that, he said, turning and looking at Jessica with half a smile and one eyebrow raised."

"I was just wondering, do you fly the same way you drive, she said coyly?"

Ellen couldn't contain herself, and broke out laughing, as she reached out and cupped his face in her hands, with a she got you smile on her face. "I'm the Man", on the land, on the sea, or in the air, he said, as he hammed it up a little.

"I'm glad you girls are doing ok, "you've been through more than enough, the last three days. "We're going to do alright," he said, taking Jessica's hand. Andy told me the Bible says that a merry heart does good, just like taking medicine. Makes you feel a whole lot better he told me, and I think we could all use a little merrier medicine. Stay in here where it's warm while I unlock the plane and check things out, I'll be back in just a few minutes."

Sliding out of the driver's seat, he closed the door and disappeared into the night. As the women peered intently into the darkness toward the darker silhouette of the plane, they could see a faint glow from a small flashlight as Josh moved about. Taking Jessica's hand, Ellen began to sing softly. *Lord you are good, and your mercies endured forever. Lord you are good and your …*

Suddenly, an enormous explosion rocked the van, and sent a ball of fire into the night sky from the direction of the Airport Terminal, a half mile away. Within a minute, Josh was back inside the van, and the three sat with their eyes fixed on the destruction, as multiple explosions continued to fill the air with balls of fire and raining debris.

"This will surly bring the Militia, and everyone else that isn't committed, down on this place. We had better get these pallets loaded on the plane. As soon as we're done, I'm going to sink the van in the pond, and then we'll cast off," he said. It's two-thirty now, we'll have to wait till about four-thirty or five, before we can take off, he said ... let's get started."

Quickly, he opened the door and jumped out of the van. Spinning around and sliding back the side door, he helped Jessica out and waited for Ellen to join them. Reaching into the van he grasped a pallet and pulled it out until the back edge hung on the doorstep.

"Ladies, if one of you will get on each side, we'll pick this pallet, turn around and walk down to the plane. Ok, he said questioningly?"

The distance to the door of the plane from the van was only about 15 feet, and a blacktop path from the access road to the dock, made the transition fairly easy, with only a slight incline. Lifting the pallet onto the deck, Jessica and Ellen stepped back as Josh slid it into the plane, and climbed in, pushed it forward. Returning to the van and repeating the procedure two more times, made quick work of transferring their precious cargo.

"It's time to take care of the van. Gather the water, food and anything else you want to hold on to, our ground transportation in going to become a submarine, he said with a grin."

In the dim light of the inferno blazing on the other side of the airport, Ellen and Jessica gathered up the remaining items from the van and carried them to the plane. Standing on the dock, the women watched as Josh started up the van, and pulled out. Turning in a wide semicircle, he pulled the lever down into low, opened the door and stepped out. The van moved quickly to the edge of the road and down the incline to the water, entering with a splash. Josh walked over to where the women were standing, and together they watched as the van floated out from the bank about twenty feet and slowly disappeared under the water.

"Now what do we do?" Ellen said, putting her arm around Jessica's shoulders, and looking up at Josh."

"I don't know about you two, but I'm all for dining on some of that Jerked meat we brought from the shop and a soda while we can enjoy them, Jessica said, waiting for Ellen and Josh to agree with her."

"All in good time my dear Lady," Josh said, smiling. We can do that while we're waiting for first light, but right now we need to get this plane untied, out on the float pond, and ready to take off."

"Ok Ellen said," What do you want us to do?"

"Go to the other side and untie the plane, he said, then open the co-pilot door on that side. On the forward end of the pontoon, you'll find an oar clamped to the top, get it and then climb onto the pontoon. After I've pushed us off, I'll tell you when to start paddling. Jessica, you help me push the plane out of the bay and get us turned out, then climb aboard

"Gotcha," Ellen said, and disappeared around to the other side of the plane. Jessica smiled, anything you say sir, as long as you feed me, she said teasingly."

"Are you ready Ellen?" Josh called out. Ellen shouted an affirmation, jumping onto the pontoon and grasping the recessed handle on the side of the plane.

Josh untied the last mooring rope form the dock, and handed the loose end to Jessica, as he pushed against the nose of the plane. Slowly the plane backed out of the slip and cleared the ends of the dock. Pulling on the rope attached to the rear of the pontoon, he swung the nose of the plane out into the float pond and brought the pontoon up against the dock.

"Climb in," Josh said, as he stepped forward to help her into the plane and closed the cargo door behind her. Opening the door to the pilot's seat, Josh untied the rope tossing it down on the deck, and pushed off, jumping onto the pontoon. Unhooking his own paddle, he called out to Ellen, and they both began paddling until the plane was well clear of the dock.

"Secure you paddle and climb in," Josh shouted, as he did the same, climbing into the pilot's seat and closing the door. No time for any preflight inspection, Josh said. Pulling down the switch cover and turning on the main switch, he turned on the booster pumps, put the levers into the flight idle position and started the engines. When Ellen was in her seat and the door latched, he began to taxi the plane down to the South end of the pond and turn it around. There he shut them down and settled back into his seat.

"Now I think it's time to pull out those snacks and the jerky Jessica's been dreaming of," he said with a broad smile. And Stewardess, could I have a soda to please."

"Yes sir, right away sir, Jessica teased, but you'll have to wait your turn. "Ladies first," she said jokingly.

With that said Josh settled back in his seat and began going over charts he had pulled out of a pocket in the door.

"What do you have there," Ellen asked, taking a sip of her soda.

"I'm just checking aerial charts for Mendenhall and Lemon creek, he said. Lemon creek drains out of the Ton grass National Forest, when we get airborne, we'll fly Northeast for a ways and swing over the Mendenhall, around Death Valley, the head of Lemon creek glacier and then West, down over the havens. Winds can be tricky up there this time of year, he said, and we're going to be making some tight turns to make our drops and land, to put you and Jessica down.

"Are you still planning to bail out after you drop us off," Jessica asked, handing Josh a large piece of jerky and a soda.

"Yea, he said, *thinking about the value of the plane he was planning to send into the Pacific Ocean.* I'm not looking forward to it, but it must be done, to protect the location of the havens. By the way, he said, pulling a small cylindrical tube and a note pad out of a bag between the seats. We'll be dropping this before we drop the supplies. Pulling a pen down from a clip overhead Josh wrote a note, folded it, and placed it in the cylinder, screwing on the cap. He then pulled out a roll of bright red plastic, with a clip on the end. Attaching it to the cylinder, he put it back between the seats.

"What was that?" Ellen said, looking down between the seats at the canister.

"Just a note to let them know that we will be dropping supplies on the next pass," he said.

Looking at his watch and then through the window behind Ellen, he could see a faint glow above the mountains, signaling dawn was approaching.

"It's three thirty-five, try to get some rest while you can. I don't want to sit out here any longer than we must, and it's going to be a difficult morning to say the least. Cramped and exhausted, Josh and the women attempted to find a position of comfort and soon drifted into a restless and fitful sleep.

CHAPTER 7

Last flight of the Lemon Lady

THE DARKNESS WAS GIVING WAY to first light, when Josh and the women were jolted awake by the rumble of a second aftershock and the wail of sirens, which sounded dangerously close to their location on the pond. Straightening up in his seat Josh could see the flashing lights as they approached on the taxi lane through the dense smoke and mist on the banks surrounding the airport.

"It's time to leave ladies, Josh shouted, as he started the engines, and allowed them to idle as long as he dared, before slowly giving them full throttle. Put on those headsets and adjust your microphones, he said, we won't be able to talk over the roar of the engines if you don't"

Josh didn't think they had been seen, but he wasn't taking any chances, once they were in the air he didn't care if they were seen or not. Even though it had been only moments since Josh had started his run for take-off, it seemed like it took forever, before Ellen and Jessica could feel the pontoons break free from the clutches of the water, and the plane begin to lift into the air. As his air speed continued to increase, Josh pulled up, and banked to the right through the smoke and low clouds, rising steadily, he made his way North.

Looking out the port side of the plane, Jessica and Ellen looked down at the flame-engulfed airport fading behind them and Lake Mendenhall and the Mendenhall glacier approaching in the distance.

"It'll take about twenty-five minutes to get to our destination, Josh said, checking his altimeter. I'm going to stay as low as I can, less chance of us being spotted, with the mountains and low clouds behind us, he said."

As they flew up over the Mendenhall glacier, Josh began to instruct the women on the procedure for dropping the supplies with the roll of the plane.

As Josh explained, Ellen and Jessica attached the parachutes to the pallets and the shock cords to the hook above the cargo door.

"Remember Josh said, when we start the drop, I'll roll the plane to the port side. Ellen, when I do, you will push the first pallet out the door, and count slowly to five. Jessica, while Ellen is counting, push the next pallet to the rear, and Ellen will push it out. Ellen, count to five and push out the last pallet. After the pallets are out, I'll level off, then pull the door forward and push it closed, make sure it latches securely. Do we understand the procedure, Josh said questioningly? We must do it right the first time, we won't get a second chance."

"We'll do fine Ellen said," giving Jessica a hug, and climbing back into her seat.

"We got your back Sir," Jessica said, Patting Josh on the back of the head and pulling on his ear. Relax and chew on this, she said, handing him a piece of jerky.

"Hey Jessica," Josh said with a smile, remind me when I start my new airline service to hire you as my first flight attendant!

As they talked, the plane began to bounce around a little.

"I'm going to have to take her up," Josh said, too much wind over the glacier this low, I'll have to keep her at about 5500 feet till we get around Death Valley and across the lemon glacier. Make sure you're buckled in good and hold on!"

Bringing the nose up Josh continued to climb making a turnover Death Valley, and heading Southeast, he slowly began making his turn west, over the end of the Lemon glacier and the head of Lemon creek valley.

"Alright ladies," Josh shouted over the drone of the engines, we'll make our presence known, and drop our message.

Dropping down quickly over the melt lakes, Josh buzzed the small melt pond just below where Ellen said the caves were, pulled up as he banked to the left and again to the right. Circling around for another pass, Josh dropped the flagged cylinder and pulled up over the end of the Lemon creek glacier. Flying south to regain altitude, he circled back from the Southeast, to make the supply drop.

Hearing the drone of the engines as the plane dropped down over the end of the glacier, Pastor Bowens and Ben raced out of the cave entrance in time to watch the plane fly by just above the treetops before turning out over the valley.

"That's my plane!" Ben shouted, look there on the pontoons, it's the Lemon Lady, he shouted." Pastor and Ben watched as the plane came around again, dropping the red flagged cylinder which landed next to the melt pond, fifty yards from where they were standing. Like a shot, Ben was out from under the cover of the trees and returning with the cylinder in his hand, unscrewing the cap as he walked back to where Pastor Bowens stood in amazement.

Ben paused for a moment to regain his breath, and unfolded the note, as Pastor Bowens stepped up beside him and looked over his shoulder.

"It's Joshua, Ben said, it's Josh!" Ben stopped to wipe the tears from his eyes, and then began to read the note aloud.

"Dad, Ellen and Jessica are with me. Our next pass we will be dropping three pallets with supplies, and then landing on the upper melt lake to let Jessica and Ellen off the plane. Ellen will explain everything. Love Josh.

"The upper melt lake," Ben exclaimed, maybe, but he won't get off again!

Pastor Bowens turned and made his way back to the entrance of the caves as Sarah and Alice emerged.

"Quick, grab our coats Pastor Bowens shouted, we've got work to do."

Ben was already around the pond and on his way to the upper melt lake less a mile away. By the time Pastor Bowens, Sarah and Alice had donned their coats, and re-emerged from the caves; Josh was rolling the plane to port as Ellen pushed the first pallet out the door. With precision, Ellen and Jessica ejected the remaining pallets and pushed the door closed as Josh leveled off.

"Ok ladies, Josh yelled out, sit down and buckle up, we're going in for a landing, and we've got to do it the first time!"

Josh banked the plane to the left, beginning his turn across the upper end of the valley. Banking hard left, and skimming the treetops, Josh leveled briefly and banked hard left for the third time before leveling off, and beginning his descent to the tiny lake, less than a mile away, and only a few hundred feet below them. As they were about to touch down, Josh had cut his descent so close that it appeared to Ellen, they were going to hit the rocks short of their watery destination. Letting out a short-lived cry, and bracing herself, Josh brought the plane down on the water, only a few feet from the bank.

Powering down, the plane settled it's pontoons into the water, and glided slowly forward as Josh turned the plane a hundred feet from the end of the small lake and maneuvered it up to the West bank before shutting down the engines.

"You do fly like you drive … Joshua Huskins," Jessica said, throwing an arm around his neck, and kissing him on the cheek. Ellen unbuckled herself from the seat and turning, reached out and taking Josh's face in her hands for a second time, planted a tender kiss on his lips.

"And I'm so glad you do," she said.

Josh sat in his seat, dazed by the loving blow Ellen had just given him. Josh's mind suddenly raced back to those high school days, when he had such a crush on Ellen that it had made him heartsick … Now eight years later he had just received the kiss he had always longed for.

Yes, there is a God in Heaven, he thought to himself, as Ellen turned, and opening the door, slid out onto the pontoon, and made her way to the bank where Jessica was waiting.

Josh quickly unbuckled, climbing out of the plane and on to the bank close behind the women.

"The sooner I get back into the air, the sooner I can get back down on the ground Josh said, taking Ellen and Jessica by the hand, he led them up the bank to a small rise.

Explain to dad when you see him, what I'm doing and why, I can't wait to get this over with," he said.

Pulling Ellen closer to him, Josh looked at her with a smile and whispered, "Thank you."

As Josh turned toward the plane Ellen continued to hold his hand until his fingers slipped out of hers, and her arm dropped to her side.

"I think something's brewing, and it isn't coffee," Jessica said teasingly, as she and Ellen watched Josh push the plane off the bank and climb inside.

"You just mind your own business little sister and start looking for your own man. I hear he's lurking around down in the Lemon," Ellen said with a smile, looking longingly at the plane as Josh restarted the engines it taxied to the far end of the little lake, where Josh began turning it around.

I think we need to pray, "Jessica said, taking Ellen's hand.

They had just finished praying when Ben came huffing over the rise.

"What in the world is he doing," Ben yelled, as Ellen and Jessica held him back.

"Just pray, Ellen insisted, I'll explain when he's in the air," she said.

Just then, the engines burst into a roar as the plane raced forward, struggling to break free from the water. Ellen's fingers dug into Ben's arm as the plane drew closer to the end of its watery runway. Suddenly the nose of the plane rose into the air just as the pontoons sliding up the bank were ripped off from the bottom of the plane by a ledge of rock. Ellen screamed as the plane roared up the narrow valley of rock and snow, struggling to gain altitude.

Freed from the weight of the pontoons Josh was able to gain enough air to clear the remainder of the obstacles, which were now disappearing in the narrow valley below him. As Josh cleared the top of the ridge and swung Eastward across the upper end of the Lemon glacier, he began a climbing bank to the left and continued to climb, until reaching the upper end of the Lemon creek valley, where he turned due West and set the autopilot. Josh looked at the altimeter.

Six thousand feet, thank you Jesus, now just get me safely back to the ground, he said to himself.

Josh quickly moved to the back of the plane and put on his parachute. Opening and sliding back the cargo door, he looked down at the two small melt lakes below him. Diving clear of the plane, he pulled his ripcord.

Moments later, as Josh hung in the air, he watched the Lemon Lady slowly fly away, and disappear in the distance. Looking up into his glider chute, Josh tested his control lines. Then looking down at the melt lakes he began to choose his course of descent. At about a thousand feet, Josh caught sight of some movement to his left. Descending in a wide spiral, he could see Jessica, his father, and Ellen, standing in a large clearing waiting for him to touch down. Glancing one last time to the West, Josh said good-bye to the Lemon Lady, as his feet touched the ground.

In less than a minute, Ellen was at his side, helping him as he released his harness, and Jessica quickly gathered up the chute and lines. As Josh turned to face his father, Ben rushed to him. Tears streaming down his cheeks, Ben embraced Josh with a hug so tight, it pinned his arms to his sides. Stepping back and holding Josh at arm's length, Ben grinned from ear to ear.

"I can't believe my eyes," he said, God is so good ... He's just so good."

Jessica stuffed the chute and lines down into the bag and hiked it up on her shoulders. Grabbing Ben's hand, she tugged him up the trail.

"Let's get home Pops, I'm cold, hungry and I'm sure you'll put me to work this afternoon, Jessica said with a laugh. We'll have plenty of time to tell our stories later."

Ellen looked up into Josh's eyes with a smile, and clinging to his arm, turned and led him up the trail toward the melt pond and the Havens.

As Andy and Max made their way up the valley, Andy tried his best to follow the ridge lines above the Lemon, where he could get a better view of the creek. It also made it easier to get around the falls and rapids, where the brush and undergrowth was almost impossible to penetrate. Max on the other hand, having four legs and being only fifteen inches tall, navigated his way through the forest unimpeded for the most part, only needing a boost occasionally, when the climbing got a little steep. By ten-forty, following Jessica's scent, Max led Andy down a hillside, to the South end of the old log that lay across the Lemon.

It appeared to Andy that the log had once rested farther up the bank than it now did, it had probably been dislodged by the earthquake. Now it had slid about ten feet down the bank and was at too steep an incline to safely try to cross. Looking around, Max was nowhere in sight, and Andy suddenly felt very alone.

"Max, Max," Andy shouted, as he looked up and down the bank for some sign of movement. "Max, where are you buddy," he shouted nervously.

Moments later, Max darted out from under a large area of mountain ferns and brush, with a large hare in his mouth, wagging his tail with excitement.

"Well, boy," Andy said, picking up the rabbit as Max dropped it at his feet. Looks like you brought in breakfast yesterday, and lunch today," good boy!

This looks like as good a place as any to take a break, and have something to eat," he thought to himself.

It'll be a long hard climb to the head of the glacier, where we can find a suitable place to cross over, and camp for the night. I'd better build me a little fire, he thought.

It wasn't long before a fire was going, and the hare was roasting on a wooden skewer he had fashioned from a small limb of a nearby tree.

Max waited patiently, licking his lips as Andy occasionally turned the meat until it was ready to eat. Removing their fare from the fire, he cut Max's half into pieces he could handle, and after they had cooled enough, fed his friend first, and then turned to his own tasty morsels. As Andy sat liking his fingers, Max suddenly jumped to his feet, and turned facing the hillside. He couldn't see anything but was aware that he and Max were being approached from two different directions.

Suddenly a huge Alaskan brown bear stood up, sniffing the air down creek about a hundred feet, and he could hear movement up the hill, coming toward them.

Without hesitation, he scooped Max into his arms, and stuffed him inside his coat, zipping it up to hold him in. Swinging his pack back onto his shoulders, he made for their only way of escape, "the old log." Climbing up the log, he used the old branches where possible, and shinnied where there were none. Almost to the bank on the other side, he felt the log begin to move beneath him as one of the roaring bears in pursuit slid off, and into the creek. Gaining the end of the log, he rolled off and hit the ground. Max leaped from inside his coat, and growling, faced their adversary now clawing his way up the log.

"Max, Max get back," Andy shouted as he crawled backwards up the bank."

Looking down he suddenly realized he had the Judge, strapped to his chest. Quickly pulling it out of the holster, he pulled back the hammer, aimed and fired, cocked and fired again at point blank range into the gaping mouth of the huge bear, as it reached the end of the log. Roaring, the bear fell heavily at Andy's feet, rolled over the bank, and into the creek below. As Andy got to his feet, the second bear was nowhere in sight, and neither was Max.

Franticly looking around, he spotted Max sniffing along the bank, and then darting into the trees and brush. Moments later Max was back, barking as if to say, "this way, we go this way!"

Andy made his way up the bank along the creek to where Max waited for him. He noticed where someone had made camp under a rock overhang not too far from the creek. Remembering portions of what he had read in Jessica's Diary, he was sure he was on the right track.

The truth was, Andy thought, if it weren't for Max's awesome nose, there really wasn't a trail to follow. As he stepped off the rocky bank and into the trees, he knew he had to do the same, "leave no trail or sign."

Stepping from stone to stone along the invisible path Max was leading him on, he suddenly found himself about a hundred feet above Lemon creek, looking down a sloping waterfall fed by a steep mountain creek. It wasn't until he moved a little farther up, to where Max sat on a large flat rock, that he saw the narrow ledge that ran behind a curtain of water spilling over the rocky ledge above him.

"Hey Max," Andy said, sitting down beside his faithful little companion. I think you're going to have to make this short trip back inside my coat."

Andy gently picked Max up, stuffing him into his coat, and zipping it up until only Max's nose was poking out.

"I don't know how I'm going to do this Max," he said, stroking his chin, and looking across the ledge at his feet."

Andy could see what appeared to be good handholds, but he knew he wasn't going to know until he finally stepped out onto the ledge and began making his way across. *With Max on the front of me, and this pack on my back, I'll have to go sideways,* he thought to himself. Standing up, and stepping out onto the ledge, he called on the Lord to help him get safely across.

Max wiggling inside his coat wasn't helping matters, as he made his way across the last few feet of the ledge before stepping into a small clearing. Andy quickly unzipped his coat and placed Max on the ground, while he re-adjusted his pack.

"Ok Max, which way now?" he said.

Max darted under the low bough of a small fir tree, and bounded from one rock to another, never getting more than a few yards ahead of Andy, as they zigzagged up the mountain side four more times before returning to the creek they had crossed earlier.

"This one is going to be a lot easier." Andy said, climbing down the bank, and picking Max up into his arms. Four large steppingstones separated them from the bank on the other side of the stream, but the waterfall to his right roused his curiosity, and he stepped farther down the bank to peer over the edge to the rocks below. To his amazement, he saw the body of a large brown bear, hanging over the edge of a second waterfall, twenty-five to thirty feet below.

I had better watch my step, Andy thought, as he made his way back up the bank to the crossing. *We don't want to end up down there, next to our dead friend,* he mused,

Stepping gingerly, he made his way across the stones, to the far bank. Andy and Max labored up the steep mountain side for a good hour, before climbing up on a large flat boulder. It was there that he and Max stopped for a healthy portion of Jerked beef, and water from Andy's canteen.

Jessica must have stopped here. He thought, as he watched Max sniff, and roll around on the rock in front of him.

"Was Jessica here buddy," he said, roughing the fir on Max's head. Andy looked around for which way Max would lead him next.

With a sharp bark, Max leaped off the rock and climbed a few yards to the West, turning and waiting for Andy to pull his pack back up on his shoulders and follow him. Andy's forty-pound backpack was now beginning to feel like it weighed eighty, and he longed to be free of its grasp. Looking down at his watch, and up into the sky, he knew he had only a couple of hours before it would be too dark to go any further.

As the evening shadows began to deepen, he and Max had crossed back and forth across the almost vertical mountainside four more times. Just as he was about to begin looking for a suitable place to make camp for the night, he and Max entered a broad meadow of high mountain grass, overlooking a small melt pond about five hundred feet long and a couple of hundred feet wide. Making their way down along the upper edge of the pond, Andy found a sheltered area where he could build a small fire and settle in for the night. Building the fire, he unrolled his sleeping bag and climbed inside, too tired to think about anything to eat. Max curled up beside him, and nestling his nose under Andy's chin, the two dosed off.

CHAPTER 8

Havens reunion

As Josh and Ellen made the climb from the melt lake back up to the Havens, they had become so engrossed in their conversation. Falling behind, they lost sight of Ben and Jessica. When they finally caught up, Ben was sitting on a large rock, and Jessica stood looking down the trail with her hands on her hips, and a well, *where have you been,* look on her face.

"It's about time you two showed up, we've been waiting here for hours," she said with a wink. And just what were you doing she added, with a look that made Ellen blush.

"Just talking, about old times, catching up on what's happened since we've been on the mountain and about Josh giving his life to the Lord," Ellen said coyly.

"I still think something's brewing, and it isn't coffee." Jessica said, looking at Josh, and then at Ellen with a giggle.

"I'll teach you not to meddle, little sister," Ellen said, and began to quickly climb toward where Jessica was standing. As she scurried up the steep trail, Jessica turned and ran over the rise, with Ellen hot on her heels, like a couple of schoolgirls.

Ben stood to his feet laughing, and holding his hand out, helped Josh up onto the rise where he was standing. As Josh stepped by, Ben began to tease a little himself about Ellen's obvious interest.

"Looks like you lit a spark, in that ladies eye," Ben said, patting Josh on the back, as he pushed him up the trail.

"Ellen's a wonderful woman, I wouldn't mind it a bit having her for a daughter in-law," he said with a chuckle.

"Things are just happening way too fast for me Pops, Josh said with a grin. I just got saved two days ago, found out yesterday you were really alive, and now you're trying to get me married off!"

"It'll all come together son, just keep praying for the Lords guidance in your life!

Pausing, Josh turned to his father, looking pleadingly into Ben's eyes

"I'm really concerned for Andy," Josh said, he needs to be our focus now, not me...

Reaching out to his father and helping him up a steep portion of the trail, Josh went on to explain how Andy had gotten hold of him, their meeting, and the story Andy shared with him at the restaurant.

"Sounds like maybe God moved Andy out of the picture for a while, not only to rein him in, but to use him to ultimately bring you into the kingdom," Ben said, pausing for a moment on the trail to catch his breath.

"Yea, I think your right dad," Josh said quietly, looking back at all of the events that had unfolded over the last three days.

"I was amazed when Max showed up in back of our store, and even more so, when Andy and I hiked up to the old camp site at the bottom of the Lemon and found Jessica's Diary. The topper was when I returned to the store and came face to face with Ellen and Jessica. I knew then that God was truly in control of everything that was happening."

"We don't always understand the reason for some of the things we do son, until we have the opportunity to look back and see that God's hand had been in it all along, Ben said. I never understood why He placed it in my heart; to establish this retreat we call the Havens, until now… You'll see what I mean when we get there."

"Dad," Josh said, I left Andy and Max there at the camp shortly before the earthquake; we agreed that if I didn't return before first light, he was to head up the Lemon without me. Max picked up Jessica's scent when we found the camp, so Andy and I had planned to follow Max, to find her and Ellen.

I'm sure if Andy survived the earthquake, him and Max are somewhere between here and the old camp, I just pray they're ok, and can find us."

"What time do you have," Ben asked, looking up into the sky.

"It's half past eleven," Josh said. Where do you think they might be?

"Well, with Max sniffing out the trail, they'd probably be close to the old log crossing below us, down on the Lemon. Close, but hours away."

"It's a very difficult and time-consuming climb, with a couple of treacherous crossings, over a large trickle of water Ellen and Jessica named Slip creek. You only rise a little over two thousand feet in elevation, but you make a hike about five miles long on a mountainside that is almost vertical and covered with dense brush and trees. The trail is almost invisible to those who don't know it, and there are no markings. If they do well, they should arrive about dark. We'll have to keep an eye out."

"How much farther to the Havens Josh asked, stopping in a clearing and looking back across the upper end of the valley, at the Lemon glacier."

"About two hundred and fifty yards, give or take a few, Ben said. We had better get up there and help take care of those pallets you dropped on us this morning. I hope you brought us something good, he chuckled."

Another two hundred yards of weaving back and forth up the mountainside, brought Josh and Ben to the Western end of a small two and a half acre melt pond. Josh took in the sight with a sigh of amazement!

Not only had all three pallets landed in a clearing within a hundred feet of each other, but there was Pastor Bowens, his wife Sarah, and the Church pianist, Alice Foster as well. They, with Ellen and Jessica were all busy emptying the contents of the pallets into backpacks, to be carried up the mountain to the caves. Josh and Ben joined in, donning backpacks and filling an arm with what they could carry.

It took three trips and as many hours to ferry everything up to the caves, including the three pallets and chutes, leaving nothing behind but brush and the wind. When everything and everyone was finally safe in the cave, Ben closed and bolted the heavy wooden door behind them.

As Josh sat down on a wide wooden bench, resting on two log rounds, he gazed around him.

"I, I don't understand … this is all so unreal," he stammered, looking around him at the simple but elegant furnishings fashioned from pallets, lodge poles, and some milled lumber. They were covered with furs, quilts and pillows, Pillows? Light, you have lights, he said … Ah, how?" Josh said pleadingly, looking at his father in wide-eyed amazement.

"All in good time son," Ben said with a twinkle in his eye. "It will be getting dark in a couple of hours, and we still have a few things to do. But first he said, let's have some coffee and a little snack before supper."

Ellen, who had been standing behind Josh, stepped around and taking him by the hand, pulled him up and led him to the long wooden table and benches on the far side of the cavern. All Josh could do, was grin, and shake his head in wonderment.

"Ellen, you could have at least prepared me a little for all of this, while we were on our way here," he said, nudging her in the ribs with his elbow.

Putting his arm around her shoulders, he gave her a hug as he continued to look around him. This all has to be a dream, he said, looking down at the coffee, jam and fresh baked bread Jessica had just placed in front of him.

"Dad," Josh said, looking across the table at his father. "I really need an explanation!"

Ben scooted back on the bench a little and leaned forward, resting his elbows on the edge of the table.

"Josh, when Mom died five years ago, it was a tough time for me. I needed to pull myself together and thought that a little time up the Lemon with the Lord would help me sort things out." "My first few days were spent at that camp you found at the bottom of the Lemon. I build that fire pit in front of the shallow cave, and made myself at home, thinking that was as far as I needed to go for my retreat. On the third night, I had a dream. "I was sitting on a rock, looking at the Lemon glacier from high up the valley. I woke up the next morning knowing that I had to continue on up the Lemon until I found the location where my dream had taken place."

Ben took a sip of his coffee. Placing the cup down on the table, he continued his story.

"It was a day's hike up the Lemon, where I found an old log laying across the creek, about three feet in diameter. I crossed on it, and made my second camp, there under a sheltered overhang of rock, a short distance from the creek. That first trip up here to what is now the Havens took me another day to make from my second camp, before I found myself standing on the bank of the little melt pond down below us."

"I stood there looking at the Lemon glacier. Although it looked like my dream, it just didn't feel right, so I began to make my way up the mountain side, from one large rock to another, taking a seat and looking across at the glacier. About a hundred yards up the mountain, I came to one and sat down, not so much to check my location, but to rest my now very tired backside. It was then as I gazed up, that I realized I had unwittingly found the stone I was looking for."

Looking across the table, Ben saw a scene that brought a twinkle to his eye and a broad smile across his face. After giving Ellen a hug, Josh had not removed his arm from around Ellen's shoulders, and now Ellen sat with her head resting against Josh's chest, as they both listened intently to his story.

Jessica, who was sitting next to Ellen, glanced across the table at Ben, giving him a wink, as she nodded in Ellen and Josh's direction. Suddenly realizing that they were the center of Ben and Jessica's attention, Josh and Ellen quickly sat up and glanced at each other with embarrassing smiles.

"You were saying, Dad," Josh said with a nod, as he leaned forward, resting his elbows on the table and looking as attentive as he could.

"Yea son, as I was saying, I found myself sitting on the very stone I was looking for, and then realized that the scene in front of me was fading, because the sun was quickly setting. I jumped up and began to look for a good place to camp for the night. As I looked up hill, the mountain side appeared to level off a bit, so I climbed up a little higher, and discovered the small grove of trees you seen outside the entrance to these caves."

"I stepped between the boughs of the trees in front of me, and found myself in a small, sheltered clearing, with a wall of stone about thirty feet high in front me, and the grove of trees I had just passed through, behind me. I set about breaking dead and dry branches off the bottoms of the trees and built a small fire. Having a bite to eat I settled in for the night. That night I had another dream."

Ben paused and took another sip of his coffee.

"If you and Ellen aren't going to have some of that bread and jam, you can pass it over here. I can still talk while I'm eating, he said with a smile."

Josh quickly pushed the bread and jam across the table, and leaning forward with a grin said, "go on Dad, I'm listening!" Ben smiled broadly and continued.

"When I woke up the next morning, I just couldn't shake the dream. I fixed me some breakfast and had a couple of cups of coffee and ..."

"Come on dad, enough already," Josh exclaimed. "The dream, tell us about the dream."

"Well, Ben said, spooning jam onto his generous slice of bread. I dreamt about ..."

Ben paused and took a bite of his bread and jam. Chewing slowly, and then swallowing, he looked at Josh with a smile, savoring the moment, as he held Josh on the edge of his seat, until Ellen couldn't contain herself any longer, and "snickering" led everyone into a roar of laughter.

"Pops, you're such a tease;" Josh said ... "get on with the story will you!"

When the laughter subsided, everyone's attention once again focused on Ben and his story.

"Josh," he went on, I dreamt I was building a retreat for hard times in some caves here on this mountain. I started out on my own in the dream, but eventually most everyone here tonight, became a part of the vision, and then the adventure. It wasn't until I began to explore farther back in the clearing I was in, that I found the entrance to these caves."

"I quickly got out my flashlight and began exploring. What I found was amazing. These caves consist of two large chambers, one directly behind the other. The one we are in now and a second one a little smaller than this. It has six alcoves or small chambers around it, three on one side, and two on the other with one small one in the rear. The one in the rear was very small and cascading down a vertical crack in the rock about two feet wide and six feet tall in the back of it, was a waterfall that disappeared into a large crack in the floor of that little alcove."

There were no other chambers or exits I could find at the time, except a crack in the low part of the ceiling over there in the back of the cave," Ben said, pointing to where Alice was busy preparing supper. "It appeared to be a natural vent, I never found out where it came out above, but there's a steady flow of air, day and night. I made sure by leaving a vent above the door in the entrance."

"That was five years ago," Josh said. How did all of this come about, how did you get all of this up here, build the furnishings, that door in the mouth of the cave, the electricity? I can't even hear a generator running."

Josh reached out and took Ellen's hand gazing affectionately into her eyes.

"How did you and Jessica end up here, how …" Ellen reached out with her free hand and placed her fingers over Josh's lips.

"Shush," she said, it's ok, Pops will eventually explain everything. "When Jessica and I first came here we felt the same way, finding a piece of heaven on earth in the midst of all this turmoil."

"God has a plan, Josh; He's always had a plan, for all of us."

Suddenly the door to the cavern opened. Pastor Bowens and Sarah stepped inside, both with a pack of wood on their backs, which they dumped at the back of the cavern, next to a home-made hearth.

"You were so engrossed in your conversation, Sarah and I took care of the evening gathering, he said. And ... by the way, I think we have a visitor down by the pond. By the glow, there's a small campfire going just below the rock bluff he said with a smile, looking over at Jessica."

Without hesitation, Jessica sprang to her feet, and made for the door with Josh and Ellen scurrying behind her.

"Wait a minute," Ben shouted, stopping everyone in their tracks. We don't know for sure it's Andy, let's show a little caution, before we announce our presence," he said! "Let's go down and quietly peek over the bluff first!"

Making everyone put on their jackets, as he donned his own, he led the small band out the door and carefully down the hill in a quiet procession to the top of the bluff. As he and Jessica slowly inched forward and peered over the edge, there lying next to the fire, was a man curled up in a sleeping bag, and a dog with his muzzle, buried under the man's chin.

"Max", Jessica blurted out, unable to contain herself!

Max suddenly sprang to his feet, with Andy following on one knee, and clutching the butt of the pistol strapped to his chest!

"Andy, it's me, Jessica," she shouted, with tears of joy streaming down her cheeks.

Looking up, Andy fell back against the bank he had been sleeping under, shouting Jessica's name as he fell.

Before he could get completely on his feet and out of his sleeping bag, Jessica was around the edge of the bluff and in his arms. The air suddenly filled with the sound of rejoicing, as those witnessing the reunion gave God the glory!

Ellen, overjoyed threw her arms around Josh's neck, kissing him and burying her face in his chest. Josh held Ellen for what seemed an eternity, before pressing his lips to her ear as he whispered.

"I think there's something brewing," and it isn't coffee, he said, giving her a squeeze and returning her kiss tenderly. Then releasing her, they joined Ben, Andy and Jessica around the little campfire, where Jessica held Max wiggling in her arms.

After putting out the fire, and collecting Andy's things, they led him back up to the Havens, encircled in Jessica's arms. What had started out as one with a dream had grown to six with a vision! Now there were eight, eager to see how God's plan for their lives would unfold, as they looked forward to their Savior's soon return.

By the time the welcoming committee made their way back into the caves, Sarah, Alice and Pastor Bowens had supper on the table. Jessica, with her arms around Andy and eyes focused solely on him, was content to leave Ellen and Josh to themselves, as they walked into the great room, hand in hand, acting as though they really were becoming attached in a more permanent way.

As they all sat down at the table, the seating arrangements took on a new persona, with the young adults holding down one side of the table, and the more seasoned facing them on the other. Nudging Josh, as he passed to take a seat opposite him, Ben leaned over and whispered in his ear.

"Getting pretty cozy there, aren't we son, Ben said with a wink. She'll make a fine Daughter In-law."

Ellen, put her arm around Josh and laying her head on his shoulder, looked across the table at Ben, as he once again sat grinning from ear to ear.

"Yes, I will Pops," she said, looking up at Josh. We just have to convince him to make an honest woman out of me; we've gone through too much together, to stop now."

Sitting up straight, she kissed Josh on the cheek, and took his hand. Reaching out for Jessica's hand she looked across the table.

"Papa Ben," I think it's time for you to pray over dinner.

Like Josh earlier, Andy sat mesmerized by his surroundings, looking in every direction until Jessica, reached up and turning his face to hers, let him know that Ben was about to pray.

"Sorry, Andy said", taking Jessica's hand and reaching across the table to Pastor Bowens. After everyone had joined hands, Ben began.

"Father, Ben said, thank you for your grace, and the love that surrounds this table tonight. Father, bless our fellowship and your bountiful provision, to the nourishment of our body's for your service we pray, in Jesus name Amen.

Ben had no sooner said "Amen", than Max resounded with two quick barks of his own, and stood up on his hind legs, looking down the table for his plate.

"Oh my," Jessica said, we forgot to set a plate for our guest of honor! "If it hadn't been for Max, Andy would never have found his way up here to us. "Poor boy, I'll take care of you," she said, getting up from the table to get a bowl.

As Jessica stood up and stepped over the bench, Max jumped up into Andy's arms, nudging him under his chin.

"If I didn't know better, Andy said, I would think we were down in Lemon town, and not up here in the wilderness next to a glacier. This is just so unreal."

Josh leaned forward and turned toward Andy, "I know how you feel, he said, but don't ask Pops to explain, he takes too long!" Turning, he winked at his father.

Ben sat through supper, savoring the meal and the conversation, as Josh and Andy, along with Ellen and Jessica, shared their personal stories. This time the rest of the company sat in awe, as their tales reflected God's unfathomable love, mercy, and grace, as well as His unseen hand in the story that now engulfed the entire company.

After supper, Ben prepared to take Josh and Andy on a tour of the caves, but first, felt it necessary to explain how the transformation took place over the previous four years.

"Shortly after finding the caves, he began, I returned to the daily routine back down on the banks. I knew what I had to do, and I needed to have a plan of action to accomplish the vision the Lord had placed in my heart. The first person I went to was Pastor Bowens. Together we prayed and sought the Lord for Wisdom and direction."

"We agreed the first thing that needed to be done, was to seal the entrance. Since I didn't have a tape measure with me at the time, I had used my walking stick as a rod for measurement and made a couple of quick sketches of the opening to this first cavern. Measuring my walking stick back at the shop, Pastor Bowens and I designed and built the door that now hangs at the entrance. We fabricated the hinges and dead bolt in the shop. I later purchased six sacks of mortar mix and packed them into two pallets along with the other tools and hardware we thought we would need for our project. I wrapped shovels; hand saws and some sticks of re-bar in a tarp and tied them down to the door."

"Later that week, Pastor Bowens and I flew the Lemon Lady around the same flight path you took Josh, making a drop like the one you made this morning, with camouflage chutes, I picked up through surplus. With the things we had prepared, here and on the ground, we headed home. Three days later, we were back and working on securing the entrance."

"It took us a week to install that door," Pastor Bowens said, and hard work it was too. We drilled four holes in the rock on each side of the entrance with sledgehammers and old minors drills your father picked up in a secondhand store. That alone took us three days. Josh reached over and pinched Pastor Bowen's biceps.

"Gotten a little soft since that project," Josh said teasingly. "But you look pretty fit, for an old duffer."

"I might have known," a chip off the old block, Pastor Bowens said, slapping his knee with a chuckle. I may be an old duffer, but your father is one too. "I'm just a tougher duffer," he said, throwing his head back with a hearty laugh.

"What were the holes for," Josh asked, leading his father back into his story.

"We placed 24" bolts into those holes Ben said, after inserting them through the door casing. Then we proceeded to lay in the rock and mortar with rebar to reinforce everything, leaving a narrow vent at the top.

"When the door is bolted, a dozen Alaskan browns couldn't force their way in here. Once the entrance was sealed, Pastor Bowens and I flew in everything we needed, over a period of three years, working on this project one week a month until it was ready to move into. That's when we brought the women up, and we've been here ever since, making occasional trips down to the banks for extra supplies when they were needed. We would sneak in and out, keeping a low profile."

"One thing I don't understand Pops," Josh said, looking at the lights attached to a series of poles around the cavern. "Where's your generator, and how do you get fuel up here?"

"We don't have a gas driven generator Josh," Ben said with a smile, ours is driven by water. You boys come with us, he said motioning them to follow him and Pastor Bowens through the archway in the back of the cavern. As they stepped through the slanted archway, and into the smaller cave, Andy and Josh were impressed.

Just as Ben had described, the six alcoves were there, but each opening, was discretely covered with heavy canvas, stretched tightly over lodge poles fitted into the rock. With small wood framed doors cut into the canvas, the simple barriers provided privacy for those who occupied the smaller caves in the walls of the cavern,

"Pastor Bowens and Sarah occupy the first room on the left, mine is the first one to the right, Ben said, motioning with his hands. Alice is in the middle one, and Jessica and Ellen have resided in the third one on the left. Now that you two have joined us, we'll be making some changes."

TURNING TO FACE JOSH, ANDY and the young women who were standing in the archway, Ben laid out the new sleeping arrangements.

"Andy, you and Jessica will be here on the left, Ellen over here on the right, in the spare alcove and Josh, you'll bunk with me."

With that established, Ben led them to the back of the cave, and the last small alcove where the opening was covered with a wall of heavy wooden planks carefully hand cut to fit the opening, and a stout door. Lifting the latch and opening it, Ben displayed his and Pastor Bowen's greatest achievement. Cemented into the back of the alcove, was a spinning water wheel encased in a galvanized splash cover. Attached to the water wheel through a series of gears was a large generator, with a very sophisticated looking control panel. To the left, protruding out of a narrow concrete cistern, a three-quarter inch pipe exited through the wooden, wall to a faucet above a fiberglass washtub outside the alcove.

"It took Pastor and me over a year to design and build this," Ben said, with well-deserved pride. "It took almost six months to install and get it running properly. While we were working on this project and digging around, we had a major water spill out into the cave. It was then we discovered that the water found its own way out, through another crack in the floor, over there, under what is now our bathroom. Because it flowed out below our water source, we concluded that we could use it for that purpose."

Josh and Andy could only stand and shake their heads in amazement. The task that Ben and Pastor Bowens had taken on was monumental to say the least.

"I can't believe you built a bathroom," Andy said, walking over and opening the door to peer inside."

"Flip on the switch on the left," Ben said, motioning Josh to move over and check out the bathroom with Andy.

Andy flipped on the light, and stepped back in unbelief, almost falling over Josh who was standing behind him.

"Just like home," Ben said, leaning against the back wall of the cave, and looking past Josh and Andy.

"We gutted the bathroom of my house, before permanently moving up here," Pastor Bowens said. We crated up the hot water tank, toilet and sink, and shoved them out of the plane on our last flight over the Havens. Prior to that, it took six flights and twelve drops to get the ready mix and mortar up here to build this beautiful work of art."

"God provided the stones of course, along with everything else we needed, we just provided the labor," Ben said, patting Andy and Josh on the back. "Let's head back into the great room, I don't know about you boys, but I could use some coffee. I'm getting pretty dry with all this talking."

Re-entering the great room as Ben had called it; they found the women gathered around one end of the table, engrossed in conversation. Noticing the men entering, the chatter became whispers, as Jessica, glancing over her shoulder at Josh, began to giggle and nudge her sister. Walking up to the table, Ben was the first to speak.

"Why is it I feel like there's a conspiracy going on here, he queried? Resting his hand on Ellen's shoulder, he gave her a gentle squeeze.

"Just girl talk Pops," Ellen responded, patting his hand as she looked up with a sheepish smile.

"I hope you ladies didn't drink all the coffee while we were touring," Pastor said, reaching out to pick up the large pot.

"You just come over here and sit yourself down Mr. Bowens. I'll stay out of your pulpit if you stay out of my kitchen," Sarah said, scurrying over to Pastor Bowens and ushering him back to the table.

"You men sit down, and we'll see if we can't find a treat, we can all have, with some coffee and wholesome conversation!"

"Yes Mama," Pastor Bowens said with a grin.

With that, the other women jumped to their feet, and began helping Sarah prepare a snack.

Max on the other hand, was content to curl up next to the hearth and finish the night's sleep he had started down by the pond, earlier that evening.

CHAPTER 9

A new leader

FTER AN HOUR OF CONVERSATION, coffee and sweet rolls, Pastor
Bowens and Sarah retired for the evening along with Alice who
after picking up and put things away, slipped out to her own
alcove for a night's rest,

Jessica sat next to Andy with her head on his chest, and cradled in
his arms, listening as Josh and his father talked about the Haven project,
and how he was able to keep it a secret from Josh.

"I still can't believe all this went on around me, and I didn't notice a
thing," Josh said, shaking his head in disbelief.

"Josh, you had just turned twenty-one when this project got started,
and pretty much out doing your own thing most of the time," Ben said.
"Then, when your Mama died, I never saw a whole lot of you. I was left
to run the store alone for the most part, so it was pretty easy to just close
the doors, take a week off every month, and not even be missed."

Tears welled up in Josh's eyes.

"I'm so sorry Dad, for letting you down like I did. When Mom
died, I blamed you and God for everything, and all I could think about,

was staying as far away from both of you as I could. Then when you disappeared, and I realized how selfish I'd been, all I had to live with every day was guilt, I never felt so alone in my life."

Ellen, who was sitting next to Josh, reached over and took his hand in hers, sharing his pain, as he expressed the emptiness that had filled his heart, and the loneliness he had endured.

Realizing the tenderness of the moment, and exhausted from the rigors of the day, Andy and Jessica excused themselves, and made their way, with Max on their heels to their small corner of the caverns for the night.

Ben reached across the table and took Josh's hand.

"Son," he said, in as fatherly a voice as he could muster, there's absolutely nothing to forgive. I just thank God, that you have given your life over to the Lord, and that you are with me now. That's all that matters."

Standing, Ben turned and gave Ellen a fatherly hug and a kiss on the forehead.

"Don't keep my boy up too late," he said.

"I'll make room for your bedroll on the left side of the alcove he said, turning to Josh, so you can be closer to Ellen. Smiling, he made his way through the archway to their room.

After pouring Josh and herself the last of the coffee, Ellen returned to where Josh sat sideways on the bench. Straddling the bench, Ellen sat down, sliding forward until her knees pressed against his. Taking his hands in hers, she leaned forward, giving him a long and impassioned kiss.

"Josh," she said tenderly", am I being too forward? If I am, please forgive me! My heart is just so full, and I don't have the words to express what I'm feeling. I've just never felt this way about anyone but you and I'm afraid now, like I have been ever since we were in high school."

"Afraid of what", he said, savoring the moment, as he tried to catch his own breath.

"Afraid of being rejected", she said, as she looked down, timidly playing with Josh's hands.

Pulling his hands out of hers, he embraced her, whispering into her ear.

"My precious Ellen," I've loved you for so many years, wanting to be more than just friends, but never feeling worthy of your attention. I was already yours this morning with that first kiss, on the plane."

Releasing her and holding her hands in his, he gazed into her sparkling blue eyes.

"Ellen," he said, if all of this isn't a dream and you're still here when I wake up in the morning, only God will be able to separate us, but I know in my heart already, He's brought us together. Everything has happened so fast, in the last three days. I shared with Pops this morning that I just received the lord as my savior day before yesterday, discovered that he was alive today, and now, he's trying to get me married off tomorrow. If you'd have me, I'd marry you without a second thought, but we both need time to pray and sort things out, especially me," he said, raising her hands and kissing them tenderly.

Tears filled Ellen's eyes as she leaned forward and kissed Josh on the cheek.

"Yes Josh, Yes," she said, sliding back to the end of the bench and standing up, still holding Josh's hands.

"I Love You, Joshua M. Huskins, and I will have you," she said, releasing him as she turned and ran through the archway to her room.

Josh's sleep was fitful to say the least, with visions of Ellen flooding his mind, and the strange silence that echoed through the caverns, between the muffled sounds of snoring and repeated trips to the bathroom throughout the night.

This intimate cohabitation was going to take some getting used to, he thought, as he climbed out of his sleeping bag and into his clothes.

Stepping into the great room, Ellen greeted Josh with a smile, a cup of coffee and a peck on the cheek.

"Did you sleep well," she said, giving herself a hug, and closing her eyes with a smile.

"Not bad, but I think the bathroom needs to be outside," he said with a chuckle.

Ben, already sitting at the table, and sipping his coffee, choked on Josh's statement, sending everyone into an uproar of laughter.

Andy and Jessica were the last to find their way into the great room, just in time to set down at the table for breakfast.

"Oatmeal with toasted homemade bread and Jam, the only thing better, would to be served first," Pastor Bowens said with a grin. Sarah slapped him on the back, with a "humph," and served Ben, who was sitting across the table first, before returning to Pastor with his bowl of oatmeal. After serving Andy, Jessica and Alice, Ellen returned with bowls for Josh and herself, nudging him over with her hip, as she scooted onto the bench.

"Something's brewing," Jessica said, once again teasing her sister, and it isn't coffee. Blowing Ellen, a kiss, with a smile, she leaned against Andy's shoulder.

No one was ready for Ellen's response, except for Josh, who glanced up with a broad smile of his own, as Ellen responded.

"It's brewed and ready to serve," she said …Josh and I are officially a couple, and with Papa Ben and Pastor Bowens blessings and counseling, we will be making that relationship a permanent one, when Josh is ready!

For one moment, everything went into slow motion.

Andy jumped to his feet. Covering her mouth with her hands, Jessica's eyes filled with tears of joy. Alice, clutching the dish towel she was holding to her breast, spilled her oatmeal into her lap. Pastor Bowens spit his dentures into his oatmeal, and Sister Sarah sat in utter amazement as the slow-motion scene erupted into "real-time pandemonium! Ben jumped to his feet and embraced Josh and Ellen, as he leaned over them from behind.

"I knew this was coming, He beamed. This unrequited love affair has been going on for years; it just took the circumstances of the present to bring it to fruition. You defiantly have my blessing, and if Pastor won't, I'll marry you myself!"

"That won't be necessary," Pastor Bowens said, after retrieving his dentures from his oatmeal, and reaching across the table for Josh and Ellen's hands. "That pleasure will be totally, mine, when the time comes!"

By the time things had settled down a little, it was mid-morning, breakfast was over, and all the morning chores were done. Max had been let out as well, but this time didn't return to Andy with a surprise that would have to be cooked.

Ben and Josh sat down at the table, with paper and pencil, as Pastor, Andy, and the women began bringing out the contents of the pallets Josh had dropped the day before, to be inventoried. Ellen carried Josh's backpack over, set it down beside him and laid his pistol and holster on the table.

"I'm glad you have this, but I pray you'll never have to use it, at least here," she said, laying her arm around Josh's shoulders.

As they went through the items, Ben was pleased that Josh had loaded up the other gear he had left in the back of the old truck, along with the food stores Ellen and Jessica had purchased at the Costco before their arrest. While the women put away the food, with Andy and Pastor's help, he and Josh stowed the other items in the bottom of the two long homemade couches in the middle of the cavern.

Ben and Pastor Bowens had made each couch from three pallets fastened, side by side, with the tops hinged in the back. They had made the ends, from pallets laid on their sides with the tops facing outward and connected by two eight-foot loge poles. An interesting concept, as the pallets on the ends, served as end tables and storage boxes as well. Then they covered the tops with foam and wool Indian blankets Ben had provided from the store. They were rugged, but pleasingly comfortable and provided an enormous amount of storage.

Josh, if you would, please put all these medical supplies you brought up, in that far couch, on the right side, end box," Ben said, as he made a notation in his inventory. What is in these tubes, Ben said, pointing to three large tubes six inches in diameter and about twenty-four inches long.

"Let me show you Pops, Josh said, but we've got to step outside... Ellen would you please grab the radio over there, and bring it with you, Josh called back."

With that, Josh led Ben and Ellen out the door of the Havens and onto the edge of the bluff where the sun was shining brightly.

Opening one end of the tube, Josh pulled out what looked like a shiny rubber mat. When he unrolled it, Ben's eyes lit up?

"It's a portable solar panel," Josh said, plugging the radio into the power bar on one end, which contained only one outlet, and a long rechargeable battery.

Turning on the radio, Josh tuned it to KJNO AM and turned up the volume. As the music ended, a world collective broadcast announcement for Juneau and the surrounding area came over the air.

The local office of the WCI, World Collective International, is pleased to announce to the people of the Juneau Collective, that the religious plague that once infested the Capitol of Alaska has been all but eliminated. Small pockets of resistance still infest some of the bush, and areas surrounding the Juneau banks, as well as areas bordering the Mendenhall wilderness. Special Forces of the collective militia will be conducting an intensive search by plane and helicopter over an eight hundred square mile area around Juneau over the next few days and are confident their efforts will end in complete success. More in the headlines today ... Josh turned off the radio, with a look of disgust and apprehension on his face.

"For the next forty-eight to seventy-two hours, we are going to have to stay invisible, if we're going to maintain this retreat for our safety and God's Glory, Josh said, camouflage clothing only and nothing that will reflect light!"

"I agree son, Ben said with much trepidation. Problem is that the weatherman said day before yesterday that we could expect nine to thirteen inches of snow by tomorrow night. I'm not sure we have time to bring across enough wood to last four or five days or not, before the snow arrives." "You know how it is Josh, snow tracks from the air, are like neon arrows. We have enough wood cut for the winter, covered, and hidden, about a hundred and fifty yards to the west, but it is not easy going. We have only brought over what was needed daily ... exercise, you know! We never expected to be hunted down out here, just forgotten, Ben said with a frown."

Ellen stood beside Ben with her arm around him, as Josh rolled up the solar panel and pushed it back into the container, tightly screwing down the cap.

"We'd better get back inside and talk to the others; we've got to get that wood over here before first snow!" As Josh stood, Ellen put her arm through his and Ben's. Together they walked back through the trees and entered the door of the havens.

As Ben, Josh and Ellen entered the great hall, Pastor Bowens could tell by the look on their faces it was time for a meeting, and that something had transpired while they were outside.

"Pastor," Josh said, laying the radio and solar panel down on the table. "If we can get everyone gathered around, we need to talk about something really important."

It took only a few minutes to gather. As they began to find a place to sit, Pastor motioned to Sarah.

"Mama could you and Sister Alice grab some cups and the pot, I think we'll need some of that coffee to help our conversation along," he said.

When everyone was seated, Josh wrapped his hands around his cup and looked down the table.

"We were just outside where I was demonstrating one of the solar panels. Tuning the radio in to KJNO, we heard a public service announcement stating that agents of the Collective Militia will be conducting aerial searches for the next three or four days over an eight hundred square mile area around Juneau. They will be looking for us or people like us, who are hiding out in the bush for the same reason we are.

Their goal is assimilation or extermination, and their preference is the latter. Wouldn't even begin to presume any kind of a leadership position here, Dad and Pastor Bowens oversee things, but if I could, I'd like to make some suggestions."

Clearing his throat, Ben stood and walked around the bench. Standing behind Josh and Andy who was sitting next to him. He placed his hands on their shoulders, as he spoke.

"For over a year and a half, six of us have lived here at the Havens unmolested and free from the harassing persecution that so many of our brothers and sisters in Christ have endured. Up till now, we've survived the cleansing that almost took the lives of Ellen and Jessica. It's now obvious to me after hearing the report, we're not only striving to survive, we're at war. The battle is not only spiritual; it's a physical one as well. I'm more than prepared to fight the spiritual one, but my age and health preclude me from being much help with the physical aspects of battle. We must be prepared to fight, as well as survive, for our sakes and the sake of those who may cross our paths as they flee the Militia. God called me, with Pastor Bowen's help, to prepare a haven for His people for such a time as this. I don't know how Pastor Bowens feels, but I think that he and I have done our part. It's time to hand things over to our young men and women, to write the conclusion to *the Lemon Creek Chronicle*, and time for the rest of us to fill the ranks as the support team. What do you think Pastor?"

"I am in total agreement, and my aching body agrees with me also," Pastor Bowens responded.

Sarah and Alice gave their ascent as well, with generous nods of approval. Josh and Ellen, along with Andy and Jessica sat in wide-eyed amazement as they looked up at Ben, waiting for some direction.

"Well, we've heard from half of us, what about the other half," Ben said with a smile. What about you two Andy, you and Jessica, what do you think?"

Andy looked at Jessica, at Josh and then at the rest of the company. "Papa Ben, I've been following Josh's lead ever since we were kids, and we've always been a team. I can't see changing anything now, my faith is in God, and I trust Josh's leadership with my life … How can we fail, especially with the kind of support we have from you seasoned saints!

"Amen," Jessica said, squeezing Andy's arm,

Ellen reached across the table and took Josh's hands in hers. Holding them tightly, she looked deeply into his eyes, and then up at Ben.

"I make a motion that we look to Josh and follow his direction. If anyone knows what to do in a tight situation, he does, Jessica and I can both attest to that!"

"I second the motion and move, that we appoint and support Joshua to oversee and direct us as the Lord leads him, for the sake of this fellowship and any who might come under our protection and provision," Pastor said, rising to his feet.

"All in favor," Ben said, raising his hand … those against. It's unanimous then he said, patting Josh on the shoulders … well Son, as you were saying." …

"Joshua's first directives will have to wait," Pastor said, until after we gather around and pray God's anointing over him, and his leadership over us."

Getting up from her seat Ellen walked around the end of the table and pulled Josh to his feet, leading him out into the center of the great room. Putting his arm around Ellen's waist Josh drew her next to him. Then placing his arm around her shoulders, he and Ellen bowed their heads, as the others gathered around them.

Pastor Bowens removed a small bottle of anointing oil from his pocked. Pouring an ample amount into the palm of his hand, he rubbed his palms together, and placing his hands on Josh and Ellen, he began to pray.

"Father, since the day you first called your chosen you have ordained leaders, leaders to minister to the spiritual needs of your people, and leaders to guide and protect your people in times of peace and war. Today Father we are at war. Today we battle the forces dedicated and now eternally committed to Satan and the Anti-Christ who has established himself against your kingdom. As the spiritual leader of this fellowship, ordained by you to that calling, I anoint Joshua Huskins, as our Leader and Commander, to guide and protect us as we stand in the gap and await your soon return."

Turning to Ellen, Pastor Bowens continued to pray.

Father, this woman, has openly confessed her love, commitment, and dedication to this man. Soon I'll have the pleasure to unite them in a Holy Covenant with you at the center of their lives and relationship. I pray a special anointing upon Ellen that you will make her a source of encouragement and a tower of strength in their relationship, as jointly they endeavor to continue in their service to you and this company. May your grace and strength empower and rest upon them, in the precious name of Christ we pray, Amen."

With tears in his eyes, Josh, humbled by the experience, shared his heart.

"To be perfectly honest folks, this is not what I expected when I stepped through the door and asked to speak with all of you about my concerns, and what I thought we might do to prepare ourselves. I am Honored, and humbled that all of you would think I have what it takes to lead this awesome group of people. I do promise you though, that with the Lords help and guidance, I'll do my very best."

Turning to Sister Bowens and the women, Josh stepped into his new role, as he encouraged them to begin preparing for the evening meal, and then took the men aside.

"Dad, I need you and Pastor Bowens to take Andy and me to where the firewood you mentioned is stored and show us the area in detail within a two-hundred-yard radius of the Havens. We need to find a way to the wood pile, that even in the snow, will remain hidden." While we are at it, we'll take the backpacks and bring four loads of wood with us on the way back. I need to know every trail, crevasse and stump that surrounds the havens, and where they are.

"The tour won't be a problem son," Ben said, but it will take all afternoon to show you everything. The trail might be a problem, and Pastor and I have something else we need to show you and Andy as well."

"That's fine with me Pops," Josh said with a grin, you are always full of surprises. It is important though, that when we go out from now on, all our clothing has to be camouflage. I brought up all the white camouflage gear we had in the shop Pops, enough for nine I think, three of each ... small, medium, and large for when the snow comes. Let's get changed and go see what you and Pastor have been hiding from us."

Thirty minutes later Josh and Andy stepped through the door, following Ben and Pastor Bowens on another tour. This time however, it was to familiarize them with the mountainside surrounding the Havens. As Andy turned to pull the door closed behind him, Max darted between his legs and took up a point position next to Papa Ben.

CHAPTER 10

The escarpment trail

AFTER WALKING OUT BEYOND THE trees shielding the entrance to the Havens, Ben led the party to the left up the face of a long sloping granite shelf that disappeared into a thickly forested area above the caves. From there, they continued to climb as they snaked their way through the underbrush and trees to a point where the forest gave way to a large clearing, covered with mountain grass, rocks, and low brush. The clearing was about fifty yards wide and a hundred and fifty yards long. It appeared to Josh to slope about 12 degrees. As he surveyed the area, the most prominent feature was the crescent shaped escarpment of granite that ran the entire length of the clearing along the upper edge. It didn't appear to be very high, but the top hung out over the bottom and looked as though it disappeared behind the crest of the hill. It was overhung with brush and small stunted trees that lined its upper edge.

With Ben, Max and Pastor still leading the way, Josh and Andy continued to follow as they moved through the clearing, stepping on the large stones that covered the ground wherever possible. When they reached the other side, it was only a short trek into a densely forested area where the firewood was neatly cut and stacked under the low hanging boughs of large thick limbed fir trees.

"At present we have about eight cords of wood hidden here under these trees." Ben said holding up one of the boughs, to reveal the wood stacked underneath.

Andy and Josh were impressed by the tremendous effort it had taken for Ben, Pastor and the women to accomplish what they were being shown, and the ingenuity used to hide and protect their source of warmth for the winter.

"Before we do anymore hiking," Pastor Bowens said, your father and I want to show you and Andy one more resource we depend on daily. "Actually, without it we couldn't survive here at all."

"You couldn't possibly be talking about the General Store, could you?" Josh said, sitting down on a boulder and winking at his father.

Pastor Bowens looked at Josh over the top of his glasses, as if to say, who told you, and then looked at Ben who could only shrug his shoulders and point to himself shaking his head no, with a smile. Josh leaned forward taking off his stocking cap.

"I knew you had to have a cash somewhere near the Havens," there wasn't enough stores in the caves to feed all of us for more than a couple of days, and the wisest thing to do would be to cash all the stores in a safe and secure place where they could be accessed, but not too close.

Ben and Pastor looked at each other in amazement, as they acknowledged with a glance that they had made the right choice in selecting Josh to take the lead for the Lemon Creek castaways.

"Let's go and take a look at what you're going to have to work with, in your new position Ben said," reaching out a hand to help Josh to his feet.

Climbing up the mountainside another hundred feet, they came to what appeared to Josh to be the western end of the granite escarpment he had noticed as they made their way across the clearing. Pressing into the escarpment, they followed a narrow trail with the wall of granite on their left and a five-foot-high berm of rocks, earth, and debris on their right.

Making their way east for about a hundred and fifty feet, the trail made a sudden upward turn to the left, through a crack in the granite wall and into a small alcove. In the back, imbedded into the rock was a heavy wooden door, fashioned very similar to the one guarding the entrance to the Havens.

"This is Havens II," Ben said, as he unhooked the latch that secured the door and pushed it aside.

Reaching into his pocket, Ben pulled out a small flashlight and walked inside to where he reached up and turned on a large battery powered lantern. The small cavern was oval shaped, about thirty feet wide and fifty feet long with a vaulted ceiling about fourteen feet high. It was filled with cases of MRE's, canned food and meats as well as dry goods of every description. As they continued to look around, Andy and Josh were shown large plastic containers of clothing of all sizes, medical supplies sleeping bags, blankets, even paper towels and toilet paper! Andy sat down on a small crate, shaking his head in unbelief at the number of provisions that filled the cavern.

"Josh … Josh," Ben repeated, looking around and expecting to see him eyeballing a special item that caught his interest.

Josh was nowhere in sight. Thinking that he had stepped out for some reason, the men began to make their way to the door, when Josh suddenly appeared in the doorway with a look of excitement on his face.

"God has provided the answer to our needs he said, motioning them to follow.

"Close it up Pops, and this time you follow me," he shouted, as he disappeared back through the crevice to the outside. When they had assembled back on the trail, Josh was busy muscling small boulders and large pieces of debris from between a tight stand of small fir trees that had grown up across the end of the trail next to the entrance of the cavern. Suddenly realizing what Josh was trying to do, Andy jumped in to help and within a short time they had a narrow path cleared through the obstruction.

"If what I think is on the other side is true, we are going to return to the Havens by a route that will never be seen from the air, regardless of the season."

With that, Josh turning sideways, stepped through the new opening, and disappeared, with Andy, Ben and Pastor Bowens following close behind. Max was already ahead of them taking the point. Moments later the men stood looking down a long narrow trail, which followed the gentle arch of the escarpment about three feet wide and unobstructed, as far as they could see, with the exception of small rocks and debris that had rolled down the back side of the berm.

"You never know what we might find up ahead," Josh said, pulling the Judge from the holster on his chest.

"Max will let us know if there's any danger Andy said." I can attest to that one myself.

"If I'm right, we should exit about a hundred feet past the far end of the clearing we entered after we left the havens." Josh said, as he began making his way down the trail.

As they moved along, Josh and Andy cleared any obstructions that had fallen into the pathway from above. Ben and Pastor Bowens couldn't believe that they had spent over four years hauling in supplies, making countless trips back and forth across that open expanse, and never knowing that the secure access they longed for, lay only thirty-five yards to their right all that time.

Ten minutes later, they emerged, pushing their way through a grove of trees and small fir's that concealed the entrance to the path.

"This is one rabbit trail I'm glad we came down," Josh said, but we need to go back to the wood pile and fetch those four loads of wood we came after he laughed."

It really didn't take as long as expected, to return and load up the wood, and within thirty-five minutes they were back at the end of their newfound blessing and making their way back down the mountain to the security of the caves and the savory smell of a much-appreciated meal.

What a tail they would have to tell tonight, Ben thought to himself, as they stepped through the door and laid their burdens down next to the hearth.

Although they hadn't accomplished everything, they had set out to do that afternoon, Josh and the men were elated with their discovery. It was a good day.

After stowing their coats and gear next to the cave entrance, the men gathered around one end of the table for some much-anticipated coffee and to discuss the afternoon's adventure.

Ben sat looking at Pastor Bowens with a sheepish smile, shaking his head in disbelief, and then turning to Josh, patted his back and gently squeezed his shoulder.

"Son, I just can't believe that with all the exploring Pastor and I did, that led to the discovery of the cave where we store our supplies, and harvested our wood supply, that we never ventured up to explore the edge of the escarpment!"

"Just human nature Dad, I read somewhere that men and rivers are much the same, they both seek paths of least resistance. You were just looking for the easiest way to get the job done, and not necessarily the best one."

"Don't put yourself down Papa Ben," Andy said, taking a sip of his coffee and reaching out to draw Jessica, who was listening to the conversation, to his side. I'm just blown away by what you, Pastor and the women have accomplished, it's amazing!

"What's truly amazing is how God provides for His own," Pastor said, as he poured himself another cup of coffee. It'll take a couple of days to really clear out the path, especially next to the Havens Two entrance, but when we're done it will be like a tunnel, but we'll have daylight in it from one end to the other. I would even venture to say that when the snow comes, we'll be protected from drifts and avalanche as well."

Mama Bowens suddenly appeared next to Jessica and removed Andy's arm from around his wife's waist.

"Let go of my help," she said, and you men go hang out on the couches, while we women get supper on the table. You might even head to the tub in the back and clean yourselves up a little before supper she said, tugging on Pastor Bowen's ear."

It was not long before Ellen and Jessica circled up the men and headed them toward the table, as Alice and Sister Bowens finished setting out the meal. Josh and Andy sat on one side of the table in the middle, with Ellen and Jessica seating themselves on each side, like a pair of bookends. The scene was similar on the senior side of the table as well, and Ben was beginning to feel a little hemmed in.

Clearing his throat, as he usually did when he was about to speak, Ben looked around the table at the other men, before making his inquiry.

"Is it just me or do you gentlemen feel like you're surrounded as well, pointing at each corner of the table. Then turning to Alice, he patted the back of her hand as it rested on the table, making her blush.

"More like protected," Ellen said with a chuckle. Besides, it makes it easier for us to get up to take care of things and serve you better she said, kissing Josh's cheek as she placed a hot dinner roll on his plate and passed the platter across the table to Sarah. Realizing he was outnumbered, and that even Josh wasn't going to come to his aid, Ben settled into enjoying the delicious meal the women had prepared. As they all enjoyed the meal and casual conversation, the tranquility was suddenly shattered by the drone of engines and the telltale sound of beating helicopter rotors.

"Sounds like the Militia is on the move," Josh said, sliding Ellen out of the way and jumping to his feet.

Josh darted quickly to the door as he strapped the Judge to his chest and put on his camouflage jacket and stocking cap. Andy was right behind him mimicking Josh's every move.

"Pops, douse the lights before we go out, and everyone else stay inside," he said, waiting for the lights to be turned off.

When the lights went out so did Josh and Andy, closing the door quickly behind them. Making their way cautiously to the trees, which obscured the entrance to the Havens, Josh and Andy crawled under them and lay down, hidden by the low hanging boughs. Lying in the shadows, they watched as the small squadron, which consisted of a spotter plane and four helicopters slowly made their way down the Lemon Creek valley toward the airport down on the banks.

"Looked to me like every one of those birds carried heat seeking devices as well as cameras and motion detectors," Josh said rolling over on his back and setting up. Since they came down over the glacier from the south, I am guessing they came around from searching over Mt. Juneau and the Salmon Creek Lake area. This late in the evening, they probably weren't looking extremely hard, and just came down the valley as the best return to the airport."

"Just like vultures in the sky," Andy said, looking for something to give them a reason to land.

Josh suddenly jumped to his feed, slapping his hand on his thigh, and spun around as he mumbled to himself ...

"What's up," Andy said, did something crawl into your pants, or what?

Reaching out to Andy, Josh gave a tug on his sleeve. "Let's head back inside, he said, we've got some serious planning to do, and there isn't much time to get things done."

All eyes were on Andy and Josh as they reentered the caverns and bolted the door behind them. Removing their jackets and firearms, they returned to the table and sat down as Ellen freshened up their coffee and slid in next to Josh.

"What was going on?" Ellen asked. It sounded like they were right over the top of us.

Andy answered her question, as he glanced over at Josh for affirmation. "Search party, looking more for a quick trip back to the banks than anything on the ground.

"So, why's Josh so upset," Ben said, walking up to the other side of the table and setting down.

"It's the pontoons, I forgot about those pontoons up on the melt lake where they were ripped off," Josh said with a deep look of concern. I have no idea if they are in the water or down on the rocks, either way we've got to get them out of sight.

They missed them tonight, but if they come this way again, in the full light of day, they'll find them, and then we'll have boots on the ground for sure, and that's the last thing we want."

"There's usually ground fog early in the morning up here, especially when we're expecting a weather change. If you're up and on your way before first light it'll give you about two hours to complete your task and get back off the rocks where you can find cover." Ben said. You don't want to be caught on the rocks, there's no place to hide up there."

Josh turned to his father, thinking aloud, he spoke.

"Those pontoons have to be sunk, either in the upper lake where they were ripped off, or in the lower lake and that means rolling, dragging, and sliding them down a five hundred-foot drop in elevation for over an eighth of a mile. My foolishness, has jeopardized everything he said burying his face in his hands."

Pastor Bowens quickly moved to Josh's side and motioned the others to gather around. Placing his hands on Josh's shoulders, he began to pray.

"Father, you know the seriousness of the dilemma we face this evening, but we know that you use the weak to overcome the strong and that we can and will do all things through you who strengthens us. Father we pray tonight for your intercession in this matter. We ask that you truly work all things for our good according to your will and plan for our lives and that you will instill in Josh's heart and mind, your strength, your peace and your character, that through him, you might manifest your leadership and strength, for your glory and our salvation, Amen.

As Pastor Bowens concluded his prayer, Josh turned around on the bench and faced Pastor Bowens and his father.

"You two have left some enormous shoes for me to fill. I'm only a three-day old Christian, and I'm already carrying a responsibility that far exceeds my experience in Christ. I really do appreciate your prayers and support, without your spiritual strength, I know I'd be helplessly lost," Thank you!

"Early rise tomorrow," Ben said looking at Josh. What do you think son, about three am? It'll give us time for some hot breakfast and an early start. We could be at the upper lake by six thirty or so."

"Sounds good to me Pops, is everyone ok with that?"

Looking around and finding everyone else in agreement, Josh took Ellen by the hand and led her to the door of her alcove, where he tenderly kissed her goodnight and retired to his own room, trying to formulate a viable plan to lay the remnants of the Lemon Lady to rest.

CHAPTER 11

Laying the Lady to rest

J OSH AWOKE TO THE SOFT glow of the light bulb, which hung in the center of the alcove he and his father shared, and a tender kiss, as Ellen hovered over him.

"Pops told me to come wake you up," she said, it's just a little past three. I'm going to go wake up Andy and Sis now, get dressed, and I'll meet you at the table.

Ellen bent over and gave Josh another kiss that sent shivers through his body, and the sudden realization that it was time for him and Ellen to talk to Pastor Bowens about marriage. As Josh sat up and rubbed his eyes, Ellen stepped through the canvas door and disappeared into the main cavern.

After rousting Jessica and Andy, Ellen returned to the great room to where Papa Ben sat nursing a cup of coffee. Pouring a cup for Josh and herself, she joined Ben at the end of the table.

"Papa, this trip to the upper lake is going to be very dangerous, isn't it?

"Yes, it is sweetheart," not because of the hike or the effort to deal with the pontoons, but because of the Militia and the extensive search that's going on. We can't all go either. We seniors will have to remain here. None of us are in good enough shape to move fast if the need arises, and we'd be more of a burden than a help. This is a job for you young men and women, but we'll be praying all the time you're out there.

Ellen reached across the table and took Ben's hand in hers.

"I love you Pops; you and Alice have been like parents to Jessica and me, ever since our folks were killed, I don't know what we would have done without you two."

"Everybody needs someone honey, even an old codger like me. When my Amy passed away, I was lost. If it hadn't been for Alice, and her loving friendship, I don't know what I would have done; she's a mighty strong woman.

After her Tom was killed in that logging accident, she faced a long road without anyone being there for her.

"I know she loves you as much as you love her," Ellen said, squeezing Ben's hand. She's told me more than once that she knows God brought you two together. I've sensed for a long time there was something brewing, and it wasn't coffee."

"I'm confused," are you Ellen or Jessica, Ben said laughingly.

"You know who I am you old tease, but I really think that there needs to be another change in the sleeping arrangements, and it's not just Josh and I that needs to talk to Pastor Bowens about a wedding."

As Ellen and Ben sat looking at each other, a broad smile slowly crept across his face.

"You've convinced me sweetheart," Ben said. Rising and leaning across the table he kissed Ellen on the forehead. I'll ask Alice today and talk to Pastor while you young folks are out taking care of business. If you and Josh would get it together, maybe we could make it a double!

As Ben was sitting back down, Josh walked through the archway and over to the table where Ellen and Ben, were still holding hands.

"What's going on here," Josh quipped, are you making time with my girl, he said with a grin?

"She's not your girl until you do some knot tying, his father shot back. If you don't marry her soon, I'm going to ask her myself."

"Ok, ok … You win," Josh said, getting down on his knees and pulling Ellen's hands out of his fathers. Ellen Michaels … I love you with all my heart, and if you kiss me one more time before we're married, I will go crazy... "Will you marry me?"

Like a bolt of lightning Ellen slid off the end of the bench, throwing her arms around Josh's neck and knocking him to the floor, as the word "Yes," echoed off the walls.

"Sounds like we're going to have a wedding," Pastor Bowens said, as he walked into the great room, followed by Sarah and Alice.

"Maybe two Ben said, as he stood and walked over to Alice. Taking her hand, he dropped down on one knee, and looked up into her surprised but radiant face.

"Alice, I'm an old man, and I don't know how much time we have left before we step into eternity, but I want to spend that time with you as my wife," if you'll have me?

Tears welled up in Alice's eyes as she tenderly reached down and caressed Ben's cheek.

"Yes Ben Huskins," I would be proud to be your wife, I've loved you too long to stop now!

As they entered the great room, Andy and Jessica, gazed at the others, with a look of bewilderment on their faces, which suddenly turned to joyful tears and smiles as Sarah filled them in on what had just happened.

"Get yourselves over here to the table and sit down," Pastor Bowens said with a laugh, calling everyone together, things are getting crazier around here by the minute."

It wasn't long before everyone was seated at the table and enjoying a breakfast of hot oatmeal, coffee and rolls left over from the evening before. After a short discussion, it was agreed that on the upcoming Sunday, after their worship service, Pastor Bowens would perform a simple but very special marriage ceremony for two couples, who could barely contain their anticipation. As Josh finished his coffee and sat the cup down on the table, he changed the subject, and focused on the task that lay before them that morning; looking at his watch he nudged Ellen, to get a little more room on the bench.

"We'll have first light in about half an hour, so we had better get ready to go. As soon as we can see to make our way up to the lake, we'll head out. I lay awake for a long-time last night thinking about how to dispose of the pontoons, when we get up to the lake. I'm going to assume they were folded up and torn apart bad, which would be to our benefit. At least that's what I've been praying for.

Andy… aside from our firearms, you and I will carry only what we need to get the task done. I think if we carry a hundred feet of rope, an ax, half dozen carabineers and a couple of Camming wedges, we should be able to move the wreckage around and get it into one lake or the other. Because the pontoons are compartmentalized, we'll have to make as many holes as we can to fill them with water and sink them. Any questions or suggestions Josh said, looking around the table, and then settling his gaze on his father."

"We're going with you," Ellen said, as she and Jessica stood to their feet.

"Whatever you and Andy will face out there, we're going to face together. Dealing with the Militia will seem like child's play compared to Jessica and me, if you try to leave us behind, she said, trying to assert herself, but realizing her smile was giving her away.

"I had already planned on it," Josh said with a smile, as he reached out and squeezed Ellen's bicep. We need all that muscle you and Jess are packing around. Let's saddle up and get this done, I'd rather focus my mind on a honeymoon he said, as he leaned over and quickly stole a kiss.

Before the four stepped out the door, Pastor Bowens and the others gathered around them, praying for their safety, and success. Then without any further conversation, the small party made their way out the door and into the crisp morning air.

Making their way down and across the three-quarter mile stretch to where the forest gave way to barren rock, they made good time, taking just over forty minutes to make the decent.

It took another twenty minutes to ascend the last half mile and two hundred feet in elevation, before they arrived where Josh had made his scraping take off into the air only days before. To Josh's delight, both pontoons lay halfway in the water with their crumpled bow's resting on the rocks at the water's edge.

"Looks like the impact simply sheared off the bolts holding the rigging onto the plane and bounced everything back to the water's edge. God is so good," he said.

"Josh, I think that if we spin the pontoons around, we'll only have to chop holes in the back ends of them in order to sink the whole thing. If we chop some smaller holes in the top, prayerfully when we push them out into the lake, they'll get far enough out that they'll sink in deep water and prayerfully a little faster," Andy said, tugging on the pontoons to see what it was going to take to get them moving.

"Good idea," Josh said, moving in to help, as Ellen and Jessica followed close behind.

Climbing out on the pontoons, Josh tied a rope to the back and tossed the other end to Ellen. Climbing off he joined Andy and Jessica as they pushed the pontoons completely into the water, and spun them around, pulling them back onto the rocks with the rope. With some effort and as the damaged bows began to sink, they were able to pull the back of the pontoons out of the water enough to begin using the axe to open the bottoms and tops of the undamaged sections.

When Josh and Andy were satisfied that they had made enough holes to adequately sink the pontoons Josh untied the rope, and with all the strength, the four could muster, pushed the pontoons out into the lake and prayed they would soon disappear. It seemed to take forever for the pontoons to fill with water, and begin to slowly sink, bow first into the icy depths of the lake.

Looking at his watch, then up at the sky and down the valley, Josh sighed with relief as the pontoons slowly disappeared beneath the surface.

Quickly gathering up the rope and axe, he stuffed them into his pack, and adjusted it on his back. With the women following him and Andy, they began making their way back across the barren mountainside, longing desperately to reach the shelter of the forest before enemy patrols with their sophisticated surveillance equipment could find them.

As they made their way down the last thirty feet of rock, where the transition began between the barren mountainside and the forest, the unmistakable sound of a helicopter filled the air as it came over the top of the glacier. Josh, grabbing Ellen's hand quickly led Andy and Jessica into a large cleft in the rocks partially covered with brush and small trees. Huddling in the back, the four pulled their camouflage jackets and hoods up around their faces and waited as the chopper swooped overhead, circled and landed a short distance away.

Although they couldn't see anything, they could hear the voices of men as they leaped from the chopper and began to make a sweep of the area. With the women behind them, Josh and Andy pulled their weapons, and prepared for what they were sure was to come. As they listened to the approaching footsteps, Ellen whispered aloud, "Father protect us." Suddenly, two uniformed Militiamen stepped into view, with automatic weapons in their hands, looking on both sides and directly into the cleft of rock where the four were huddled.

"I could swear I saw movement and four heat sources as we came over the glacier," one of the men said, peering again into the rock cleft and looking intently up and down before turning away and motioning his companion to follow.

"I'd rather be policing the streets of Juneau than up here in this desolate place, the other man retorted, hunting down those crazy religious freaks is a waste of time as far as I'm concerned.

Be thankful friend, we could be rotting in the Lemon Creek Prison or worse yet, facing execution ourselves.

Moments later the whine of the helicopter rotors rose overhead and then slowly disappeared down the valley. Josh moved cautiously out of the cleft in the rock, before calling the others to follow. Without any hesitation, they quickly made their way into the shelter of the trees, and began their way back to the Havens, rejoicing in the miracle they had just experienced and listening to Ellen as she sang, "He hideth my soul in the cleft of the rock, and covers me there with his hand!"

ABOUT THIRTY MINUTES AFTER JOSH, Andy and the women had left; Ben and Pastor Bowens climbed the granite shelf just outside the entrance to the Havens. They took up a position just inside the trees where they could see the smaller melt lake and the ridge the group would be taking to the upper lake, as well as the face of the Lemon glacier. Sitting side by side on a slab of granite, both Pastor Bowens and Ben searched the landscape before them with field glasses. It wasn't long before Ben spotted the group as they left the cover of the trees and began the short climb to the upper melt lake.

"I see them, there, just to the left of the lower lake, breaking out of the trees," Ben said, with a ring of excitement in his voice.

Pastor Bowens glanced at Ben and then quickly finding his quarry focused his binoculars, zooming in on the young group as they picked their way up the steep narrow trail and around the two small snowpacks between them and the crest of the granite ridge. When the group finally crested the ridge and disappeared out of sight, Pastor reached over and placed his hand on Ben's shoulder.

"Let's pray," he said, gazing at glacier.

The first rays of the morning sun lit up its face with a heavenly glow, as the two men bowed their heads. When Ben and Pastor finished praying, the face of the granite ridge below the point of Josh's take off became easier to study with more light, and the men began to scour the mountain side from top to bottom looking for sign of the pontoons but found nothing that looked out of place. It was just a little over a half hour later that Pastor Bowens spotted the group as they rose over the crest of the ridge with Josh in the lead.

Ben was overjoyed that they were returning so soon. It could only mean that their mission was a success, but he could not relax until they were safely into the shelter and cover of the trees, and off the granite escarpment. As Pastor Bowens watched the men and women make their descent down the mountain, Ben kept a wary eye, as he scoured the sky with his binoculars and listened intently for any sounds that might indicate impending danger.

As Ben searched the sky above the glacier, a dark speck suddenly appeared in his field of vision from the Southeast, as the unmistakable sound of a helicopter rang in his ears.

"Where are they?" Ben shouted, as he frantically watched the approach of the helicopter which was about to break over the edge of the glacier.

"Almost to the bottom," Pastor shouted back, "almost to the bottom!"

Ben and Pastor's hearts pounded, as the helicopter broke over the edge of the glacier and descended down on top of Josh, Andy and the women.

Coming almost straight at them, Ben and Pastor Bowens watched as it made a banking turn to their right less than a quarter of a mile from them, and swoop down, landing in a clearing not far from where Josh and his group had been only moments before. Looking intently through their binoculars, Ben and Pastor watched as four uniformed men with weapons emerged from the helicopter and began searching the area.

"Ben, those two men, there on the left, their looking right where Josh and the others disappeared from sight", Pastor said, jumping to his feet.

"Sit down Pastor; sit down before they spot us up here. Remember, they have cameras on that bird that can read the label on a soup can from space."

Moments later, as Pastor and Ben watched from their vantage point, the militiamen climbed aboard the helicopter.

Rising into the air and hovering briefly, the nose suddenly dropped, and it moved off to the west, passing within a hundred yards of where they sat motionless on the hillside. Raising his binoculars to his eyes, Ben searched the area where the helicopter had landed. To his utter amazement and joy, he watched as Josh, and then Andy and the women seemed to climb up out of a crack in the rock only feet from where the two militiamen had stood moments before.

Ben and Pastor Bowens watched for another thirty minutes, as the small group made its way up the mountain, moving quickly across the clearings from one forested area to another until they were just beyond the melt pond, before descending to the Havens to meet them.

As Josh stepped through the thick grove of trees that sheltered the entrance to the Havens with Ellen at his side and Andy tugging Jessica behind him, Alice and Sarah burst between Pastor and Ben, to embrace the couples as though they had been gone for months instead of only hours. With everyone talking at once, the excitement escalated, until a shrill whistle brought a deadening silence.

"Let's take this joyous occasion inside, before they can hear us down on the banks," Josh said, laughing. "Besides, I really need some coffee!"

Stepping inside, the Lemon Creek Warriors put down their packs, Jackets and firearms beside the entrance and made a bee line to the well-used table, sliding onto the bench with some moans and groans, but overjoyed to have once and for all, laid the Lemon Lady to rest. Sarah and Alice had a large pot of navy bean soup and fresh baked cornbread waiting on the hearth, along with plenty of coffee and a special treat that made Josh grin from ear to ear. Sitting in the middle of the table, was a bowl filled with packets of powdered French Vanilla creamers!

By twelve thirty, the tales of the Lemon Lady saga, and Lemon creek miracle, had been told and retold until it was indelibly etched into everyone's mind, and God had been fully glorified. As the women finished cleaning up, Andy stood and walked over to where Josh was reclining on one of the large sofas.

"Hey Josh, I was just thinking about the new escarpment trail. If you're not too tired maybe we could use this afternoon, to clean up the trail and clear out the rest of the debris next to the storeroom. The women could scope things out and bring back what they need from the storeroom. We could haul back more firewood as well."

"That's a great idea," Josh said, sitting up and motioning to Pastor and his father, who were once again engrossed in deep conversation. Andy, would you gather the women together too. We will just have a huddle here on the couches to let everyone know what we are planning. Then we'll get ready and head up to the escarpment."

After the meeting, the women were excited to investigate the new trail, and were ready and waiting at the door with their gloves in hand before the men had even gotten up from the couches.

"Are you guys going to get the lead out, or do we have to vote in a new leader." Ellen quipped, blowing Josh a kiss as he sprang to his feet, strapped on his gun, and slipped on his coat and hat.

"Just remember ladies, you may be Queens of the caves in here, but outside, we're Kings of the mountains," Ben said, with a hearty laugh.

Ten minutes later, Josh led the women, with Andy, Pastor and Ben following, through the thick grove of young fir trees that concealed the entrance to the escarpment trail. This is amazing, and incredible; the accolades flowed as the women slowly made their way down the trail behind Josh and Andy. Ben and Pastor fell behind as they took their time, clearing rocks and other debris from the trail, widening it wherever possible.

By the time Pastor and Ben arrived at the entrance to the storeroom, the women were busy inside loading up stores for the Havens. Josh and Andy had completely removed all of the trees and rubble, removing even the small stumps and roots which had been embedded in the trail. Pressing onward, they found Andy and Josh working intently on removing debris and boulders from the last hundred feet of the trail. Joining in, they quickly completed the task, climbed up the bank and hiked down the last hundred feet to the woodpile.

Loading up their backpacks with firewood, they returned to the storeroom, where the women were waiting. After closing and securing the door, the troupe began making their way back down the escarpment trail, which now seemed to everyone, more like the Egan Drive expressway between Lemon Creek and Juneau. It was with deep feelings of elation that everyone marched into the caverns and laying down their hard-earned treasures, settled in for the night in the warmth and security of God's wonderful provision.

CHAPTER 12

A new back door

AFTER A LIGHT SUPPER OF leftovers and coffee, everyone was ready to turn in. Beginning with Pastor and Sarah, the residents of the Havens took their leave, one and two at a time, to hit the shower and bed. The rigors of the day had left everyone exhausted beyond measure. Josh and Ellen sat alone in the great room; waiting for Jessica to let her know when the shower was vacant. Moments later Jessica appeared, and with a wave, returned to Andy. With a deep sigh, Ellen rose and made her way through the archway, leaving Josh to fall asleep as he waited his turn.

Once again Josh found himself awakened with a kiss and Ellen hovering over him, with the sweet smell of scented soap clinging to her body. In the glow of the light, as it shone through her hair, she looked like an angel. Josh ached everywhere from the labors of the day, and longed for a hot shower and sleep, but as he lay there on the couch, in Ellen's arms, he knew that tonight, his shower would have to be a cold one.

"Honey," Josh said, as he sprang to his feet and staggered to the archway, two more days and then ... Josh disappeared into the darkness.

With a smile, Ellen returned to her room and lay listening to the sound of running water, as Josh enjoyed his long-awaited turn at the shower.

It started as a low rumble that gently coaxed most everyone out of a deep and restful sleep. Sarah and Alice had been up since six and the smell of fresh brewed coffee and flapjacks waft through the archway and into the adjoining chamber. Looking at his watch, Josh saw it was well past eight in the morning. Now, instead of being very tired, he was immensely hungry and climbed out of his sleeping bag, anticipating a hot cup of coffee with some of that vanilla creamer he had the night before.

Stepping out through the canvas door, Josh came face to face with the love of his life, who greeted him with a kiss that made his knees buckle. He was putty in her hands, and he knew it, as Ellen led him by the hand into the great room and over to the table where his father and Pastor sat engrossed in early morning conversation. Josh and Ellen had just sat down when the earthquake hit, traveling like a freight train, it rolled up the valley, underneath them and beyond the Lemon glacier as the caverns shook violently, then all was silent again.

Jumping to their feet, Josh and Ellen helped Alice and Sarah off the floor, walking them over to the table where Ben and Pastor sat pulling themselves together. The coffee pot had moved about six inches and rested on the edge of the iron grate it sat on. Picking it up and moving it back, Josh was overjoyed that it had been spared. After helping pick things up that had fallen, and pouring coffee for Ellen and himself, he refilled Pastor and Ben's cups before returning to pot to the hearth.

It was then that Andy ran into the great room, motioning for everyone to follow him into the adjoining chamber.

"Hurry, you won't believe this, you just won't believe this," he said, turning and rushing back through the archway.

Josh and Ellen were the first to enter and investigate the alcove where he and his father had just spent the night. The back of the alcove lay on the floor in shattered pieces, and a new archway stood before them. It was about six feet wide and tall enough that Josh could step through it without hitting his head. The most amazing thing was the cold blast of air that hit Josh's face, and the light from outside, that filtered down from another opening about fifty feet away and eight to ten feet higher than the cavern floor.

Handing Josh, a flashlight, Ben pushed him through the opening, as he urged Josh forward. They entered a chamber about ten feet high, fairly level for about fifteen feet and then slopping upward toward the light where it narrowed to an opening about five feet wide and six feet high. Beyond the opening, Josh and Ben could see trees.

"Let's step out through the opening Josh," Ben said, I want to see where this comes out.

Pushing back the bough of a small fir tree that partially covered the cave entrance, Josh stepped out into the fresh morning air with Ben clamoring on his heels.

"I knew it, I knew it," Ben shouted as he walked over to the granite slab, he and Pastor Bowens had sat on the day before with their field glasses. Josh lets head back in and cover the opening so we can keep our heat in, then we'll have some breakfast and talk this over, God has blessed us beyond measure this morning!

Returning to the alcove Ben and Josh leaned what was left of the canvas partition over the opening. Before reentering the great room, Ben stopped to pull out some paper and a couple of pencils from a small box.

"Now for some breakfast and coffee," Ben said, patting Josh's shoulder and escorting him to the table where Ellen waited impatiently.

As Alice poured them coffee, Ben began to draw a crude map of the caverns with the new back door the Lord had created and its relationship to the escarpment trail.

"We now have a secluded trail from the caverns, all the way to the woodpile, he said excitedly. Unless we have boots on the ground, there's absolutely no way to see a trail or spot any movement. I think we have enough material stacked behind the bathroom to build a door for the new entrance and make it secure. We will have to get it done today and tomorrow he said, pausing as he thought to himself for a moment.

"Come on Pops, Josh said, taking away his father's paper and pencils.

My mind won't work until I feed it some coffee and pancakes, then we can start forming work parties."

Ben looked at Josh with a frown that soon turned right side up as a smile formed on his face.

"You are right son," Ben said, pulling his coffee cup to him and taking a sip. Alice placed a stack of pancakes in front of him, and tenderly ran her fingers through his snowy white hair.

After helping the other ladies get everyone served, Ellen sat another large plate of pancakes down in the center of the table, and seated herself next to Josh. Leaning over and laying her head against Josh's shoulder, Ellen looked up smiling.

"One more day," she said, and then turning to Pastor Bowens she added, what's the sermon about tomorrow Pastor?"

"Wives obey your husband's," he said, laughing as he gave Josh and Ben a nod and a wink.

Not much ever fazed Ellen, but this time for some reason, Pastor's answer left her blushing and looking down at the table with a little girl smile on her face.

"Oh Pastor ... I never know whether to take you serious or not," she responded, you and Papa Ben are the biggest teases I've ever known!"

"Part of my Pastoral duties," he said grinning, looking over the top of his glasses. "Since Ben is my only elder and advisor, it's his duty to tease as well."

"That's ok, Ellen said with a smile, we women have our duties. Oh, by the way, just how badly do you teasers want supper this evening?"

"Bad enough to behave myself, but there's always tomorrow, he said with a chuckle and a wink."

After everyone finished breakfast, Josh returned the paper and pencils to his father, and focused on the new door they would be building. Finishing their coffee, the four men stood and headed into the second chamber where Ben led everyone to the area behind the bathroom. It was there that ten sticks of eight-foot tongue and grove two by sixes, and eight remaining bags of mortar mix were stored. These they removed and carried to where the new opening, had been created.

"Josh, up in Havens II on the back wall of the cavern, is a wooden box about four feet long and a foot square," Ben said. "In it is two more sets of hinges and some threaded rod with nuts and washers attached, as well as the other things we'll need to set the door in place. As soon as you and Andy can get it down here, we can get things going."

"We're on our way," Josh said, slapping Andy on the back and heading into the great room to get their gear. Moments later they slid behind the tarp and out the new entrance to the escarpment trail.

THIRTY MINUTES LATER, JOSH AND Andy were back, toting the long wooden box down into the chamber through the new opening, and setting it down, watching while Ben and Pastor assembled all the pieces together.

"Looks like you two have done this before," Josh said.

When the door was finished, they stood it on its end, against the wall of the cavern. The whole process had taken less than forty minutes.

"That was the easy part," Ben said. Now you and Andy are going to have to go to work, while Pastor and I finish the casing and have some coffee, he said with a grin."

Handing Josh and Andy each a short, handled sledgehammer and a minor's drill he led them up to the new entrance. Dropping a short plumb line down each side of the entrance, and using a tape measure, he marked three spots with a pencil.

"I really need you boys, so don' go hitting each other with these hammers, he said. Six holes and each one has to be at least six inches deep."

Ben showed Josh and Andy how to use the drills by hitting and rotating them each time, and then stepped back.

"Good luck boys", he said, I'll send Ellen to fetch you for lunch …

Josh and Andy decided that one should start at the top, while the other began at the bottom, so as not to leave lumps on each other's heads.

While wisdom comes with age, youth does have its advantages, and by the time, Ellen called up from the alcove to summon Andy and Josh to lunch, only a hole and a half remained. Before Ellen could get back into the great room, Josh and Andy had raced past her and were standing at the end of the table begging for coffee!

"Considering how long it took for your father and I, with you two young men hard at work, we should be able to start installing the door sometime tomorrow", Pastor Bowens, said, as Josh and Andy seated themselves next to him and Ben.

"How about an hour after lunch," Andy whispered with a snicker, looking at Josh with a twinkle in his eye.

Ben leaned into the table, what did you say about an hour after lunch? ...

Josh turned to his father with a smile.

"We only have one and a half holes left to do, and we'll be ready for you and Pastor to put that door where it belongs. While you're doing that, Andy and I will gather the stones and mix the mortar, so you and Pastor can lay them in. We might be working in a little artificial light for a while, but I'm sure we can get this job done before supper!"

Ben and Pastor were amazed to say the least. As the women finished setting the table, the men sat and planned the remainder of the day, with the hope of really being able to finish by nightfall. After Alice and the other women had set the soup and hot rolls on the table, they were directed by Pastor, who spoke very seriously, to seat themselves next to their significant others.

"Before I pray, I just want to say, the reason I asked you to seat yourselves this way was because ... Alice and Ellen have been thinking significantly all morning about these two others, pointing at Ben and Josh, and need some special attention," slapping the table, and laughing so hard tears came to his eyes.

Pastor Bowens," Alice squealed, you said there would be no more teasing today! I think we should use your anointing oil on you, and pray for your fibbing tongue she said, as she tried to hold back her own laughter.

Ellen on the other hand, took advantage of the pandemonium. Turning Josh's head, and pulling him to her, she planted the biggest kiss yet on Josh's lips, as Josh struggled "weakly". Silence filled the cavern as everyone gazed intently at Ellen's unbridled passion.

As Josh regained his composure, Ellen looked down the table with her chin raised in a defiant gesture and a smile on her face.

"He was mine before, He is mine now, and tomorrow he will be mine without question!"

"On that note, let's pray," Pastor said, wiping his eyes with his napkin.

By twelve forty-five, with lunch tucked away behind the men's belts, the men were hard at work. As Josh and Andy worked feverishly, to finish drilling the holes in the rock, Ben and Pastor hung the door in its casing, and readied the bolts that would be set into the stone at the entrance. By two in the afternoon, Josh and Andy were muscling the door and its casing up to the entrance where Ben stood with the long bolts, and Pastor with the hack saw in his hand.

After drilling the remaining holes, Josh and Andy had leveled the area where the door would sit with flat slabs of stone and mortar. Ben had attached a three-foot piece of soft rubber hose to the bottom of the door as a sweep, to keep cold air and varmints from entering under the door, once it was in place. Up and outside the opening, it took a few minutes to turn and set the door in place, but once standing, it looked like a piece of art! With the large brass deadbolt Ben had installed, it was a work to behold.

Opening the door in its frame, Ben stepped through and inserted the bolts through the holes and then into the stone, carefully measuring the distance from the head of the bolts to the casing, and then cutting that amount of the other end of the bolts with the hacksaw. The next step involved threading a large washer and nut onto each bolt after it had been reinserted through the casing, and the nut and washer spun up until the bolt could be reinserted into the holes in the stone. Once that was accomplished, Josh used a wrench to tighten the nuts up against the backside of the casing, locking the casing into place. With a few adjustments, the door opened and closed easily.

It was now three in the afternoon and the sun was beginning to wane in the West. Andy and Josh being resourceful young men had managed to gather more than enough rocks and small stones to complete sealing up the space around the new door. Andy and Josh busied themselves, mixing up the mortar for Pastor and Ben as they finished tying in the rebar to the bolts for added strength.

"Hey Pops, do you and Pastor think we have enough time for a coffee break after using up this first batch of mortar," Josh asked hopefully.

"I was just about to suggest that, even if you hadn't asked," He smiled. "I need some of Alice's sweet rolls and coffee to carry me through to supper. We're doing real good," Ben said.

Josh set the five-gallon bucket of mortar on the threshold and began handing rocks and small stones to Pastor and Ben as they laid them. Pastor worked one side of the door and Ben the other, with Andy handing up the rocks to Josh. By the time they had used up the first bucket of mortar, the wall on both sides of the door had risen over two feet high and a foot wide.

"Ok Ben said," getting to his feet, fifteen minutes … If we get started again by four, we'll only have two hours before it's too dark to see without a light bulb.

By three forty-five, Josh was mixing the second bag of mortar and by four, Andy and Josh were busy passing rocks and stones to Ben and Pastor, who worked as though they had been, masons all their lives. By the time Josh mixed the last bag of mortar, the entrance was sealed, except for a small area at the apex of the opening. It was in that space, Ben folded the last piece of wire mesh from the box, into the shape of a triangle about ten inches long and two inches wide on each side. Laying in some mortar, he placed the wire in it point down and flat side up, placing stones around and on top with mortar until the only opening left was the one with the wire secured inside. Putting the last stone in place, Ben stepped back, closing, and bolting the door.

Looking down at his watch, Josh pushed the button on its side, lighting up the dial of his faithful Timex. "Five fifty-eight he said."

As the men began making their way down the incline to what used to be Ben and Josh's alcove, Jessica appeared in the opening.

"Finished or not, Sister Bowens and Momma Alice said to call it a day and get your backsides to the table. Just make sure you stop at the wash tub first, they said."

Before Andy could open his mouth, Jessica disappeared into the great room. The men could hear laughter and giggles as they made their way to the large tub at the back of the cavern, where they used the bathroom and freshened up before filing into the table. Josh and Andy walking stooped over much like Pastor and Ben.

"Look Ellen cried here comes four little dwarfs, looks like Sleepy, Pappy, Teasy, and Droopy. Poor little men, come here and sit down, rest your weary bones while we get you something good to eat!"

"Especially you Mr. Teasy," Alice said, as she grinned from ear to ear at Pastor Bowens.

Sitting down at the table to fresh brewed coffee, was a welcome sight. Pastor Bowens however felt a little uneasy, suspecting he was going to get a real hazing from the women for his antics earlier in the day. The women did have a little something planned for Pastor, but seeing how tired him, and the other men were from their hard day's work, took pity, and lovingly served them a well-earned supper. After supper, Sarah chased the men over to the couches while she and the women cleaned things up, before joining them in the center of the great room.

Sarah, being the eldest of the women, and assuming the position as Matron of the group, began to lay down the law for the four men who were too tired to resist.

"Pastor Bowens, tomorrow is Sunday, and you have important duties to perform, so off to bed … Now, shoo!"

"Yes Mamma," he said, getting to his feet and heading for the archway, too tired to argue.

As for you other men, no more talking. We women have things to prepare for tomorrow. As tired as you are, you should all be in bed as well. Andy before you go, you should step outside and call Max, he's been out for several hours now. Ben, you, and Josh can sleep here on the couches for tonight since your room doesn't exist anymore; we'll make other arrangements tomorrow.

Jumping up and going to the main entrance, Andy found Max curled up, and waiting patiently to be let in. Rushing over to where Jessica stood with the other women, he made a whimpering request for his share of the evening meal, which Jessica served him, with loving words of endearment, scratches behind the ears and repeated pats on the back

"You don't do that to me," Andy teased.

"When you get down on all fours, wiggle your backside and pant, I will," Jessica responded.

In an instant, Andy was on the floor of the great room on his hands and knees, shaking his butt and whimpering for attention. Jessica, laughing, knelt and began scratching behind Andy's ears.

"How about a kiss too," Andy said, getting up on his knees and hanging his hands as though he were begging.

"I don't kiss dogs, only my husband, and he's not here," she said. Now get to bed, before I have Papa Ben come and put you outside!

The women roared with laughter, but restrained themselves, "They had a Wedding Cake to bake!"

CHAPTER 13

Wedding bells and the bear

IN SPITE OF THEIR LATE-NIGHT vigil, the women were up early the next morning, preparing breakfast, and taking care of last minute items for the day's special event. The first ones awakened by the aroma of freshly baked biscuits, gravy, and coffee, was Ben and Josh, who were sleeping in the great room. Kicking off their blankets, they pulled on their boots and shirts, making a beeline for the table, as Alice filled their cups. Moments later, Ellen and Alice joined the men at the table for coffee. Sitting down beside Ben, Alice slid a small jewelry box in front of him, with a smile.

Clearing his throat, Ben opened the lid of the box and moved it to the center of the table turning it around as he did. Josh pulled it to where he and Ellen could see it contents, discovering two sets of wedding rings.

"Kids," Ben said tenderly, when moving to the Havens these were the only treasures brought with me, leaving everything else down on the banks.

The set of rings on the top, I want you and Ellen to have, they belonged to your mother and me. I just pray that they will fit both of you. A few years before your mom passed away, we put them away, replacing them with gold bands that were looser and more comfortable on our aging hands. The bottom set belonged to your grandfather and Grandmother, who did the same as their hands gave way to old age. Alice and I tried theirs on, and they fit just fine. Try on Mom's and mine, and we'll see how they fit."

Josh and Ellen could not hold back the tears as they took out the rings and tried them on. As Ellen slid the engagement and wedding ring on her finger, they fit perfectly as did Joshes wedding band.

"Papa, I'm so honored that you would share your life with me like this, and I love you more than words could ever express ... "thank you", Ellen said tearfully.

Standing to his feet, Josh moved around the end of the table. Bending over, he embraced his father tightly, and then moved around to Alice, whom he embrace from behind, and kissed her cheek.

"I'm going to be so proud to call you Mom, he said. "You're one precious and special lady!"

As Josh and Ellen placed the rings back into the box and closed the lid, Ben picked it up and handed it to Andy who had just come into the room with Pastor Bowens.

"You had better take good care of this box," he said. You are not only Best Man today, but also the Ring Bearer as well."

"Does that mean that Jessica will be the Maid of Honor and Mama the Old Maid," Pastor Bowens said, with a chuckle.

"Don Bowens," Sarah said with one eyebrow raised and a scolding tone in her voice. You are treading on thin ice this morning. I'm a Brides Maid, and no more teasing unless you want to preach on an empty stomach.

"Yes Mama," Pastor replied, no more teasing. "Brother Ben, would you please pass the gravy," he said with a grin.

As everyone sat around the large table, portions of scripture flooded Ben's mind, and tears of joy trickled down his cheeks.

All the believers were together and had everything in common. Every day they met together in their home, and broke bread together with glad and sincere hearts, praising God." Thank you, Father, for using me to provide this refuge for all of us who now live here, and those you will send our way, thank you, he prayed.

After breakfast and having put things away, the women moved into the center of the great room and joined the men on the couches, where Pastor Bowens opened in prayer and Alice led the small congregation in a time of A- Cappella worship.

In the cavern, the voices of eight sounded like a choir as the worship resonated from their hearts and off the walls. After another time of prayer, seeking God's blessing and continued protection over the Havens, Pastor Bowens shared a short Sermonette.

"This morning, I want to take us back to the book of Matthew and reflect a little on chapter twenty-four but more specifically on verses twenty seven through thirty one.

"For as lightning that comes from the east is visible even in the west, so will be the coming of the Son of Man. Wherever there is a carcass, there the vultures will gather. "Immediately after the distress of those days "the sun will be darkened, and the moon will not give its light; the stars will fall from the sky, and the heavenly bodies will be shaken." At that time, the sign of the son of man will appear the sky, and then all the Nations of the earth will mourn when they see the Son of Man coming on the clouds of heaven, with power and great glory. And he will send his angels with a loud trumpet call, and they will gather his elect from the four winds, from one end of the heavens to the other."

"Jesus Himself tells us that His coming as a thief represents only that He comes suddenly and without warning, not that he will come sneaking in to gather up His church and then sneak out again. The whole world will see His coming and mourn! Then and only then will all those who have laid down their lives for Him and His kingdom be raised to newness of life, to rule and reign with him. Then those of us who are alive and remain, will be caught up, to be with Him in the air! This is our blessed Hope!

My precious friends, it is for this hope that we are gathered here in this haven He has prepared for us, as we await His coming, ministering to one another and to those who He will send to us. When they come, and I know they will come, Christ will use us to meet their need for His Glory. Then the end will come for the world, as God pours out His wrath upon it, but for you and me, it will not be the end, "it will be the "beginning!""

Bowing his head Pastor Bowens prayed a closing prayer, as Ellen, led by the Holy Spirit began to sing, "He Hideth my Soul." As everyone recalled the events of the previous Friday morning, a spirit of peace seamed to settle upon the great room, which turned to rejoicing as preparations began for the wedding ceremony.

The sudden barking and scratching at the door of the great room brought everyone's conversations to a stop as Jessica cried out," We forgot about Max", and rushed to the door. As Jessica swung it open, max rushed in and straight to the hearth, where he curled up on the warm stones. Looking out through the door, everything was a swirl of white as snow fell heavily in blizzard like conditions.

Josh stepped out the door and closed it behind him, only to return moments later, shivering and brushing a heavy blanket of snow from his shoulders.

"There's about ten inches on the ground already. If it keeps coming down like this, we could have two to three feet by tomorrow. This should bring the Collective's searching to an end, at least until the weather changes, which won't be for a while, he grinned."

It was almost one in the afternoon, when Sarah pulled Pastor Bowens aside and quickly whispered in his ear, that it was time to get the other men in their places for the ceremony. Turning she disappeared back through the arch and into the second cavern. Pastor Bowens lined up Ben, Josh and Andy on the left facing the archway, and he took up a position on the right, where Jessica soon joined him.

As Alice and Ellen entered the great room with Sarah in the middle, Jessica began the A- cappella wedding March. As the women came to the end of their march, Pastor Bowens stepped forward. Alice and Ellen were radiant Brides, both dressed in their white camouflage pants, and white blouses. They wore blue scarves draped over their heads, held in place by white paper roses, pinned on the side. Ellen and Alice glowed, as they looked at Josh and Ben with anticipation.

"Who gives these women to these men?" Pastor Bowens said.

"I do", said Sarah smiling, as she stepped forward with Alice and Ellen, and then moved to the side, joining Jessica.

"Gentlemen, would you come and stand next to your Brides," Pastor said, motioning with his hand.

Ben and Josh almost tripped over each other as they scurried to get into their places next to Alice and Ellen.

"Gentlemen, please take the hands of your respective Brides."

"We're gathered together today to join these men and these women in a Holy Covenant with each other and with God, to be the center of their lives and these unions.

After leading the couples through their vows, Pastor called Andy forward with the rings, which the couples exchanged with tearful joy. Then, spreading out his hands Pastor Bowens gave his pronouncement.

"Forasmuch, as Ben Huskins and Alice Foster, and Joshua Huskins and Ellen Michaels, have consented together in the presence of this company in Holy Matrimony. And have witnessed the same before God, having pledged their love for one another, and declaring the same by giving and receiving a ring. I pronounce that they are husband and wife, in the name of the Father, and the Son, and the Holy Spirit! "What God has joined together, never let man put asunder!"

"You may kiss your Brides," he said, with a look of satisfaction on his face.

After a few moments however, Pastor Bowens began clapping his hands and shouted jokingly.

"Enough, enough, if you don't stop and take a breath, these will be the shortest marriages I've ever performed!"

With that comment, the entire company burst into laughter, releasing a time of celebration that lasted well into the afternoon.

It wasn't long before everyone gathered around the small cooking table, where a delicious sheet cake covered with creamy white icing lay waiting. As four hands, held one trembling knife to cut the wedding cake, the frenzy began. In less than fifteen minutes, nothing was left of the cake, but the frosting licked from the fingers of the ravenous eight who washed it down with fruit punch and laughter. Even Max was playful, caught up in the excitement and enjoying his unhealthy share of the cake.

IT WAS A LITTLE AFTER four, when Pastor Bowens made his way to the end of the couch where Josh and Ellen sat gazing at one another like love starved teenagers.

"It's time to send you two off on your Honeymoon adventure before it gets dark," he said, with a grin. A place has been prepared in the back of Havens II, but you need to get to the escarpment trail before the snow gets any deeper and to the cavern before dark. We'll take care of Mom and Pop Huskins here, so they will have a little privacy as well, but you better get going".

Josh and Ellen, who didn't have to be told twice, were suiting up, and putting on their parkas before everyone was able to gather at the new rear entrance, to see them off for the night. As Jessica hugged her sister, she kissed her cheek and stepped back with a twinkle in her eye. "Coffee's done," she said!

As they prepared to make their way up to the door, Andy unzipped Josh's coat and patted his chest.

"Just wanted to make sure you were packing the Judge," he said, zipping Josh's coat back up, and handing him a large flashlight and two pair of snow goggles.

"Everything you'll need is already there," Sarah said, giving Ellen and Josh a motherly hug.

"If you're ready, I've got the door son," Ben shouted down from above the anti-chamber where everyone was gathered.

Stepping up to the door, Josh and Ellen pulled their snow goggles down over their eyes and synched their hoods tightly around their faces, as Ben opened the door to a cold wintery afternoon. The snow was now about two feet deep as they stepped through the door and into the woods, listening as the door slammed shut against the cold winter weather sealing the rest of the Havens family inside.

With Josh breaking trail in the fading light, it took almost fifteen minutes to make their way to the entrance of the escarpment passage as Ellen clung tightly to Josh's coat tail. Once through the trees and into the entrance, they were able to remove their hoods and snow goggles as they took turns brushing the snow off of their gear before continuing down the escarpment trail to Haven II.

As they stood there in the quickly diminishing light Josh drew Ellen to him and kissed her, generating emotions that threatened to overcome them before they could reach the safety and comfort of the cavern. With a longing look, Ellen took Josh's hand, and began to lead him down the trail. Five minutes later, they stood at the entrance of the cavern where Josh unlatched and pushed open the door. Scooping Ellen up into his arms, he turned sideways and carried her into the cavern. Setting her down on a stack of boxes, he turned and closed the door, sliding the heavy bolt into position and securing their wedding chamber.

With flashlight in one hand and Ellen securely pressed to his side with the other, the newlyweds made their way to the back of the chamber, where much to their delight they found a bed fit for a King and Queen. Piled six deep, were sleeping bags unzipped and spread out upon two large pieces of foam remnants from the work done on the haven's homemade couches. These were covered with a fitted flannel sheet. A full-sized flannel sheet and another unzipped sleeping bag took care of the covers. There were even three large pillows, and two robes draped across the end of the bed.

"Sister Bowens said there was fresh water and punch inside the ice chest, and sweet treats in the one next to it," Ellen said, sitting down on a small barrel as she began removing her boots and snowsuit.

"I'm so full of cake and punch already; I don't think there's any room left, Josh said, picking up one of the robes and modestly stepping behind a row of boxes to undress. As Josh stepped out from behind the boxes in his thigh length robe, Ellen began to chuckle.

"What's so funny," Josh said, looking down at himself and then up at Ellen, who was now nestled seductively under the flannel sheet and holding out her hand with a gesturing motion, for Josh to take his place at her side.

"It's not you sweetheart, she said, as Josh turned down the lamp to a soft glow and slid under the sheet next to her. It was a note I found underneath one of the pillows, from your father."

Reading it again aloud to Josh, they slid down under the covers laughing.

"*Don't worry kids, there's a honey Pot next to the front door! Stay in and stay warm*", Love Pops.

During the storm, their love and life together found consummation in the divine nature of God's plan for their lives.

CHAPTER 14

Avalanche

THINGS JUST WERE NOT THE same at breakfast without Josh and Ellen. Everyone looked forward to having them back, even if they were only two hundred yards away. Jessica stood and walked around the table several times.

Everyone assumed that the newlyweds were returning Monday morning after spending their wedding night in the seclusion of Havens II, Jessica mused as she ceased her pacing and sat down, resting her elbows on the table with her chin in the palms of her hands. Now it was Tuesday!

"When those two realize they can't live on love and MRE's, they'll be knocking on the door, and begging to get in," Pastor Don said with a chuckle.

"It's only been a day and a half. We'll check on them this afternoon," Ben said, turning to Alice and giving her a tender kiss on the cheek. "We need to bring down some stores anyway, and we are just about out of firewood."

Taking another sip of his coffee, he looked across the table at Pastor and Andy.

"I did some measuring in the antechamber at the rear entrance. It looks like we can bring down and stack almost a rick of wood where it will be out of the way. There is also more than enough room to store our coats, boots, and winter gear", as well". Andy leaned into the table and paused a moment before speaking.

"I was wondering what you had in mind for sleeping arrangements, considering we have lost Ben's and Josh's quarters to the new entrance. As Pastor shared with us on Sunday, we're expecting more guests. Do you have a plan Pops, for adding some rooms, or do you have another cave up your sleeve you haven't told us about yet?"

Sister Sarah spoke without a moment's hesitation.

"Easily solved," she said. Ben has moved his belongings into Alice's quarters. We will move Josh into Ellen's. As for our future guests, we could probably create two more rooms between Ellen and Josh and the bathroom, but that kind of stuff is up to you men. We women have enough to do, just taking care of our four little Dwarves, nodding her head at Pastor.

"Especially Pastor Teasy," Jessica added, as she stood and gave him a hug before beginning to clear the table.

The great room filled with laughter as the women began picking up after breakfast, and the men prepared for the afternoon trip to Havens II. By eleven-thirty, everyone was in the process of putting on their winter gear when a rapid pounding at the rear entrance, sent Andy running through the antechamber and up to the door. Ben and Pastor Bowens stood below with weapons in hand. Slowly, Andy unbolted the door and allowed it to open slightly as he peered through the crack...

"It's Josh and Ellen," he said, swinging the door open, as Josh pushed Ellen through, ahead of him.

"Close the door quickly, and bolt it," Josh shouted, turning and pointing his handgun at the door until Andy had it closed and secured.

It didn't take long for Josh and Ellen to remove their gear, or the rest of the group to join them around the table in the great room, both appeared visibly shaken. As their breathing slowed and the adrenalin rush began to subside, everyone waited patiently but filled with apprehension, until Josh cleared his throat, and began to speak. Sarah and Alice, after starting a large pot of fresh coffee, joined the others at the table.

"As we were preparing to leave Havens II yesterday, about two in the afternoon, we opened the door in the face of the biggest Kodiak I've ever seen. When he saw us, he lunged into the doorway, but couldn't get in. His head filled the whole door. I pulled out the judge and emptied all five rounds at his head. When he pulled back out, Ellen slammed the door closed and threw the bolt. For almost half an hour, it sounded like all the hordes of Satan were outside that door, and then everything went silent.

"Five-point blank rounds, and all I did was tick him off," Josh said, shaking his head, and reaching for the coffee Alice had just poured for him.

After taking a couple of sips and giving Ellen a comforting hug, he continued.

"We waited for the longest time, at least an hour or so, before I attempted to open the door again. When I did, we discovered the door was savagely clawed up, leaving deep scars in the wood. There was blood everywhere, but no bear in sight. It was starting to get late, and there was no way we were going to get caught in the dark with a wounded bear, so we hunkered down till this morning before attempting to venture out of the cavern again."

"I was terrified," Ellen said. "Josh made me close and bolt the door behind him when he went out, I thought I was going to die waiting—until he came back in again"!

Ellen sat with both arms wrapped around her husband, nestling herself under his arm and her head pressed against his chest. Tenderly kissing Ellen's forehead, Josh took a deep breath.

"I had reloaded with 45 Cal. Colt hollow points before going back out this morning. I only went a short way past the crack in the escarpment. The blood trail led to the right and out into the forest where our wood supply is stored. When I realized we had a chance, I went back for Ellen, secured the door to the cavern, and we headed back down the escarpment trail for home. It wasn't until we came out of the trail at this end, and looked up across the clearing, that we saw him stand sniffing the air. When he caught sight of us, the race was on. He couldn't have been more than a hundred feet behind us when you opened the door and let us in."

"There's nothing more dangerous than a wounded bear," Ben said, especially when it stands between us, and our source of warmth and food. How big do you think it is son, eight hundred, a thousand pounds?"

"More like twelve to fourteen hundred, and better than nine feet standing," Josh said, the head had to be more than three feet wide. I'm not positive, but paw prints had to be fourteen inches at least."

As the company sat talking, Max lay at Andy's feet, his hair bristling and a low growl emanating from his throat, which left the hairs standing on the back of everyone else's neck.

It was apparent to all that their new nemesis had taken up an offensive position outside the Havens. The question now, was how to bring him down without jeopardizing anyone's safety.

"Do you hear something, or is it just me," Andy said, sitting up straight and turning his head slightly, trying to focus in on the sound that suddenly filled everyone's ears.

"Helicopters," Josh said, and their right on top of us! We need some eyes… Andy, strap on your pistol and grab your AR7. We'll go out the front like before, better cover under the low boughs."

Even though they were in a sealed cave, the doors seemed to act like eardrums, which magnified the sounds emanating from the outside. In less than three minutes, Josh and Andy were suited up in their winter camo's. Standing at the door, they put on their goggles and pulled their hoods around their faces

"Two taps twice, to let us back in," Josh said.

Then without another word, they disappeared through the door, which Ben closed and bolted behind them. Circling the small clearing in front of the entrance, with their backs to the rock wall, they moved to the narrow grove of trees, which guarded the entrance to the Havens. Moving into the trees Josh and Andy began burrowing in under the low hanging boughs and three-foot-deep snow, until they could clear away just enough snow to see the small melt pond and upper end of the lemon valley, through the trees.

Andy and Josh couldn't believe their eyes. The huge Kodiak stood pawing the air, on the far side of the frozen melt pond, facing the mountain and roaring defiantly. Two Collective helicopters hovered only feet above the snow flanking the giant bear on the east and west sides. In the middle, stood four uniformed militiamen with automatic weapons, and less than thirty feet separated them from sudden death!

"It's obvious they don't know anything about bears," Andy whispered, this doesn't look good… "for them I mean".

Suddenly the bear charged. Before the last echo of gunfire ceased from the automatic weapons, two of the men were down, and the snow red with blood, as the wounded giant took down the third of its four assailants. Then with a roar, the mighty bear fell to the ground at the feet of the fourth. The survivor of the bloody melee, seemed frozen in the moment, as did Andy and Josh who had just witnessed the carnage that lay before them.

In an instant, the terror of the moment gave way to a new and more ominous threat that drove the lone survivor trudging desperately to the safety of the helicopter closest to him, which now sat belly deep in the snow. The second helicopter suddenly rose straight up and turned to the Northeast, as a sound more ominous than those of the helicopters filled the air.

"Avalanche," Josh cried, rolling in unison with Andy over on his right side. The two men watched in amazement as the entire snow crest of the two-thousand-foot-high basin above them, descended the mountainside. As the helicopter, which had landed began to rise into the air with the militiaman still standing on the landing gear, the quickly descending wall of snow and debris arrived. Plucking the helicopter from the air and sweeping away the carnage on the ground, the mountainous river of snow cleansed the steep mountain side as it continued to the upper reaches of the Lemon creek valley another three thousand feet below.

Josh and Andy lay motionless, reeling from the amazing saga, which had just unfolded in front them. Once again, God's mighty hand had covered the small band of believers, and the Havens would continue to serve as a refuge for its occupants and those who God would lead to them. The men watched intently, as the remaining helicopter made repeated circular passes over the area, looking for heat sources and survivors.

Flying directly toward where Josh and Andy lay hidden, the helicopter turned east, and made one more pass before descending to the banks, and what Josh was sure would be a grueling inquisition for those who survived. Only after the helicopter had disappeared, did Andy and Josh back out of their hiding place and retrace their steps along the rock wall to the door of the Havens.

Josh rapped twice on the door, paused, then twice again. A few moments later, the door opened. Six people with questioning faces immediately helped the men out of their gear and ushered them to the table. Everyone gathered around, anxiously waiting to hear about the drama, which had unfolded outside the safety of Havens door.

CHAPTER 15

A prophetic word

F OR OVER FORTY MINUTES, JOSH and Andy alternately recounted the calamity that had unfolded outside the Havens. It became apparent to everyone as they listened, that God had pitted their foes against each other, and then used the snow-covered mountainside to cleanse the battlefield. It was almost ten past one, when Josh stood, and instructed everyone to gear up for a trip to Haven II and the woodpile.

"I'm thinking the Militia will be back in force in the morning, combing the mountain side for wreckage and bodies, before any more weather sets in. Ladies, you need to make as many trips as necessary to bring down enough stores for a week. The men and I will do the same for our wood supply," Josh said, pulling his parka back on and zipping it up. Before leaving the Havens, Josh pulled out four five-gallon buckets from the back of the cavern and had Andy fill them with water.

"I'm sure that blood around the Havens II door will draw unwanted guests if we don't clean things up a little, Josh said, snapping the lids down tightly on the buckets. With two on each bucket, it will be easier to carry them up"

"Be careful, the last thing we need is to encourage another avalanche while were up above," his father said, donning his own parka and adjusting his snow goggles.

Josh led the party out of the Caverns and up to the entrance of the escarpment trail. By dusk, both men and women had made three round trips for wood and stores. With a little effort, they had also managed to clean up the alcove and door at Havens II as well. Cold and tired, they entered the Havens and unloaded their burdens.

While the men stacked the last of the firewood in the antechamber, Ellen made a fresh pot of coffee and began helping the other women prepare the evening meal.

After cleaning up, Andy, Josh, and Pastor Don made their way to the table, while Ben made a short detour to a storage pallet under one of the couches. Moments later, he arrived at the table with a cardboard box and took a seat across from Josh.

"I wasn't sure why I brought this up from the shop Josh, but now I'm glad I did," Ben said, as he pushed the box in front of his son.

To his amazement, as he opened the box to reveal its contents, he found a new, multiple channel and programmable scanner.

"This is awesome Pops," Josh said excitedly. "I can have this programmed from memory in about fifteen minutes, but we can't get a signal in here, we're under too much rock."

"Not a problem," Ben said reaching under the end of the table and pulling a roll of wire out of a small wooden box attached to the table leg.

"I mounted an antenna to the back side of one of the large trees in front of the caverns, and buried the wire after we moved in. The radio wouldn't work in here without it, and we enjoyed the music!"

When Josh finished programming the scanner, he attached the antenna wire, turned up the volume and adjusted the squelch.

After thirty minutes of listening to the traffic on the scanner, Josh turned it off. Picking up the paper he had been writing on, he began to read his notes to everyone, now gathered around the table for dinner.

Tomorrow morning at 08:00 hours, three helicopters with seven men on each will be heading our way. Pilots and crews of two, will remain on board, there will be twelve pairs of boots on the ground outside of our front door.

Josh laid down the paper and looking pensively at the back wall of cavern, took a long sip of coffee before continuing.

"Some heavy snow could bring us some peace if it would finally come," he said, forcing a smile. "Tomorrow we'll pray for the best and prepare for the worst. They're going to be focusing all their attention from the far side of the melt pond down to Lemon Creek for sure. They will be flying all around us, so pray for snow tonight to cover our tracks, just in case they can get a peek through the trees between here and the escarpment.

Jessica and Sarah placed the large pot of stew and rolls on the table, and everyone held hands as Pastor Bowens bowed his head to pray.

Father, we come to you with grateful hearts this evening as we prepare to partake of your provision. We ask for your blessing on our meal, and upon those who have labored so diligently to prepare it for us. Lord, thank you for watching over us today, for keeping us in the hollow of your hand, and we pray that you will cover us with a blanket of new snow tonight, to hide us from the enemy's searching eyes, Amen.

When dinner and clean- up were done, Jessica helped Ellen get Josh's things settled into their alcove, and a bed prepared, before taking Andy by the hand and leading him to a much-deserved rest. After another strenuous and difficult day, everyone was eager to make his or her way to the comfort of a warm bed and a night's rest.

Before making his way to bed, Josh climbed up to the rear entrance, and opened the door. With flashlight in hand, he peered into lightly falling snow. By first light, Josh was back at the rear entrance and carefully opening the door. To his delight, the snow was less than a foot from the top of the door, and it was still snowing heavily. *We will have to dig ourselves out to break trail to Havens II, but it means no boots on the ground for the Collective Militia today,* Josh thought. As the smell of fresh brewed coffee and pancakes drifted under his nose, he quickly closed and bolted the door, making his way into the great room, where Pops and Pastor Don sat listening to the scanner.

"You should hear this," Ben said. "The banks were buried under more than three feet of snow, and everything is grounded."

Josh scooped up a cup, filled it with coffee and slid onto the bench next to his father. Moments later Ellen stood behind him, tilting back his head and gazing down into his eyes.

"Why didn't you wake me you rascal," she quipped, ruffling Josh's hair before going for her own cup of coffee.

"Enjoying married life I see," Pastor Bowens said, reaching for a pancake as Sarah slapped the back of his hand.

"More than you will be, if you don't wait for the others," she said.

Josh grinned as Pastor wrapped his hands back around his coffee cup and waited for the others to take their seats. When everyone were seated, he gave a nod to Josh.

"Would you ask the blessing this morning son," Pastor said, folding his hands and bowing his head.

As Josh began to pray, a peace fell upon those sitting around the table and enveloped them like a warm blanket. Josh found himself speaking words, which were not his own as the Holy Spirit moved in his heart and mind through a prophetic word of encouragement.

My children listen to my words and do not fear, for your redemption is near. What I have begun, I will finish and those I have called will come. Have I not told you I am with you always? I have covered you with my covering, anointed you with my anointing. Labor faithfully, trust in Me, and you will live to see My Glorious coming!

Josh sat trembling, as the entire company sat engulfed in a sudden outpouring of the Holy Spirit, speaking in tongues and weeping tears of joy and gladness. Along with the Baptism of the Holy Spirit, Josh received a special anointing, as Pastor Bowens poured his entire bottle of oil on Josh's head, the Lord imparted into his spirit a wisdom and understanding, surpassing his age and experience.

It was almost eight in the morning before the small band of believers began to look hungrily at the now cold plate of pancakes on the table.

It was not long, however, before Sarah had them warned up again. They were quickly consumed, as everyone continued to rejoice in God's peace and exceeding grace.

As Josh and the other men made their way out the rear entrance to clear the trail to the escarpment, Ellen helped the women clean up, and then made her way into the rear chamber to pull down and fold the laundry that had been hanging since Monday afternoon. After sorting the clothes and laying them inside the doors each room, Ellen took hers and Josh's to their room, tossing them on their bedroll. Before treating herself to a hot shower and some personal pampering, she folded them and opened the wooden crate where Josh kept his things. There she found his journal and began to read.

Tuesday, November 5th, 2019. I have been born again, and everything is new. For the first time in the last five years, I've found peace!

With tears welling up in her eyes, she quickly closed the cover and placed the journal into the pallet on top of Josh's clothing. Her mind suddenly raced back ten years, to when she became a high school freshman. *It was a time when Josh Huskins seemed to fill every waking moment of her life with longing, and an unrequited love.*

Josh was the most popular boy in school and although She was also very popular, her fear of Josh's possible rejection, had robbed her of the dream she held in her heart throughout those High School days. Even after Graduation, they had always remained close friends, in and outside of the church, until Josh began drifting farther away, and eventually stopped attending church altogether.

Ellen dropped to her knees on the blanket-covered foam that served as a bed. She slid forward to her stomach and rolled over on her back, gazing up into the shadows of the caverns ceiling.

When the opportunity came for her to escape the disappointments, which continually surrounded her there on the banks, she had flown to Seattle Washington to live with a widowed Aunt and attended college at Northwest

*University in Kirkland. Until the tragic deaths of her parents, which brought
her back to the Lemon Creek community, new friends, and a new choice of
direction in her life, had brought respite from the deep sense of loss that had
held her heart captive for so long.*

As Ellen lay on the bed, the tears began to give way to a smile and a
deep sigh, as she began to focus on the present and not the past. Josh was
now her husband, and she truly possessed the love that had unknowingly
belonged to her all along.

With the sound of voices at the rear entrance, Ellen scrambled to her
feet and quickly made her way to the antechamber. There she embraced
Josh with a kiss, and sliding her arm around his waist, walked into the
great room where the other women were busy placing lunch on the table.
Josh and the men had spent all morning digging out and re-opening the
trail to the escarpment, following the snowfall during the night and the
day before.

While the company sat around the table enjoying the hearty chicken
noodle soup and fresh baked rolls, Ben as usual, cleared his throat before
speaking.

"While we were out this morning, I saw black tail sign up near the
entrance to the escarpment trail. I also heard some bleating," he said. The
blacks are in rut this time of year and will be heading down below fifteen
hundred feet soon now that the snow is getting deeper."

"A venison steak would sure taste really good," Andy said, raising his
bowl, to drink down the last of his broth.

"Well, Ben continued, I was thinking, that a nice fat doe would help
feed us well into next year and provide a great roast for our thanksgiving
dinner to boot. What do you think Josh, are you up to doing a little
hunting out beyond our wood supply early in the morning? We'd have to
use snowshoes to get around out there, but I think we would do all right."

Josh's eyes lit up, as he savored the idea of bagging a big doe, or even
a big buck for that matter.

"It's a man thing Pops," he replied. "You would have to hog-tie and
gag me to stop this boy from going with you!"

"And this one as well," Andy chided. "Where Josh goes, so do I, "well at least most of the time", he said, looking at Ellen with a grin.

"Jessica and I get the back strap," Ellen said, holding a knife in one hand, a fork in the other, and licking her lips.

"Only if the two of you tan the hide and chew the leather to make moccasins for Josh and I," Andy said. "Otherwise, you'll just have to settle for the heart and liver."

Laughing, Andy tried to jump up from the table and run, but Jessica and Ellen tackled and took him down before he could get very far. As they playfully roughed him up, Josh and Ben stepped in to rescue one of their own. Max leaped in to comfort his master with whimpers and a generous face licking, as Jessica and Ellen burst into tears of laughter that sent the whole company into an uproar, before settling down to the morning chores.

While Josh, Andy and Ben began preparing for the next morning's hunt, Pastor Bowens sat at the table with his Bible and notebook, laboring intently over his Sunday message.

"Do you mind if I hook up the radio Pastor and see if I can find some music we could listen to for a little while," Jessica asked.

"Not at all, Pastor Bowens said, as long as you pour me another cup of coffee and sit for a spell. I need a little break anyway."

Jessica plugged in the radio and hooked up the antenna wire. After pouring herself a cup of coffee and refilling Pastors, she sat down and turned on the radio.

Tuning to KTOO FM, the radio suddenly filled the great room with some wonderful contemporary classical music that brought Sarah, Ellen, and Alice to the table as well, for coffee and a break. Much to Pastor Bowens delight, it also brought a plate of Alice's sugar cookies. It wasn't long before everyone was gathered around the table again.

As Josh dipped the last bite of his sugar cookie into his coffee the music ended, ensued by a comprehensive weather report. Everyone listened intently as the announcer warned of an impending snowstorm that threatened to bury the Juneau and surrounding area under another five feet of snow.

"We haven't had this much snow since two thousand nine, Ben said, and then it was for the whole year, not just the month of November."

"It looked like snow this morning, when we were clearing the trail, maybe we should think about doing our hunting this afternoon, if it snows tonight, we might not get a chance tomorrow," Josh said, walking toward the door of the great room.

Opening the door, Josh peered out into the grey afternoon.

"It's not snowing now, but it doesn't look good," he said, closing the door and returning to the table. Andy and Ben rose from their seats as Josh approached.

"If we suit up and leave now, we'll have about four hours to hunt, make a kill and get back before dark, Ben said, are you young fella's game?"

"As game as what we're after," Andy said, with a grin.

Fifteen minutes later, the men were hiking up the path to the entrance of the escarpment trail, with their rifles, and snowshoes strapped to their backs.

CHAPTER 16

Black tail hunt

I T WAS THREE THIRTY, WHEN Pastor Bowens decided to turn off the radio. He was concerned there might be militia patrols still flying about while the other men were out hunting and plugged in the scanner instead.

Adjusting the squelch, he turned up the volume, and went back to sipping his coffee and re-reading the scriptures he had chosen for Sunday's message. Much of the traffic was from the airport concerning rapidly changing weather conditions. That changed however, with a report from a militia helicopter crew who had just found and arrested two couples, hiding out at the Taku Lodge on the far side of the Juneau ice field.

"We need to pray for those people, Jessica said, if they went that far to escape the mark, all that awaits them on the banks is death."

The scanner suddenly came alive again, as the pilot announced he would be returning along a direct route, which would bring them across the Lemon glacier and down the Lemon Creek valley.

"That's only a twenty-six-mile flight or so," Pastor said, thinking aloud.

As they continued to pray, the hunting, party was included and Ellen began to pray for their safety, and that they would remain invisible to the helicopter now heading their way. With an Amen, Pastor stood and strode to the door. Opening it, he and the women, could see the snow falling heavily. More than a foot of new snow had fallen, since the hunting had party left. As snow began to swirl in through the open door, Pastor closed and bolted it.

Reaching the far end of the escarpment trail Josh, Ben and Andy donned their snowshoes and with rifles in hand, stepped out into the forest, trudging past their well-covered winter's supply of firewood. Since the wind was coming up valley, Josh led the hunting party down the north side of the timberline to keep them upwind from any game they might encounter.

Finding a large tree, whose lower branches lay buried in the deep snow, Josh pushed a hole in the snow where the party could crouch and step in under the branches. Inside next to the trunk, the ground was bare and dry. Moving around to the side facing southwest and just west of the small melt pond, Josh cleared away the snow so that he, Andy and Ben could have a clear view of the pond and the small clearing.

Cupping his hands over his mouth, Josh began to make short braying noises as they stood and gazed through the increasing snowfall. It had been almost an hour since Josh had begun braying, when Andy caught some movement coming through the trees on his right.

"Josh," Andy whispered, Right side, hundred feet.

Ben and Josh slowly turned as Andy raised his rifle. Stepping into the clearing was a huge Black tail doe, and not ten feet behind her was the largest buck Josh had seen in years.

"Go for it son," Ben said, as he slowly moved back, giving Josh room to turn and aim.

Josh and Andy's shots were so close together, it almost sounded to Ben like only one shot, had been fired. The three quickly emerged from their snowy blind, and making their way to the game, began to quickly field dress the animals. By the time they were finished and had covered the area with snow to hide the blood and entrails, it was snowing so hard it was difficult to see as they began to make their way back into the shelter of the forest.

The men had just made the tree line, when the blinding snow began to swirl around them, and the sound of the rotor blades of a helicopter above them made them drop to their knees. Suddenly, from out of the swirling snow several large objects, hit the snow-covered ground, one after the other. As the men knelt there in the blinding snowstorm, the sound of the helicopter seemed to rise into the air and move quickly to the southwest. Moments later, after silence had only briefly returned, an enormous explosion echoed across the Lemon valley, as a ball of fire filled the evening twilight.

"I don't know what that was all about, but we had better get ourselves out of here now," Josh said.

He was just about to jerk the buck up onto his shoulders when Andy stopped him.

"Did you hear a moan," Andy said, turning to Ben, who also thought he heard something,

"There it is again," he said, looking at Ben and Josh.

Quickly Andy moved out into the clearing where they had seen the objects fall.

"People; Josh, there are people out here, and they're alive!"

Josh dropped the deer, and steadying his father with his hand, they moved into the clearing where Andy knelt, helping a woman to her knees. Quickly Josh and Ben moved to the other three people half buried in the deep snow, uncovering their faces and helping them as they attempted to catch their breath.

"We've got to get these people to the havens, Josh said. We'll never make it before dark going back through the escarpment trail. I can just make out the melt pond through the snowfall. We're only about a hundred yards from the front door if we cut straight across."

"I'm with you son,' Ben shouted back. 'Do you think you can walk; he asked the four shivering newcomers?'" They all responded weakly with a nod.

Gathering the newcomers together, Ben comforted and encouraged them as best he could while Josh and Andy stowed their game and snowshoes under the large tree they had used for a blind and returned to where Ben and the others were waiting.

Reaching into Andy's backpack, Josh pulled out a twelve-foot piece of rope and unwound it. Quickly he tied a small loop in each end, giving one end to Andy. He had him slip his hand through the loop and grasp the rope. Josh placed two of the people between Andy and his father, and the other two between his father and himself.

Slipping his right hand through the loop and grasping the rope, Josh began breaking trail through the deepening snow toward the warmth and safety of the Havens.

Breaking trail through five feet of snow was no easy task. After about thirty yards, Ben moved up front, Andy to the middle and Josh fell back to the rear. Another twenty yards and Ben moved back, giving Andy the lead for another thirty yards or more, and once again handed Josh the reins. Josh knew they were getting close; he could just make out the stand of trees in the darkness, which guarded the Havens entrance, but now the climb was uphill.

PASTOR BOWENS AND THE WOMEN waited impatiently around the table, each longing to hear a rap on the door from the men returning, or some traffic on the scanner; the silence was deafening. Suddenly the scanner broke the stillness with a mayday.

"Mayday, mayday, this is alpha 027 to base, do you copy, do you copy base?"

"Copy 027, report."

"Base, we just crossed the glacier into Lemon Creek valley, heavy snow, 0 visibility, and high velocity crosswinds... we're losing altitude, over!"

"Alpha 027, dump cargo, I repeat, dump cargo and proceed to base. Do you copy 027, over?"

"Copy base, dump cargo and return to base, 027!"

As the scanner went silent, those gathered around the table suddenly heard the helicopter, as it seemed to pass directly above the Havens. The front door of the cavern began to vibrate as the helicopter barely missed the tops of the trees, which guarded the entrance. Moments later the scanner again broke the silence.

"Alpha 027 base, do you copy base?"

"Copy 027, report."

"Base, cargo has been ejected, we're gaining some altitude, but we're lost. Proceeding on instruments only, stand by base."

"Base, standing by."

Once again, the scanner went silent, as Pastor Bowens bowed his head and began to pray.

"Father we …"

"Alpha 027!" rang from the scanner in a high-pitched voice. 027 to base, we're blind, instrumentation failed, we're …"

The screams of dying men echoed from the scanner, bouncing of the cavern walls until the actual sound of the explosion replaced them and reverberated through the closed cavern door.

Everyone quickly joined hands, as Pastor once again bowed his head, and began to pray for the men who were still missing, and those who were thrown from the helicopter. Intercessory prayer flowed like water from living springs for the next forty minutes, until a loud rapping on the Havens door brought everyone leaping to their feet.

Ellen was the first to reach the door, pausing until she heard two more, distinctive raps and silence. Swinging the door open Ellen stepped aside. Josh led the exhausted caravan of rescuers and the rescued into the great room, still holding on to the rope.

As though this scenario had been practiced time and time again, Sarah and Alice started a fresh pot of coffee, and began adding noodles and other stretch items to the large pot of Soup simmering on the hearth.

Ellen closed and bolted the door as Jessica began helping the men and their new guests out of their wet clothing while Ellen provided towels and blankets.

By the time, they made their way to the table; bowls of hot soup and fresh brewed coffee were waiting for them, along with a barrage of questions for Josh, Andy and Ben. Josh raising both hands, waved them in the air,

"Later, Josh said, I'm sure they have as many questions as we do. "Let's give our guests a chance to recover, eat their soup, and get warmed up."

The two men and women, all in their early twenties, looked around the great room with bewilderment, much the way Josh and Andy did when they first encountered the retreat. As Ellen studied the faces of their new guests, one of the young women looked vaguely familiar, but she couldn't make a connection at that moment.

Jessica and Ellen carried over the two short benches sitting by the main door of the cavern and placed them at the ends of the table.

"Twelve, Ellen said, we now have a table of twelve."

"Pastor, would you lead us in prayer," Josh said, as he bowed his head and reached out for Ellen's and his father's hand.

Much to Pastor Bowen's surprise, their new guests immediately bowed their heads as they joined hands to pray.

Heavenly Father, we praise you and give you all the glory as we gather around this table tonight! Thank you, Father, for your guiding hand of protection, for bringing home our loved ones, and using us to provide this sanctuary for those you have sent to join our company. Bless the food Father, as we take nourishment from your bountiful provision, in the precious name of our Lord and Savior, Jesus Christ.

Waiting until everyone was almost finished eating; Josh broke the silence, mimicking his father as he cleared his throat before speaking to their guests.

"I know you're probably feeling a lot of anxiety right now, having been tossed out of a hovering helicopter into a freezing snowstorm, and drug through armpit deep snow to a warm, well-lit hole in the ground, but that will all be explained to you later. Right now, I think it would be best if we introduced ourselves to you and found out who you are and where you're from."

"To begin with, my name is Joshua Huskins, and leader of this company of believers. Sitting next to me is my wife, Ellen."

Andy was the next to speak, as he placed his arm around Jessica's shoulders.

"I'm Andy Bridgeport, and this is my wife Jessica, Ellen's sister."

Gesturing with his hand across the table, Andy looked at Pastor with a smile.

"This is my precious wife Sarah, the one who is really in charge here at the Havens, and I'm Pastor Bowens, he said with a wink."

Everyone's eyes then fell on Ben who was standing behind Alice, with his hands resting on her shoulders.

"My name is Ben Huskins, founder of this refuge, and this is my wife, Alice.

The two young couples sat pensively for a few moments as the dark-haired man sitting next to Andy, looked at his companions before speaking.

"My name is Richard Devon he said with trepidation, still uncertain about their new circumstances, and this is my wife, Linda. We're recent graduates of Northwest College in Kirkland Washington, and until a year and a half ago, served as youth pastors at First Assembly in Ketchikan."

Looking across the table to the other couple sitting next to Pastor and Sarah, Richard nodded.

"My name is Todd Prichard, and this is my wife Jan. As with Rich and Linda, we directed the worship ministry in the same church in Ketchikan."

Ellen and Linda gazed at each other, each searching their memories, and trying to recall a time in the past, when Linda's face suddenly broke into a broad smile. Ellen, Ellen Michaels, we were in school together in Kirkland until you had to leave because of deaths in your family, right?"

"Yes, Ellen replied", *now recalling the classroom discussions and the many occasions she and Linda spent in the commons with other students, discussing the signs of the times, and how close it must be for the Lords return.* Urgency was the by-word back then.

Suddenly, the tension and apprehension, which resided behind the smiles and cordial remarks, vanished. With the realization, there was a connection, a personal relationship tying the twelve together through Ellen and Linda, a corporate sigh of relief seemed to emanate from everyone at the same time, especially from the four new castaways.

While everyone sat around the table after dinner, nursing a fresh cup of coffee, the newcomers sat spellbound as Ben recounted how the Havens began. Then sharing the high points of the Lemon Creek chronicle, he finished with Pastor's help; recounting the events, leading up to their being dropped on the Havens doorstep and God's providential placing of the hunting party.

"It's getting late, Ellen said," I think it's time to acquaint our guests with the bathroom facilities, and get them settled for the night."

"Bathroom," Linda said, with a puzzled look on her face.

"Just like uptown," Josh said. "We also have hot running water and a shower," he added with a grin.

The two words hot and shower in the same sentence brought beaming smiles to the faces of Todd and Jan. Rich and Linda could only shake their heads in amazement.

It wasn't long after hot showers and devotions led by Pastor, that the couples were bedded down on the nine-foot couches in the center of the great room. As everyone else made their way to their rooms for the night, Josh, Ben and Pastor quickly discussed the next day's agenda, from the early morning retrieval of their game, to introducing the newcomers to the Havens, it's rules and routines.

Tomorrow was going to be a very busy day, Josh thought to himself, slipping into bed next to Ellen, he quickly dosed off to sleep.

CHAPTER 17

Meat and greet

B Y SIX THIRTY THE NEXT morning, Josh and Andy were already making their way through the deep snow, to retrieve the venison they had killed the evening before.

Nearing the tree on the edge of the clearing where they had placed the deer, the men were amazed at how the blowing and drifting snow had completely erased the deep trail their party of seven had made as they fought their way back to the Havens. Burrowing through the snow on the backside of the tree, Andy and Josh retrieved their game and the snowshoes they had left behind.

Packing their game back to Havens II was no easy task, even though it was less than a hundred yards. Struggling through the deep snow on snowshoes with an extra hundred plus pounds on their backs left the men exhausted, by the time they reached their destination.

"If we had a fire going, I'd be cooking as we speak. I can just taste that steak," Andy said, licking his lips.

"I'm with you there," Josh answered. "The sooner we get these animals cut up, the sooner we can make that idea a reality."

Entering Havens II, he emerged moments later with some rope, and two pieces of heavy rebar, one about two feet long and the other less than a foot.

Wrapping the rope around the short piece, he climbed up onto the earth berm on the outer side of the trail and reaching as high as he could slid the rebar into a T shaped crack in the face of the granite escarpment. Then making slits between the bones and tendons of the rear legs of the buck, he inserted the two-foot piece of rebar tying the rope in the center. With Andy lifting the deer, he took up the slack in the rope. Tying the other end off on a large boulder, they hung, skinned, and quartered their game.

Setting aside what they were taking back to the Havens with them, the men temporarily stored the venison just inside the door of Havens II until they could return later in the day to hang the remainder of the meat where it would stay frozen and secure from predators. Taking the right shoulder and right rear portion of the doe, Josh and Andy headed back to the Havens.

It was nine by the time Josh and Andy joined everyone around the table for coffee. After a brief discussion, everyone was looking forward to venison, instant mashed potatoes, and canned kernel corn with some hot rolls for dinner.

While the women began preparing for cutting up the venison, and getting things started for lunch and dinner, the men finished their coffee, discussing how to hang the remainder of the meat to keep it frozen and secure.

After tossing around a few ideas, Andy spoke up with what everyone agreed would be the best solution.

"Josh," Andy said, scratching his head. "If I remember right, you still have two or three carabineers and some camming wedges in you backpack, from our excursion to take care of the Lemon Lady's pontoons. I was thinking that there are several cracks in the top of the granite alcove above the door of Havens II. If we could climb up and attach one of the camming wedges at the top, and two or three carabineers down the back side, we could hang the meat high and out of sight, to keep it safe."

"That's a great idea!" Turning to his father, Josh continued. "Pops, didn't I see a small cargo net somewhere in all those stores at Havens II?"

"Yea, it was tossed against the wall of the cavern, and right behind the honey bucked I left for you and Ellen on your wedding night," Ben said with a chuckle and winking at Josh over the top of his coffee cup.

Pastor Bowens and Andy broke into laughter, as Rich and Todd looked on a little puzzled, until Josh explained.

"Ellen and I, along with my father and Alice were just married four days ago.

Between him and Pastor Bowens, they'll tease your sox off if you give them a chance, so be forewarned," he said with a grin. "Rich," how would you and Todd like to get a firsthand look at what we've been talking about, and an idea of where you're at in the light of day, instead of a blinding snowstorm?"

"That would be awesome;" Todd blurted out without hesitation, and then paused. "But when the militia loaded us up on the chopper, it was without gloves, coats or hats, he said disappointedly."

"Come with me," Andy said, standing and placing a hand on Todd and Rich's shoulders. "We'll take care of that right now!"

It wasn't long before Rich and Todd emerged through the archway, in their new winter camos with gloves and stocking caps in hand, grinning from ear to ear.

"We have winter gear for Linda and Jan as well, and plenty of clothing stored up in Havens II to provide a few changes for all of you, but we'll take care of all that later," Josh said. "Right now, we had better get this show on the road!"

After suiting up Josh checked his backpack to make sure everything needed was still where he had left them and threw some more wedges and carabineers for good measure. Putting it on his back, he led the men out the back door of the Havens. The first stop was behind the large granite stone outside the door, where Rich and Todd gazed across the upper end of the valley at the Lemon Glacier, the small melt lake and the frozen two-acre pond below them. Turning, Josh led the party up through the winding snow path, to the escarpment trail and eventually to the door of Havens II.

Rich and Todd, overwhelmed by everything they saw and experienced, could not believe their eyes as they stepped into the large cavern for the first time. Pastor Bowens was delighted to take Todd and Rich on a tour, while Josh, Ben and Andy tackled the climbing project.

Taking off his backpack, Josh looked up at the roof of the shallow alcove at what appeared to be a long crack about an inch and a half wide. *Now the only problem, was getting to it*, he thought to himself.

Turning to his right, he noticed several cracks running up the wall, with each one leaning more toward the back of the alcove. Josh was sure he could use the smaller camming wedges to climb the wall and ultimately insert a larger camming wedge, into the crack in the roof.

Once set, he could run the rope through the wedge, and the men could lower him down to the floor of the entrance.

Attaching a carabineer to the loop on a small camming wedge, Andy and Ben gave Josh a boost up to where he could reach and insert the first wedge into the vertical crack about ten feet off the ground. With the help of the rope and pulling himself up high enough to attach another wedge in the continuing crack, he was able to scale the wall to the top in five-foot increments, until finally reaching out and inserting the larger wedge into the crack running across the roof of the alcove. Passing the end of the rope through the carabineer attached to the wedge, he quickly made a loop in the rope and inserted his foot. While the men below held the rope, Josh swung out as they lowered him to the ground.

Andy already had the small cargo net waiting at the door.

"All I could find to wrap the meat in was a couple of white twin sheets," Andy said, holding them out to Josh. "I thought maybe we could cut them each in three pieces to wrap the six quarters we have left."

Sounds good to me," Ben echoed. "What do you think Josh?"

"It's not like saran wrap, paper and tape," he replied, but it will have to do. "We'll just trust the Lord will keep our meat fresh for us, He's taken care of everything else so far, hasn't He."

As Andy and Ben held the ends of the sheets, Josh marked them into thirds with a short cut, and then finished cutting them up.

After wrapping the quarters, Andy and Josh placed them in the cargo net and gathered up the corners, clipping them together with a large carabineer. Tying a more secure loop in the end of the rope, Josh attached his last carabineer to the rope and then to the one holding the cargo net together.

"Almost time to hang our groceries," Josh called out. "Andy, would you stand on the edge of the net and hold really tight on the rope for me?"

As Andy stepped up to meet Josh's request, Josh began climbing up the wall using the rope. Climbing up above the first two camming wedges, he released them allowing them to slide down the rope, and then returned to the floor. Once at the bottom, he reinserted a wedge deep into a horizontal crack and pressed the rope into the carabineer attached to the wedge.

"Ok guys, he said," let's hoist up this meat!

With Josh in the lead, Andy and Ben helped raise the laden cargo net to the roof of the alcove. Once up, Josh laid a half hitch around the rope, and two more around the loop, before coiling up the remainder, and tucking it behind the rope going up the wall.

"I love it when a plan comes together," Andy said, trying to imitate an old TV character.

"So do I," Josh said, leaning back against the opposite wall of the alcove and looking up at their venison swinging above their heads, so do I!

AFTER THE MEN HAD GONE, it didn't take long for the women to get out the knives and the old hand operated meat grinder Sarah cherished almost as much as the seasoned cast-iron cookware she had used most of her life. Carrying the small worktable from the kitchen area to the washtub in the back of the second cavern, the women washed the shoulder and hindquarter, before cutting twelve generous steaks for the evening meal. The rest of the venison, after Sarah and Alice boned it, was cut into small chunks and fed through the grinder by Ellen and Jessica, while Linda and Amy portioned and wrapped it in saran wrap.

When the work was finished, Ellen stood back looking at the pile of ground venison.

"Thank God for His provision and Costco," she said with a smile. "Jessica and I bought two boxes of this wrap on our last trip to the banks, and almost paid for it with our lives, but this morning makes it worth the effort."

"I don't understand," Jan said, bursting into tears. "I just don't understand all of this. I'm thankful to be alive, and for all of your kindness and generosity, but we missed the Rapture! Unless we all die a martyr's death, we have no hope of heaven. I just can't believe I missed the Rapture; I thought my life was right with the Lord!"

Jan sank to the floor sobbing uncontrollably as Jessica, Ellen and Linda rushed to her side. Raising her up, they led her into the great room to the couches. Comforting her as best they could, the women allowed her to weep until she was able to regain some composure, before attempting to speak to the ominous questions, which now seemed written on Linda's face as well. Lifting Jan's chin with her hand, Ellen looked into her eyes and spoke with a loving forcefulness and authority that not only snapped Jan to attention, but Linda as well.

"Jan, Jessica and I have faithfully and lovingly served our Lord and Savior all of our lives, since we were five and seven. Pastor Bowens, Sarah and all those who reside in this Haven are, and have always been, devout followers of Christ all their lives."

Ellen paused for a moment, as she continued to hold Jan's gaze fixed on herself.

"Now, there are only two answers to your question. Either Christ and everything we have professed to believe in is a lie, or the rapture has not yet occurred. We choose to believe the latter, and when Pastor Bowens and the men return, we will sit down after supper, and he will explain in detail, why we continue to hold on to the hope we have in our Lord and Savior. "Ok", Ellen said, kissing Jan's forehead as she held her hands.

Jan nodded, forcing a smile and wiping her eyes with the soft towel Jessica handed to her. Brushing her hair back from her face, she reached out and grasped Linda's hand, pulling her down beside her on the couch.

"I'm so sorry for my behavior," she said, looking around her. "Everything has just been so overwhelming and happening so fast. I've just been so confused through all of this."

"That goes for me as well," Linda said, still trying to fight back her own apprehension. "Things just haven't been happening the way we were taught, and we weren't prepared for all of this. When the economy collapsed, the currency changed and persecution of Christians and the church started big time, we were sure Jesus would come at any moment. We've been on the run with our husbands for over a year and a half now, and even they feel we missed the rapture. When the militia captured us, we were sure we were going to become Tribulation Saints."

"I felt cheated, no I felt robed, when they threw us out of the helicopter like garbage, like I had missed the last opportunity to seal an eternity with Christ," Jan said, beginning to tear up again.

"God never intended for us to seek death, in order to gain life," Sarah said, reaching over and patting Jan's' hand. "His desire was that we be willing to face death for His sake, knowing that eternal life was ours, in spite of the circumstances."

Alice walked up to the women wiping her hands on a towel as she spoke.

"It's going on one in the afternoon ladies; it will take the rest of the afternoon to prepare for supper, so we had better get snapping. Ellen, the venison needs to go back out into the freezing weather. I think it would be a good idea if you and Jessica took it up to the men, to be placed in the safe they have been preparing. With Linda and Jan's help, Sarah and I will get things ready for supper, and you can help finish up when you get back"

"Good as done Mom," Ellen said, as she grabbed Jessica's hand and headed for the bench where the portioned venison was wrapped and stacked.

Splitting up the meat, and packing it into a couple of backpacks, Jessica and Ellen suited up in their winter gear, donned the packs and headed out the back door for Havens II.

As Josh leaned against the wall of the alcove, Pastor, Rich and Todd emerged carrying the two remaining large pieces of foam, sleeping bags and the last large tarp remaining in storage, placing them out on the trail.

"With the addition to our company, I thought we had better begin making a more suitable place for them to find some privacy than the center of the great room," Pastor said, placing his hand on Josh's shoulder, and adding "Sir", with a wink.

"Andy and Dad both brought up the packs for firewood as well," Josh said, pushing himself away from the wall. We'll go load up the wood, and if we have everything squared away here, we'll head back for the Havens when were done."

Todd and Rich were now both wearing fresh packs, laden with several changes of clothing for themselves and their wives, as well as toothpaste, brushes and other personal care items that filled the cavern. Swinging their packs off their shoulders and placing them on the pathway next to the other items, they followed the party to the area where the wood supply lay hidden under show covered tree boughs.

Seeing all of the firewood neatly stacked under the trees that surrounded him, Rich reeled under the confusion, which suddenly flooded his mind. Reaching out to Pastor Bowens, he fell to his knees, looking up into the faces of his hosts, as Todd stepped up to his side, to aid his friend. With a look of bewilderment across his face, he spoke with timbre in his voice.

"Since the moment we were thrust out of the door of the helicopter last night, everything I have experienced has been amazing. I can find no words though, to express the nagging question, "Why", why is all of this here, when there is no hope! Obviously, the church has been taken out, or the world would not be in the condition it is in now. Only those who become martyrs and do not receive the mark of the beast will have any hope of salvation. Death without the mark is the only hope left. Why, why are you here, why do you maintain all of this, when there is no hope?"

Pastor Bowens dropped to his knees in front of Rich, and weeping, wrapped his arms around him.

"My precious, precious brother," he said. "God placed us here for you, to reveal to you and yours, the truth, and restore the hope and joy this world has taken away. Tonight, after supper, we will gather, and God Himself will reveal the truth to you, and restore your faith through His precious Word. Until then, take heart and rest in the reality that surrounds you."

CHAPTER 18

Mid-tribulation Eschatology 101

A FTER LOADING UP THE BACKPACKS with wood, Josh led the party back up to the escarpment trail, and to the alcove, where Rich and Todd donned their packs, and picked up the foam, sleeping bags and tarp. As the men were beginning to leave, Andy saw Jessica and Ellen coming down the trail, with Max leading the way. Moments later, everyone stood visiting in front of Havens II.

"Honey, Mom had us bring the ground venison up to you, to be stored in the safe you were building, Ellen said," looking around. "If you show us where it is, we'll put this meat away."

'It's right in front of you," Josh said, trying to hold back a grin.

Ellen looked at the other men, and then at Josh. Placing her hands on her hips, she gave them all, the look.

"It's right there in front of you", he said again. Then pointing up, Ellen's eyes followed his finger to the cargo net hanging from the roof of the alcove.

"Joshua Huskins, you teasing rascal, you're just as bad as your father, and you too," she said, turning to Pastor Bowens. "Now you all get that net down here right now, so we can put this meat in there, or I'm going to tell Mom, "she said, laughingly.

It took only a few minutes to lower the cargo net, while Andy retrieved a couple of empty flower sacks from inside the cavern. Loading the ground venison in the sacks and tying them closed, Josh and Andy placed them in the cargo net. Raising it again, they tied it off, secured the door and the party of eight headed back to the Havens. As twilight began to settle in, so did Andy's appetite.

"How big are the steaks, Andy said, licking his lips? I hope dinners on."

"There was only enough for eleven," Jessica teased. "I hope you saved the heart and the liver," she said, remembering his remark from the day before.

As everyone entered the Havens, and began hanging up their gear, Ben looked around him considering all of the changes that had occurred in such a very short time. Reaching out, he placed his hand on Pastor Don's shoulder.

"Don," he said, it was not that long ago these caverns seemed so enormous with just the six of us here. "They have grown so much smaller in the last two weeks, and so much has happened, it seems like twelve months have gone by instead of only twelve days."

"I know what you mean," Pastor responded. "It is nice to see my congregation growing though, and I am very excited, about our devotional this evening. Pray with me Ben, that the Lord will give me wisdom, to explain His plan of redemption in these final days before He comes to call us home!'

While the rest of the party moved on into the great room, Ben and Pastor Bowens stood in the antechamber. After joining hands and bowing their heads, Ben then reached, up and placed his hand on Pastor's head as he began to pray.

"Father, today as we stand amid trials and a period of tribulation like humanity has never experienced before, so is the faith of your elect, tested even to the point of death for your names sake. Lord we have with us now, those who you have brought to us, whose lack of understanding has robbed them

of their blessed hope and the joy they once had. I pray for Pastor this evening, that you would instill in him a double portion of your Holy Spirit. Enable him Father, to explain through the simplicity of your word, and without man's vain attempt to interpret what never needed interpretation, your plan for this time. As your great day and our redemption approaches, strengthen our resolve, to lay ourselves upon the altar, whether through life or death in your service. For each one gathered here tonight, renew and restore our hope, our peace and our Joy, in the name of our Lord and Savior I pray, Amen!"

After washing up, Ben and Don joined the rest of the company in the great room, where everyone was gathering around the massive table that had become the social center of the Havens. Pastor took a seat at one end of the table and Ben at the other. After Alice and Sarah finished serving the venison steaks, they sat down next to their husbands. As everyone joined hands and Pastor prayed, Max lay quietly next to his bowl of venison and whipped potatoes, licking his lips in unison with Andy, as they both anticipated a hearty Amen.

"I'm so overwhelmed by all of this, Todd said, cutting into his steak and savoring the aroma before taking his first bite. It is just so hard, to wrap my mind around it all. I don't know what I've looked forward to more today, this awesome meal, or Pastor Bowen's insight on why we're still here, and why hope thrives when there should be none".

"All in good time son," Pastor mumbled, as he relished Sarah's cooking and washed it down with a generous sip of coffee. "I'm sure that tonight the Lord will satisfy both your appetites."

Conversation filled the air with a buzz, as the company devoured every morsel of the sumptuous feast the women had prepared. For the new arrivals, the perils of the present became more distant, with the peace and joy that filled the great room.

When supper was finished, Pastor Bowens excused himself briefly, while Jessica and Ellen cleared the table, and Alice started a fresh pot of coffee for their meeting. Returning with Bibles, Pastor passed them out to the four new members of his congregation and called for everyone else to gather around the table with their Bibles as well.

"Before we pray, it's important for you Todd and Jan, and you Rich and Linda, to understand that what I'm sharing with you tonight is simply God's Word. It is not a personal interpretation. I don't believe that God ever intended for us to interpret his word, only that we should study it, obey it and rightly divide its truth by living out its precepts with fear and trembling. With that said, let's pray."

After praying for God to open their hearts and minds to His word, Pastor opened with a question.

"What and who are the saints of God," he said.

"According to everything I've been taught, a saint of God is a person who has accepted Christ as Lord and Savior. He or she strives under His blood covering, to live their life to its fullest for God, through the power of the Holy Spirit, Rich said", looking around the table for affirmation.

"I always believed that when you accepted Christ as your savior, you were saved, done deal. You don't become a saint until after you die or the rapture", Jan said questioningly.

"The truth God's word teaches us, is that salvation is a journey," Pastor said. "It begins when we accept Christ's provision for our salvation, and ends, or is complete, when we die in that personal relationship, or we are changed when Christ comes to gather his bride the church to Himself. All those who are actively seeking and living their lives for Christ through this journey are called His Saints."

"The Apostle Paul alludes to this journey in I Corinthians 1:18 where he states that, the message of the cross is foolishness to those who are perishing, but to us who are *being saved;* it is the power of God. It's important we understand that the Saints of God are all those who are in the faith, alive and serving Him, as well as those who have died and are now in His presence.

There are two things which all of us sitting here at this table cannot deny! First, the mark of the beast is present, and the only way to escape death and persecution from this world order, is to receive its precepts and the mark. Second, hundreds of thousands have become martyrs for the cause of Christ, and many are alive and remain, like us who have not received that mark.

Does this mean that we have missed the rapture, the blessed hope that each of us has longed for, or if we don't die a martyr's death, all is lost. I don't believe so, and I'm going to explain to you why I believe this to be true, by simply giving you the scriptural facts, without trying to interpret them, and then you can judge for yourself."

"Let's go first to a passage in Matthew that we have all read before, chapter twenty-four, and we'll read what Jesus says to us in His own words about His second coming to gather His Bride, His Church, to Himself."

"Let's start with verses thirty-seven through thirty-nine."

Opening his Bible, Pastor Bowens read the passages. Pausing, he laid his Bible on the table and continued.

"The first thing we need to address, is the belief that the tribulation saints are those who fail to make the rapture and are forced to meet a martyr's death in order to gain heaven. Jesus, in the passage of scripture we just read made a very clear and pointed statement. He said, *'As it was in the days of Noah, so it will be at the coming of the Son of Man.'* "How was it in the days of Noah? When it came time for Noah and his family to enter the ark, God's word says that God brought the animals to Noah and the ark, and when everyone was on board, God shut them in."

"He closed the door, and only those who God had called were saved. According to Jesus, own words, when He comes to gather up his elect, his church, only those who are in Him will be saved. Just as it was in the days of Noah, once the door was closed, no one else got on or in the Ark."

"When the Father closes the door to the church age, with the return of Christ for his bride, the door to the marriage supper of the lamb, will be closed."

"If what you're saying is true, Rich said, with a look of terror on his face, we truly have no hope left, because we missed the rapture!"

"No, my young friend, we have not missed the rapture," Pastor said.

"How can the rapture not have occurred, we've faced unbelievable tribulation and persecution, and now the mark of the beast. God said He would take us out of this world and that his children wouldn't taste of His wrath," Jan said, tears welling up in her eyes.

"You're absolutely right, Pastor continued, but God's wrath doesn't begin until the eighth chapter of Revelation, and after a period of silence for about half an hour. "The tribulation wrath the church experiences is not God's, it's the wrath of the antichrist making war against the Saints of God. God begins pouring out His wrath on the earth and humankind, beginning with the trumpet judgments. This is halfway through the great tribulation period. Turn with me quickly to the book of Daniel, and the seventh chapter."

After reading verses nineteen through twenty-seven, he again laid his Bible down on the table and continued.

"The fourth kingdom Daniel is speaking about here is that of the antichrist! He makes war against the Saints of God for a time, times, and a half a time, or a period of three and a half years. At the conclusion of that period of testing, Christ will return for his bride, and the body of Christ will have victory!"

"Why would God test his church?" Todd said, leaning into the table and wrapping his hands around his coffee cup.

"Because", Pastor Bowens replied, not all those who profess the name of Christ are truly His. Only when our faith is put to the test will the faithful be separated from the unfaithful, the wheat from the tares, and the sheep from the goats. Jesus alludes to this in the book of Matthew in chapter seven.

"Simply acknowledging Christ is not enough. He tells us that we need to have a personal relationship with Him to be considered by Him, as His own."

"Pastor, how can you be so sure of all this?" Linda said. We were taught that Jesus was coming as a thief in the night and that no one would know the day or the hour of His coming."

"Before we go on Linda, let's turn back to Matthew twenty-four and let Jesus answer those questions for you. Jesus says, that after the distress and the trials His elect will face at that time, the sun will be darkened, and the moon won't give its light; the heavens will be shaken, and the stars will fall from the sky. Jesus goes on to say, then I will appear in the heavens and all the peoples of the earth will mourn when they see me coming on the clouds of heaven, with power and glory. Then Jesus said, 'I will send my angels with a trumpet call, and they will gather my elect, from the four winds, from one end of the heavens to the other.'

"When Jesus stated that He would come as a thief in the night, He didn't mean that He would come sneaking in to gather up His church, and then sneak back out again. He only meant that He would come unexpectedly! In this passage of scripture, Jesus says that He is coming in clouds of great glory and the whole world will see Him and mourn. Then he will gather His Saints to Himself, with the whole world watching! You're right in your assertion that no one will know the day or the hour of His coming, but Jesus Himself said that we would know the season, if we were watchful."

Picking up his Bible, Pastor turned quickly to the sixth chapter of Revelation. Placing his finger between the pages, he closed the book and gripped it tightly in his right hand as he spoke.

"The sixth chapter of Revelation deals with the opening of the seven seals on the scroll in heaven. The first four seals deal with the four horsemen of the apocalypse. It's during this time that the antichrist comes into power, deceiving the world with false hope and false miracles.

The world sees him as a savior, as he makes war against the saints of God, using them as a scapegoat for all the worlds' ills. When Jesus opens the fifth seal, the souls of those who had been slain, because of the word of God and their testimony, called out for judgment upon those who had taken their lives. They were told to wait until those who were to be killed as they were, had been fulfilled.

"The opening of the sixth seal directly reflects Jesus' statement in Matthew chapter 24, finding it's fulfillment somewhere near the halfway point in the seven-year tribulation period.

Placing his Bible down on the table once again, Pastor folded his hands and paused for several minutes, allowing what they had read and what he had just said, to sink in.

"Seeing this passage of scripture in context, with what Jesus said concerning His return to gather up His Saints in Matthew twenty-four, what would you say were the definitive factors?"

"Well, I guess it would be the signs in the heavens, the sun, moon and stars, the sky rolling up like a scroll and Christ coming in clouds of glory," Rich answered.

"Have any of you witnessed this event since you accepted Christ as your Savior?" Ben said, looking around the table.

"Neither have I! I assure you, if we had missed the rapture of the church, there would be absolutely no doubt in anyone's mind. When my Lord and Savior comes to gather me up to Himself, He's going to come in clouds of great glory, and the whole world is going to see me go. He will not come sneaking in, and I will not go sneaking out!"

CHAPTER 19

A conclusion and a new beginning

"I KNOW IT'S GETTING LATE," PASTOR said. "I don't want to send you all to bed tonight exhausted, and with more questions than you have answers, so I think it's time for a little break., and we'll finish up afterwards."

Laying down his Bible, he pulled over his empty coffee cup, and waited as Ellen made her way around the table with a fresh pot of coffee. Moments later, Alice and Sarah stepped up with two large plates of sugar cookies.

"Baked them the day of the earthquake, while you men were building the back door," Alice said.

"If we hadn't wrapped them up and hid them, they would have been gone by now," Sarah concluded with a smile. "They will make good dunkers though."

Later, with the cookies devoured, and everyone's cups refilled, Pastor Bowens took a sip of his coffee and reopened his Bible to the book of Revelation.

"I've given you a lot the think about, and I'm sure you still have some questions. Rest assured God has the answers. Turn in your Bibles to Revelation chapter seven."

As everyone opened there Bibles, Linda sighed, as she read ahead, quoting aloud the words in bold print. 'The Great Multitude in White Robe's.'

Thank you Jesus, for our blessed hope Pastor thought, as he cleared his throat and re-opened the Bible study with a short prayer.

Picking up his Bible, he read verses nine and ten. Then dropping down to thirteen and concluded with verse fourteen.

"Note verse fourteen, Pastor Bowens said." *"These are they who have come out, of the great tribulation".*

"Beloved, these peoples are the raptured church. Included in them are those who did not receive the mark of the beast on their hands or their foreheads! Turn with me to revelation chapter twenty and lets read verses four through six."

Looking down the table after reading the verses, Pastor laid down his Bible and stood to his feet.

"There are only two mass resurrections spoken of in God's Word, concerning Christ's return and end times judgment. The first one is the resurrection, unto everlasting life, our blessed hope, and the second one unto judgment, the great white throne judgment. If those who were beheaded, for not receiving the mark were included in the rapture of the church, the first resurrection, then our blessed hope remains, and our Savior's return is imminent!

The two young couples sat in silence as each pondered the scriptures and logical deductions Pastor Bowens had presented to them. Then, one by one, the hopelessness and despair that had filled their hearts were replaced, with a fresh and renewed hope that made their faces shine and their eyes sparkle. In one spontaneous moment, as the Holy Spirit began to move in everyone's hearts. The rest of the company gathered around the couples with a rejoicing that filled the great room, reverberating off the walls of the cavern in glorified praise, with tears of relief and overwhelming joy!

As the elation began to subside a little, Alice who sat at the end of the great table with her hands raised to the Lord and tears of joy coursing her cheeks, trembled as the Holy Spirit began speaking into her heart, and words began to flow out of her mouth in a prophetic utterance.

Listen carefully to my words, and know I am, that I am! I am the Alpha and Omega, the Beginning, and the End. Those things, which have been ordained since the beginning, now, are coming to pass. Throughout the earth, I have called my children, who are filled by my Spirit, to be beacons of light to those who have not received the mark of perdition, but who still do not reside under the wings of my salvation. Soon, the Father will give the command and the trumpet will sound, my Bride will be received and the chosen of Israel will be sealed. Watch and pray my faithful, for I will never leave or forsake you. Stand in the power of my Holy Spirit, and labor as you have been called, for your redemption truly is near!

The power and presence of the Holy Spirit was so strong, the peace and joy that each experienced so great, no one could stand. For over two hours, twelve saints of God lay on the cold and uneven stone floor of the cavern, lost in the life-giving power of His presence. Slowly, the company one at a time, began making their way up and onto one of the benches around the table, staring at one another in joyful bliss.

Cradling their wives in their arms, Todd and Rich wept freely, but no longer in fear and doubt. The faces of the two couples radiated with God's peace and understanding.

Still overwhelmed by the power and presence of the Holy Spirit, Pastor Bowens bowed his head and prayed.

"Precious Heavenly Father, Lord and Savior, thank you for your mercy and grace, and for the power of your restoration in our spirits tonight. Now Father, as we retire to our beds, bring rest and renewed strength to our bodies. Fill our hearts and minds with your peace and watch over us as we sleep, in Jesus name we pray, Amen."

Slowly, each couple rose and made their way to the comfort of their beds, and each other's arms, with the Spirit of God and His hand resting over the Haven, He had ordained and prepared.

Josh sat at the end of the table in the great room for a long time, with his hands wrapped around the warmth of his coffee cup. As he pondered the lifetime of events, which had occurred over the last twelve days, he could taste the saltiness of his tears as he raised the cup to his lips.

It's amazing he thought, how wonderful the simplest things in live can become when the reality of everything around you cries 'eternity is at the door'. I'm only twenty-five years old, been a Christian for seven days, married for four and Christ is coming at any moment, calling me out of this reality and into another.

Taking another sip of his coffee, Josh pulled his journal in front of him. Opening it, he took out a pen, and turning to the page opposite his last entry, he began writing.

November 15th, 2019/4:00 AM … *Couldn't sleep, so I got up and made the coffee this morning. I never thought vanilla creamer could taste so good. I feel old before my time, and there is a cry in my heart, that I haven't been able to share with anyone, even my precious Ellen. I'm going to try to write it out this morning if I can only find the words.*

Savoring another long sip of his coffee, Josh sat and pondered what was going on in his heart, before picking up the pen. After a long pause, he began writing.

Where will I go; when each passing minute has finally gnawed through the shell of my existence, and the vacuum of eternity withdraws the last vestige of my life, through the breach that time has made? I do not know the place; yet I dream of it often and believe! Tightly in my grasp, I clutch the promise and cling to the hope that drives away the darkness, binding the hands that would snatch my treasure from me, if they could. Wrap around my heart the scarlet thread from Rahab's window, and bind me to the rock of my salvation, for my bones are weary and my soul longs to enter into His rest. How I long to hear the words "well done" and to feel His loving arms of welcome about my shoulders, but I know my time has not yet come and I must endure, until He calls me safely Home.

Returning the pen to the sleeve in his leather-bound journal, Josh closed, and pushed it aside. He was just raising his cup, when he felt

Ellen's gentle touch as she placed her hand on his shoulder. Leaning over, she kissed his cheek.

"Good morning honey," she said with a smile, sliding on to the bench next to him and setting down her cup next to his. "You're up early this morning. I didn't sleep well either, just too much excitement I guess."

Josh turned, and sliding his arm around Ellen's waist, pulled her to him, and kissed her tenderly.

"Right now, you're all the excitement I want," he said, kissing her neck and growling playfully, as Ellen struggled weakly to escape, with a giggle.

"Humm", Ben cleared his throat as he and Alice strode into the great room. "I see you two are up early this morning."

"Yea", Josh touted back.

"It looks like you and Mom aren't sleeping in this morning either," Ellen said, laughing.

Pouring himself a cup of coffee Ben joined Josh and Ellen at the table as Alice began digging through the cookware.

"Sarah and Pastor will be out soon, would you mind giving me a hand dear," Alice said, looking over at Ellen. "We'll start getting things ready for breakfast."

Ellen quickly drank down the last of her coffee as she scurried over to where Alice was busy mixing up a large bowl of pancake batter.

It wasn't long before Sarah and Pastor made their way into the great room, followed by the new members of the company. When Andy and Jessica finally pulled themselves out of bed and made their way into the great room, it was only six o'clock in the morning, and breakfast was just being set on the table. Joining hands after everyone had taken their seats, Ben led in prayer and Pastor closed with a hearty Amen, while scooping two pancakes onto his plate before Sarah raised her head and opened her eyes.

"Don Bowens," Sarah exclaimed,

"Ah, ah," Pastor said with a grin, don't mess with a man of God, the bears will get you. Says so right there in Second Kings chapter two.

"It also says that it's better to go live on the corner of the roof than share the house with an unhappy wife in Proverbs twenty-five, twenty-four. That's Sarah paraphrased of course, she said, looking at Pastor over the top of her glasses with a gotcha smile!

There seemed to be a new freshness, a sweet scent in the air Ellen thought, as she glanced around the table. The great room seemed to be bathed in a brightness that the sixty-watt bulbs attached to the poles in the cavern, couldn't possibly produce. Sipping her coffee, and slowly savoring each bite of her breakfast, Ellen listened to the conversations going on around her, until the sound of Josh clearing his throat, as he began to address the company, captured her attention.

"IF I COULD HAVE EVERYONE'S attention, we have some important matters to discuss this morning," Josh said, clearing his throat again and taking a quick sip of his coffee. "Most are general M and O's for the next couple of days, but we do have a couple of serious matters involving recent Collective activities, which will require us to take some offensive measures. Those we'll discuss later."

"I don't want to sound totally ignorant," Jan said questioningly "But what are M and O's?"

"I'm sorry," Josh said, pausing, as he folded his hands and leaned into the table where he was sitting.

"M and O stands for maintenance and operations. Aside from the daily chores of cleaning and meal preparation, supplies and firewood need to be, brought down from stores. Then we have the job of dividing the remainder of the second chamber into more sleeping quarters, since our family has now grown by four... I hope that helps."

Jan answered with a blushing nod. "Sure does," she said, "you learn something new every day!"

Taking another sip of his coffee, Josh continued.

"To begin with, we still have the lodge poles, door and canvas that once covered the alcove which is now our back door. I believe I saw a number of poles and some two by two's, along the wall in Havens II, if I'm not mistaken."

Ben nodded, as he opened the inventory book. Josh had asked him to bring it to the table during breakfast.

"According to my records, we should have more than enough materials to provide some privacy for our new family members he said," patting Rich on the back. "If we get started this morning, we should have them moved in before supper tonight, and still have time to take care of stores as well."

"Mom, I'm sure you and Sarah have the meal situation well under control, so I won't even think about stepping into your territory."

Josh grinned.

"You're such a smart young man," Sarah responded, as she reached over and patted the back of Pastor Don's hand. "Maybe with your help, there is still hope for my husband," she said, struggling to hold back her laughter.

"This is such an amazing place." Linda paused for a moment as tears welled up in her eyes. "God's grace is so complete during all the evil that surrounds us. I love you all, and I'm so thankful for the privilege to be a part of the family of God, especially this family."

"We're blessed as well," Josh said, hugging Ellen, who sat leaning her head on his shoulder.

"While the women take care of the Havens, we men will take care of the stores, and bring down the materials needed for our construction project this afternoon. Does that sound agreeable to everyone? Good, then we'll consider that taken care of. The last two items will take some explaining, before we talk about how to facilitate them."

Again, Josh cleared his throat as he opened his notebook, perused his notes and then looked up at everyone, whose gaze was now fixed on him.

"Since the day of the bear, Pastor, Pops and I have been monitoring the scanner as often as possible, and some interesting news has come to our attention. Evidently, the bear incident last Tuesday created quite a stir down on the banks. Along with that, there have been eight different sightings of Kodiak bears in and around the lower Lemon Creek area. Because of this and the loss of two helicopters, the Lemon Creek valley has been declared closed to all public and Militia personnel. All helicopter flights have been redirected, over the Mendenhall to the north and over the Salmon Creek valley to the south. Fixed wing flights over the valley have to remain above ten thousand feet. This closure is to remain in effect until after spring thaw. It looks like we have been granted a reprieve for the next five and a half months or so. Because of the earthquake damage and bear intrusion, everything east of thunder mountain road, and the north, south end of Anka Street has been cordoned off, and fenced. Anyone attempting to enter the area without expressed permission, will be arrested or shot by the Collective Militia. Barricades and fences have also been erected on the north side of Lemon Creek and along Lemon Creek Road west of what's left of the correctional facility."

"That sounds like great news," Todd said.

"It is," Josh continued, but here's our problem. We have ears of a sort, but we're blind. Unless we post a guard twenty-four seven, we have no way of knowing what may be coming our way, and we don't have those resources."

"It sure would be nice if we had the security system from your store down in Lemon town," Andy blurted out. "And all that other high-tech stuff buried under what's left of the Costco."

"My sentiments exactly," Josh said, setting his cup down on the table and clearing his throat. "It's my intention to make an incursion into Lemon Creek to bring back what we need to put some eyes on the outside of the Havens."

Ellen suddenly bolted upright, gripping Josh's arm with a look of disbelief on her face, as the entire company seemed to gasp in unison. Raising his hands, Josh motioned for everyone to quiet down, until he once again had the company's attention.

"Please, I've given this a lot of careful and prayerful consideration. It will take some effort, but I'm sure I can make it down in about two days and return the same way I came, nine days ago. I just wanted to let you know what I'm thinking, "when" is another matter, and the weather has got to be just right."

Silence seemed to reign for the longest time, before Ben stood, and spoke.

"I can't stop you son, but it would be pure foolishness for you to attempt something like this alone."

Following Ben's example, Andy stood, looked at Jessica, and then at Ellen before he spoke.

"I've said many times, that I've been Josh's shadow and followed his leadership ever since we were kids. In all these years, he has never let me down. Josh, if you think that making this decent into lemon town is necessary, to ensure the safety of the Havens, I'll go with you in a heartbeat. Besides, I've jumped as many times as you have, and I know there is another glider chute on the shelf in the back of the store."

"Son, you said there was a couple of issues that needed our attention, what's the other one?" Ben said, as he sat back down next to Alice.

"I don't think the helicopter went all the way down to Lemon Creek in the avalanche," Josh responded. "If it didn't, we need to make sure it does. I want the Militia as far away as possible from our location here at the Havens, if they decide to return to the incident site. If the chopper didn't go all the way, maybe we could do some salvage work of our own, before sending it the rest of the way down," Andy added. "The surveillance equipment installed on those helicopters is pretty high tech, and we have the power to make them work, if they haven't been destroyed."

Pastor Bowens, being the most pragmatic of the group, leaned forward, and resting his forearms against the edge of the table, spoke directly to Josh.

"In theory, I couldn't agree with you more Josh, but from a practical perspective, is it really worth the risk? After all, you just told us that we have at least a five-month reprieve, before we might have an encounter with the Militia."

"Pastor," Josh responded. From a practical perspective, was all the time, effort and danger involved in building this retreat, worth the risk you and Dad placed yourselves in? When you're doing what you know in your heart is right, it ceases to be a matter of risk, and becomes a matter of faith and trust in God's faithfulness doesn't it? I would much rather stay here in the safety of the Havens with Ellen, and those I care for. It was you and Dad, who placed the burden of leadership on my shoulders, now I need all of you to understand, and follow that leadership, as I prayerfully try to follow the Lord's. As Dad said, I can't do this alone. I believe with all my heart, it needs to be done, to ensure our ability to accomplish what the Lord has called us to do. The question now is, will you help and support me in this decision?"

After bowing his head, and exhaling a deep sigh, Pastor looked up into the faces of those gathered around the table before responding to Josh's question.

"Thank you, Josh, for reminding me, that our reason for being here is for God's glory, and not simply our own self-preservation. I'm with you son, till death or rapture, you just continue to follow God's direction as He speaks to your heart!"

Taking Ellen's hand, Josh reached over for Jessica's, as the company joined hands. Bowing his head, he led in a closing prayer. While the women began picking up the breakfast dishes, the men donned their winter gear, and prepared for the short trip to Havens II. As Josh pulled up his hood, Ellen pushed the list Sarah and Alice had prepared for supplies into his hand.

"I love you Joshua Huskins," she said, giving him a quick kiss on the cheek, before scurrying back into the great room.

CHAPTER 20

Big cats and ravens

B Y ELEVEN IN THE MORNING, Josh, Ben, and Andy had filled the antechamber next to the rear entrance with almost a rick and a half of firewood. Pastor Bowens, Todd and Rich had brought down all of the stores on the women's list and were returning with the first load of building materials, when all the men met on the escarpment trail near Havens II.

"It's just a little past eleven," Josh said, helping Pastor Don remove his pack, and lowered it to the ground.

"The women are preparing to put some lunch on the table soon. Dad, Andy, and I will go and get what's left of the materials we need, and then we can all head back to the Havens together."

"Sounds good to me, I'll just sit right here on my pack and wait for you young fellers to come back and help me get loaded up again," Pastor grinned.

"Who you are calling a young feller," Ben said, with a wink. "I feel older than you look."

Patting Pastor on the shoulder, Ben followed Andy and Josh as they made their way to the entrance of Havens II.

"By the way," Pastor called out, "we forgot to get the box of large zip ties, they're next to the door, right hand side."

Ben responded with a nod, and a wave of his hand as he stepped into the alcove and out of sight. Minutes later, Josh appeared with the ends of half a dozen four-inch lodge poles on his shoulder and a small carton under his right arm, followed by Andy, with the other end of the twelve-foot poles on his shoulder. After securing the door to the storeroom, Ben joined Andy and Josh, taking up a position between them. As they made their way along the escarpment, Josh led Ben and Andy around the other men, and continued down the trail. Todd and Rich helped Pastor to his feet, repositioning his backpack. Then, picking up their own, they resumed their trip to the Havens.

Jessica stood outside the rear entrance, waiting impatiently for sign of the men's return. As she looked up the trail, a quick movement caught her eye and lifted her gaze to a large granite rock to the left of the trail. Leaning out to her right, she could make out the head of the biggest mountain lion she had ever seen. It was apparent the huge cat was watching the unsuspecting men coming down the trail. Quickly she stepped back through the door of the Havens and dashed down into the antechamber where Ben kept his hunting rifle, leaning into a niche in the wall. Chambering a shell, she returned to the door and slowly stepped out into the trail.

Jessica could now hear the men talking as they approached the last turn, before descending to the rear entrance. She watched as the lion raised its head, peered up the trail, and then settled into a crouching position, ready to spring. Quickly, she raised the rifle to her shoulder, taking aim at the back of the big cat's head, and held her breath. Just as Josh rounded the corner, the lion leaped into the air, and Jessica's shot rang out! Everything suddenly melted into slow motion, as the huge lion folded in mid-air and rolled onto Josh, Ben and Andy, as they fell backwards into the narrow snow- lined trench.

Jessica chambered another shell and shouldering the rifle, crouched as she began sidestepping her way up the trail toward the men, now sprawled under the lion and lodge poles. Seeing the lion was dead, she sank to her knees, as Ellen and the other women, hearing the shot emerged from the cavern entrance. With a bound, Max leaped over her in a defensive rage that suddenly snapped Jessica back into the reality of the moment.

"Jessica," Ellen shouted, as she rushed to her sister's side. Kneeling in the snow, she wrapped her arms around Jessica's trembling body.

"I was waiting for Andy, and I saw the lion, I got the gun and..."

"It's alright Sis, you did good," Ellen said, taking the rifle and handing it to Sarah, before helping Jessica to her feet. "Come on lets help the guys get out from under this big kitty, so we can all get inside where it's warm."

Dropping his pack to the ground, Todd rushed forward to help Andy side out from under the lodge polls. Together, they lifted the poles up on their shoulders until Ben could get to his feet.

The men continued to raise the poles until the huge cat slid down, and onto the trail at Jessica and Ellen's feet. As Todd, Ben and Andy passed the poles back to Pastor Bowens and Rich, Ellen and Jessica pulled Josh to his feet, shaken, but grinning from ear to ear.

"Jessica Michaels Bridgeport," Josh said, throwing his arms around Jessica, and hugging her tightly. "I'm so glad your parents raised you and Ellen right. What a shot!"

As Josh turned, Ellen leaped into his arms, kissing him tenderly and burying her face under his chin.

"I hate to break up this wonderful reunion, but I think we need to move this stuff and ourselves inside, and we'll deal with the cat later," Pastor Bowens said. "Besides, I can smell the coffee, and I need to use the restroom."

Laughter and relief filled the air, as everyone began moving toward the rear entrance of the cavern, passing poles, packs and building materials as they went. When everyone was safely inside and the door secured, the men removed their gear, while the women returned to the great room and began setting lunch on the table.

While the others made their way into the great room, Josh quietly slipped through the small door of the little alcove, which offered the only source of privacy for him and Ellen. Making his way to a small recess in the back, he knelt in front of a shelf of rock that jutted out into the tiny room. Bowing, he rested his forehead in his hands, as warm tears coursed his cheeks.

God, you are so good, Josh thought to himself. His mind suddenly flooded with visions of the last thirteen days. Less than two weeks had passed, since he had stepped out of the courthouse in Juneau and into this chronicle of events that now, swept through his mind.

It was Ellen's gentle touch, which pulled Josh away from his musing as he turned and watched her drop to her knees beside him. Putting her arm around his shoulders, she leaned her head against his, and gave a gentle squeeze.

"It's almost too much to comprehend sometimes isn't it," she said, kissing his cheek.

"Thirteen days, it's only been thirteen days, and yet it seems like a lifetime has passed by…"

Josh sat back on his heels and ran his fingers through his hair as he gazed up at the dimly lit ceiling.

"Ellen, I'm torn between staying here in the safety of the Havens with you and going back down on the banks. I know the Lord's hand is on us, and that He'll watch over me, today is a testimony to that, but the battle between duty and desire is a tough one."

"I have no doubt you will make the right decision," Ellen said. Just know that I have complete faith in your judgment, and in the Lord. Let's head in with the others, and have some lunch, I'm starved."

Pulling Josh to his feet, Ellen led him through the door to the archway, and into the great room.

ENTERING THE GREAT ROOM, JOSH walked up to the table behind his father and placed his hands on his shoulders, while Ellen headed to the cook table to get soup and sandwiches for Josh and herself. Leaning over his father, he watched as Ben quickly drew a sketch of the pole placements for Rich and Linda's quarters and passed it over to Pastor Don.

"Looks good to me Ben," Pastor said, washing down the last bite of his sandwich with a sip of coffee. "Once these poles are up, we will be able to place Todd and Jan in between Rich, Linda and the newlyweds." Grinning at Josh, he swilled down the last of his coffee before rising to his feet.

"We had better get started though, if we're going to have this little project done, and the kids into their new quarters before supper."

Standing and stepping around behind his son, Ben pushed Josh down onto the bench at the end of the table where he had been sitting and motioned for Ellen to sit down beside him.

"You two enjoy your lunch; there will still be plenty of work to do when you're done."

Patting Josh on the shoulder, he made his way through the archway and disappeared into the rear chamber of the Havens, with Todd and Rich following close behind.

Sliding onto the bench, Ellen placed a bowl of soup and a sandwich in front of Josh, then reached for her own, bowing her head to pray. As he took a bite of his sandwich, Andy entered the great room. Striding over to the hearth, he poured a cup of coffee and sat down across from Josh and Ellen.

"I got the cat on a small tarp and managed to drag it as far as the escarpment trail. That lion must weigh at least two hundred pounds if not more," he said, taking a drink of his coffee. "The shot hit behind the right ear and exited through the left eye. I didn't know Jess could shoot like that."

"Jessica and I have been shooting since we were big enough to hold a rifle," Ellen said proudly. "She takes after her big sister."

"Well Josh, looks like we got the cream of the crop. "Doesn't it,"

Andy said with a smile. "By the way, as I was coming back down the trail, I spied half a dozen Ravens drifting around to the east of the melt pond, so I went and borrowed Pastors field glasses. I climbed up on the granite slab by the back door to look. Your right Josh, the helicopter didn't go down to the Lemon, it's hung up on the ridge with two of its blades sticking up through the snow. Josh dropped his sandwich onto his plate and leaned into the table.

"You said there's Ravens, and you're sure it was chopper blades you saw?" Josh said.

"With Pastors glasses, you've got to be kidding. I could see the Collectives insignia and the helicopter number on the door, zero two five, sticking through the snow. There's thick brush and tree cover to within thirty feet of it, if we come in from the west, off the other end of the escarpment trail, and drop down about two hundred yards."

Josh leaned on his elbow, cupping his hand over his chin and mouth, as he closed his eyes and mused over Andy's report. Then sitting up straight he spoke, looking over at Ellen, then intently at Andy.

"If the Ravens are gathering, either the bear or bodies are exposed. First light Andy, we've got to be at the west end of the escarpment trail by first light in the morning." Do you still have Pastor's field glasses available?"

Andy nodded.

"Good, let's go and take another look."

Jumping to his feet, Josh strode through the archway and turned into the antechamber, making his way to the door at the top of the rise. Andy, following close behind, paused briefly to pick up Pastors binoculars he left lying on the woodpile and joined Josh at the door.

"What happened to Josh," Alice said, turning from her work at the prep table to find Ellen sitting alone, and hovering over her soup and sandwich.

"Ravens," Ellen said glibly. "Those scavengers have led Andy and Josh to the helicopter that crashed in the avalanche. Pray with me Mama, things are constantly changing around here with every passing minute.

We need to pray God will give Josh wisdom, and protect our men, especially when they are outside of the Havens."

Alice gathered the other women around the table with Ellen, and together they entered a season of prayer for the men, praying for grace as the company of twelve prepared to fill the unwritten pages of the Lemon Creek Chronicle.

Closing the door behind them, Josh and Andy climbed up onto the huge slab of granite near the rear entrance. The sun shone brightly on the mounds of drifted snow, even though ominous dark clouds hung on the western horizon. Raising the field glasses to his eyes, Josh searched the mountainside below the slow circling Ravens, who intermittently would dive and rise again from his field of vision. With Andy's help, he was soon able to locate the helicopter just as Andy had described it. Josh watched intently, as the huge black birds would land, and leap down through the open door of the helicopter, returning moments later with chunks of flesh in their beaks. Quickly he lowered the glasses and turned away from the grizzly scene, knowing what lay ahead of them when he and Andy would make the trek to the chopper in the morning.

"I'm not looking forward to what we'll find tomorrow," Josh said, wiping his eyes with the back of his hand. "It's going to be an ugly mess inside that helicopter, but we'll have to go in, if we want to salvage any of the equipment and ordinance that might still be useable."

"Snow's packed good," Andy said. "I think we can do pretty well on snowshoes, and the tracks will cover easier with new snowfall. What do you think Josh?"

"I think you're right; we'll stay inside the tree line as much as possible, and weave through the brush on the upwind sides. Let's head back inside, and discuss tomorrow, over coffee!"

Josh placed the field glasses back in their case, as he and Andy turned and re-entered the Havens. Walking into the great room they found Ben and Pastor Bowens sitting at the table with mallets in hand, placing more grommets along the edges of the newly cut tarps for the partitions they were building.

"Todd and Rich are cutting and notching the poles we measured up," Ben said, laying down his mallet. "What are you two fellas' up to?"

"Getting ready to dispose of that cat," Josh said, after some coffee and planning for tomorrow.

"Planning?" Ben mumbled, as he took a sip of his coffee.

"Yea, Andy responded, pushing Pastor Bowen's field glasses into the center of the table. Thanks for letting me borrow these, they came in real handy.

"What were you looking for?" Laying down his mallet and joining in the conversation, Don reached for his coffee cup, and discovered it was empty. "Hey Josh, while you're getting coffee for you and Andy, could you fill me up again please?"

After making sure everyone had a fresh cup, Josh returned the pot to the hearth, and sat down at the end of the table.

"While Andy was moving the cat up to the escarpment trail, he saw a number of ravens gathering down the mountain to the east. That's when he borrowed your glasses to check things out." Josh paused to take a sip of his coffee. "He discovered that the helicopter didn't go over the bluff as I had suspected. We went back out to have another look, and decided that early in the morning, we're going to make a trip down there, and see what we can salvage. So, we thought we should come in, have a cup, and make some plans."

"One's mind does work better over a cup of coffee," Ben said, with a grin. "What do you two have in mind exactly?"

Folding his hands, Josh leaned into the table, pursing his lips before he spoke.

"We need to take some tools with us, wrenches, screwdrivers, pry bar and a hammer," he said, pausing briefly as he looked at Andy for some input. "Other than side arms, I can't think of anything else. Depending on what we can salvage, I don't want to overburden ourselves on the way back."

"I think maybe we should take along some rope, a couple of wedges and carabineers, never know if we'll have to roll that bird to get to anything we might want," Andy interjected.

"It sounds to me like the two of you have things covered pretty well." "Here's how we're going to put the partitions together," Ben said, pushing a drawing over to Josh. "If you and Andy can start installing the poles, Pastor and I will finish these grommets…

"Let's do it," Josh said, rising to his feet. "Our family's growing, and we need more rooms!"

CHAPTER 21

Scavengers

FOLLOWING HIS FATHER'S DIAGRAM, JOSH and Andy drilled pilot holes and lagged the lodge poles together, each piece structurally reinforcing the other, like building a bridge. With Rich and Todd holding the pieces in place, it took only a couple of hours for the young men to assemble the superstructure for the partitions.

"I can't believe the forethought that went into gathering all of this hardware together," Andy said, let alone getting it up to Havens II from the banks."

Inserting the last lag bolt and ratcheting it into place, Andy stepped back with Todd and Rich, to admire their hard work.

"Every time we go up the escarpment trail to get stores it's like going to Wal-Mart!"

"Isn't that the truth," Todd said, reinforcing Andy's statement.

"I was overwhelmed when Pastor Bowens first took us to Havens II. Even our wives couldn't believe the things we brought back with us."

"What do you say we all head into the great room for some coffee, we'll see how Ben and Pastor are doing with the grommets."

Josh had barely finished his sentence, before Andy and Rich were entering the great room. Placing his hand on Todd's shoulder, they followed laughing, as Rich and Andy dashed to the hearth, only to be stopped, by Sarah's upraised hand.

"You boys take a seat, and I'll get your coffee and a little something to go along with it," she said with a smile."

Pastor and Ben sat at the other end of the table, engrossed in coffee conversation, the finished tarps lay neatly folded on the floor between them.

While Josh and Todd took a seat the women served coffee, and what Ellen called drizzle cake. Joining the men around the table, Linda led in prayer. With an "Amen", Linda's prayer was punctuated by a bark, as Max stood on his hind legs at the end of the table, looking for his share of the desert. Laughing, Jessica stood, placing her plate on the floor for Max, she went to the worktable to get another piece for herself.

"I'm assuming everything is together and ready for these tarps," Ben said, looking down the table at the young men.

"Everything but the doors," Josh replied. "All the one by two's are still up in Havens II. We'll go and bring those pieces down, soon as were done here."

Standing to his feet, Ben walked around to Josh and handed him a piece of paper, resting a hand on his shoulder.

"Just a short list of things we'll need to finish up. "When you get back, we'll stretch the tarps, then frame, and cut out for the doors. We can finish making the doors tomorrow. That will free you and Andy to take care of the cat and explore the wreckage downhill. Will that work for you son?"

"Sounds good to me Pops."

When they were finished, Josh and the other young men made their way to the rear entrance suited up and began the short hike to havens II.

Stopping at the entrance of the escarpment trail, the big can still lay on the tarp where Andy had left it, the four men each taking a corner began carrying the dead animal down the trail to the other end, where they placed the carcass just inside the tree line and out of sight. From there, Josh and Andy would be able to drag it to the canyon on the west side of the trees, the next morning.

Entering Havens II, Josh filled his father's list, while the other men gathered up the one by two's and headed back down the trail. After locking up, he lagged, taking advantage of the privacy, and spent some personal time, in prayer as he walked along.

Twenty minutes later the men were busy installing the tarps, stretching, and lashing them to the lodge poles with the large zip ties. It was after five, when six tired men made their way into the great room and found their places, as the women finished placing supper on the table, and joined them for the evening meal.

The venison stew and hot roles never tasted so good, Ben thought to himself.

"There's nothing more rewarding than a good day's work and an awesome meal like this one to finish it off," he said, savoring his stew, before spooning it into his mouth. "Ladies you truly are a blessing!" With nods, and other affirmations, the men agreed heartily, with pleas for seconds, which the women graciously met.

After the evening meal, Josh gathered the men around one end of the table, to discuss the next day's plans. An hour later, they all trudged wearily to their beds, seeking the shared warmth of their spouses, and a well-deserved night's rest. Before retiring, Josh stoked the fire in the great room and checked the Haven's doors, making sure everything was secure for the night.

Pulling back the covers, Josh slid into bed as Ellen's warmth seeped into his tired aching back. Cradled in her arms, the day's events melted into a fitful sleep. Hours later, the hard-fought battle for sleep, gave way to the early morning rumble of a passing tremor, and by four in the morning, all hope for sleep was lost. As he and Ellen joined the others in the great room, a second tremor hit. It's violent shaking, left everyone clinging to the edge of the table, and sent Andy springing to the hearth to save the brewing pot of coffee from becoming an early morning casualty!

Cheers rose from everyone, as Andy grasped the handle and pushed the teetering pot of coffee away from the edge and back over the glowing coals.

"As much as I like to eat, I'm afraid I couldn't survive very long without coffee," Pastor said, looking longingly at the pot on the hearth.

"That must be why we brought up sixty-four three-pound cans," Ben said with a chuckle.

Picking up the large pot, Ellen began moving around the table filling cups, as Alice carried over the sugar, spoons, and Josh's favorite creamer.

"I know the Bible talks about fruit of the vine and living water as a beverage at the marriage supper, but I don't think coffee is on the list," Alice touted. "Maybe we should start praying for deliverance, before the Lord comes."

Pastor Bowens, who had just raised his cup to his lips, inhaled his first sip and began a coughing spell that brought Sarah to his aid, rubbing his back, and reassuring him that prayer does change things.

"Just pray, if it's the Lords will, coffee will be on the menu," she said, looking at Alice with a wink.

After a quick breakfast of oatmeal, and a lengthy discussion about the foray to the downed helicopter, Josh and Andy suited up, and donned their packs with the tools they had gathered the night before. With kisses, hugs, and final words of encouragement, they stepped through the rear entrance to the Havens into cold crisp air and lightly falling snow.

IT DIDN'T TAKE LONG FOR Josh and Andy to reach the far end of the escarpment trail and the woods. The mountain lion lay where they had left it, under a fresh blanket of snow. Disposing of the carcass, was the first item on their list, and the men wasted no time dragging the big cat through the trees to the crevasse on the far side of the forest where their firewood was stored.

Stepping back, the men picked up the back side of the tarp and rolled the carcass over the edge.

"This is one job I'm glad is out of the way," Andy said, folding up the tarp and stuffing it into his backpack.

"I'm just glad that it was the cat on that tarp, and not me," Josh mumbled, leaning over the edge and peering down at the mountain lion sixty feet below. "If it wasn't for Jessica's intervention, things could have been a lot different. Let's get away from here, before we end up joining our friend down below. This snowbank doesn't look too stable."

Turning, the men made their way back into the trees, as Josh led the way down the mountain side. Following their plan, they stayed just inside the eastern tree line, until the forest began to thin out. There they quickly made their way through the open areas, until they reached a small, forested area, overlooking the steep cascading mountain side. Pulling his father's field glasses out of his pack, he surveyed the mountainside to the southeast, looking for the telltale rotor blades of the downed helicopter, to get their bearings.

"I don't see a thing," Josh said, scanning back and forth across the ridge to the east. Lowering the glasses, he rubbed his eyes.

As Josh began to raise them again, Andy tapped him on the shoulder.

"Maybe you should check to the west," Andy said with a chuckle.

As Josh turned around, he stood in amazement, as he gazed at the rotor blades glistening in the early morning sunlight, less than fifty yards away. The helicopter lay buried in the snow and balanced precariously on the edge of a thousand-foot drop to the upper reaches of the Lemon Creek valley below them.

"Thank you, Jesus," Josh said, exhaling deeply.

The helicopter lay with its belly toward the men, and the tail hanging out over the snow-covered mountain side. The ravens were already gathering, but detecting the men's presence, they were content to circle overhead as Andy and Josh made their way around the nose of the helicopter and up to the open and twisted pilot's door.

Peering inside, Andy rolled back in disgust.

"Even though frozen, the exposed flesh of the bodies inside had been stripped to the bone by the ravens, leaving a macabre scene, which left both men shaken. Nonetheless, they were resolved to the task of entering and removing the bodies to salvage the surveillance components they hoped had remained undamaged. Josh and Andy moved away from the helicopter a short distance and compacted the snow in the bottom of a shallow snow cave, where they sat down to discuss what to do with the bodies, and how to secure the helicopter during their salvage operation.

"That lone tree there on the left should hold it down," Andy said. "We have enough rope to reach from the landing gear to the tree, a couple of times."

"Sounds good to me, but I think we should tie-off on the front and rear of the landing gear, and not at the same point. We need to get that done before we try to extricate the bodies. We'll take care of them the same way we did the lion, over the edge and let nature do the rest.

"Well," Andy sighed, the sooner we get going the sooner we can dispose of these bodies. "I counted four, before I turned away."

"That was my count too," Josh said, pulling on his gloves and getting to his feet. "Let's do this."

It didn't take long to secure the aircraft, and after doing so, Josh prepared to enter the helicopter.

Tying a scarf over his nose and mouth, he pulled down his snow goggles to cover his eyes, then he and Andy opened the side door behind the pilot. Carefully Josh climbed down into the helicopter and began to untangle the bodies. Breaking frozen limbs where necessary, he pushed the first militiaman up through the opening.

Carrying, and dragging the body until it was clear of the helicopter, Andy rolled it over the edge and down the nearly vertical mountainside. Returning, he began dragging the second body away from the helicopter and disposed of it, as he had the first.

"Andy," Josh called out. "I'm going to need some help with these other two. Can you climb in here with me?"

"Be right there Josh... just let me suit up."

Covering his nose and mouth as Josh had done, and pulling down his goggles, he carefully descended through the opening. Before moving the first two bodies, Josh had removed their side arms, radios and automatic weapons which now rested in a corner. The pilot and co-pilot were still strapped in their seats, and hanging toward the downside of the cockpit, frozen in the positions the crash had left them.

Josh drew his knife and cut the seat belts of the co-pilot first, and then those of the pilot. Breaking the limbs of the corpses, was a distasteful process, but necessary, to extract the bodies from the aircraft. Once they had ejected the last two bodies, they dragged them away from the helicopter and sent them to rest with their comrades at the headwaters of the Lemon Creek valley.

"Thank God, this part of our re-con is over," Andy said, removing his goggles and the bandanna from his face. "I don't think I could have stomached much more of this."

"I know what you mean, but this is only the beginning. We may have to send more of these men to face God's judgment by our own hands, before our Lemon Creek chronicle comes to an end."

Looking at his watch, Josh stood to his feet, and removed his backpack.

"Let's gather all the loose items together first," he said, firearms, ammunition, and radios, especially the radios. "I found a bag with two chargers; I think I can alter the frequencies so we can use them ourselves. There's also some cargo storage under the tail we need to check out as well."

"Sounds good to me," Andy said, making his way to the rear compartment door of the helicopter. If you don't mind Josh, "I'll check that out first, I'm not ready to climb back down into this bird quite yet.

"Not a problem brother, I'm not too excited about it myself. Hold on, and we'll check it out together, its only quarter past eight."

Joining Andy, they brushed away the snow covering the compartment door, finding it necessary to use a pry bar to gain access. Inside they found a complete medical kit, emergency provisions and a box of C4, complete with timers and detonators. By the time they had gathered all the lose salvage; the small snow cave was filled with more than they could carry back to the havens, and they still hadn't removed any of the hardware mounted on the helicopter.

Beginning with the bottom of the Helicopter, the men located two cameras, and what they assumed was a heat seeking sensor of some kind. These they removed with the tools they had brought, and placed them with the other salvaged items, leaving the wiring exposed.

"Andy, I'll climb back inside and see what's on the other end of these wires. Be prepared to loosen any nuts, if they hold what we need to the floor."

"Gotcha," Andy replied, as Josh made his way around to the door of the helicopter and climbed down inside. At the bottom and directly in front of one of the jump seats was a pedestal, bolted to the floor. Attached to the top, was a laptop computer, two joy sticks, and a small control panel.

"Andy, dig down into the snow, toward the back of this bird, there should be four bolts grouped together. We need to pull them," Josh shouted.

Scraping away the snow in the area Josh had directed, Andy exposed the four half inch bolts, and placed a box-end wrench over one of the nuts.

"Found them!" Start with the top left and move around clockwise," Andy shouted back.

Thirty minutes later, the pedestal lay in the snow cave on the tarp Andy had pulled from his backpack. The men sat at the entrance and discussed how to get their booty back to the Havens, or at least to Havens II.

"There's just no way we're we going to be able to pack all this back up to the trail," Josh said. "It sure would be nice if we had a sled about now, he mused out loud."

Just then Andy recalled a placard he had seen between the seats in the rear of the helicopter. "Do Not Inflate Inside of Aircraft."

"I can't give you a sled Josh, but would you settle for an inflatable raft?"

CHAPTER 22

Family time and reconciliation

J OSH WASTED NO TIME SCRAMBLING up onto the helicopter and quickly disappeared inside. Moments later the life raft appeared through the opening, followed by Josh, grinning from ear to ear. Laying it in the snow, he pulled the cord and stepped back as it inflated.

Dancing for joy, Josh fell backwards into the raft, and slid into Andy. Knocking him forward onto himself, they slid downhill a short distance, before hitting a small tree and filling the raft with snow. When the laughter subsided, Josh looked at his watch. Rolling out of the raft he gave Andy a hand up, and together they dumped the snow from the raft before, sliding it over to the snow cave.

"This is awesome little brother; we can fit everything in here. With me pulling and you pushing, we'll have things up to Havens II in no time."

"We'll need our rope," Andy said, but I think we should load up and move everything up the mountain, away from here before we untie it, just in case we've loosened something up."

"Agreed," Josh said, let's get started.

As the men were loading the raft with the things they had salvaged, Josh picked up the box of C4, and paused.

"Andy, before we untie the rope, let's set a small charge under this bird, enough to dislodge it from its perch and send it down to its previous occupants. I'll set the timer for fifteen minutes, to give us time to get a safe distance away. What do you think?"

"Sounds good to me, fifteen minutes should put us well up into the trees before it goes off. Everyone at the Havens is going to wonder what's happened though."

"I'm sure there will be some worry," Josh said. "But it will give them some incentive to pray, and we need God's continued covering every minute."

When they finished loading, Josh set the charge and the timer, while Andy untied the rope, and attached it to the raft. Pushing and pulling, the men made the best time they could, considering they were wearing snowshoes, and it was beginning to snow heavily. They had covered about seventy-five yards, when Josh threw the rope around a large tree, and tossed the other end to Andy, who quickly pulled himself up beside Josh. Clinging to the tree, they turned and watched as the charge went off. The helicopter disappeared in a ball of fire as the remaining fuel in its tanks exploded, then reappeared momentarily before dropping out of sight over the mountain side in an avalanche of snow.

"We're about a hundred and fifty yards from the escarpment trail," Josh said, looking at his watch. "It's twenty to twelve right now, with the Lords help we should be there by noon or a little after. I asked Pops last night, if he and the other men could meet us there, so we should have plenty of help."

"I can smell the coffee already," Andy said, turning to take up his position on the other end of the raft.

'Our part is almost over."

Patting Andy reassuringly on the shoulder, Josh took up the rope and began breaking trail up the mountain.

"That's what I appreciate so much about you and your leadership," Andy said, "You always plan ahead!"

Zigzagging through the woods made the going easier, but it took a little longer than Josh expected, to climb back up to the escarpment trail. None the less, when they arrived reinforcements were waiting, and Pastor Bowens was the first to spot them through the trees.

"Praise God you're both alright," he said. "When we heard the explosion, everyone fell to their knees and began to pray."

"What happened down there boy's," Ben asked, embracing the men, and then stepping back to allow them access into the shelter of the escarpment trail. As Andy stepped past, Josh pulled the raft up to the entrance and tied it off on a large stone.

"Again, the Lord's blessed us with unexpected provision; you wouldn't believe what we've brought back with us. The explosion was of our making, we found some C4, and used a little to send the helicopter down to the Lemon, so it's no longer on our doorstep," Josh said, brushing the snow off his shoulders.

"There will be plenty to tell around the table tonight, but for now, let's get this stuff packed and hauled down to the Havens, before I run out of steam."

Rich and Todd quickly began to transfer the hard-earned treasures Andy and Josh had salvaged, to the empty backpacks brought up with them from the Havens. Within a short time, everything was loaded and on the men's backs, except for the pedestal and its components, which Josh shouldered himself. Leaving the raft deflated and folded, inside the door of Havens II, everyone began trudging down the trail to the warmth and security of the Havens.

Snow was still falling heavily, as the men emerged from the escarpment trail and into the forest.

"Only a hundred yards to go and we're home," Todd said, hiking his pack higher up on his back. "I can't wait to take a look at these components Josh; we'll be a high-tech installation for sure now!"

"That was my hope, you can't fight what you can't see or hear. It will help even things up, so we can also be hunters as well, and not just the hunted. The fate of the Collective Militia is already sealed for eternity. We won't seek confrontation, but we will fight to protect ourselves, and those who call upon the Lord and haven't received the mark of the anti-Christ."

"Well said Josh," Pastor said, pausing to catch his breath. "Like Joshua against the Amalekites God will give us the victory as well. Physical death is nothing compared to what awaits those who sold their souls to Satan. If we must send some to their reward early, so be it!"

As the men rounded the last corner to the rear entrance of the Havens, Jessica stood like a sentry at the door, with Ben's rifle in hand, and a (why did it take you so long look on her face), which melted away as Andy stepped into view.

Carrying their packs into the center of the great room, the men sat them down between the couches, and made a beeline for the table, and six fresh cups of coffee. As Josh stepped up to the end of the table, Ellen rushed into his arms, and buried her face against his chest.

"I try so hard to be strong when you're gone, but sometimes the anxiety is just more than I can bear," she said, kissing him tenderly before returning to help the other women with preparations for the evening meal. Taking a seat at the end of the table, Josh bowed his head and with a deep sigh, began to pray.

"Father, I am so grateful for your provision, for your mercy, and covering over each of us. Thank you for watching over Andy and myself, for the blessings you have provided for us today, and bringing us all safely home. Be the center of our fellowship this evening we ask in Jesus name, Amen."

Pausing from their work, the women gathered around the table with their spouses, as Josh and Andy attempted to paint a verbal picture of the morning's events. They related their story as best they could, without going into the grizzly details of the deposition of the bodies, except that they were sent to the Lemon, along with the helicopter. The great room rang with laughter as Andy told how Josh's dancing for joy, had sent them both down the hill in the raft, to a shower of snow. Everyone rejoiced over the Lord's provision, thankful that the last remnants of the Militia's presence had been removed from their doorstep.

While the women returned to their preparations, Josh and the men retired to the center of the great room, to take a look at the items brought back from the helicopter. Todd could hardly wait to get his hands on the pedestal and get a closer look at the controls.

RICH AND TODD UNLOADED THE backpacks, spreading their contents out on the floor between the couches, as Ben and Andy examined, separated, and inventoried the items. Carefully, they placed the side arms, automatic weapons and munitions inside a pallet under the couch closest to the front entrance.

"I'll take the transmitter and detonators to my quarters," Josh said. "The C4 I'll store in a safe place I discovered, until it's needed."

"These little things are amazing," Ben said, holding one of the tiny detonators in his hand. "With the flip of a little switch, you can choose to time or remotely detonate a charge. "They keep making things smaller all the time, I'm impressed!"

"You'll be even more impressed, when I'm able to assemble this surveillance equipment," Todd said, affectionately caressing the control center Josh had so carefully carried back to the Havens. This will definitely give us a, one-up on the Militia, or anything else that comes too close to our front door. The cameras are multi-directional with night vision and remote controlled with these joysticks. This stuff is really high-tech."

Picking up one of the cameras, Josh held out the cable ends toward Todd.

"Besides a heavy duty twelve-volt transformer, how much of this cable will we need to get this stuff operational?

"About two hundred and fifty feet of the cable would do, along with a soldering tool, connecters, and a marginal list of other electrical supplies, but unfortunately we don't have any electronics store close by," Todd said derisively.

"Don't worry, I'll have them for you soon, I plan on going shopping early next week. Make me a list of what you'll need, and I'll have it airmailed," Josh said with a grin.

When everything had been carefully put away, the men sat and talked until Ellen and Jessica, pulled their husbands to their feet, and gave the dinner call. Jessica led the men to the table, with the exception of Pastor Don, who having smelled the fresh dinner rolls, was already seated.

"It's about time you fellas got here, your holding up the show," he said with a twinkle in his eye."

"Pastor Bowens," Sarah said sharply, of all people you should know that man shall not live by bread alone!"

"True my love," he said with a smile, but it sure does help. "We're supposed to eat our bread with a glad heart, and my heart will be full of joy when my stomach is full of your delicious rolls!"

Ruffling Pastor s hair, Sarah placed a large plate of rolls on the table in front of her husband with a smile, before returning with a bowl of venison stew, which Pastor savored while everyone took their seats.

Bowing his head, he prayed, and closed with a hearty Amen. Ellen and Jessica chuckled in response to the brevity of his prayer, and the size of his appetite.

"That's ok young ladies," Pastor responded, looking down the table over the top of his glasses. "I still have some chuckles of my own."

Jumping to Pastors defense, Ben interrupted.

"Shame on you two, you should have more respect. After all, Pastor is a man of the napkin... ah, I mean the cloth," he said, winking at Jessica and Ellen. The look on Pastor's face sent everyone into an uproar of laughter.

As Josh finished his dinner, Ellen stood, and leaning over, wrapped her arms around his shoulders, whispering in his ear. Receiving a nod of affirmation, she straightened up, and spoke softly to those still seated around the table.

"Josh needs some rest and a little TLC, so we're going to say goodnight, we'll see you in the morning."

Josh stood to his feet, with his arm around Ellen's shoulders, and with hers around his waist, the two swayed around the table and through the archway, to their little corner of the Havens.

With Ellen's help, Josh undressed and wearily made his way to the shower with a large towel around his waist. Moments later, Ellen could hear the soft moans as the warm water began to wash away the stressful events of the day. Joining her husband, she washed and massaged his back, before sending him off to their room and savoring a few more minutes of the shower's warmth for herself.

Stepping through the simple door of their quarters, and latching it behind her, Ellen could hear Josh's labored breathing in the darkness, as he lay sleeping. Sliding into bed beside him, she brushed the hair from his face, and kissed his forehead before pressing her cheek against his chest. As Josh moved restlessly in his sleep, reliving the events of the day, Ellen bit her lip and began to pray. She knew in her heart, there was more to the story than what he and Andy had shared at the table and prayed the Lord would cleanse his heart and mind, from the darkness of the day's events. As Josh's body began to relax and his breathing became less labored, Ellen drifted to sleep with Josh nestled securely in her arms.

It was three twenty in the morning when Josh slipped out of Ellen's arms, dressed, and made his way into the great room. He wasn't surprised to find Andy sitting at the table with his hands wrapped around a cup of coffee. Pouring a cup for himself, he slid onto the bench across from his best friend and gazed into his tear-filled eyes.

"It looks like yesterday impacted us both more than either of us were willing to admit. I didn't sleep much either," Josh said, taking a long sip of his coffee before setting his cup back down on the table.

"Those were people Josh, and I just dumped their bodies down the mountainside like they were garbage. I know it had to be done, I know what we did was the right thing to do, but I just feel sick inside."

"I know what you mean, but we have to keep a proper prospective Andy, and remember that they are the enemy, they made their choice.

Physical death is nothing compared to what awaits them when they stand before our God, and their righteous judge.

"You've been a Christian a lot longer than me," Josh said, reaching across the table and clasping Andy's hand. "But I think that in times like these, what we need to do is just pray, pray that the Lord will give us the strength, wisdom and understanding we need in His ability, and not our own."

"Your right, Andy said, placing his other hand on top of Josh's. "Let's pray."

Bowing his head with a shaky voice, Andy began to pray as his eyes again filled with tears. Weeping together in prayer, Andy and Josh sought God for inner strength, and the resolve to face the events and trials they knew would be coming. With their planned excursion back down to the banks, in search of cable and components for their security system, both men knew it was just a matter of time before the Collective Militia would realize they had not completely eradicated the Christian resistance, as they had thought.

Once Sarah and Alice were up, and banging around as they prepared for breakfast, it didn't take long before the entire company was gathered around the table, coffee in hand, and steeped in deep conversation. It was almost eleven, when Pastor Bowens finally gathered everyone together around the couches for their Sunday worship service. Once again, the great room resounded with choired voices, as twelve precious souls found renewed strength in pressing closer to their Lord and Savior.

CHAPTER 23

Staying ahead of the storm

F INISHING THEIR SUNDAY AFTERNOON MEAL, the company dispersed throughout the Havens, some to relax on the couches in quiet conversation, and others to find much needed rest in the comfort of their quarters. As usual, the men sat huddled around the table, nursing a fresh pot of coffee and listening to the scanner for an updated NOAA weather report.

Josh, who sat pensively rotating his cup in a counterclockwise motion, listened quietly as the men conversed. When the weather report for Juneau came on the air, he slowly raised his cup, and took a sip. The men listened intently as the national weather service painted a dramatic picture of the worst snowstorm to hit the Juneau area since the winter of 2012.

"Coupled with winds out of the northeast in excess of eighty miles an hour, this storm could become the worst recorded in panhandle history," the announcer concluded.

A profound silence filled the great room.

"That was some winter we had in twelve," Pastor Bowens said, taking a long sip of coffee. "Remember Ben, how long it took you, and the boys to dig me and Sarah out? We had eighteen feet of snow that year and twelve-to-fourteen-foot drifts almost everywhere else."

"How could I forget, that was the year the world was supposed to end, along with the Mayan calendar. Between that storm and the National elections, it did become, the "beginning of the end" for our nation. The results of that election didn't change anything; the damage was already done and irreversible. The stupidity of the next four years though, turned our country into a socialist republic with a woman serving as a National Governor for the Anti-Christ.

Leaning into the table, Andy looked around at the other men and then focused on Pastor Bowens and Ben.

"Think about it for a minute, from the year our nation became the United Socialist States of America in 2016, the church has faced three years of unprecedented trials, persecution, and the martyrdom of millions of saints around the world. Didn't I read in Daniel and Revelation that the Anti-Christ would make war against the Saints of God for three and a half years, and overcome them, but God would give them the ultimate victory?"

"Yes, you did Son."

Bowing his head, Ben took a deep breath.

"Jesus said no man would know the day or the hour of his coming, but he did tell us that those who were truly looking for Him, would know the season, and that season is truly upon us. Jesus said in Luke 21:28, "When these things begin to take place, stand up and lift up your heads, because your redemption is drawing near."

Setting down his coffee cup, Josh spoke for the first time since the men had gathered around the table.

"Judging from the report we just heard, we have our work cut out for us. We have at the outside, only seven days to bring everything together, before this storm arrives. Rich and Todd, would you gather everyone together around the table for a meeting. We have plans to make."

As the men went to gather the others, Josh pulled out a note pad and pen from his breast pocket and began making a list of priorities. When the others took their seats, Ellen and Jessica poured a fresh round of coffee before taking their places at the table. Josh then cleared his throat and began with a word of prayer. After closing, he looked up at his father as he spoke.

"I apologize for interrupting your conversation earlier, but as the announcer began to expound on the pending weather forecast, all I could picture in my mind was our lack of preparation, and the pending trip to the banks Andy and I have been planning."

"So you're still going through with it," Ben said, looking at Josh with an uneasy trembling in his voice.

"Yes," said Josh, because of the pending weather, we'll be leaving early Tuesday morning, and with God's help, be back two days before the storm is due to arrive. We have to think ahead of the storm and prepare for the worst. I have a plan, but most of the work will have to be done by all of you, while Andy and I are gone."

"Once the storm arrives, we'll be sequestered for a long time, so we will have to work hard and fast to get everything done.

"If we can expect as much snow if not more than what fell in 2012, on top of what we've already accrued, we need to build a tunnel between here and the escarpment trail. If we can't, we'll have no way to secure supplies from Havens II or get firewood."

"The snows already over five feet deep now," Rich said. "How do we create a roof over the open trail between here and the escarpment that would support so much snow and not cave in?"

Josh stood in order to have room to move, as he gestured throughout his explanation.

"We'll use tree limbs," he said, they already have a natural downward curve, and the heavily needled branches will catch the falling snow, allowing it to build up until it forms a covering. If we lace the branches together, embedding the butts of the branches alternately in the snowbank on each side of the trail, it will support the new snow layer overhead. The freezing weather and snowdrifts will secure our trail well into the spring."

"Where will we get all these branches," Todd said, looking as puzzled as Rich had been before Josh's explanation.

"We'll cut them from the forest at the other end of the escarpment trail, while we're moving our firewood into the protection of the trail, back toward Havens II."

Ben and Pastor Bowen's mouths dropped open with Josh's statement.

"There's more than six cords of wood stacked under those limbs, we couldn't possibly move it all into the trail, even if we had room and fourteen days instead of seven," Pastor blurted out.

"Who told me, we can do all things through Him who strengthens us," Josh responded, looking down the table, at eleven wide-eyed faces. "With Todd and Rich's help, Andy and I will have the trail covered before dark tomorrow night! If anyone else wants to help, we can do a better job and get it done even faster. The other items on this list, you will have to complete over the next five days, while Andy and I are gone."

"What else do we need to take care of besides moving firewood honey?" Ellen asked, reaching out and placing her hand over his in a gesture of support.

Taking a deep breath, Josh slowly exhaled and continued.

"Aside from moving as much wood as possible under the escarpment, the antechamber needs to be filled with as much firewood as it will hold. You'll need to make sure there is enough food and supplies brought down from Havens II, to last a minimum of two weeks. Bring extra blankets, clothing, and personal items. Pray for wisdom and the Holy Spirit's guidance in your choices. Todd, I want that list of supplies you need to utilize the equipment we salvaged before tomorrow night. I'll do everything possible to fill it and get it all back here to you."

"I'll have it for you in the morning," Todd said, with a ring of anticipation in his voice. He could hardly wait to see all that high tech equipment in action.

Clearing his throat, Ben turned to Alice who handed him a box which he placed on the table in front of Josh.

"Son, I knew you were determined to make this trip back down to the banks. I took the liberty of working on these radios you brought back from the helicopter. They are re-programmed. Prayerfully there set on a frequency much lower than the Militia, or anyone else would consider monitoring. None the less, we'll work out a few simple code names and words over coffee in the morning, just in case."

For the first time since the weather report, Josh's face shone with an ear-to-ear grin, which suddenly raised everyone's spirits.

"Is there anything else we need to be aware of before we call it a day? It sounds like you're going to work us all pretty hard tomorrow, and I need all the rest I can get," Ben said, with a chuckle.

"No, I think that's enough for tonight, but if you wouldn't mind Andy, I could use your help repacking my chute. Jumping isn't a problem for me, but the landing is a real bummer if the chute doesn't open properly."

Andy stood and patted Josh on the back.

"Not a problem," he said. I just pray the other chute you packed down at the shop, works equally as well.

IT WAS JUST A LITTLE past three in the morning, when Josh walked into the great room, poured a cup of coffee, and sat down at the table across from his father. Ben was busy working on a list of code words, followed by a short meaning for each one. Josh sipped his coffee, watching intently until Andy joined them, and Ben paused from his ciphering.

"I'm assuming you men are packed and ready to head out at first light. I've been watching the two of you pack and repack for days now. I figured I should ask just in case there was something I could help you with other than the radios," Ben said, looking over the top of his glasses, without raising his head.

Finishing, he laid down his pen. Sitting up straight, he looked across the table.

"Any chance one of you gentlemen could refill my cup. I think I spent too much time writing instead of drinking my coffee, and I like mine hot."

"Not a problem Pops," Josh said, springing to his feet. "I need a warm-up as well."

Grabbing the pot, he filled his father's cup, topping off his and Andy's before returning it to the fire and taking his seat.

"Looks like you've finished the code words," he said, as he poured the second pack of vanilla creamer into his coffee, and stirred it in.

"The codes I've put together will be enough to get us by for now. As we discussed yesterday Josh, your code name is Sun 1, yours Andy is Moon 2, and we here at the Havens will be Stars.

I've written the code words and their meanings on these two small pieces of paper, one for each of you."

Ben slowly pushed one in front of Andy, and then Josh.

"I'm not going to tell you, don't get caught with these on you, just don't get caught at all! I found two more batteries in the things you brought from the helicopter and charged them. You should be ok, if we keep our transmissions short."

Reaching down beside him, Ben produced the batteries, setting them on the table in front of Josh.

"Maybe you can commandeer another charger while you're down below, and recharge before heading home. I know this is important and necessary, but I still wish there was some other way. I pray the Lord will give me the confidence Ellen has, she's a tower of strength for all of us," Ben said, bowing his head."

Reaching across the table Josh took his father's hand, as Andy stood and placed his on-Ben's shoulders.

"Let's pray Pops. Let's pray for the wisdom, strength, and boldness we'll all need for the next few days. When this is all over, we'll really be able to celebrate Thanksgiving with rejoicing."

While the three men were praying, the rest of the company joined them, entering the great room until the circle of twelve was complete. As Josh finished praying, an air of peace settled upon, everyone and the tears turned to laughter as the women began preparing an early breakfast before sending Josh and Andy on their way.

As they gathered around the table, Ellen and Jessica clung to their husbands, savoring every moment with the realization that the next four days of separation would be a true test of their faith and resolve, as they placed their men in God's hands.

"Do you still plan to take the high road across the face of Thunder Mountain," Pastor Bowens said. "It seems to me that way would be more difficult than taking the lower trail through the valley." "Actually, it will be easier going," Josh said. "We've got a heavy crust on the snowpack, and very little brush. We'll also have better cover by staying just inside the tree line. With our snowshoes, we should be able to make good time. I'm figuring Andy and I should be able to dig our way under the snow-covered boughs of nice fir below Heintzelman Ridge before dark for shelter and slip into the store just after dark tomorrow evening. We'll have to hole up under the old bridge on Lemon Creek, up by the quarry until dark, once we make it to the bottom."

"From there on, we'll have to play it by ear and shoot from the hip," Andy said with a grin.

"Praise the Lord, its pancake time," Pastor Don said, as Alice and Sarah stepped up to the table with two large platters.

Linda and Jan followed close behind, filling everyone's cup with fresh coffee. When everyone had their fill of homemade jam and pancakes, Josh and Andy drank down the last of their coffee before getting to their feet, and making their way to the antechamber, followed close behind by Ellen and Jessica.

As the men suited up in their white camo's, Jessica and Ellen helped them with their packs, side arms and automatic weapons. Placing Josh's parachute at the top of his half-filled backpack Ellen carefully cinched it down.

With hugs, kisses and tearful words of encouragement, Josh and Andy stepped through the door, and into a cold blustery morning. Bending low, the men began making their way through the newly made tunnel of tree boughs the company had laid with much effort the day before. Josh and Andy were elated, when they reached the escarpment trail, where they could stand up straight again, and readjust their packs before making their way to the other end of the escarpment.

With much trepidation, Josh and Andy donned their snowshoes, and stepped out of the shelter of the escarpment trail. Following the same trail, they had taken a few days before, they made their way to the crevasse where they had disposed of the mountain lion carcass. Making their way uphill along its edge, they made their way around its upper end, and back down to the tree line on the opposite side. Staying just inside the trees, they were able to make reasonably good time, despite the difficult terrain, and had covered almost two miles by the time they stopped for a breather.

"It's just a little past eleven," Josh said, looking at his watch. "We should be able to make it to the forested area just above what's left of the correctional facility by dark at the rate we're going."

"Not if I don't get a little something to eat and a chance to catch my breath," Andy moaned.

Making his way over to a small granite outcropping, Josh dropped off his backpack, and stomped down a small area of snow where he and Andy could sit down with their backs against the rock.

"You're right he said, there's no need to push it. Ellen packed us a dozen pieces of venison sausage wrapped up in this morning's leftover pancakes. That should take the edge off till this evening, when we can heat up a couple of MRE's."

Taking off his gloves, Andy blew into his cupped hands and rubbed them together, anticipating wrapping them around at least six of those rolled up pancakes. Carefully, Josh pulled out their late morning fare, and unwrapped the blessing Ellen had prepared for them. Uttering a short prayer, Andy and Josh quickly devoured every morsel, before stuffing the wrapper back into Josh's backpack.

CHAPTER 24

Down to the Gastineau banks

ALTHOUGH THE DISTANCE TO THEIR destination was a little more than five miles, the rugged terrain across the upper regions of Thunder Mountain to the area below Heintzlemann Ridge, was compounded by the deep snow. Nearly exhausted, from the ordeal, Andy and Josh were able to get within a quarter mile of their halfway point, as light began to fade. Pausing to catch his breath, Josh turned to Andy, clearing his throat.

"How you are doing little brother, think you've got enough strength to break trail for the next few hundred yards?"

"I think so Josh, but it would sure help to take five before I step up to the front."

"You got it," Josh said, falling back into a snowbank.

It was more like ten minutes before Andy stood and stepped past Josh, turning to give him a hand up, before continuing. Their destination was a dense stand of timber a little over three hundred yards away, and they had to reach it before dark. They didn't want to take any chances using a flashlight so close to town. To make matters worse, they would have to cover this last distance in the open, as they traversed a well-known slide area to gain the shelter of the trees on the other side.

Andy paused before stepping into the open and bowed his head.

"Father, we're entering a very dangerous area, we pray for your guidance and protection. Make us invisible to wandering eyes and keep the snow firm beneath our feet, in Jesus' name."

"Amen," Josh said," Let's get this last stretch behind us, I could really use something to eat and a night's rest."

"Step lightly," Andy responded, "We'll be across in no-time."

Hiking his pack higher up on his back, Andy moved out. Josh followed step for step, aware of the ever-present danger that the snowpack could slide from under them at any moment. It took them almost twenty minutes to cross the open slide area and enter the dense cover of the trees.

As Josh began looking around in the fading light for the largest fir, suitable for their shelter, the crack and ominous sound of shifting and sliding snow echoed off the cliffs of Heintzlemann ridges eastern end, above them. Josh and Andy instinctively dove headfirst into the snow behind a large fir, kicking off their snowshoes and digging franticly under its snow-covered boughs as a mountainous wall of snow and ice poured over them through the trees, and continued down the mountainside. Josh was the first to reach the trunk of the tree, followed by Andy, spitting, and sputtering as he dug the snow from around his face and out of the hood of his parka.

"Thank you, Jesus," were the first words Andy heard, as Josh rolled over on his back, and dug into a breast pocket for a flashlight. Turning it on, the light revealed Andy half buried in the snow, with only his head, shoulders and arms protruding into the small cave created by the snow-bent lower branches of the tree.

"That was close, are you alright Andy?"

"I will be as soon as you help dig me out."

Drawing his knees up against his chest, Josh spun around. Lying on his stomach, he slid over to Andy, handed him the flashlight, and began digging the snow out from above him, until he could drag himself forward into the tiny donut shaped cavern. It was Andy this time who mouthed the words, "thank you Jesus", as the men surveyed their accommodation for the night.

The snow-free space under the tree was about eight feet across, with a two-foot diameter trunk supporting the snow roof, three feet above their heads. The ground beneath the tree, was covered with a dense layer of dry needles, and enough dead branches to keep a small fire going through the night.

While Andy dug a large hole in the snow wall on the upper side of the tree, Josh lay on his back, kicking and breaking off the branches, which protruded into their retreat. Breaking the smaller branches off a large dry limb, Josh worked his way up to where Andy had opened up a three-by-three-foot area in the snow wall, and about two feet deep. Pushing the branch up through the snow roof above the opening, he produced a chimney when the branch protruded through to the outside.

With the same branch, he produced tunnels on each side sloping away from where they would build their small fire, for the melting snow to run away from their shelter. The final touch was to produce another opening on the downhill side, for ventilation. Removing their packs and firearms, Josh began building a small fire with dry needles and some of the broken branches, while Andy spread out the remaining needles to insulate the cold, hard earth beneath them.

Un-zipping his backpack, Andy produced two MRE's, a small pot, and two tin cups. Packing the pot full of snow, he placed it in the middle of the small fire and leaned the MRE's against the burning prices of wood.

"Won't be long, and supper will be ready," he grinned. Then, reaching into a breast pocket, Andy produced two packets of vanilla creamer, which he tossed to Josh.

"Only have enough of Pop's instant coffee for two cups each, so enjoy. I figured one for tonight and one for morning!"

Tears filled Josh's eyes as he investigated the grinning face of the best friend he had ever known.

"Andy, you have always been, and will forever be my brother," he said, reaching out and grasping Andy's hand. "I love you Man."

"Whoa, where did I hear that before," Andy said, with a puzzled look on his face? "Oh, I know, it was on a Budweiser commercial."

Leaning forward, Josh pushed Andy into the wall of snow behind him.

"You'll always be my Bro, but you're still the biggest stinker I've ever known," he said, jabbing Andy in the ribs before rolling on his back, and laughing tearfully.

When their food was ready, the men ate their warmed MRE's in silence. Periodically Josh stoked the small heat source between them. Savoring each sip of their coffee, they discussed the next day's events, and then made a brief radio communication with the stars before trying to get some much-needed rest.

As EVERYONE SAT AROUND THE table in the Havens, waiting for a transmission from Andy and Josh, the radio suddenly filled the great room with Josh's voice for a moment, and then went silent.

"Sun One to Stars, Stars, do you copy?

Ben almost dropped the hand-held radio, as he raised it to respond.

"Copy Sun One, go ahead," he said, with a quiver in his voice.

"Sun One, Moon Two ... snug, stop 1...hail, stop 2 ... heart, encompass."

"Josh says that they are safe and secure for the night above Lemon Creek. They will contact us tomorrow night, and they send their love to everyone," Ben said with a smile.

Jessica and Ellen hugged each other tearfully, as everyone around the table sighed in unison, joyful that the men were safe and secure, at least for the time being. Moments later, the words "copy, stars out", broke the silence, as Andy and Josh stoked the fire and settled in for the night.

Josh and Andy awoke abruptly to a flurry of ice crystals filling the air around them. The wash from the rotor blades of the helicopter passing above, forced snow through a large hole above their heads. The chimney above their small fire had grown to a foot in diameter through the night.

Both men quickly slid to the downhill side of their sheltering tree and waited until the sound of the helicopter faded away to the west before venturing forward, and peering up through their, now enlarged chimney.

Pulling the hood of his parka up over his head, Josh forced his way up through the opening, and stood to his feet. Digging up through the snow on the downhill side of the tree, Andy did the same, standing in amazement as he surveyed the devastation caused by the avalanche the night before. Pulling themselves inside, they met at the upper side of the tree trunk.

"God's hand was truly covering us last night," Andy said, motioning Josh to go look from the downhill side of the tree. "All the snow that once covered this mountain side, along with everything else, looks like it's now in the Lemon."

Josh scrambled over to the opening, and standing, inhaled deeply as he took in the overwhelming sight that unfolded in front of him. Thousands of trees lay broken and splintered, littering the rest of the Forrest, which lay bent to the south beneath the weight of compacted snow and ice. Getting his bearings, he slowly withdrew into the shelter of their retreat, and rejoined Andy.

"What do you say we get another fire going, I sure could use that other cup of coffee to go with this creamer," he said, pulling the small packet out of his pocket.

"I'm with you on that, and we can use it to wash down some of this." Reaching into his backpack, Andy pulled out a small bulging paper bag, and unrolling the top, handed it to Josh.

"It's from Pastor Bowen's private stock. He said the only other one he's shared it with was Pops, when they were down on the Lemon a while back."

Waving it under his nose, Josh licked his lips as a broad smile formed across his face. It didn't take long with the dry needles and branches, to get a hot smokeless fire going and the heaping pot of snow securely planted on its glowing embers. When the water was boiling, Andy quickly filled their tin cups, and added the instant coffee. Using a twig, Josh carefully stirred in his vanilla creamer and savored the aroma as he raised his cup, to Andy with a nod.

The men took their time, eating their fill of the jerked meat, and slowly drank their coffee, savoring every sip. It wasn't until snowflakes began falling through the now gaping hole above them, that they considered the time.

Looking at his watch, Josh took another bite of jerky and washed it down with the last of his coffee, standing to his feet he looked up the mountainside.

"Andy, it's almost nine thirty. The snows starting to come down hard, and I don't think that helicopter will be coming back. They were probably just surveying the area before weather set in. I think we had better saddle up and begin making our way down to the Lemon."

"Sounds good to me," Andy responded. "But I think we should consider holing up on the south side of the Lemon in the trees. It looked to me like the bridge and most of the creek is buried under the avalanche."

Clearing away more snow, Josh and Andy donned their backpacks, and climbed out from under the shelter of the tree boughs. The snowshoes they had lost when they dove into the snow before the slide, were swept away, but the avalanche had brought a blessing. The snow was now not as deep, and what there was had been compacted by debris. Nonetheless, the trek down the mountainside in the heavily falling snow, and endless obstacles, took more than four and a half hours.

IT WAS WELL PAST TWO in the afternoon when the men found themselves standing on the hillside, just above where the old quarry bridge should have been. Instead, they looked down upon a hundred-yard-wide snow and ice dam, which had buried the bridge, Josh estimated, some twenty feet below where they stood. Water was already beginning to flow over the leading edge.

"We have got to get across before the water breaches the dam, or we won't have a chance of getting to the other side," Josh said, grabbing

Andy's coat sleeve, and dragging him down onto the dam, littered and barricaded with debris.

"Make for the other side, and don't look back," Josh shouted, searching desperately for what he thought would be the easiest route. Without hesitation, Andy leaped forward into the falling snow and disappeared around a mound of snow and tree limbs. Josh chose a path to the left, where he could see the rising water, and attempt to stay ahead of its leading edge as it flowed across the dam.

Josh's heart sank as the water ahead of him, flowed under a sloping tree trunk and quickly disappeared over the trailing edge of the dam, causing the snow and ice to collapse, and creating an instant chasm between him and the safety of the other side. Running up the trunk of the leaning log, Josh reached the end and leaped with all the strength left in his aching muscles.

He landed hard on the other side, but could feel the ice and compacted snow, giving way' as he dug franticly to pull himself away from the crumbling snowbank beneath him. As Josh made a last desperate attempt to save himself, Andy reached out, dragging him to safety. With Andy's arm around Joshes waist, the two men staggered to the south bank of the Lemon. There they lay in the falling snow until they had rested long enough to make their way to the safety and shelter of the trees.

"Are you okay Josh. You didn't injure yourself, did you? I haven't seen a broad jump like that since we were doing track in high school. You'd have been home free if the snowbank hadn't fallen away just before you landed."

"Thanks for being there Andy. I thought I was going to beat you to heaven for sure."

"Not a chance Brother. We're going together."

"If we don't get out of the open, we may get there together sooner than we want to," Josh said, as he stood and pulled Andy to his feet.

Facing the five-foot wall of snow that covered the road, once again their hearts sank as they considered the time and effort it was going to take to break trail into Lemon Creek for the next mile and a half.

Pushing their way through the snow to the base of the hill, they took turns breaking trail, as they worked their way up the hill. It took half an hour to make their way around the edge of the hill, to where they could look down the old haul road, to where it ran into the end of Anka Street.

As Josh and Andy stood catching their breath, headlights suddenly appeared, rounding the corner off Ralphs way, and moving steadily in their direction. Both vehicles carried flashing yellow lights, but it wasn't until they were halfway to the old bridge in the dim light that they were able to make out the dump truck with a bull nose plow, and the grader following behind as they cleared the road.

"Something is up," Andy said, settling back in the snow, as he and Josh watched their approach.

"Thank you, Lord," this could be our ticked home. Josh quickly pulled out the radio and turned the small knob to scan.

Within minutes, they were listening to chatter between the drivers of the equipment clearing the road.

"Hey Gus, what're we cleaning this old haul road for again?"

"What you got in your ears Mac, snow? The big boys are going to blow up an ice dam at the old bridge in the morning, and they need it open. Just follow me in and out and push that snow out of the way."

Josh immediately began breaking trail down the hill toward the old road, with Andy following close behind. Reaching the bank above the edge of the road, they waited and watched as the equipment passed below them.

"Look, on the back of the grader, those tines are only a couple of feet off the ground. When they come back, past our position, we'll climb up on the tines and get a free ride into town, at least to the end of Anka Street, and leave no sign of our presence."

Andy's response was a pat on the back and an arm around Josh's shoulders, as the men squatted, with only their heads visible above the snow. With the radio turned down low, and still set on scan, they waited and watched as the equipment rounded the corner to the old bridge, pushed out enough snow to turn around, and headed back toward them.

"Ok Mac," slow and steady on the way back. We get overtime credits for this job, so let's do it right. We'll return to the yard going down Anka street."

Josh turned to Andy, grinning from ear to ear, to find him wearing the same expression.

Huddled together with his arm still draped across Josh's back, Andy bowed his head.

"Father, we serve you with such joy, amazed at how you continually fulfill your promise to never leave us or forsake us. Your loving protection and provision is evident in every circumstance, and we are so thankful. Continue to watch over us and give us victory over our enemies we pray in Jesus' name, Amen."

"Get ready Andy, here they come. I'll break us out to the road. We'll have to run a little, so keep it close."

Josh waited until the light from the floods on the grader had passed their position, and quickly slid down the bank, with Andy on his heels. Both men hit the road running. Slipping on the freshly ploughed road, Andy stumbled, but quickly regained his footing. Josh reached the grader first.

Grasping the framework supporting the rip tines, and with some effort he pulled himself up to a sitting position to one side. As Andy caught up and got a hold on the tines, Josh reached out and clasping Andy's other hand, pulled him aboard.

The men sat in silence and enjoyed the ride into town. As the grader passed the end of Ralph's Way, Josh gave Andy a nudge.

"As soon as we come up in front of the shop, we'll jump off. Stay in the road until their far enough away for us to move out."

The men were surprised to find the space between the shop and the sign pro building shoveled out. The front of the shop stood covered with piled and drifted snow, well above the roofline, leaving only the upper portion of the east end exposed.

"Andy let's go around next to the Pro building, and then cut back behind the shop. That way we can dig and push our way to the door without leaving a visible trail from the road."

"I really pray that what we came for is still here," Andy quipped, as they both jumped over the new ridge of snow left by the grader and made their way toward the side door of the Pro building.

Stepping past the end of the building, they made a left, and began breaking their way through chest high snow, around to where Josh guessed the door to be. Snow sliding off the roof, had left the rear of the store looking much like the front, and forcing the men to literally tunnel their way to the back of the store.

"I know it's here somewhere," Josh said jokingly, tearing snow away from the back of the building until he found the edge of the door casing.

Kicking and pushing the snow behind them, Josh and Andy cleared away as much of the snow as they could from the door. Carefully Josh slid the key into the lock.

CHAPTER 25

A perilous journey home

INSTINCTIVELY, JOSH THREW THE SWITCH as he stepped through the door, and to his amazement, the light came on. Walking straight to the security monitor, he turned it on. He and Andy danced arm in arm as four windows appeared on the screen, and the images indicated the system was intact.

"As much as I would like to just stretch out and take a load off, we had better take care of business before we do anything else. Andy, you look around the front, I'll check the garage and then we'll start pulling what we need."

With a nod, Andy was through the door into the front of the store. As Josh turned and stepped through the door to the second storeroom, everything looked just as he and the women had left it fifteen days earlier.

Josh suddenly stood overwhelmed by the realization that the lifetime of events he had recently lived through, had been condensed into only fifteen days. It was as if time itself had stood still, while he dwelt in the upper reaches of the Lemon valley. Andy's voice, and the sound of his footsteps in the other room, snapped Josh back into the reality of the moment. Turning, he quickly stepped back into the main storeroom and closed the door.

"Everything for the most part, looks just like you and I left it before heading up the Lemon," Andy said. "By the way, where's that other glider chute? If it's going to be my way home, I want to keep it close and safe."

"Top shelf, against the back wall," Josh responded. "Trust me, Andy. I packed it as good as you packed mine. The rest will be up to the Lord."

Walking over to the shelf by the back door, Josh took down a toolbox. From it, he pulled a couple of needle nose pliers and flat bit screwdrivers. Handing one of each to Andy, Josh turned and disconnected the cables from the security monitor.

"Andy, you take down the two cameras in the store front, and I'll get the one in here and over the back door. When you have the cameras, release the clips holding the cables and we'll pull them through and coil them up."

"I'm on it brother, no problem."

As Andy disappeared back through the door, Josh set about pulling down the camera in the second storeroom, and then moved outside, stepping through the back door, he dug out the snow above the door and remove the camera there. Finished, he closed the door. Removing the clips holding the cables he pulled them into the main storeroom.

"Here are the cameras from the store side, the cables are free, when you're ready to pull them."

"Awesome, go ahead and pull the cables, coil them and lay them in the bottom of this larger backpack, I'm going to pick us out a couple of semi-automatics, just in case. The Taurus Judge is great, but slow in a pinch."

As Josh stepped through the door into the store, Andy began pulling the cables and coiling them. He had just placed the last one in the backpack, when the back door flew open, and a young girl rushed in with a small bundle in her arms.

"Help me, help me please, their right behind me, please," she screamed.

Before Andy could react, two militiamen rushed through the door, one grabbing the young girl, and the other pushing Andy up against the wall, with an automatic rifle barrel under his chin.

Josh, who was just about to walk into the room quickly, stepped back out of sight. Moments later, a third man entered from outside.

"Commander Jenson, we have two in custody," shouted the militiaman, pressing Andy to the wall.

Looking at the young girl, the commander spoke harshly.

"If it wasn't for the baby, I'd put you down right here and now, but that will have to wait for a while." "And you, I've seen you somewhere before. Yes, in Juneau, at that restaurant. You had a friend with you, where is he?"

Andy quickly glanced toward the door leading out to the garage, and then downward at the floor. Drawing his revolver, the commander cautiously made his way toward the door, and readying himself, kicked it open. At that moment, Josh stepped through the door from the storefront, taking out the militiaman holding Andy with two quick shots, and the guard holding the young girl with a round to the chest. As Andy grabbed the girl, pulling her to the floor, the commander spun around and fired two rounds, one hitting the door casing, the other grazing Josh's left shoulder. Without hesitation, he returned fire, hitting the commander once in the arm and twice in the chest, sending him reeling into the garage.

"Get her into the other room," Josh shouted. Grabbing an automatic rifle off the floor, he rushed through the back door and into the cold night air, anticipating more militiamen, but to his surprise, there were none. In the shoveled area between the buildings, a grey double cab pickup with the Collective emblem on its hood and doors, sat idling, everything else was silent.

"Oh, thank you Jesus," Josh breathed out loud.

Turning, he quickly made his way back into the store, calling for Andy and the young girl to come out. Grabbing a large towel, he wrapped it around the monitor, and with some dishtowels, wrapped the cameras, stuffing everything into the backpack. Looking up, Josh began throwing orders like a drill sergeant.

"Andy, get this young lady a coat from out front, and a warm blanket for the baby. Fill your pack back up with anything we can eat without heating, and while you're at it, pull four boxes of 45's. I'm going to take our new charges out to a warm truck, with the equipment, and don't forget your chute," he called out. Taking the girl by the arm he led her out the door.

Andy's mind was still reeling, as he climbed into the front passenger seat of the truck. Josh had already backed into the street, and was pulling forward, before Andy got the door closed.

"Whoa Josh, let me catch up a minute. Where are we going?"

Without a word, Josh slowed down as they approached the corner in Anka street where the recycling yard used to be. There he stopped at the gates, in the eight-foot-high fence which now blocked the end of Anka street at the corner. Without hesitation, the two Militia security guards at the gates unlocked and swung them open, coming to attention as Josh drove through. Turning into the lot, and driving to the far end, he stopped for a few minutes, watching intently in the rearview mirrors, as he spoke.

"That was so close," Josh said, resting his forehead on the steering wheel. Laying his pistol in the seat, he began to shake.

"I just killed three men, "he muttered," and I don't feel any remorse, "I'm just glad we escaped."

A trembling voice from the back seat suddenly caught both men's attention.

"Mmm … my name is Jamie," she said softly, "and this is my daughter Missy. Thank you for saving us."

"Thank the Lord, Jamie; He's the One who saves. "We're just here to serve Him," Andy said, wiping the nervous sweat from his face.

"You're Christians?"

"Yes," Josh responded. "Those men were enemies of God, who sold their souls to the Anti-Christ. We'll explain later. Right now, we need to pick up some supplies and find a way home."

As Andy turned to face him, Josh continued.

"Andy, out on Old Dairy Road, there are two stores, just this side of Crest Street. One is an audio and video store and the other is a Radio Shack. They will be our last stops, before we look for a plane, just like we discussed last night, only sooner than we expected."

"Okay Big Brother, let's head for Yandunkin Drive before any more of these devils advocates show up."

Josh pulled down a little used stretch of paved road, which came out on the Glacier highway. Turning right, they began making their way toward the airport, crossed Egan Drive and made their way onto Old Dairy.

As they neared their first stop, four squads, were dispatched from the Airport, in search of the men Josh and Andy had left on the floor of the Shop.

"Commander Jensen and his men were last reported pursuing a suspect with a small child, in the Anka street area of Lemon Creek. Proceed with caution and keep an eye out for squad ninety-one," the dispatcher concluded."

Turning into the parking lot, Josh drove to the rear of the store, parked, and waited until four squads passed by with lights and sirens making their way to Egan drive. Lights were still on in the back of the store, and as Josh stepped out of the truck, a young man backed out the door with a trash bag in each hand. Stepping forward he placed the muzzle of the forty-five against the young man' neck, speaking quietly and deliberately.

"I would like to borrow some supplies from the store, if you'll help me gather them together, it won't be necessary to use this pistol, do we have an understanding?"

The man nodded his head nervously, and pulled the door open, as Josh followed him into the store with his hand on the man's shoulder.

Reaching into his breast pocket, Josh pulled out the list Todd had given him, and handed it to the young man, reaching around his left side.

"Do you have these items in this store?" he said, spinning the man around so he could see his face.

Both men stepped back, in surprise!

"Josh, Josh Huskins?" I thought they gave you a permanent hair cut with all the other religious fanatics. Should have taken the mark Man. It doesn't hurt near as much as the ax."

"Zip-it, Pete, and fill that list, before I put you down, and fill it myself. I never had time for your low life antics in school, and I certainly don't now!"

Holding his hands up palms out, Pete nodded his head. Turning and picking up a shopping basket, he walked through the store, picking out the items on the list. Pulling down two, one-hundred-foot rolls of video cable, and placing them in the basket he turned and set it on the floor in front of Josh.

"That's it man, now what? Looking up he saw Andy standing behind Josh with his Judge leveled at his chest.

"One last item," Josh said, reaching over and pulling a large roll of duct tape off the display next to him. "Turn around and get on your face Pete, hands behind your back."

"I might have known you two would still be hanging together. Are you still playing second fiddle to this jock Andy? You two are a couple of real losers."

Grabbing Pete by the collar, Josh thrust him to the floor and secured his hands behind his back with the duct tape. Then he bound his feet before rolling him on his side.

"Pete, I'm going to do something I've wanted to do to you for years."

Tearing a piece of tape off the roll, he firmly placed it over Pete's mouth, and slapped him on the side of the head. Andy couldn't hold back the laughter, as he and Josh made their way to the back door, turning out the lights as they walked out.

BEFORE CLIMBING INTO THE TRUCK, Josh and Andy popped the tonneau cover on the back and looked inside. Stowed in the bed of their escape vehicle, was enough armament and supplies to equip a small company of men. Grabbing what appeared to be a small canvas duffel Andy unzipped it. It contained an aluminum cooking kit, which he quickly dumped out into the parking lot, and refilled, with the contents of the shopping basket.

"Let's roll, we need to find a ride home," Josh said, and climbed behind the wheel.

As Andy climbed in, Josh turned on the headlights, and paused for a moment, before jumping out of the cab, and running over to a utility truck where a pair of cable cutters hung on the side. Grabbing them, he quickly returned to the truck and threw them on the floorboard.

"I just remembered, we have a gate to go through next to the Glacier fire station, before we can get across the runway, to the float pond."

Putting the rig into reverse, he backed up and quickly pulled out to Old Dairy and turned left. Three hundred yards down the road, he made another left onto Crest Street, and didn't stop until they reached Yandukin. There he turned off the lights, and crossed the intersection, letting the truck slowly idle forward.

"The fire station is manned twenty-four seven, but the crew on the night shift spends all their time on the computer scanning porn or glued to the television. Pray no one is looking out the window."

Quietly driving up toward the gate, Andy quickly jumped out, while the truck was still rolling. Running up to the gate, he clipped the cable, and pushed it open as Josh drove through, then climbed back in without missing a beat.

"You two are amazing," Jamie breathed, as she attempted to quiet her nursing baby.

Josh pulled quickly out across the tarmac, where several small planes were tethered, then made a quick left and right across the taxi lane, repeating the same maneuver across the runway to reach the access road to the float pond.

Driving slowly down the road, Josh began looking for an Otter. He knew there were three other outfitters in the area who had Otters, two were Christians, the other a sworn atheist. The Otter was one plane he knew very well. They were halfway down the pond, when Josh found what he was looking for, and quickly pulled over. Turning to Andy and Jamie, Josh took a deep breath.

"Jamie, your becoming a part of our party was unforeseen, but that's ok. We'll take care of you and Missy as best we can, but for now you'll have to trust us. Josh is my name; my brother here is Andy. We are about to commandeer an airplane to get us back to a place of safety. While Andy and I get the plane ready, I want you and the baby to stay right here in the truck, do not get out for any reason until Andy or I come and get you. Do you understand?"

"Yes, she said," nodding her head and drawing Missy close to her, pulling the covering over the baby's head, and leaning back in the seat.

"Andy let's get everything out of the back and down on the dock, After I break into the plane then we'll load up. It won't take me long to get it started once we're all in."

When they were outside and standing at the back of the truck, Josh spoke quietly.

"Andy, we're not going to be able to follow our original plan. With Jamie and the baby, this blessing in the back of the truck and the supplies we've acquired, the chutes are useless. I'm going to have to land this plane next to the Havens."

"Are you sure you can do this, big brother?" With the varied cloud cover so low and the ceiling catching the top of Thunder Mountain, you'll be flying by the seats of 'both' our pants."

"If I put it down on top of the pond, and keep the nose up, our landing should be short, going uphill. As for the clouds, we'll just have to trust the Lord. It's all in His hands anyway, Josh sighed. We'll let Stars know what we're planning so they'll be ready."

"What-ever you say Josh, you haven't failed me yet, and I know the Lord's hand is on us."

The men quickly unloaded the bed of the truck, packing everything down to the dock, by the plane. It took Josh only moments to gain entry, with the screwdriver, he had stuck in his pocket. Within twenty minutes, everything was aboard, including Jamie and the baby.

"Only one more item," Josh said. "I want to make another submarine!"

Heading back to the truck he left Andy scratching his head, with a puzzled look on his face.

As before, he made a wide ark on the float road, and steered the truck down the bank before stepping out onto the pavement. Returning to where Andy knelt untying the last tether on the plane, they pushed off, not waiting to see the truck slide beneath the surface.

Josh looked at his watch.

"It's eleven forty and won't be light enough to fly for six hours at least. There's a small estuary on the other side of the pond. We'll wait there until first light. My plan is to fly up the Salmon creek valley, and down the Lemon Glacier. I'll fly over the Havens, make a wide turn and land."

"I think I have a new nick name for you," Andy said, punching Josh's shoulder.

"And what would that be?" he replied.

"I think I'll start calling you Cuttinit," Andy said with a grin. "It really fits, cause you're always cutting it way too close!"

Josh could only drop his chin and shake his head at Andy's silly, but all too true remark.

"Andy," Josh said with a grin of his own. I'll forgive you, if you'll help me paddle this plane to the other side of the pond.

"Let's grab the paddles off the pontoons and go for it Josh, I'll race you there," he said jokingly.

"Right after we contact Stars, I'd better try it now before Pops doses off."

Pulling out the radio, Josh turned it from scan to the programmed settings his father had set and keyed up the radio.

"Sun One to Stars, Sun One to Stars, Stars do you copy?"

"Copy Sun One, you're late."

"Sorry Stars, long story ... on wetmac, snug, two extra cartons both pluses. Can't leap, coming down hard, castle west side dash A.M. Heart, Princess One, Princess Two and Court … Sun One."

"Copy Sun One, castle west side dash A.M. Knees …Stars out."

After translating on paper, Ben read aloud Josh's transmission to the whole company, who sat all evening, waiting eagerly to hear from the men, especially Ellen and Jessica.

Josh says they're safe on a plane on the float pond. They have two more passengers both female. They can't jump, so they're going to try landing on the snow on the east side of the Havens early in the morning, and they send their love to Ellen, Jessica and the company. There's only one way Josh can come in, where there aren't any trees or large brush, and that's across the pond and up the mountain side."

"You answered knees," Linda said, what does 'knees' mean?"

"We'll be praying, Ben responded, and I think that's what we should do right now."

CHAPTER 26

Home and counting coup

IT WAS ALMOST TWO AM by the time Josh and Andy paddled the plane into the mouth of the small estuary and turned it around facing the float pond. Their arms ached as they climbed back into the plane and settled into their seats. Jamie and the baby lay asleep on the deck in the back. It didn't take long for Andy to join in their slumber, as he lay his head against the window and bulkhead seeking a position of comfort.

"Some Co-pilot you turned out to be," Josh mumbled, as Andy began to snore in between sighs.

Josh dosed and woke up several times through the remainder of the night. By five AM, he was awake, thinking about the events of the previous two days' until it was light enough to fly. It was quarter to six when he nudged Andy and Jamie, letting them know it was time to get into the air.

Pulling down a headset he handed it to Jamie and explained why she needed to wear it.

Then adjusting her microphone, he helped her buckle up. Buckling up and adjusting his own headset, he and Andy ran through the preflight checks, making sure that both power levers were in the flight idle position. Then making sure the switch guard was down, he turned the master switch to start, switched on the booster pumps and after running his inspections started the engines one at a time, letting them idle, before moving the plane through small patches of fog and into the float pond. A low bank of clouds hung above them and down the Gastineau channel at about eight hundred feet. Looking around for any movement along the runway to his left, Josh slowly gave the plane full throttle. The pontoons struggled to break free of the water's grip. A sigh of relief filled the cockpit as the Otters nose finally came up and they lifted into the air.

Breaking over the channel, Josh held their altitude at about six hundred feet until he could see Vanderbilt hill road, down on his left. Bringing up the nose, he took the plane through the low clouds.

Breaking through, he slowly banked to the left, flying up the valley along the north slope of Mt. Juneau and south of the Salmon creek reservoir. When they reached forty-five hundred feet, Josh banked to the left, and crossed over the south end of the Lemon glacier.

"Andy, it looks like the cloud ceiling is about forty-eight to forty-nine hundred feet, we'll stay at forty-five until we drop over the foot of the glacier and make our turn to land."

"If it's the same up the Lemon as it was up the Salmon, the low clouds should end just below the Havens. Looks like that big storm is coming in early," Andy said, looking to the west.

"It sure does, lets pray it doesn't push those low valley clouds up the Lemon before we get down on the ground."

Pulling the radio out of his jacket pocked, Josh keyed up.

"Sun One to Stars, copy?

"Copy Sun One …

"Stars, we're moments from the castle, out."

Dropping over the foot of the glacier, Josh made a wide banking turn along the southeast face of the mountain side, behind the Havens. Flying down the valley about a mile, he made a hard hundred and eighty, bringing the plane back up the valley again. Lining up with the six hundred- and fifty-foot-long clearing which quickly rose up the mountainside in front of the Havens, Josh drew in a deep breath.

"Hold on, we're going skiing," he said.

Pulling back on the throttles, and dropping the plane's pontoons down on the snow, like a goose landing on a pond, he kept the nose up.

A blinding wall of blowing snow rose as the plane sank into the snowpack and glided up the hillside. Pulling the throttles all the way back he killed the engines and held on.

As the plane quickly began to slow, it suddenly spun to the right and came to a stop, facing back down the mountainside.

"Good job Cuttinit," Andy said, with a nervous laugh.

Jamie sat crying softly, clutching Missy tightly against her chest, and rocking back and forth to comfort herself and the baby.

Looking out the window on his right, Andy could see Todd and Rich breaking trail through the deep snow, with the rest of the company following close behind. Within minutes, the cargo door on the port side of the plane was open, and the air filled with the voices of thirteen people, all trying to speak at once. It took Josh a few minutes to collect himself, and get the company to quiet down, so he could speak.

"First order of business," Josh shouted. "Let's get our guests, the cargo, and ourselves into the Havens, then we can talk!" Like ants, the company emptied the plane and began making their way back to the Havens. As Andy and Ben began to leave with their share of the cargo, Josh stopped them.

"Wind's coming up the valley ahead of that big storm," he said "I've got to do something with this plane; we can't leave it sitting here like a road sign. Wait for me up the trail, and pray my idea works."

Climbing back into the plane and sliding the cargo door closed, he jumped into the pilots' seat with a couple of Bunge cords in his hand. Setting the flaps, he secured the stick with one of the cords and tied the pilot's door open with the other. Re-starting the engines, Josh pushed the throttles forward, the engines revved up, and the nose dropped momentarily as the plane lurched forward. Slowly it began sliding back down the tracks left by the pontoons when they landed. Climbing out onto the edge of the door, he reached in and pushing the throttles all the way forward, turned, and leaped from the plane.

Andy and Ben stood in astonishment, as the plane, barreled down the mountainside, rose briefly into the air, and disappeared as it plummeted down into the valley with an explosive roar. It took a few minutes to find Josh, who lay buried under the snow. Dragging him to his feet, they help him back up the hill, to where the last pieces of cargo lay in the snow. As the weather-front and low clouds moved up the valley, they gathered up the cargo and made their way to the Havens.

Emerging through the trees, Josh and Andy found themselves standing at the junction, where the bough covered tunnel and the escarpment trail came together. Crouching and turning down hill, they made their way to the rear entrance of the Havens. Passing through the entrance Josh paused, rubbing his gloved hand across the door.

"You'll never know how gland I am to see you," he said, it' good to be home!

JESSICA AND ELLEN WERE WAITING in the anti-chamber, as the men made their way inside. Closing and bolting the door behind them, they began removing their gear with the women's help. Sidestepping Ellen, Ben made his way into the great room with a smile on his face, as Jessica and Ellen greeted their husbands in the privacy of the anti-chamber. Between hugs and kisses, Andy turned toward Josh, grinning ear to ear.

"We should go on these excursions more often," he said, as Jessica kissed him again with passion in her eyes.

Josh and Ellen turned, and retreated to their quarters, discretely slipping inside, Ellen wrapped the tie around the door handle.

It was just before noon, when the couples made their way into the great room, with Ellen and Jessica blushing against the gazes and smiles of their Havens family.

"It's good that you could finally join us," Pastor Bowens said with a twinkle in his eye. "I hope you got rested up after such an electrifying three days. Jamie has filled us in with bits and pieces where she and Missy came into the story, but I think you two still have a lot of talking to do after lunch."

"And we will be all ears," Sarah added, as she, Lind, and Jan sat down large bowls of venison stew on the table. Alice followed with two large pans of cornbread. The women then took their places, as everyone held hands and bowed their heads. Ben led them in prayer.

After lunch, Josh and Andy meticulously retraced each moment of their three-day ordeal, with a clarity, that at times sent a shiver down Josh's spine. There was a moment though, as Andy recalled Josh's last words to Pete, and the slap on the side of Pete's head after taping his mouth shut, that everyone, especially Ellen and Jessica broke into roaring laughter. Most of his life, Pete had been a living example of Proverbs 29:11, known for his foolish and annoying talk.

The laughter came to a sudden halt however, as the scanner reminded everyone of the reality that surrounded them.

Squad ninety-two of the Militia Security Guard, hastily confirmed that a twin-engine Otter was missing from the float pond, and it was registered to Commander Darrel Jenson of the local Militia Guard. The plane had been seen last, flying south, disappearing onto the low clouds over the channel, there was no one in the tower at the time, monitoring the radar.

"Jenson, 'Commander Jenson?' That was the name of the militiaman I shot in the store," Josh said, reeling from the connection.

Ben reached over and placed his hand on Josh's shoulder.

"Son, of the three men you shot, this Jenson fellow survived. His most serious wound was in his upper left arm, shattered the bone. The two shots to the chest bruised him good but didn't penetrate his Kevlar. He recognized you and Andy from an encounter at the Breakwater Inn earlier this month, just before the amnesty period ended. He is hopping mad, and swears he will find you two, if he has to search from Vancouver to Barrow.

"How do you know all this Pops? Where did you get all this information?"

"The airwaves have been on fire, since late last night. Between the scanner and the radio, Pastor and I stayed up in shifts, to stay on top of all the traffic. If this part of the world didn't know who you two were before, 'they do now.' I'm sure your pictures have been on every television within a thousand miles of here."

Josh took a long sip from his coffee cup, and asked for a refill, reaching out for a couple of vanilla creamers from the bowl in the middle of the table.

"Andy, could you go and grab that small duffle you loaded, you know what it looks like."

When Andy returned with the bag, Josh nodded across the table.

"Give it to Todd will you, thanks Bro."

"Todd, I promised you that I would get what you needed to give us eyes, and God knows that we are going to need them now more than ever. Everything on your list is there, including the surveillance equipment from the store, the rest is up to you. You will give the orders on this one, and we'll get things where you want them. The full storm will be on us by tomorrow night, and we need to have things up and working before then. Can you, do it?"

"I can do anything with the Lords help," he said, placing the contents of the bag on the table like a young boy, laying out the pieces of a new erector set. "You are so awesome Josh; I love you Man!"

'Now where did I hear that before," Andy said, winking at Josh with a wide-eyed grin.

While the women cleaned up after lunch, the men gathered around the couches to open and inventory all the hardware, pulled out of the back of the militia truck. Todd opened Josh's backpack and began pulling out the video cameras, his eyes lit up as he pulled out the monitor.

"Hey Josh, did you know that your security monitor is actually a nineteen-inch television?"

Everything came to a standstill, and all eyes fell on Todd, as he held up the small flat screen TV.

"Gentlemen, with a makeshift antenna, we can watch the news!"

Josh was amazed that he had never noticed. It was something his father had picked up, and had a friend install shortly after they opened the store.

"That's awesome Todd, KTOO channel four has a transmitter, digital and VHF across the channel from Lemon Creek. It's line of sight from here, right down the valley.

"Would the wire mesh antenna I put up for the radio work for the TV as well," Ben asked?

"It should, let's check," Todd said, carrying the television over to the table.

Plugging it into the extension cord from the light pole, he removed the antenna wire from the box under the table and attached it to the television. As the TV flickered on Todd tuned to channel four. Ironically the programming had been preempted by a special breaking news bulletin. Everyone gathered around in amazement, as Josh and Andy's pictures flashed across the screen. The focus had now turned to the Militia vehicle, which apparently had not completely sunk in the pond. Finding none of the munitions and armament in the vehicle, was a disparaging turn of events for the local Militia detachment.

"Let's finish up our work," Josh said, turning and walking back to the munitions sitting in the middle of the room. "Let's see what the fuss is all about."

Turning off the television, Todd went with the men, as the women talked amongst themselves.

Aside from sleeping bags, a new assortment of MRE's, flashlights and a base radio, Ben logged an array of military grade weapons. Quickly he wrote down what Josh called out.

"Four nine mm MP-5N machine guns, two SMAW's Pops, their shoulder launchers, for grenades, mortars, and laser guided missiles. Four SASR M4 carbines, and four modified pistols with holsters, 45 cal.

There are four ammo boxes, and two boxes containing two rockets, two mortars and two grenades."

"With the weapons we've already collected, C4, and all of this, we could really go out with a bang," Andy said. "I just pray it never comes to that before the Lord takes us out of this world for good."

Picking up the last large bag, Josh unzipped it. Inside were six Kevlar body suits.

"No wonder the Commander is so upset; you've shot him, sunk his truck, crashed his airplane, and taken all of his toys. That would be enough to make any man angry," Ellen said, as she walked over to let the men know, coffee and a snack was on the table.

Pastor Bowens didn't have to be told twice. Moving the TV out of the way, Josh sat down. Clearing his throat, he spoke with as much authority as he could muster.

"I want to settle the matter right up front, concerning this television. When it came into the Havens, it came as a monitor for the security cameras. Although it is a blessing to know we can receive TV signals, its primary use will remain, to serve as a monitor for the security system Todd is going to create, with our help. It will not be used, for entertainment. However, at the appropriate time each day we, we will tune it in for local, national, and world news. Does anyone have any objections?"

There was a long pause, before Ben spoke up.

"I agree with Josh, the news will give all of us something to look forward to each day, but we have more than enough to do, and our time is certainly going to be full before the big storm rolls in."

"Settled then," Josh said, looking around the table. Todd, if you don't mind, after we're finished here, we'll get our heads together and begin laying out a plan for your project."

"Sounds good to me," he responded, quickly pulling two cookies off a large plate, as Linda sat it down on the table, and Jan began pouring coffee.

Taking a sip of coffee, Josh turned to his father and Pastor Bowens.

"Where are we, with the firewood, and bringing down the stores we discussed on Monday?"

"Everything we'll need for the next two weeks is stored behind you along the wall, and covered with a small poly tarp, that part is taken care of. As for the firewood, we have about two thirds of it moved. We started with what was farthest away and worked out way back toward the escarpment trail.

"That's awesome Pops, we'll leave it at that for now. Once we have our security system in place, and this storm settles in, I'm going to invest in some rest and relaxation. It's time I work at being a husband for a little while. Putting his arm around Ellen, Josh gave her a gentle squeeze, and tenderly kissed her forehead.

CHAPTER 27

A day of Thanksgiving

JOSH'S EYES SUDDENLY POPPED OPEN with the sound of Max barking, which had awakened everyone. As he sat rubbing his eyes, the tremor hit, rolling under them, and disappearing somewhere to the east. Ever since Max and Andy joined the company, Max had become their early warning system. It wasn't long, before the members of the Havens family were gathering around the table, looking for a hot cup of coffee.

"The tremors seem to be diminishing in intensity but moving faster. The last three especially," Ben said.

Sarah poured him a cup of coffee as he sat down at the table.

"You can say that again," Rich moaned, still trying to rub down the Goosebumps on his arms.

Jamie sat on a bench at the end of the table holding Missy in her arms, nursing the baby, and a cup of coco Alice had made for her.

"Does this happen all the time up here," she said.

"Quite often sweetheart," Alice responded, sitting down beside her.

"We even had one that created a new back door for us, the one you came through when you arrived."

"You're looking pretty chipper this morning, for being up so early," Josh said, as Pastor Bowens took the cup Sarah handed him and sat down next to Ben.

"The day before our Thanksgiving celebration, is always a great day," he said. "It's always filled with joyous anticipation, for the feast that's just around the corner."

Patting his belly, he gave a nod and a wink to Sarah, as she sat down next to Alice and Jamie.

Besides that, we set Thanksgiving back a week, because you and Andy were going to be down on the Banks Thanksgiving Day. Now our celebration will be twice as joyous, because you're both back with us, safe and sound!"

"Here, let me hold that little girl," Alice said. "Then you can enjoy your coco."

Josh paused for a moment and reflected on the events of the past week. It had taken six long days to run and secure the wires, cables, and cameras for their new security system, while Todd repaired equipment and made minor changes to set up a new and modified control center. Now the new control center pressed against the east side of the Great room. It look impressive.

The winds predicted by NOAA were upon them, and the heavy snowfall had already buried the tunnel they had created with the tree boughs under three and a half feet of snow. For the last three days and nights, the snow had fallen in blizzard conditions, but spirits were high. In spite of the torturous weather outside, the Havens was filled with a warmth and security that only the Lord could provide.

"Hey sweetie, whatcha thinking so hard about," Ellen said, sliding onto the bench beside her husband. Kissing his cheek, and laying her head on his shoulder, she looked up at him questioningly.

"Nothing really," Josh said, just thinking about this last week. The days have been so full, and gone by so quickly, it's hard to believe we're almost to the end of November. Do you realize that in another month, we'll be entering into two thousand twenty?"

"I know, it's hard to believe it's been eight years since we graduated, another four and we'll both be halfway to retirement," Ellen said laughingly. "Just think of everything that has happened worldwide in the last eight years"

Sitting down across from them, Andy jumped into the conversation while Jessica went for their coffee.

"Jess and I were talking about this same thing last night before we went to bed," he said. "Just think about everything that's gone down Biblically since two thousand twelve. Then the world economy was about to flat line and did. Then we had a short-lived World War three in the Middle East at the end of two thousand fourteen. That ushered in Lord Chris, and I use the term loosely, as our now world leader, who we know as the anti-Christ."

Jessica slid in next to Andy, placed his coffee in front of him, and sat hers down on the table. Taking a sip, Andy continued where he had left off.

"By two thousand sixteen he had negotiated an Israeli and Palestinian peace treaty. That opened the door to the building of the third Tabernacle. It was completed in seventeen. Now the world thinks he is their Messiah.

"Don't forget the new world church order, which sprang into existence that year as well," Jessica added. "It was shortly after that, when worldwide persecution began for those saints of God, who wouldn't join, and it's still going on. Millions of saints have been martyred and still are, especially now, since the mark of that beast has been fully instituted."

Joining into the conversation, Pastor Bowens spoke up.

"I've shared this with you many times but let me read a portion of Matthew twenty-four to you again, beginning with verse fifteen through verse twenty-nine."

After reading the scriptures, Pastor laid down his Bible, and took a sip of his coffee before continuing.

Jesus himself tells us that the sun will be darkened, the moon will not give its light and the heavenly bodies will be shaken. The Apostle John gives us a more descriptive narrative in the book of Revelation. These events are in conjunction with Christ's return and the rapture of his Church. Only one more event stands between us and our Savior's return, the visible signs in the heavens, and could happen at any time. When we see this, and immediately after the distress of these days we're in, our redemption will be at the door.

Everyone's attention became suddenly drawn to the far end of the table, where Jamie sat in tears, looking at Alice for some reassurance.

"I... I've never asked Jesus to come into my life, but I haven't received that terrible mark either. Can I still be saved? Can Missy and I still go to heaven with you when Jesus comes?"

Handing the baby to Sarah, Alice reached her arms around Jamie and held her tenderly.

"Sweetheart, only one simple act stands between you and an eternity with Jesus. All you have to do is believe in Him, ask Him to forgive your sins, and fill you with his Spirit and presence."

"Oh, I do, I really do," Jamie said, wrapping her arms around Alice and holding her tightly.

"Let's pray," Alice said, motioning the other women to gather around them. "We'll all pray with you. Just speak to Jesus from your heart."

Sobbing, Jamie poured out her heart to a loving Savior and, in that moment, became a member of God's family, and the loving Saints who surrounded her.

After breakfast, the women cleaned everything up. Then they began preparing for the evening meal and the feast Pastor Bowens so eagerly anticipated.

For the remainder of the day, the men took care of the daily chores, made a trip to Havens II for some items the women needed, while clearing the tunnel and escarpment trail of snow. Ultimately, they ended up around the new security center, listening to the scanner, and discussing the events unfolding down on the banks. After supper, everyone gathered around the security center, as Todd transformed the monitor into a television, to watch the evening's local and national news.

THE MORNING OF THE HAVENS Thanksgiving celebration was a busy one. The men huddled around one end of the table in the great room, steeped in conversation judging from the news casts, pockets of Christian resistance fighters had emerged, once the lines had been clearly drawn, by those who had received the mark. The world and national news rang with accounts of resistance fighters taking in and protecting those who still had not received the international mark of the New Collective. International Militia forces were perplexed, because these pockets of resistance fighters were able to appear and disappear without a trace and fighting only in self-defense.

"That's because God's Hand covers his own, and not even the powers and principalities of the air know where they reside," Pastor Bowens said, raising his cup, with a nod of his head.

Taking a long sip, he sat the cup down, and folded his hands. "The fighting isn't over for us either; we've just been given a reprieve by the weather. When spring comes, so will the Militia."

"Well, if that's the case, we had better take advantage of this time the Lords given us and enjoy all of his provision. One day at a time, we'll celebrate with Thanksgiving, starting today, and every day, until His return," Josh said!

"Here, here," Rich said, holding up his coffee cup!

As the men toasted Josh's Proclamation, Ellen stepped up to the table with a handful of CD's and handed them to Todd.

"The world won't be playing this kind of music anymore, but we still can, and I know the CD player still works on the radio. Would you bless us with some Holiday cheer," she said?

With a twinkle in his eyes, Todd jumped to his feet, and quickly made his way over to the security center where the radio had been set up. As he inserted a CD, the great room filled with warmth and joy.

Every heart and face glowed with God's grace and the realization that Christmas was just around the corner.

The Thanksgiving feast and celebration that day left the company filled to overflowing with the Lord's bountiful love, and provision. Pastor Bowens, unable to hold any more, finally succumb to a long winters nap, on the end of one of the couches. Nestled in pillows and supporting a Pendleton blanket Sarah had draped over him, he found respite from the cares of the troubled world that surrounded him.

From that momentous occasion, the hours melted into days, the days into weeks and the weeks into months, as the Havens Company settled into the daily routines and adventures of surviving the hardest winter to hit the Alaskan panhandle in over a hundred and fifty years.

CHAPTER 28

Jenson plans for revenge

I T WAS MID-APRIL OF TWO-THOUSAND twenty, when Commander Jenson's pent-up anger and frustration, found respite. The early spring thaw and unrelenting rains quickly devoured the snow on the banks and raised the snow level steadily every day. Resolutely, the Commander began planning a strategy for dealing with the Christian fanatics, or CF's, as the local Militia now referred to them. It was several weeks before his plans and the weather begin to reconcile themselves, but when that time came, Commander Darrel Jenson, unleashed his furry, with a vengeance.

Blood flowed as hundreds of the 'unmarked', were mercilessly hunted down. They were either shot or transported to Juneau, and publicly executed by guillotine at the rear of the Capitol Building.

Commander Jenson was sitting at his desk, when his assistant's voice rang over the intercom.

"Commander, Sergeant Brokers is here with an urgent report concerning CF's making their way up the Lemon Creek valley."

"Send him in Dunn, and bring me some more coffee," Jenson snapped.

Escorting the Sergeant in, Lt. Dunn filled the Commanders cup, and turned to leave.

"Leave the pot here, and bring back two more cups, I want you in on this briefing as well."

"Yes Sir," Dunn replied, and quickly left the room.

Returning with the cups, he filled them. Handing one to Sergeant Brokers, he took the other and sat down facing the Commanders desk. Even though completely healed, Jenson favored his left arm, and sat rubbing it slowly as he spoke to Brokers and Dunn.

"Let's have that report Brokers, I have other business up Lemon Creek, maybe we can take care of everything at once."

Sergeant Brokers cleared his throat and took a sip of coffee before opening a folder. Handing copies of the report to the commander, and Lieutenant Dunn, he leaned forward in his chair.

"As you can see, we discovered a group of CF's, hiding out in a derelict house at the end of Laurie Lane, in the Salmon Creek subdivision. After a forty-five-minute standoff, we lost two men, but took out eight of the CF's, three children and five adults. The remainder, we believe to be ten or twelve escaped into the bush heading north and east into the Lemon Creek valley, somewhere above the old Lemon Creek Trail, three days ago. Low clouds and heavy fog has made surveillance by chopper impossible, but we do have two squads in pursuit and in constant radio contact with dispatch."

"Dunn, what's the current weather report?"

"We had a low of forty-one last night Sir. Expected high of fifty-eight this afternoon, and current temperature is fifty–six. Clouds are expected to rise to forty-eight hundred feet by Thursday afternoon with a visibility of eight miles, Dunn concluded.

Commander Jenson looked at his watch and pushed his chair away from the desk. Picking up his cup, he walked over to the window of his office and looked out briefly before turning around.

"Brokers, call your men back, and get them equipped for an extended pursuit. I want ten men standing by, and ready to roll out at zero six hundred hours tomorrow morning. Dunn, we will have a military surveillance satellite available to scan the Lemon Creek sectors by twelve hundred hours. I want you on top of this. Have the coordinates on my desk as soon as those CF's are located. They will also be looking for my downed choppers; we lost two of them up that valley last year."

Lt. Dunn quickly scribbled his notes on the back of Brokers report, as the Commander took his seat again.

"Brokers, any word on Huskins or Bridgeport yet? I'll have the heads of those two CF's on poles in front of my office if it's the last thing I do!

"We've had no word or contact yet Sir, but there is a chance they might be part of this group we're looking for now. They seem to be well armed."

"Dunn, contact the D.O.D. If they detect anyone on those satellite scans of the Lemon Creek sectors, I want close-ups; I want to see the plaque on their teeth, 'understood?'"

"Yes Sir," Dunn replied, becoming more anxious as the commander's rage began to build.

"Brokers, you're the C.O. on this mission, if Huskins or Bridgeport are a part of this group of CFs, I want to be notified immediately! Don't let me down Sergeant."

"Yes Sir," Brokers hammered out, with a solute.

"Thank you, Gentlemen, this briefing is concluded," Jenson hissed, rubbing his left arm as he stood. "Dunn, get my car, and meet me in front of the building in five minutes, the executions begin at sixteen hundred hours, and I don't want to be late."

"Right away Sir, will there be anything else?"

"No Dunn, just get the squad, and make it snappy!"

It was five minutes to four when Dunn pulled up at the rear of the Capitol building, next to the van holding the eight CF's captured the week before. There Commander Jenson stepped out of the black SUV. Making his way through the crowd to the observation platform, he took his seat with the Collective Council, presiding over the Southern Alaska constituency.

Dunn remained in the car, looking intently at the large stainless-steel guillotine, placed over a modified manhole. A Militiaman with a fire hose would conveniently wash away all signs of each execution, into the city sewer system. The bodies would be placed, in cardboard coffins, then transported to the new waste management facility in Lemon Creek, to be incinerated.

With clenched teeth, Dunn watched as each of the condemned prisoners, five men and three women, were led before the Council and then to the platform. There, their heads were placed into a stock, their body's strapped face down onto a metal bench, and their hands to the platform. With Military precision, the executioners would step back in unison and with the press a button; send another DF to meet their precious maker.

"The sooner they get rid of these fanatics, the better", he thought to himself. He had to admit though; there were times when he wished it were Jenson's head stuffed in that infernal machine. He was just as much a fanatic as those he was so obsessed with hunting down.

Forty minutes had passed, when Dunn saw the Commander stand and step down from the platform. Jumping out of the driver's seat, he scurried around the front of the SUV and opened the door with a solute, as Commander Jenson entered the vehicle. Closing the door, he stepped forward, and opened the rear door for the Council President, Karl Ostenberg, who quickly slid inside jerking the handle out if Dunn's hand, as he slammed the door shut.

As Dunn climbed into the driver's seat, Ostenberg's voice filled the SUV with his venomous rhetoric.

"I will never understand these, Christians! They are defiant, fearless, and cling to their 'faith' with the tenacity of a pit bull. I'm tired of these executions Jenson, I'm through being publicly disgraced by their willingness to die for a God that doesn't exist. I don't care how you deal with them, but it will no longer be here on my doorstep. Do you understand Jenson? There will be no more public executions in Juneau!"

"Yes, Consul Ostenberg," the Commander replied, visibly shaken by the Consul's tirade. I understand ... I will have the Guillotine removed immediately!"

"Driver," Ostenberg barked. Take me to the Convention Center on Willoughby Avenue."

Pulling up in front of the Convention Center, Dunn made his way around the car and opened the door. Before stepping out, the Consul reached forward and griped the epaulet of Jenson's coat.

"Don't forget Jenson, when I look out my office window tomorrow morning, I want to see that edifice of Christian rebellion gone from my sight! Gone, do you understand ... gone!"

"Yes Consul, I will see to it personally," Jenson said, reaching for his cell phone, as he spoke.

After the Consul had entered the building, Dunn climbed behind the wheel and waited until the Commander finished his conversation and put away his phone.

"Where to now Sir," Dunn quipped?

"Drop me off at the Militia Motor Pool on Mill Street, and then return to the office. I'll contact you there. A truck, trailer and Crain are on their way to the Capital Building as we speak. I will be overseeing the removal of the Guillotine, and its transport to our facility in Lemon Creek. One more thing Dunn ..."

"Yes Sir."

"Assign a couple of men to remove the manhole cover at the end of cell block A. Since Consul Ostenberg wasn't specific, we will continue to feed the blade from the view of my office window instead of his"

With the addition of an administration building at the rear of the secured parking area, the Juneau Police Station had become the new Juneau Militia Headquarters, complete with barracks' and commissary for fifty men, an armament center, and Helipads for six helicopters.

Dunn swelled with pride, as he drove down Alaway Avenue, and into the Headquarters compound. Stopping at the gate, he rolled down his window.

"Private, call the barracks, I want a two-man detail to meet me outside the west end door of cellblock A, in ten minutes."

"Yes Sir, ten minutes Lieutenant Sir."

Spinning on his heels, the guard picked up the phone, and Dunn drove to the administration building. As he stepped out of the car and made his way to where the two Militiamen stood waiting, his cell phone rang.

"Dunn, I'm leading a convoy passed Vanderbilt as we speak. Are things ready for our arrival?"

"Yes Commander, I have a detail ready and standing by."

"Good, I want to get this equipment set before dark. Our E.T.A is fifteen minutes."

With hurried instructions, the men secured a pry bar and removed the manhole cover. Tipping it on edge, they rolled it to the end of the building, and leaned it out of the way.

By eighteen hundred hours, the last of the quickly fading light had disappeared in the west, the tool of Jenson's obsession, slid into position.

"Good job today Dunn," Jenson said glibly. When these CF's are finally eradicated, I'll see you get extended R and R somewhere nice, maybe Hawaii or the Bahamas."

"Yes Sir, I'll be looking forward Sir."

"Zero six hundred Dunn, and don't be late. Tomorrow is going to be a big day, I can feel it in my bones," Jenson said. Rubbing his left arm, he walked to his car, climbed inside, and drove out the gate.

IT WAS THREE THIRTY IN the morning, when Josh was awakened. Gently shaking his arm, Ben whispered into his ear.

"You need to get up Son, we've got company coming, and it looks like trouble is right behind!"

Quietly slipping out of bed, he quickly dressed and met with Andy,

Todd and his father as they gathered around the security center, in the great room.

"What's up guys," he queried, still rubbing his eyes, and trying to focus his attention on the radio traffic Todd was monitoring.

Todd finished writing down his notations and stood.

"Let's gather around the table with some coffee, and I'll fill you in on what's going down, or maybe I should say, what's coming up. And it doesn't look good."

When everyone had filled their cup, and were leaning into the table, Todd pulled his notes in front of him.

"The early thaw and rain down on the banks, has unleashed a resurgence of Militia activity. It's literally been a bloodbath, with hundreds of Saints who have survived the winter, now being sought out and shot, or publicly executed at the Capitol Building. Jenson is on a rampage. Right now, there are approximately twelve mark-less, making their way up the Lemon. They left behind five adults and three children dead, after a stand-off in a Salmon Creek subdivision.

"Shooting children," Josh stammered.

"It's Jenson's orders, 'If their mark-less, their dead' Ben said," shaking his head and wiping the tears from his eyes.

"Does the Militia have any idea where the twelve are now? Do they have boots on the ground in the valley?"

"Josh, the Militia was called back at four in the afternoon, three days ago. It appears they're scheduled, to be redeployed this morning, on two helicopters, five Militiamen and crew in each. These birds are carrying fifty calibers. A military surveillance satellite is scheduled to conduct a scan of the valley at noon, they will be looking for the mark-less and those helicopters that went down last year. "We've got to develop a plan of action now," Josh replied. We can't wait until the Militia gives us a location before we act. Andy, we're going to need six backpacks, automatic weapons, grenades, the C4, and all the ammo each person can carry.

"I'll take care of it as soon as we're done here," he responded.

Todd, you, Ellen, and Jessica will make up team one. Once we know the location of the mark-less, you and the women will move as quickly as possible to make contact and lead them to the Havens. Rich, Andy and I, will take up a position where we can cover your retreat."

"Josh, what about the SMAW's? I think you or I should be packing one of them with us," Andy said, placing his hand on Josh's shoulder. "Those grenades and mortars would come in real handy, not to mention the rockets."

"Good call Andy," we can spread the additional armament between us. Josh looked down at his watch.

"Well Gentlemen, it's almost four, and the others will be getting up in another hour or so. Let's see how much we can gather before breakfast. I want to be moving out by seven. They won't launch those helicopters until full light. They'll run a search pattern on the way up, so we need to be in place before eight. Dad, could you take care of the radios? We'll need all four, one for Todd, Andy Ellen and Me."

"It's good as done Son. I've always known the day would come when we would have to make a stand. At least this time we will definitely have the advantage."

Pulling himself to his feet, Ben made his way to the security center where the handheld radios were stored.

CHAPTER 29

Battle for the Mark-less

B Y FIVE THIRTY THAT MORNING, the Havens was buzzing with activity. Alice and Sarah busied themselves preparing breakfast, with Linda and Jan's help. The Lemon Creek Six, as Andy had so aptly named himself and his counterparts, were already in their Camouflage pants and tee shirts busy putting on their body armor and placing the remainder of their gear in the center of the great room.

Ellen and Jessica talked quietly as they took turns adjusting each other's body suits.

"Are you ready for this Sis?" Jessica whispered.

"I was ready when we were in the Lemon Creek Detention Center. This had to happen eventually. I just wish I had more time with my husband, but then we'll be together for eternity."

"Me too Sis, but today isn't over yet. We're going to rescue those people, and still be home for dinner!"

Putting on and buttoning up their jackets, they made their way to the table and some hot coffee.

Setting down at the security center, and using the infrared devices attached to the cameras, Todd began a hundred and eighty degree sweep to the south of the Havens. Looking due west, he slowly scanned the mountainside below them, for any kind of heat signature within range of the cameras. Switching to camera two, he continued his sweep to the east. Todd found nothing significant until the camera swept across two tiny heat sources just west of the lower melt lake below the glacier.

"Josh, come take a look at this," Todd shouted. "I've got heat sources."

Using the telephoto lenses on the camera, Todd zoomed in on the targets.

"I think I've found our group of Mark-less," Todd said, sliding over so Josh could look at the monitor. "They're camped right on our doorstep."

As he leaned forward, he could see the flickers of firelight on the screen.

"How many yards did we figure the small melt lake was from our location Pops," Josh said, turning to his father as Ben stepped up to view the screen with the other men.

"About a thousand yards Son, or roughly half a mile, give or take a few feet. Those images look to be a couple of hundred yards this side of the lake though. I think they're about eight hundred yards out Son, not much more than that."

"We had better get something warm inside us before we head out," Josh said. Turning, he headed for the table and another cup of coffee.

Breakfast was short, as the biscuits and venison gravy, were washed down with coffee and hurried conversation. One thing Josh was good at was quick thinking, and it only took a short time to lay out a plan for getting to the Mark-less. Rescuing them was another matter entirely. Everything depended on taking out the helicopters before they could use those fifty's they were carrying. Josh took a sip of coffee and paused briefly before reaching out and tapping Andy on the shoulder.

"Andy, remember where we hid from the Militia the day, we sunk the pontoons? "That small plateau between us and the melt lake, wasn't it a couple of hundred feet higher than the lake?"

"I'm sure it is Josh; it might even be a little higher. It overlooks the area where the Mark-less are camped."

"That's where we'll set up. We'll have high ground advantage and the element of surprise.

"Why do you men keep calling these people Mark-less? If they aren't bearing the mark, surly they must be Saints," she said questioningly.

"Not necessarily so," Josh responded. They may not have received the mark, but they may not have received Christ as their Savior either. Our Jamie is a good example. She didn't come to us as a Christian, but she most certainly is now!"

Jamie sat at the other end of the table holding Missy in her arms, and grinning from ear to ear.

"We'll know soon enough," Andy said. Standing... he drank down the last of his coffee.

With Josh following close behind, Andy walked over to their gear, and began helping Rich, Todd and the women suit up.

"Everyone wearing Kevlar?" Josh asked, as he helped Ellen and Jessica with their side arms.

When the women were ready, he and Andy made sure Todd and Rich were set, before strapping the Judges to their chests, and holstering their automatic pistols. When everyone's parkas were on, Josh and Andy helped them with their ammo packs, and then donned their own. Andy carried only the munitions for the SMAW, and an automatic rifle. Josh carried their ammunition in his pack and slung the grenade and rocket launcher over his shoulder.

"God's storm troopers," Pastor Bowens exclaimed.

Gathering, in the great room, fourteen Saints joined hands as pastor prayed. Ending with a tearful Amen, he looked around. There were no dry eyes, as the Lemon Creek Six tearfully embraced the rest of the Company. Each knew that even with a victory over the Militia, eventually they would face the full force of Commander Darrel Jenson's demonic obsession.

"It's time," Josh said, taking Ellen by the hand. As Ben opened the front door of the Havens, and stood to the side, Josh and Ellen led the small band of Christian soldiers out into the damp morning air. Closing and bolting the door, Ben rushed to the security center, where those left behind, followed the six down the mountainside on the monitor, until they disappeared into the distant trees.

MAKING THEIR WAY ALONG THE north side of the small melt pond, Josh directed the party to spread out, keeping six to eight feet between them. This way they would be less likely to leave any sign that might be visible from the air. Skirting the many patches of snow, which remained between them, and the shelter of the forest was difficult, and slowed their progress immensely. Halfway to their destination, the six regrouped, to snake their way through the trees until they found themselves on the west side of the small plateau which Josh, Andy and Rich would descend upon.

"If my bearings are right, we should be about a hundred and thirty yards north of our Mark-less. The only place they can put Militia on the ground is about a hundred yards to the southeast," Josh said, kneeling down and scraping out a map in the moist earth.

"Josh, how are we supposed to make contact," Ellen said? "They may shoot first and ask questions later. We look more like Militia than Tribulation Saints!"

"Wait here and let them come to you. You'll know what to do when the time comes. As soon as those helicopters take off, we'll take them out with the rockets. If they get a chance to use those fifties, things could go wrong in a hurry. When the Mark-less see they have help, they'll be looking for friendly's, that will be your signal. They'll be running uphill to your location, so make sure you take up positions that will give you the best visual advantage."

As Josh took Ellen in his arms, Jessica held Andy's face in her hands. Standing on her toes, she kissed him tenderly and stepped away.

"I'll see you at the Havens for lunch," she said, and don't be late!"

Following Josh, Rich and Andy began making their way to the vantage point they were looking for. On the brow of the plateau, overlooking the southern face, Josh found a shallow crevasse about twenty feet long, and four or five feet deep. Flanked on the east and west ends by large boulders, the rear was covered with dense brush and small trees. As the men settled in and leaned against the wet stone, Josh pulled out his field glasses. The Mark-less below them were huddled back-to-back, between two fires.

"Andy, I count six men, two women and four children, they look like pre-teens. Call team one and let them know what will be coming."

Pulling out his radio, Andy keyed up. "Team two to team one, copy?"

Moments later, Ellen's voice rang out.

"Go ahead team two."

Andy passed on the information and cleared, just as the familiar sound of helicopter rotors filled the air. Josh watched through his field glasses, as not two, but three helicopters came up the valley.

"I think we're one rocket short," Josh said, as Andy opened the munitions box. Pulling out a rocket, he handed it to Josh. Pulling out the other rocket, and a mortar, he set them aside to have them ready!

BROKERS SAT IN THE CO-PILOTS seat of the lead helicopter. Behind him and the pilot, two Militiamen sat operating the surveillance equipment. To his left and his right, two troop carriers with the fifty calibers, zigzagged their way up the valley. As they approached the small melt lake directly ahead of them, a voice came over the com.

"Sergeant Brokers, I have heat sources, ten o'clock, and a thousand yards ... 'Over'."

"Did you copy that Alpha One, Alpha Two? Swing to the south and put boots on the ground between that melt lake and those CF's, then I want you in the air and using those fifties. If you have any ammo on those birds when we return to base, I'll use those guns on you myself!

"Copy Sergeant, sir!"

"Looks like the middle chopper is surveillance," Josh said, so we still have two with fifties. Are you two ready for this?"

"Let's do it," Rich said, with a thumbs-up. To be absent from the body, is to be present with the Lord!

As the troop carriers descended in a wide turn, they touched down less than a hundred yards from the Mark-less, who quickly began to retreat up the mountainside. The Militia had barely cleared the helicopters, when Josh stood, took aim at the one nearest to them and fired!

The war was on, with an explosion that roared across the mountainside. By the time he had reloaded the SMAW, the second chopper was in the air and strafing the hillside as it rose toward them through the smoke and flames. Again, Josh fired, amid a hail of fifty caliber rounds that filled the air with flying stone shrapnel that cut and stung their faces.

As the second rocket found its mark, an explosion that ignited the air with a suffocating ball of fire, scorched the ground. Debris rained down on them. Automatic weapons fire soon followed, as the Militia's attention turned away from their quarry, and focused on the hillside. Rich and Andy quickly stood and returned fire, as Josh surveyed their situation.

"I count eight," Josh shouted, three on the left and five on the right."

Suddenly Josh threw himself across Andy and pushed Rich to the bottom of the crevasse.

"In coming he cried, they've got a SMAW!

Within seconds, a grenade bounced off the large boulder behind Rich, and exploded in the brush behind them.

"God help us," Josh cried, as rage and fear welled up in his heart in chorus.

Shouldering the SMAW, he fired the mortar Andy had pulled for him, down the hill to his left.

When the smoke cleared, there was no weapons fire from that sector, but there was from the right, the far right!

"Ellen," Josh shouted, as he clamored to his feet.

Rich and Andy quickly stood with Josh, searching intently for the locations of their own, in the midst of the firefight taking place at the bottom of the hill. Without hesitation, they climbed out of the crevasse. With their automatic weapons echoing in overlapping bursts, Andy and

Rich made their way down the hillside, taking out two of six adversaries before tumbling to the ground in a hail of gunfire.

Rushing down the hillside, to the right of their position, Josh leaped off a shallow precipice and into the air, his automatic rifle in one hand, and pistol in the other. A scream tore from his lips, as everything suddenly slipped into slow motion. Firing simultaneously, the air filled with an explosion of gunfire. Josh could feel the pounding against his chest, as his parka exploded into a cloud of goose down. Dropping to the ground, he gazed momentarily into the morning sky, and lost consciousness.

When he came to, he lay cradled in Ellen's arms, as Todd examined him, and then turned to Andy, who lay next to him in a fetal position, holding his chest.

"I feel like I've been hit in the chest repeatedly with a sledgehammer," Josh said, trying to raise himself, only to fall back into Ellen's arms.

"They're going to hurt for a while, but I think they'll be ok," Todd said. Thank God for His Grace and Kevlar!"

It was almost forty minutes before Andy and Josh were able to stand. As his head cleared a little, Josh looked down at his watch. It was almost ten-twenty.

"Where's Rich," Josh asked, looking around at all the unfamiliar faces.

Ellen's eyes welled up with tears.

Rich is dead," she said. He didn't make it, we also lost two of the group we came to rescue. There are fifteen of us all together.

"What do we do now Josh?" Andy asked with a grimace.

"We need to bury our dead and find cover before the surveillance satellite begins its pass over the valley," Josh wheezed. There's a small crevasse deep enough to hold our dead at the foot of a rock slide a hundred yards up the hill. We'll bury them there. There's also a shallow cave near-by, that we passed this morning, where we can huddle until the satellite passes over.

Suddenly, a familiar voice filled the air, as Ben called out to the Lemon Creek Six over the radio!

"Does anyone copy," he said.

Pulling the radio off her belt, Jessica responded.

"Princess Two, go ahead Stars."

"Forget the code stuff," Ben responded. "We want a status report."

Jessica's lip began to tremble, and her eyes filled with tears. Reaching out, Josh took the radio from her hand and keyed up.

"Pops, we have three dead, two mark-less, and T … Todd didn't make it. Andy and I are wounded, but ok."

Looking at the ten ragged souls in front of him, Josh paused and asked the man standing closest to him, "Are you all Christians?" With a nod of the man's head, Josh re-keyed the mike. "We are fifteen Saints in all," he said.

CHAPTER 30

The Lemon Creek Massacre

A SCREAM EMERGED FROM THE BACKGROUND, as Linda responded to the news of Rich's death, and a sudden burst of emotion flooded the hearts of those huddled around Josh as a collective moan rose into the smoke-filled air.

"Pops, we can't get back before the surveillance satellite begins its photo scan. We will bury our dead on the plateau above the melt lake and take shelter in a shallow cave until you can give us an all clear. Do you copy?"

"Copy Son, we're monitoring as we speak. The world is coming apart, massive eruptions are occurring everywhere. We'll talk when you get home, take care."

As Josh handed the radio back to Jessica, the roar of an ascending helicopter filled the air as it dropped to the south, made a three-hundred-and-sixty-degree circle around their location and flew west, disappearing into the valley below.

"I wondered what happened to that third helicopter," Josh coughed out. "I'm sure Jenson will get some interesting photo's when they get back to the banks."

SERGEANT BROKERS SAT, DEFIANTLY BEATING his fist into his thigh, as the pilot turned the helicopter around, and sat it down on the helipad. Within moments, Commander Jenson's voice rang over the com.

"Brokers, I want those pictures in my office stat ... do you copy?

"Yes Sir, I'm on my way as we speak, sir!"

Turning in his seat, Brokers investigated the face of the security officer as he removed the thumb drive from the USB port on the computer and placed it in the sergeant's hand.

"We'll debrief, after my meeting with the Commander," he said.

Sliding out of the helicopter, he ran to meet Lieutenant Dunn, who stood holding open the door of the Administration building.

"If you don't have what he's looking for on that thumb drive, we may be the next one's to face the blade," Dunn shouted, leading the way to the Commanders office.

Opening the door, Brokers stepped inside, as Dunn turned to leave.

"I want you in here too Dunn and bring a pad and pen with you! And more coffee too, while you're at it!"

When Dunn returned, Commander Jenson and the Sergeant sat looking at the large flat screen monitor on the wall behind the Commander's desk. With glaring, detail the entire battle unfolded before their eyes, recapturing the daring charge down the mountainside, and the hail of bullets, which brought the battle to an end.

Then they appeared, fifteen souls standing in a semicircle around the two most wanted men in the Alaskan province, and with them, the two women he had arrested, the day before the Juneau Prison disappeared into the earth. Zooming in on the CF's as the helicopter circled, Jenson couldn't believe his eyes—Everyone was waving.

In a rage, he hurled his cup into the screen, with a shattering impact. Spinning in his chair, he unleashed a tirade that left Brokers and Dunn visibly shaken.

When Jenson's anger began to quell, he leaned into his desk addressing his subordinate's in a manner totally out of character, which for Brokers and Dunn, only added insult to injury.

"Gentlemen, at twenty-two hundred hours last night, two volcano's erupted along the Pacific rim in Southeast Asia, and Yellowstone has turned into a cauldron of fire and smoke. In a week the smoke will be so thick around the world, you won't be able to see the sun at noon. The world Collective is in an uproar, and civil unrest is growing. Now, to make matters worse, I have these men, these CF's within my grasp, and I can do nothing, at least for the next seventy–two hours. Ostenberg will be next on my list if he doesn't back off. I will have my revenge, and no one will deprive me!"

As the Commander talked, the phone rang in Dunn's office. Excusing himself, he answered the phone and quickly returned.

"Commander, that was the DOD. They finished a prescheduled event early and have begun photographing the valley as we speak. Results should be ready by one o'clock this afternoon."

"Good, now maybe I'll get some answers. Brokers, complete your debriefing, and have your report on this desk by three this afternoon."

"Yes Sir, Commander, sir."

"Dunn, contact procurement, I want another monitor here within the hour. When those digitals come in, I want to see them immediately, understood?"

"Yes Sir."

"Gentlemen you're dismissed ... and Dunn, bring me another cup and some fresh coffee."

TENDERLY AND WITH GREAT CARE, they carried their brothers up the mountainside. Josh led the solemn procession to the place where they would be, laid to rest. Zipping the bodies into sleeping bags, the men laid them in the narrow crevasse, as the entire company carefully filled it with stones and tears.

It was just a short distance to another crevasse the men had passed only hours before. Shallow at one end, it deepened until turning into a small cave, where Josh directed his new charges and team inside.

"We didn't have time at the grave side to pray," Josh said. "I'd like to take that time now and say a few words before we do. We have not had time to learn each other's names, but I'll tell you who we are. My name is Josh; this woman at my side is my wife, Ellen. The couple on my left is Andy and his wife Jessica. Sitting in front of you is Todd. Rich is the name of our brother who sacrificed his life for Christ this morning."

"We are part of a group of people who have taken shelter in the upper reaches of this valley for several years, just over a half mile from here. We will go there as soon as we know the satellite surveillance has been completed. Once there, you will be taken care of, and all your questions will be answered. Let's bow our heads and thank God for His grace and mercy!"

As Josh finished praying, Ben's voice echoed through the cave. Taking out his radio, he responded.

"This is Josh, go ahead."

"Son, we just picked up a radio transmission from a Lieutenant Dunn to a Sergeant Brokers, seems they started the surveillance earlier than expected. It's now completed, and the photo's transmitted to the Militia Administration Center. Evidently, the Sergeant was called in for a briefing. You and your people are probably in the photos. You're clear to come home!"

It was almost half past one, when Josh gathered everyone on the east bank of the small melt pond, below the main door of the Havens. Keying up his radio, Josh verbally knocked on the front door.

"Come on in, Son," Ben said. "It's warm, cozy, and foods on the table, we have you on visual."

"Copy Pops, we're coming in!"

As the ten newcomers stood gazing up at the snow- and ice-covered mountain in front of them, searching for some sign of their destination, one of the young men spoke up.

"Is that where you're taking us," he said, there's nothing up there but wilderness!"

A broad smile quickly formed across Andy's face.

"Yes, and I'm sure you'll have a lot more questions very soon, Andy said, with a laugh."

Again, spreading everyone out, so as not to leave a heavy trail, Josh and Andy led the way around the pond, and up the hill, where they gathered in front of the tree-sheltered entrance to the Havens. Jaws dropped, and the newcomers gazed in amazement, as the heavy door embedded in the rock wall, opened.

"Looks like rain, we had better get inside," Andy said, as heavy drops began pelting the company.

SERGEANT BROKER IS HERE COMMANDER, Dunn announced over the com.

"Bring him in Dunn and bring a pen and pad with you. You'll be staying."

As they walked in, Jenson sat clicking through images on his new TV monitor.

"Good job Dunn, I like this larger monitor. Have a seat gentlemen, and I'll start these pictures from the beginning."

As Brokers took a seat, Dunn stepped back through the door, returning moments later with cups and a pot of coffee.

Clicking through the photos, Jenson began to point out details in selected images, zooming in with unbelievable clarity.

"These first few photos cover the avalanche destruction on the lower Lemon, the night before I was gunned down by Huskins and Bridgeport," he said, rubbing his left arm.

Skimming through the next series of photos, Jenson stopped at image fourteen, zooming in on the south side of the valley.

"Here gentlemen is the remains of 027. They went down in a snowstorm while transporting four CF's back to our facility from the Taku Lodge.

Moving across the valley, and slightly east of the wreckage, he then zoomed in on what was left of a twin-engine plane, it is numbers still plainly visible on a twisted wing.

"This gentlemen, is what is left of my Otter, which was stolen by Huskins and Bridgeport! And here, moving slightly northeast, is what is left of 021, pulled down by an avalanche, in the Great Alaskan Brown fiasco!"

Pausing for a moment, he took a sip of his coffee, and moved on to the last three photographs.

"These, Mr. Brokers, are of your debacle!"

The last three photos covered the upper end of the valley, just below the glacier. The north and south photos showed nothing of interest, but the image covering the melt lakes disclosed volumes, as Jenson zoomed in on the area where the engagement took place.

The mountainside as it ascended to the brow of a small plateau lay strewn with wreckage of the two helicopters. Bodies of the Militiamen and Aircraft Personnel lay where they had fallen, a testament to the violence of the battle. As the Commander continued to move through the gruesome scene, Dunn counted uniforms, and confirmed personnel losses, except for Brokers and the surveillance crew. Noticing something peculiar, Brokers spoke out abruptly.

"Commander, I see something, move up and to the left ... there just below those small trees."

Moving into the upper left quadrant of the photo, Jenson found what had caught Brokers attention. Zooming in, the three sat in amazement. The photograph had caught the CF's descending in single file into the mountainside, with Josh Huskins pointing the way in.

"This picture was worth the effort and troop loses," Jenson said defiantly. "Now we know where they are!"

"Alright," Brokers said, with a sigh.

Turning in his chair, Jenson looked at him over the top of his coffee cup.

"You're not out of the woods yet Sergeant, alive yes, but only by a thread.

"Dunn ... I want exact coordinates for that hole in the ground. Schedule continuous surveillance flights over that sector for the next seventy-two hours. Have them stay high, out of reach, and report anything that moves looks unusual or out of place."

Standing and walking around his desk, Jenson stood behind Sergeant Brokers with his hands griping his shoulders.

"Sergeant, I'm going to give you an opportunity to save your sorry head from the blade. I want you to handpick five men of your choosing, and gear-up for an extended march. You will be driven to the Lemon Creek trail head tomorrow morning, at zero six hundred. From there you will proceed up the valley, seeking out and investigating these three crash sites. I want pictures, body counts, flight record data and detailed reports for each site. I will personally rendezvous with you in four days at the engagement site, with a company and air support. Do not let me down Sergeant. If you do, I'll bury you with the men you left there."

"Yes Sir, Brokers stammered, thank you sir."

Picking up the control for the TV monitor, Jenson switched the input to the local dish network, and tuned to NBC or the evening news broadcast.

"You're dismissed Brokers, I think it's time you get started making preparations."

"Yes Sir, Commander sir," Brokers replied!

Standing, he quickly made his way out of the Administration building, and into the Militia barracks.

"Dunn, is there any more coffee left in that pot?"

"I'll make a fresh one Sir," Dunn replied, and quickly left the room to Jenson and the news broadcast.

When he returned, Jenson was on the edge of his seat, as the News Anchor and a panel of scientists sat discussing the sudden disappearance of known stars used for celestial navigation and the rise in geologic activity around the world. Turning, Jenson spoke with a timbre in his voice, that made Dunn feel a little uneasy.

"We may be closer to the end than we want to be. It's going to be survival of the fittest Dunn, and I'm at the top of the food chain in our little part of the world. It pays to know people in high places my friend— keep that in mind!"

CHAPTER 31

Peace in the eye of the storm

A S THE TEN NEWCOMERS FILED through the door, an overwhelming sense of awe filled their faces with wide-eyed unbelief. The room suddenly filled with murmuring and a flood of unanswered questions.

"Welcome home Son," Ben said, with tears welling up in his eyes.

Alice stepped forward embracing them both, as she kissed Ellen's cheek.

"There's no way we're going to seat twenty-three people at once," she said, ushering Josh and Ellen to the side. "Why don't you take Andy, Jessica and Todd to freshen up a bit, when you come back out, I'll have hot coffee and some food waiting for you?

"Let's get something warm in you folks," Sarah said, guiding everyone to the table.

Pastor Bowens quickly seated their guests and joined them as Sarah and Alice served, with Jan and Jamie's help. Without hesitation, Josh led the way to the smaller chamber, where he, Andy, Todd and the women cleaned up, changed clothes and tended to their wounds, before returning to the great room.

In the privacy of their quarters, Ellen carefully cleaned the deeply bruised wounds on Josh's chest and abdomen, as tears coursed her cheeks.

"You know this isn't the end," she said with a ring of consternation in her voice. "It's only a matter of time before Jenson and his minions come, and ultimately overrun our sanctuary."

Reaching up, Josh grasped her shoulders, and pulled her down against his chest, holding Ellen as close as his wounds would allow. Brushing her hair aside, he kissed her tenderly.

"I'm ready, with you at my side, and Christ in my heart, to face whatever lies ahead. The prophecy of Matthew twenty-four concerning the sun, moon, and stars, is finding it's fulfillment as we speak. The only thing left is our catching away, and the revelation of the Anti-Christ. God's Righteous Judgment will soon avenge the blood of His Saints. Our duty now, that we have done all we can do, is simply to stand our ground, and submit to the Lord's will."

As Josh raised himself to a sitting position, Ellen helped him to his feet and handed him a fresh tee shirt from his chest. A smile broke across his face as he held it up before putting it on. In bold army drab were printed the words "Soldier of the Cross."

By the time Josh and the others made their way into the great room, their guests had eaten. They had gathered around the couches and on the floor between them, which was carpeted with tanned bear and wolf pelts. Ben and Pastor Bowens sat among them, answering questions, and retelling the story of how the Havens came into being. Taking Jessica and Andy in tow, Sarah led the rest of the group to the table, where Alice Jan and Jamie reset the table and joined them for an early supper.

Just as Jamie began to eat, Missy stirred in her makeshift cradle Ben had made for her.

"You just sit there and eat your dinner Jamie," Sarah said, Grandma Sarah will take care of our little girl. I've munched on enough for two people today."

As Josh and his small band discussed the day and the prospects for the days to follow, they consumed more coffee than food. Setting up a defense parameter around the Havens was going to be an immediate priority.

How well they laid their plans, would determine how long they could hold out, once their location was discovered. One advantage would be the growing darkness Ben said would occur because of the geologic activity around the world.

"Hey pops," Josh shouted across the great room. "Can we borrow you for a few minutes?"

"What can I do for you Son," Ben said, making his way to the table.

"We need a little clearer picture concerning the volcanic activity. Has there been any further news since this morning?"

"No there hasn't Son." Looking at his watch, he paused for a moment.

"Let's have Todd switch the monitor over and hook up the antenna. I think it's time to watch the local and international news."

Jumping to his feet, Todd made his way to their makeshift security center. Turning the TV monitor around where everyone could see it, he switched from the security cameras to the antenna and turned on the television.

"It's so hard to believe all of this is here in the middle of nowhere," a voice rang out.

Those sitting at the table remained where they were. Todd turned up the volume and returned to his seat. Everyone sat mesmerized, as the local news anchors described the morning's battle, now called the "Lemon Creek massacre".

Lies flowed like melt water from Commander Jenson's lips, as he described how a small army of over fifty CF's ambushed his twenty-man patrol. Using rocket launchers and armament previously stolen by the outlaws, Josh Huskins, and Andy Bridgeport, the CF's Ring Leaders.

"My men didn't have a chance," he continued.

"We now know the exact location where these CFs are holed up," he stated emphatically.

I have satellite photos showing these religious fanatics marching single file into their den less than a hundred yards, from where their heinous crime was committed! They're not only fanatics, but they're also stupid. In five days, I will fall upon this scourge like fire from the sky and eradicate them from the face of the earth. Then we truly will have peace and safety!"

"In other news tonight," the commentator continued, worldwide unrest continues to grow, along with the thickening blanket of smoke and ash, now covering eighty percent of the planet. As we enter a full Moon cycle, the Sun and Moon both appear as blood red spheres in the sky. Scientists predict that within three to four days, both bodies will totally disappear.

This will plunge the earth into a surreal and terrifying darkness. For humanity, this catastrophic event will produce the long-feared equivalent, of a nuclear winter without the radiation. Around the world, peoples of every nation are preparing for the worst, as military and police forces prepare for the civil unrest, they are sure is to follow. National and World news will follow after the station break."

The great room became a buzz of conversation, as Josh leaned into the table. Collecting the attention of those sitting there, he cleared his throat, and took a long sip of coffee.

"According to Jenson, we have only four days to prepare for an all-out assault on our location.

I'm pretty sure they'll be concentrating their search from Slip creek to the base of the Lemon glacier, and up the northern and southern slopes. Jenson thinks the shallow cave we rested in is our refuge. He will hit it first, and I don't think we should disappoint him. Any ideas on what we can do to arrange a special greeting?"

"I don't know about a greeting, but I do have an idea for a diversion that may save all of our lives," Andy replied.

Leaning into the table, he looked at Josh with a twinkle in his eye.

"With the exception of what little of the C4 we used to move that helicopter last year, we still have almost ten pounds of it left. That cave we rested in goes down and back almost forty feet. If we were to place enough of that C4 in the back, and detonate it remotely, it would create the illusion they had buried us alive. I'm sure they won't put boots on the ground until they search for heat sources and soften things up a little from the air, when they do, we'll collapse the cave. I don't think Jenson, or his men will want to excavate just to look for bodies, especially with the air filled with smoke and ash from the eruptions."

Everyone setting at the table looked at Andy in disbelief, until Ellen broke the silence with a spirit of rejoicing and a prophetic word, as she stood and raised her hands in the air.

"I am coming," says the Lord. With my left hand, I will hide you from the enemy and with my right hand; I will draw you unto myself in clouds of glory and a trumpet call. Tarry and look to the east, for your salvation is at hand."

When the excitement and rejoicing, gave way to quiet anticipation, Josh stood and spoke to Andy, as the entire company, gathered around them.

"God has given His conformation to your proposal, now we need a plan to implement it! Let's pray."

Amen's echoed in the great room as Josh concluded his prayer for direction, and safety. While Alice and Sarah helped their guests prepare for some much-needed rest, all of the men joined Josh around the table.

"The first thing we need to do is set up twenty-four-hour monitoring of all Militia and air traffic radio transmissions," Josh said emphatically. "Todd, if you'll take the first short watch until ten this evening, I'll take the second until six in the morning. After that, we'll make out a roster of eight-hour shifts, to continue until this thing is over. Secondly, we need to figure out how much of that C4 we'll need to do the job. We want to cave in the roof of the cavern, not create a crater.

As Josh paused to take a sip of coffee, one of the men rescued in the morning's battle spoke up.

"Josh, Sir". My name is Mitchell, William A. "I'm an ex-Marine, one of the last to leave Afghanistan in fifteen. I spent two tours there as a demolition expert. I'm sure I can give you what you want Sir.

"You're the man William," Josh said with a sigh of relief. "Only one thing though, he continued."

"Yes Sir," William shot back with military decorum.

"Please don't call me Sir, "he said with a grin... "Just call me Josh".

Andy, who was sitting next to William, turned. Taking his hand, he gave him a brotherly hug, which, William heartily returned.

"Welcome into the family Will, you had better get some rest. Tomorrow is going to be a long day for all of us, as if today hasn't been already."

"On that note," Josh said, standing and stretching his arms. "I need to do the same thing before my watch comes up. We'll discuss this more over breakfast in the morning. Rest in the Lord.

FOUR AND A HALF HOURS later, with a fresh cup of coffee in hand, Josh relieved Todd from his watch.

"There's been a lot of traffic Josh, but I only noted what I thought was important. Jenson's on the prowl."

"Thanks Todd, I'll check them out. You had better get some rest, we'll talk in the morning."

Settling down on the backless stool, and donning the headset, he began reading Todd's notes covering the last five hours of radio traffic.

-6:50 PM Volcanic activity increasing, Mt. Fuji Japan, Shisha din AK, Pavloff AK, Redoubt AK, Mt. Rainer WA, and Colima Mexico. Minus tides and Tsunami warnings along the entire Pacific rim.

-7:43 PM All air traffic in and out of Juneau International closed due to low or no visibility above four thousand feet. The only things flying are Militia helicopter patrols on an as needed basis.

-9:35 PM As of 9:00PM this evening, martial law has been declared in the greater Juneau area, and cities across the nation. Panic and looting is increasing with the deepening darkness caused by the dust cloud, which now completely covers the earth.

-9:48 PM Jenson just called for a special meeting with his lieutenants, *thirteen hundred hours tomorrow afternoon. Mentioned Lemon Creek CF's and something about strike force. Looks like Jenson's' coming...*

Pushing the notepad away from him, Josh leaned forward and folded his hands. The weight of the previous six months, which had rested so heavily on him, seemed to vaporize as he prayed. Peace like a warm blanket draped across his shoulders, drove away the last vestige of anxiety that had for so long gripped his heart. Wiping the tears from the table, he pulled the notepad back in front of him, and began to formulate a plan in preparation for Jenson's eminent visit.

CHAPTER 32

Jenson's grand reception

I T WAS MAX'S PAWS ON his thigh, which alerted Josh to Andy's presence. "Good morning big brother," he said, placing his hands firmly on Josh's shoulders. Looks like you have been busy while I was tossing and turning all night. You've always been the man with the plan."

Josh patted Max on the head, scratching behind his ears and rubbing his neck before turning to look into Andy's smiling face.

"Not much activity last night, at least anything we need to be concerned about. Why couldn't you sleep?"

Stepping back, Andy motioned for Josh to follow him to the table.

"Turn up the volume, and let's have some coffee."

"That's probably why you couldn't sleep... too much coffee last night," Josh said with a chuckle.

Grabbing his cup, he followed Andy to the table, filling it before setting down. Wrapping his hands around its warmth, he savored the aroma as it waffled up from the cup.

I could never drink too much coffee," Andy said, tipping his cup to Josh before taking a sip and licking his lips with a grin. "I've just got a lot on my mind with all that's been happening, and my body aches in places I didn't know I had. I think our story is quickly coming to an end. I must admit Josh; I'm looking forward to it with anticipation. What about you?"

Josh rubbed his chest and abdomen, acknowledging his own discomfort, and took a sip of coffee.

"I'm with you, but I think there are a few more scenes that need to be played out before the Lord writes 'The End', to the Lemon Creek Chronicle. I wrote one last night, and I pray that it plays out like it's supposed to."

"So do I, are we going to set up for Jenson's arrival, and plant the C4 today?"

"As soon as we've had something to eat, and I gather things together. It's five-thirty now. As soon as Will is up and ready, we'll talk about the plan."

By six AM, the women were busy preparing breakfast, and tending the children. The men, sat attentively around the table with coffee in hand, as Josh assigned work details.

"Dad, I need you and Pastor to take Pat, Mike and Peter with you up to Havens II. Show them around so they can familiarize themselves with the area. It may take two trips, but we need to secure more supplies and replace our depleted firewood."

"I'll Have Sarah make a list of the things we need," Ellen Said. Refilling Josh's cup, she made her way around the table with the pot.

"Andy, Will and I will make our way to the cave, get the charges set, and find a suitable location to operate the transmitter," Josh continued. "On our way back to the Havens, we'll plant the rest of the C4 in some strategic locations just in case our ruse fails to convince Jenson that he's eradicated us from the face of the earth."

"What about monitoring the radio traffic Son," Ben said. Turning, he saw Jessica was already at the station with the earphones on.

"Well, I guess that answers my question," he said with a chuckle.

As Ben turned back around, the women flooded the table with fresh baked biscuits and venison gravy. In an instant all conversation ceased. Pastor Bowens thanked the Lord for the food, the women who prepared it, and the oven Ben had built over the firebox.

"You can tell Ben and Josh are related," Andy said grinning. "They're always thinking ahead."

A hush fell over the table and conversation ebbed, as the men relished Sarah and Alice's biscuits and gravy. Ellen soon followed with the pot, refilling their half-empty cups with fresh hot coffee.

"I 'aven't eaten anyting dis goot for veeks," Peter said, devouring his breakfast. "I most olready be in 'eaven and ditunt knowit."

"Give that man some more biscuits and gravy," Sarah shouted laughingly, before he realizes where he really is.

Laughter erupted around the table.

When the men had eaten their fill, and began preparing for their assignments, the women and children filled the empty benches in anticipation of the second round of breakfast. A sense of reprieve and peace filled the great room, until Jessica suddenly jumped to her feet. Tearing the earphones from her head, she turned and with a calm but urgent voice, called to Josh across the cavern.

"Commander Jenson is on the move," she shouted. "He's coming with a full troop, five helicopters, two with fifty cal's and rockets, one troop, one surveillance, and his command. Lift-off is 1300 hours this afternoon!"

"Sounds like he means business this time, and we have only five hours to prepare for his arrival," Josh said, strapping the Judge to his chest and pulling on his Jacket.

Calling Will over to where he stood, Josh handed him the backpack containing the C4, and the small satchel with the detonators and remotes.

"Let's get this show on the road," he said. Calling for Andy to join them, they headed for the front door of the Havens.

In an instant, Ellen and Jessica stood in front of their men, embracing them momentarily, before letting them slip through the door and into the dark dust-filled morning.

IN LESS THAN TWENTY MINUTES, Ben, Pastor Bowens and the other three men were marching down the escarpment trail. Nearing the door of Havens II, Ben paused. Un-slinging his rifle he raised it quickly to his shoulder and chambered a cartridge. Stepping slowly around the corner where he could see into the alcove, a grin slowly spread across his face. He lowered his rifle.

"Ha-a," Ben shouted, stomping his feet.

Suddenly, an enormous raccoon darted out of the alcove. Scurrying up the trail ahead of them it ran hissing, as it looked back over its shoulder. Without hesitation, Ben and Pastor led their charges into the chamber where they began to fill their packs with the items on Sarah's list. Stepping out the door, Ben lowered the cargo net. Removing what was left of the venison, he stowed it in his backpack, and pulled it up on his shoulders.

"We'll take these things back to the Havens, have a quick cup, and then head back up here to the firewood reserves," he said. "We should have everything done by noon if we're quick about it.

"Quick you say," Pastor Bowens chuckled. "I can still do everything I did as a young man, but quick is no longer in my vocabulary. Methodical yes, deliberate maybe, but not quick... quick is an adjective which I no longer use."

Looking at Ben, Pastor Bowens gave him a wink.

"We had better be getting back to the Havens," he said with a grin. "I'll need that 'quick' cup of coffee to keep me going.

LEADING THE WAY AROUND THE upper side of the small melt pond, Josh paused on the edge of the bluff. Turning, he knelt down on one knee.

"If we double time it, we should be able to reach the cave in less than thirty minutes. I sure wish we had some way to draw their fire and give them something to shoot at."

"I already thought of that," Will said, un-slinging the SMAW from his shoulder. "I only brought one rocket though, cause it's all we'll need. I figure I'll load it, brace it up with some rocks pointing out of the mouth of the cave, and attach a detonator to the trigger. It should be enough to launch the rocket in their direction."

Josh and Andy looked at each other in amazement, as broad grins coursed their faces.

"This here transmitter is set up to detonate three charges at different times. When they home in on the launch location, and fire back, we can blow the cave."

"That's an awesome plan," Josh said. But 'we' won't blow the cave, I will! "Andy, you and Will are to head back to the Havens after we get set up and plant the rest of the C4 as we discussed earlier this morning."

Andy began to voice an objection but stopped as Josh held up his hand.

"If things don't go well, I need you and William back at the Havens, with the rest of the family. If we pull this off, I'll make my way home after Jenson and his men make their way back down the valley to the banks.

Looking at his watch, Josh quickly turned and headed across the mountainside, leaving Andy and Will to scurry behind as they attempted to catch up. A low ceiling of clouds, dust and ash hung over the valley like a dirty brown shroud. What light was able to penetrate left the landscape before them looking like the sepia-colored print of an old photograph. Nearing their destination, they clamored to the top of the bluff, pausing briefly at the small crevasse and pile of stones which marked the hallowed ground where their fallen were laid the day before. It was only another fifty yards to the entrance of the cave, where Josh led the way into even darker recesses.

Quickly he lit a flare, and tossed it to the ground, repeating the scene in the middle of the cave and again as he reached the bottom of the descending cavern. Andy stood next to Will as he studied the ceiling and walls for the best place to position his charges, and quickly swung the backpack from his shoulders. Kneeling down, Will began drawing in the dirt with his finger. Glancing up periodically, to recheck his decision for placement of the charges, Will suddenly stood to his feet.

"I think I'm ready to do this," he said, "but I'll need your help to place the ceiling charges."

"Just tell us what you need," Josh said, as he stepped forward and looked down at Will's drawing on the floor of the cavern.

It took less than forty minutes to set all the charges, including those placed on the ceiling of the cavern, with great difficulty. As the flares began to burn out, the trio quickly moved to the mouth of the cavern, where Andy helped Will load and place the SMAW. Josh stood outside of the entrance, gazing pensively down the valley, and then up the mountain side toward the Havens. Grimacing, he rubbed his chest and abdomen to relieve the pain of the growing bruises on his torso.

"Josh," Will called out, "come and check out this rocket placement, and tell us what you think. The detonator is attached, and it's ready to go."

Josh moved quickly back into the mouth of the cavern and looked intently at the SMAW's placement.

"You're a God-send," he said, patting Will on the shoulder. He looked at Andy with a grin and a nod of his head. "The only thing left to do now is find a place for me close enough to set off the charges, but far enough away to survive the blast, and onslaught of Jenson and his Militia."

Standing in the mouth of the cavern, the three men looked intently down the mountainside toward the east, and the smaller of the two lakes below the glacier. After only a few minutes, Andy pulled a small pair of binoculars from his pocket.

"I think, yes... thank you Jesus," Andy said, slipping the binoculars back into his pocket. "Come-on guys. It's time to get you settled in Josh. I've found the perfect place."

Descending the mountainside, Andy came to a halt about thirty yards from the water's edge. There, a huge slab of stone about five feet thick had come to rest. Getting down on his stomach he slid forward. With his flashlight he peered into the dark recess beneath.

"Josh, there's enough room in there for you to lie stretched out on your stomach. There's no way they could get a heat signature through five feet of stone. We can place a few smaller stones in front of the opening to conceal you from the side. What do you think?"

"I think you two had better tuck me in and get those charges set on the way home. When you get back to the havens you can monitor everything down here on the cameras. I'll be fine, and besides, I can take a little nap before Jenson arrives."

"Ok big brother," Andy chided. "Slide your bottom inside and we'll tuck you in."

REMOVING HIS PACK, JOSH LAY on his belly and slowly pushed it into the narrow fissure beneath the massive granite slab. Wiggling his way through the opening, he slid into the small chamber, amazed at how much room there actually was. On his left, a small opening under the northwest side of the boulder left a clear view of the cavern entrance as he looked up the mountainside. On his right, the fissure sloped back about seven feet, leaving ample room for him to stretch out under the three-foot-high ceiling. Turning around he stuck his head and shoulders back through the opening.

"What a strange looking creature," Andy said laughingly. "It's amazing what you find living in the rocks near this glacier."

The laughter, which erupted over Andy's impromptu remark, brought an immediate release of the building anxiety over the pending encounter. Tears coursed the cheeks of the men as they lay in the rocks facing each other.

Reaching out, Will grasped Josh's wrist and placed the remote in his hand. "The first setting will launch the rocket. When they begin firing back, settings two and three will detonate the charges, one, two and three in that order."

Folding Josh's fingers over the remote, Will stood and helped Andy place some stones haphazardly in front of the opening as Josh settled in. Kneeling in front of the opening, the men prayed. Then rising, they began making their way back toward the Havens, leaving Josh to wait for Jenson's arrival in the solitude of his tiny stronghold.

Pressing the button on his watch, the face lit up with an eerie glow in the semi-darkness. Setting the alarm for twelve-thirty, Josh pulled the collar of his jacket up around his ears and laid his head against his pack. Hoping to get a little rest, he maneuvered to find a position of comfort. Thinking upon the endless possibilities the day could bring, he slipped into a shallow and fitful sleep.

As ANDY AND WILL MADE their way up the mountainside toward the Havens, Will, with the eye of a demolition expert, placed the remaining C4. With military precision, he set his charges in places where they would produce the most shrapnel. As they began to make their way around the small melt pond, Andy paused to look at his watch.

"It's almost eleven-forty-five Will. We had better get inside just in case Jenson makes an early start."

Quickly covering the last fifty yards, the men paused again, as they heard the ominous sound of beating rotors echoing up the valley.

"I just knew this was going to happen," Andy shouted, stomping his foot and lashing out at the boughs of the fir tree in front of him.

William pushed Andy through the boughs of the trees guarding the entrance to the Havens. As they approached the entrance, Ben quickly opened the door and ushered them inside.

"We've been following you on the cameras ever since you came over the ridge above the melt lake," Ben said, helping Will and Andy remove their gear.

"Jenson's here early," Andy shouted, and moved quickly to the security table where Todd sat monitoring the cameras. "We could hear the helicopters coming as we reached the front door."

With the joystick in hand, Todd nimbly swung the cameras to the west and zoomed in on the ridgeline where the low ceiling of clouds and dust hung over the narrow valley. Moments later, the aircraft began to emerge from the semi-darkness. As they approached, two gunships and a troupe carrier swung to the southeast, while two smaller helicopters moved to the northeast and passed directly overhead. Quickly, Todd maneuvered the cameras back to the small melt lake and zoomed out to reveal the scenario which would soon play itself out before the eyes of the entire company. Fixated on the small TV screen there in the great room, they joined hands, as twenty-three voices rose in unified prayer!

It wasn't the alarm, but the roar of the approaching helicopters that snapped Josh out of his short-lived rest, to hit his head against the mantle of stone that covered his hiding place. Quickly pushing his pack aside, he rolled onto his stomach and leaning forward, looked up into the dirty brown sky through his narrow stone window. The first aircraft to come into view was the troupe carrier on his left, and then the two gunships which flanked it on both sides. The two smaller aircraft hovered to the northwest of his location. Josh held his breath as the gunships and troupe carrier began to descend upon their intended target. As they moved into a position facing the entrance of the cavern, he set the remote to one and pressed the button.

With a flash, the rocket emerged from the mouth of the cave, striking the forward blades of the troupe carrier. With a deafening roar, it dropped nose first into the mountainside below the cavern in a ball of fire and debris. Moments later the gunships unleashed a hailstorm of fifty caliber rounds into the mouth of the cavern. Setting the remote to two, he pressed the button, then to three and quickly pressed again as the leading gunship fired two rockets into the mouth of the cave.

Instinctively, Josh thrust his backpack into the narrow window and buried his head as a thundering firestorm engulfed the mountainside. Moments later, Josh moved his pack and watched intently as the two gunships descended through the smoke to land below the now buried cavern, less than seventy yards from his lair. Within seconds eight Militiamen, automatic weapons in hand, were on the ground and moving into the blast zone searching for any signs of life from their fallen comrades or resistance from the CF's, they now presumed to be buried beneath the rubble.

Josh lay motionless, as if his muscles had turned to stone. Suddenly, a down draft filled the air with choking dust, and the sound of beating rotors pounded in his ears. Like an armadillo, he slid to the bottom of the chamber, pressing himself into the narrow crevasse with his chin tucked against his chest, and his back to the openings. Huddled in the tiny cleft, he listened intently as the whine of the engine and rotors slowly ebbed into silence.

Slowly Josh unfolded and pushed himself to a position where he could see the shadows of two men in the bright searchlights of the helicopter as they climbed out.

"Brokers, get over there with your men, and secure this area. I want everything within a hundred yards of that blast site covered before I return to base, and I'm leaving here in thirty minutes."

"Yes Sir, Commander," Brokers stammered. "Will there be anything else Sir?"

"I want you back here with a full assessment Brokers," Jenson barked, looking at his watch. "And now you have only twenty-eight minutes!"

Josh rolled back into the shadows as Brokers clamored down from above him and quickly made his way across the mountainside and up to his men. Twenty minutes later, the Sergeant stood in front of Josh's tiny portal, looking up into Commander Jenson's scowling face. Josh listened intently as Brokers gave his report, and Jenson unleashed a tirade of venomous filth upon his subordinate, from the slab of stone above him.

"Brokers, I wanted bodies, and all you can give me is a cavern full of boulders?" "You and four Militiamen will remain here for the next forty-eight hours. Look for another entrance. I want constant radio contact and I'll be monitoring your traffic. You screw this up, and I will personally send a gunship up here, to take you out!"

"Yes Sir," Brokers shouted.

Turning on his heels, he fled Jenson's wrath, to the respite of his comrades. Selecting four of his best men, he took up a position near the rubble of the cavern and waited for Jenson and the rest of the contingent to move out. Josh sighed with relief, as Jenson boarded the helicopter and it rose into the air.

"There's five men between me and the safety of the Havens. How am I going to get around them," Josh thought to himself?

Rolling to his left and gently sliding the stones aside, which concealed his hiding place, he could see the beginning of the brush and scrub trees, which ran below the bluff.

From where Brokers and his men had stationed themselves, he might be able to conceal himself," He thought, but getting there would be tricky.

Lowering his head onto his forearms, Josh whispered a prayer before slowly emerging from his lair, just out of their line of sight. Turning to face them, instead of his destination, he made himself as small as possible, and began inching his way across the mountainside. Using every large stone and boulder, he could find to break up his cowering silhouette, he slowly made his way to the shelter of the brush and trees. A sickening odor of burning flesh rose from the debris of the downed troupe carrier, forcing him to hold his breath as long as he could, before gasping for air and repeating the torturous process until he had made his way up-wind and through the gruesome scene.

Pointing to the microphone attached to his helmet, Brokers gave the sign to his men, to mute their mikes.

"Alright guys," Brokers barked. "If there are any CF's still breathing up here, we need to find them, and put them out of our misery, otherwise Jenson will take us out to get his pound of flesh. Thompson, get up on that ridge above us and do a one-eighty. Dellers, you're on the radio."

Looking at his watch, he reached out and spun Dellers around to face him.

"It's thirteen-forty-five Dellers. At fourteen hundred, contact the base and inform them that the blast scene is secure, and we are widening our perimeter. It will be your responsibility to report every hour on the hour as to our progress. If you fail to report, you won't have to wait for Jenson to deal with us, I'll take care of you myself, clear?"

"Yes Sir, clear," Dellers stammered.

"Roberts, you and Phillips come with me. We're going to spread out towards that boulder Jenson took off from, thirty yards between us and sweep to the west. If anything moves, shoot it!"

As Brokers and his men spread out to his right, Josh moved as stealthily as he could to the west. Keeping the trees and brush between him and the men. He had almost made it to the West side of the small bluff, when the air around him, became filled with ricocheting rounds. The lookout Brokers had stationed on the rise above them had spotted him.

Josh's heart pounded in his chest, as a sudden rush of adrenalin coursed through his veins. Stealth was no longer the issue. Instinctively, he knew his only hope, and that of those in the Havens, would be to out-run his pursuers. If he could lose them in the deep woods along slip creek, he could climb the mountain and make for the escarpment trail. Firing five quick rounds at his assailant Josh turned and ran a zigzag pattern to the west to put distance between himself and his pursuers.

The entire company of the Havens sat mesmerized, eyes glued to the small monitor, and ears straining to hear the radio traffic emanating from the scanner.

"Thompson, report, report," Brokers shouted.

"One CF, 100 yards northwest of your location," Thompson retorted.

Ellen and Jessica stood behind the men, wrapped in Ben's arms, as tension grew within the great room, and the pursuit, closer to the small melt pond below the Haven's front door.

"I see him, I see him," Todd shouted. "There, coming over the ridge."

Moments later three Militiamen appeared, with their automatic weapons blazing up the mountainside. A unified gasp filled the great room, as Josh's back arched, his arms rose into the air, and his body tumbled to the ground on the edge of the small melt pond.

Will quickly withdrew the small transmitter from his pocked, switched it on, and held his thumb over the third button, waiting as Brokers and his men approached Josh's position. The Militiamen were about thirty yards from where Josh had fallen, when he thrust his thumb down on the button, and the monitor suddenly filled with a blinding flash. Without hesitation, the entire company fled the safety of the Havens, and in unison descended the mountainside. Gathering around Ben, and Ellen who cradled Josh in her arms, the company broke into tearful prayer.

Will, Todd and Andy, weapons in hand, cautiously made their way to the blast site. Three bodies lay in the rubble. Turning to leave, they were startled, as one of the Militiamen suddenly turned his head and gazed at them with glassy eyes.

"You CF's," Brokers breathed. Inhaling sharply, his head dropped with a hiss.

CHAPTER 33

In Clouds of Glory

J ENSON AND HIS CONTINGENT HAD just set down at the base, when Thompson's traffic came over the com, and Brokers began shouting orders to Roberts and Phillips. Jenson listened intently as the chase began to unfold. Moments later, he grabbed the microphone, barking orders as he opened the door of the command helicopter and climbed out.

"Gunships, prepare for lift-off, we're going back up," he shouted. "Everyone else, stand down."

Running to the gunship closest to him, Jenson climbed aboard as the helicopters lifted into the air and began their swift ascent up the lemon valley.

Tears coursed Ellen and Ben's cheeks as Josh gazed up into their faces, and Andy approached, kneeling at his side.

"What's all these tears for," Josh said, breathing out each word from behind a forced smile. "I really don't feel a thing."

Reaching up with his right hand, Josh wiped away the tears from Ellen's cheek.

"No tears in heaven," he breathed.

"Will went to get a blanket," Andy said, placing his hand on Josh's shoulder and giving him a gentle squeeze. "As soon as he returns, we'll get you on it, and back into the Havens. There's still a couple of Militiamen on the mountain and we need to get back inside." Moments later Will arrived.

Everyone had been so focused on caring for Josh, that no one heard or noticed the gunships, until they came roaring up out of the valley, and into view. Fifty caliber rounds tore up the mountainside, as the gunships circled the Havens Company, driving them into a tight cowering mass of terror. As the helicopters landed on the south side of the little melt pond, with their armament leveled at their quarry, Jenson defiantly leaped to the ground and strode to a position between the gunships.

"Patch me into the speakers and turn up the volume, "he roared over the com. "I want to gloat over this moment before I send them to their non-existent God. Today the victory is finally mine!"

The venomous and sickening filth, which erupted from the commander's mouth, echoed back and forth across the valley like thunder. Violent anger welled up in Jenson's heart, leaving him reeling as he raised his hand in the air.

"Fire," he cried, defiantly dropping his hand.

In a blinding flash, time suddenly seemed to stand still. With a thunderous roar, the dark sepia colored sky tore open, and rolled up into brilliance beyond description. Every eye beheld the King of kings and Lord of lords as a trumpet blast turned the windows of the gunships to dust, and left Jenson screaming in terror, his face buried in his hands.

Just as suddenly, the semi-darkness returned in the midst's of gunfire that tore the mountainside apart on the opposite side of the melt pond. To the utter amazement of Jenson and his men nothing remained of the CF's, they were gone! After regaining their composure, Jenson and his company circled the pond and examined the site where their quarry had once stood. Nothing remained but a large pile of clothing, shredded by the fifty-caliber gunfire. It was then that one of the men noticed a small dog above them, which turned and disappeared into the trees.

"Follow that animal," Jenson roared. "I don't know what's going on here, but we aren't leaving until I find out!"

Quickly, three of the men made their way up the mountainside and pushed their way through the trees. Moments later a Militiaman appeared, waving his arms and gesturing to follow.

"Commander, you've got to see this," he said, and disappeared back through the trees.

With the remaining men, Jenson made his way to the top of the rise and pressed through the thick tree boughs. In wide-eyed amazement, he stepped through the door imbedded in the granite wall, and into the great room of the Havens. As he surveyed the room, his eyes fell upon the table where the monitor sat and stared at the gunships sitting on the bank of the melt pond. Quickly he strode to the table. Taking the joystick in his hand, he rotated the camera as he surveyed the landscape from east to west. Pushing a button in front of the monitor, the image suddenly changed, and a local news commentator filled the screen, with a special CBS news report. Jenson and his Militiamen stepped back encircling the monitor and listened intently.

"Just moments ago, the world was plunged into total chaos, as Lord Chris, who has been residing in Jerusalem for the last year, erected an edifice of himself in the Holy of Holies of the new Temple, declaring himself to be God and supreme ruler of the world! He has vowed to destroy all who refuse to bow to his Lordship."

A dogs sudden barking turned Jenson's attention away from the monitor in time to see Max, who had been hiding behind the heavy door, dart out of the cavern and disappear into the trees.

Moments later, terror struck the hearts of Jenson and his men as a harmonic tremor rose in pitch to a deafening roar. Time, again seemed to stand still, as the Havens and its occupants disappeared in a cascade of flowing stone. The liquefied Glacier suddenly filled the upper reaches of the Lemon and Salmon Creek valley with a pyroclastic flow, which soon filled the Gastineau channel, beneath its searing fingers. This is not **The End...** It's just **The Beginning!**

Epilogue:
Scarlet Thread

Where will I go; when each passing minute has finally gnawed through the shell of my existence, and the vacuum of eternity withdraws the last vestige of my life, through the breach that time has made? I do not know the place; yet I dream of it often and believe! Tightly in my grasp, I clutch the promise and cling to the hope that drives away the darkness, binding the hands that would snatch my treasure from me, if they could. Wrap around my heart the scarlet thread from Rahab's window, and bind me to the rock of my salvation, for my bones are weary and my soul longs to enter His rest. How I long to hear the words "well done" and to feel His loving arms of welcome about my shoulders, but I know my time has not yet come, and I must endure until He calls me safely Home. Louis L. Claassen

About The Author

Louis L. Claassen currently serves as an ordained minister, and Bible teacher, in Northeastern Washington State. Throughout his life and ministry, as an artist, poet, writer, and orator, he has shared his gifts and the truth of God's word with a sincere and deep-seated passion.

The father of two adult children, he was born and raised in the Pacific Northwest and currently resides in the Davenport farming community with his wife Talafaipea, from the beautiful Polynesian islands of Samoa. There, the author holds the high-talking chief title of Salaivoa Lui, as an acknowledgement of years of service to family and community. Throughout his life, art in its complexity of media and the written word, have become the tools of self-expression, which he uses daily as he answers God's call upon his life.